SLAVE
AND *Sister*

SABRA WALDFOGEL

Slave and Sister by Sabra Waldfogel

Copyright © 2014 by Sabra Waldfogel. All rights reserved.

Cover Design: Zetah Design, www.zetahdesign.com
Interior Design: Patti Frazee, www.pattifrazee.com
Author Photograph: Megan Dobratz, www.studiotart.com

Library of Congress PCN: 2014900927

ISBNs:
978-0-9913964-3-6—Ebook
978-0-9913964-4-3—Print

Sabra Waldfogel, Publisher
www.sabrawaldfogel.com

Published in Minneapolis, MN

For my mother, of blessed memory

Table of Contents

Prologue

The Union Scouts

On a warm afternoon towards the end of May, three years after the outbreak of the Civil War, a troop of twenty blue-coated men rode warily through the northern Georgia countryside. General Sherman's army was a few miles away, just having tangled with the Confederates at a place called Cassville. The Confederate army was in retreat, so far away that Sherman had lost sight of their position, and these men from the 10th Ohio Cavalry had been sent to find out where they were waiting for the next fight.

Captain Endicott and his second in command, Lieutenant Randolph, rode together. Endicott, slight and pale, with light brown hair and gray eyes, was an Ohio man who had rushed home from Abolitionist Oberlin College to sign up as soon as he heard about the shots fired at Fort Sumter. Randolph, taller, broader, his skin swarthy, his hair dark and wavy, was a New Yorker who had come to the war as a photographer. Once in the Union Army, he learned that a man with a keen eye had greater value as a scout. He was mustered in as a private early in 1863, and after surviving the bloody Battle of Chickamauga last September, he had become a lieutenant.

The road was packed dirt, but it was wide and even. On either side were cotton fields. The plants were choked by weeds, but the crop hadn't been burned to the ground, as they'd seen in the bushwhacked counties along the

Tennessee border. They passed a plantation house that looked the worse for wear, the paint peeling and the windows dusty. But it was standing, and whole.

They saw no one on the road and no one in the fields. The fighting at Cassville, which had been close enough to echo here, had frightened the local people into staying in their houses.

Down the road, on the right side, the open fields gave way to a slight hill covered with a thick growth of trees. Randolph said, "I don't like that thicket."

Endicott said, "Neither do I. Can you see anything?"

"No. That's what worries me."

It was a good vantage point, if you were waiting for a battle.

Endicott halted, as did the rest, and he addressed them. "We split up, ten men on the road, ten men behind. Remember, we aren't here to do battle. We're here to draw fire so we know how many there are. After they start shooting, we don't linger." He said to Powell, his second lieutenant, "You and your men approach them from the road. Randolph and I will take the rest and we'll scout them from the rear."

All of these men, with the exception of Randolph, had mustered in together in Ohio in 1862 and had been fighting together ever since. They had all been on scouting and picket duty, both dangerous, in Virginia, Tennessee and Georgia.

Powell and his men rode towards the trees. Randolph, Endicott and the others left the road, looking for the back of the hill.

Before they were in rifle range, the air began to fill with smoke from black powder and the sulphur smell of powder exploding. The shots came in a steady stream. More than their twenty men. Was it fifty? Or a hundred?

The land behind the hill was heavily wooded, too. There might be a thousand men hidden in the trees. Endicott's men, looking for a way through the growth, were met with a steady stream of fire. They couldn't see through the trees, and the horses were unable to maneuver. One of the horses was hit. It screamed and reared, and a second shot felled it. Unhorsed, its rider was shot before he could run. He dropped to the ground, screaming in pain.

Endicott called out, "Get out of the line of fire!" His men maneuvered their horses through the trees as best they could. They spurred the horses as the shots continued to come at them. In a moment, they were lost in the trees, with only the sound of hooves to tell they were there.

Randolph said, "I'll see to Robson." Before Endicott could stop him, he dismounted, crouched low, and wove his way through the trees toward the man who had fallen. Robson lay on the ground, moaning now, his tunic soaked with blood from the wound in his chest. It was too dangerous to lift him, too dangerous to stand in the rain of fire. Randolph grabbed Robson by the legs and to drag him away. Robson cried out and then he was quiet.

Randolph let go Robson's legs. Still crouching, he looked for Endicott, his vision obscured by black smoke. Keeping as low as he could, Randolph ran through the trees, trying to find a way out of the thicket.

"Randolph! Over here!" It was Endicott.

"Where are the horses?"

"Lost! Follow me!"

Stumbling, they ran together, away from the barrage. Despite the sun, it was dark in the thicket, even darker because of the smoke from the guns. Even here, the air reeked of sulphur. They ran without getting their bearings, not knowing where they were, until they could hear the shots but were out of their reach. They slowed. Panting, Randolph said, "I see a break in the trees." It was a path. "Let's hope it leads to a road," Endicott said.

They followed it, and came onto a dirt road, narrower than the one they had left. They could see beyond the trees to cotton fields again.

When they stopped, Randolph asked, "Are you all right?"

Endicott looked down to see the hole in his right sleeve. He moved his arm and groaned in pain. Randolph said, "Take off the tunic and let me see."

The sleeve of Endicott's blouse was streaked with blood. Underneath, there was a graze, ugly but not deep, in his upper arm near the shoulder. Endicott said, "Nothing serious."

Randolph poured whiskey into the wound and bound it with his handkerchief. Endicott said, "That should hold it." He reached for his rifle and groaned in pain again.

"Can you shoot like that?"

Gritting his teeth, Endicott said, "I'll have to."

They walked slowly, doubly vigilant now that they knew the Confederates were nearby. There could be an army in the next thicket and just beyond.

They had walked less than a mile when they saw it.

"I'll be damned," Randolph said. He was looking at a flagpole, and atop it flew the Stars and Stripes, which fluttered prettily in the slight breeze. Next to the flagpole was a sign that said "Kaltenbach," and a driveway.

In surprise, Endicott said, "Is there another regiment already here? Holding this place? I thought we were the advance troop."

"Let's find out."

Endicott held his rifle ready, despite the pain in his arm, and they walked slowly down the driveway.

3

The gravel of the driveway had been recently raked and smoothed. There were shrubs planted on either side, magnolias as tall as young trees, intensely fragrant, which had been recently pruned. As the driveway curved, they saw flower beds, which had been kept free of weeds. There was an expanse of lawn, which looked as though it had been tended.

Even in his apprehension, Endicott thought of his family farm, where his mother took good care of the front yard. He had not seen a Georgia plantation that looked house-proud, like a Northern homestead.

It looked peaceful. But both men had been soldiers long enough to know that peace was deceptive, and could be shattered with a single shot.

On the steps of the house stood a group of about ten black people, women and children clustered in the center. They were flanked by four men armed with rifles, who held them ready. A voice came from the center of the group. "Who are you?" she asked, and when she pushed back her straw hat they both saw that she was white.

Randolph and Endicott didn't lower their rifles. Endicott asked, "Are there Union men here?"

"No," she said. "Just you."

"Who put up the Union flag?"

The woman to her right spoke. She said calmly, "We did." Her face was the color the former slaves called medium brown, and even a glimpse of it showed that she was pretty, with a rounded face and a dimple in each cheek. She wore a neat calico dress, and over it, a clean apron. Her hair was hidden by a white kerchief. Despite her slave's attire, she stood very straight. If she were a soldier, her commander would be proud of her bearing.

Endicott asked, "Are you for the Union?"

"We all are."

Endicott's right arm ached unbearably. "Then put your rifles down."

She nodded to the four armed men, who lowered their rifles and laid them on the ground at their feet. Randolph and Endicott lowered their guns. When Endicott slung the gun over his unwounded left shoulder, he gritted his teeth against the pain.

Endicott said, "My name is Captain John Endicott. This man is Lieutenant Thomas Randolph. We're both attached to the 10th Ohio Cavalry, and we've just skirmished with the Confederates not far from here." He looked at the white woman. "Who are you, ma'am?"

"I'm Mrs. Adelaide Kaltenbach. My husband owns this place." She turned to the pretty ex-slave. Mrs. Kaltenbach said, "This is Rachel Mannheim, who manages it."

Randolph and Endicott looked at each other in surprise at the surname. Most slaves—or recently freed slaves—referred to themselves by only a Christian name.

"How do you do, sir," Rachel said. Her speech was clear and grammatical, not at all like someone born a slave.

Mrs. Kaltenbach gestured to one of the men who had been holding a rifle, who stepped forward. He was darker than Rachel, with broad shoulders and muscled arms. He wore a cotton shirt, plain blue trousers, and boots dirty with the mud of the field. She said, "This is Miss Mannheim's cousin, Charles Mannheim, who looks after the crop."

Endicott asked Adelaide Kaltenbach, "Where is your husband?"

She said, "He's away, fighting."

Endicott asked, "For the Confederacy?"

"Yes, to his regret. He's with the 18th Georgia in Virginia, God help him."

"Is he a Union man, too?"

Rachel was the one to reply. "Mr. Kaltenbach has always been a Union man, since before the war."

More and more surprised, Endicott asked, "Do you people know about the Emancipation Proclamation? That you're free?"

Another of the former riflemen, a short, sturdy man, said, "Miss Rachel read us the Emancipation Proclamation when it came out last year, and she and Miss Adelaide explained it so we could understand it."

So Miss Rachel Mannheim could read, too. Endicott, who had borne the news of freedom to many slaves in Georgia and Tennessee, asked, "What did you make of it?"

To his surprise, the sturdy man answered. "It said that we're forever free, and we can come and go as we please, and get paid wages for the work we do, and defend ourselves, and join the Union Army to fight for freedom."

Randolph said, "That's as neat a summary as I've heard from anyone."

Adelaide said, "May we offer you some refreshment? Even if it's only water?"

Endicott swallowed hard at the thought of fresh water. "Lieutenant Randolph and I would be greatly obliged."

Rachel turned to a woman who was so small that both men thought she was a child until they saw her face. She was very dark, African black, and her eyes were wide with apprehension. She held a small white boy, about five years old, tightly by the hand. Rachel said to Endicott, "This is Mrs. Minerva Davis, who looks after the house." Endicott nodded. Rachel said, "It's much too hot to stand in the sun. Please, wait on the piazza. Minnie, would you get these men a drink of water?"

When Minnie brought them water, she watched them drink it gratefully, and she said to Endicott, "Sir, are you wounded?"

Endicott said, "It's not serious."

"But it pains you."

Randolph said, "You can't ride or shoot like that." He asked Adelaide, "Might we stay for a day on your land? So Captain Endicott can rest?"

Between the two women, Adelaide Kaltenbach and Rachel Mannheim, passed the easy look of people who knew each other well. Adelaide nodded, and Rachel said, "I think we can do better than that. There's plenty of room in the house. We can make up the bedrooms, and we can give you dinner, too. And tend to that wound of yours."

Endicott was so startled at this courtesy from an ex-slave and her former mistress that he blushed. "We don't mean to trouble you."

The complicit look, and the nod. Adelaide said, "It's no trouble at all. Please come into the house."

Both men had been on grand plantations in Tennessee—they'd been headquartered in the home of one of the biggest planters in Marion County, outside Chattanooga—and they knew right away that this was the house of a small planter. The walls were painted a plain white, and the floors were a plain varnished oak. Like the grounds, the house was well-kept. The Turkey carpet in the hallway wasn't new, but it had been lightly used, and the colors were bright. Someone took care to beat the carpet and sweep the floor.

As they stood in the entryway, Endicott murmured to Randolph, "What do you make of it?"

Randolph looked at the pleasant house, which seemed untouched by the war, but he was thinking about the Union flag and the ex-slaves who understood so well that they were free. "Damnedest place I ever saw," he said.

Part 1

Chapter 1

Mules and Slaves

Rachel stood against the wall in the dining room, waiting for her master and mistress to finish their breakfast so she could clear the table. She had been in this room before, to wax the great mahogany table, brush the velvet seats of the chairs, and help Ezra the butler polish the silver, kept locked in the sideboard. "Take special care with them candlesticks," Ezra told her. "Missus prizes them. They're for the Jewish Sabbath." Marse and Missus were Israelites.

But Rachel was new to helping Ezra serve and clear, and she was still afraid that she would spill something on Missus' silk dress, or worse yet, drop one of the fragile plates that had come all the way from Germany.

Missus said, "Adelaide is being willful and won't leave her room."

Marse chewed a mouthful of eggs and said, "What's the matter?"

"She says she misses her nurse." Missus set down her fragile coffee cup hard against the fragile saucer.

Marse said, "You told me she didn't need a nurse any more. That's why I sold her."

Like every slave on the place, Rachel knew that Esther had been sold away. Now she knew why. She stood quiet against the dining room wall, feeling uneasy in her stomach.

Missus said, "She doesn't. I don't know why Adelaide is still so upset."

Marse looked at the biscuit on his plate, liberally smeared with marmalade. He said, "She's old enough for a servant of her own. A maid."

"Well, give her one. God knows we have enough useless girls around the place." Missus looked at the silver coffee pot on its silver tray. She said, "It's still tarnished." She shook her head. "Even though I slapped the girl for it last time, and told her to polish it bright."

Rachel vividly recalled the slap and the words that accompanied it. Missus told her she was lazy and insolent, and had called her *Neger* and *Affe*, words no less hurtful because they were in German.

Marse said, "I'll see to it."

Later that day, Aunt Susy said to Rachel, "Marse want to see you." Rachel's mother died when she was five and as an orphan, she had grown up in the kitchen under the eye of Aunt Susy, the cook.

Rachel's eyes went wide. "Did I do wrong?"

Aunt Susy said, "No, honey. He smile when he ask me."

Aunt Susy took Rachel to see Marse in his study. Rachel had come to this room to clean the hearth, sweep the floor and tidy the big desk. Behind the desk was a shelf of books, which she dusted every week. The room smelled of the cigars that Marse smoked and that Missus hated.

Marse sat in the big chair before the fire, his big body filling the chair. He nodded at Aunt Susy and Rachel was alone with her master.

He said, "Come here."

She came closer. He put his big hand on her shoulder. She dropped her eyes, as she should. He said, "Look at me."

She had never looked him in the face before. Now she raised her eyes to the big red face with its double chin and the dimples in both cheeks.

He said, "Miss Adelaide needs a servant. I want you to be a servant to her."

So she was the useless girl who would serve her master's daughter. "Yes, Massa," she said.

"You can start today."

"Yes, Massa.

In a gentler tone than she had ever heard from him, he said, "You take good care of young miss." Before she could reply, he patted her on the shoulder. "You can go now."

Rachel knew Miss Adelaide by sight, but Miss Adelaide, who never came into the kitchen, didn't know her. Aunt Susy led Rachel up the back stairs to Adelaide's room, where she tapped on the door before she opened it. She said, "Miss Adelaide, this is Rachel. Your daddy wants Rachel to be your maidservant."

Rachel kept her eyes down, but she had learned how to see without looking up. In the middle of the room was a big bed, twice as big as the bed in the room that Rachel shared with Aunt Susy under the rafters. It was pretty and dainty, but the girl who sat on the bed was tall and wiry, with big dark eyes and a headful of unruly dark hair. "How do, Miss Adelaide," said Rachel, looking at her bare feet.

Adelaide said crossly, "She's just a baby. What can she do for me?"

Aunt Susy said, "She'll do whatever you ask her. She's a smart gal, and capable. Now I'll leave her with you."

Adelaide, still cross, looked at her new servant and said, "Can you brush my hair?"

Rachel had never touched a white person's hair. "No, miss."

"Can you fix my dress?"

She could sew a pillowcase, but she had never sewn a dress. "No, miss."

"Can you sing to me?"

She wasn't good at singing, either. She began to worry. How could she take care of Miss Adelaide? "No, miss."

"Can you tell me a story?"

She knew stories to tell. Relieved, she said, "Yes, miss."

"What stories do you know?"

"I know Br'er Rabbit."

"Esther used to tell me stories," Adelaide said, her cross face momentarily sad. "But she didn't tell me about Br'er Rabbit." She patted the edge of the bed. "Sit with me and tell me."

Rachel looked at the beautiful white coverlet on Adelaide's bed. Adelaide said, "It's all right to do what I tell you."

Rachel sat, but she kept her eyes down.

Adelaide asked, "Why are you looking at your lap?"

Rachel said, "Missus says I'm not supposed to look Marse or Missus or young miss in the face."

Adelaide said, "I can't talk to you unless you look me in the face. So you can."

"You won't tell Missus?"

Adelaide grinned. "Mama won't know."

Rachel swallowed hard and began her story. "One day Br'er Fox got mad at Br'er Rabbit and decided he would catch him."

"What for?" Adelaide interrupted.

"To eat him!" Rachel said. "He got some tar and mixed it up with turpentine and made a baby out of tar."

"A baby?"

Rachel warmed to the telling. "Like a doll-baby. He put it in the road and waited. Along came Br'er Rabbit—Hop! Hop! Hop!" She pretended to be a rabbit and it made Adelaide laugh. She must be doing right. "Br'er Rabbit saw the tarbaby and he said, 'Good morning!' But the tarbaby didn't say a thing. Br'er Rabbit said, 'Is you too haughty to talk?' but the tarbaby didn't say a thing. 'Is you deaf?' he said, but the tarbaby didn't say a thing."

Adelaide laughed again.

Rachel said, "Br'er Rabbit got so mad that he hit the tarbaby on the head. And his hand got stuck! Couldn't pull loose."

"Silly!" Adelaide said.

"Br'er Rabbit said, 'If you don't let me loose, I'll hit you again!' But the tarbaby didn't say a thing. He hit the tarbaby with his other hand, and it stuck too. He got even madder, and he kicked the tarbaby. One foot, then another. Both stuck fast. Then Br'er Fox jumped out and said, 'Now I've got you!' Br'er Rabbit cried out, 'Br'er Fox, whatever you do, don't throw me in that briar patch!'"

"What did Br'er Fox do?"

"He said, 'That's what I'll do! I'll throw you into that briar patch!' And he grabbed Br'er Rabbit and threw him right into that briar patch. Thought he'd done him in." She paused. "But guess what?"

"What?" Adelaide said, laughing with delight.

"Br'er Rabbit got right up. He laughed at Br'er Fox and said, 'Fooled you! I was born and bred in a briar patch!' And he hopped away, just fine, laughing at Br'er Fox."

Adelaide clapped her hands and laughed. "Now I should tell you a story."

Rachel waited for her to tell it, but she got up, walked over to the shelf across the room, and pulled down a big book. "What's that?" Rachel asked.

"It's a book full of stories. They're special. From Germany. Do you want to hear a story?"

"Yes, miss."

Adelaide opened the book and turned the pages. She said, "This is a story about little Red Riding Hood." As Adelaide read the story of the brave little girl who outsmarted the wolf, Rachel looked at the pictures. The little girl in her red cape. The dark forest, so different from the pine woods of Georgia. The wolf, on his hind legs, as tall as a man. She sat side by side with

Adelaide on the bed, both of their heads bent over the pages, sharing the big book between their laps.

When Adelaide finished, Rachel pointed to the page. "Them little black marks. Is they the story?"

"They're the words. What you read." Adelaide looked up in surprise. "You don't know how to read."

Rachel shook her head.

Adelaide's cheeks were pink with excitement. "I could teach you."

Rachel said, "We ain't supposed to."

Adelaide poked Rachel in the ribs, as though she and Rachel were friends. "We aren't supposed to." She laughed. "But we will."

Later that day, Aunt Susy said, "You did right, going to Adelaide. She told her papa she liked you."

Rachel dropped her eyes and fidgeted. She wasn't sure about Adelaide, especially the promise about reading. Slaves weren't supposed to read. They were punished if they did. Was it all right because Adelaide ordered her to?

Aunt Susy bent down and drew her into her arms. "Honey, even if they is crazy, what they say, we do."

The next day, Aunt Susy let her carry up Adelaide's breakfast on the heavy silver tray: a plate of toast and marmalade in a silver pot. Marmalade was special, Aunt Susy told her. It came all the way from England, and it was made from oranges.

Oranges were for Christmas. Even though the Mannheims didn't celebrate Christmas, they gave gifts to their slaves and to each other. The slaves got lengths of cloth for new clothes, but Rachel, who lived in the house, saw the gifts that sat beside Adelaide's plate on Christmas day. Rachel didn't begrudge Adelaide a stuffed bear or a doll from Germany. But she yearned, with all her heart, for a Christmas orange like Adelaide's.

Adelaide looked up from her plate to see Rachel staring at the marmalade pot. "Do you want some?"

"I shouldn't."

"There's plenty," Adelaide said. "Mama will think I ate it." Rachel hesitated, and Adelaide grinned. "We'll fool her. Like Br'er Rabbit."

Rachel carefully daubed a piece of toast. Adelaide said, "You can have as much as you want. We have lots more." Rachel heaped the toast and took a big bite. The marmalade was sweet and sour at the same time, and it tasted the way an orange smelled when the peel came off. She closed her eyes so she could taste it better.

"Ain't it wonderful?" Adelaide said.

Every morning, the two girls ate breakfast together, and Adelaide took down the book for a reading lesson. She was delighted with Rachel's progress. "You're a good reader," she said, her eyes dancing.

"You is"—Rachel corrected herself, using the proper talk Adelaide was also teaching her—"you are a good teacher."

Rachel, who was braver with Adelaide now that she saw her every day, asked her new mistress where her mama and daddy used to live before they came to Georgia.

Adelaide said, "They came from Germany before I was born."

"Like them stories."

Adelaide said, "My daddy says they left because Jews couldn't own property, or go to school, or vote. The Germans said they couldn't."

"Was they slaves?"

Adelaide pondered this. "I don't think so." She looked thoughtful. "But Jews were slaves, a long time ago. Do you know the Passover story?"

Rachel shook her head. Passover meant helping Aunt Susy sweep the breadcrumbs out of the kitchen, dust off the special dishes, and struggle to cook without cornmeal or flour.

Adelaide said, "The Egyptians put the Jews to work, making bricks, and they beat them when they didn't work hard enough."

Puzzled, Rachel asked, "When was the Jews slaves in Egypt?"

"A long time ago. In Bible times."

"But not now."

"No. Not now."

When Marse wanted to see her again, Rachel knew how to find his study on her own. He gestured to her to come in, and said, "You're a smart gal."

She was afraid again. There was safety in stupidity. She had seen Aunt Susy, the wisest person she knew, act stupid around Marse and Missus.

"Do you know what we grow here?"

"Cotton, Massa."

"How many bales of cotton?"

"I don't know, Massa."

"Three thousand acres, two thousand in cotton, a bale an acre. How much is that?"

She was torn. Adelaide had taught her how to count, but she didn't know if it was all right to say. She said, "Two thousand bales, Massa."

He looked pleased. "How much do we get for a bale?"

She didn't know, but now he was talking about his favorite subject, money. "Five hundred pounds to a bale, ten cents a pound in Savannah. That's fifty dollars a bale. How much will three thousand bales bring?"

Interested in spite of herself, she said, "I'd like to know, Massa."

"One hundred and fifty thousand dollars," he said, and his face reddened with pride. "That's what the crop made last year."

"Is that a lot of money, Massa?"

He laughed. "A lot of money!" He smiled as though he were pleased with her.

There was more to learn than reading. There was figuring, too. She asked Adelaide if she knew how to figure.

Adelaide said, "I can, but I hate it. It makes my head ache."

"Can you teach me?"

Adelaide had a book to show her. "It's called arithmetic, not figuring."

Whatever it was called, Rachel found that it came easily to her. She could do sums in her head, and she could multiply and divide, too. The next time Marse asked her about the price of cotton—"It's up to twelve cents a pound. How much would I get for a bale?"—Rachel had to bite her tongue. She wanted the figuring to stay a secret.

When Rachel came into Marse's study to dust and straighten she saw the newspaper strewn across the desk. She had never touched it before, but now that she knew how to read, she hesitated before it, longing to know what the "little black marks" said. If Missus found her reading, she'd be punished.

Marse had already read it and left it open. He would never know if she read it herself. She touched the page, her hands shaking, startling at the rustle the paper made. The page said "Commercial Intelligence", and she struggled through it, reading about the news from the cotton exchange: not just the price of cotton in Savannah, but in Charleston, New Orleans, and a place called London.

So that was how Marse knew about the price of cotton. And now she could know, too.

Drawn in, she turned the pages to read about the world the newspaper described—the world of politics, which she didn't understand, and the newest in ladies' bonnets, even though she would never wear one, and the round of parties, balls, and visits in Savannah and Charleston, even though she would never go there. There were darker things in the paper, too—notices for auctions, where slaves and mules were sold at the same time, and described in much the same terms, and announcements about runaway slaves.

She thought she heard a rustle, like the sound of a silk dress, and she leaped up to grab the dusting cloth and tell Missus she'd been straightening the paper, not reading it. Her heart pounded. But no one came in. She must have imagined it. Her heart still pounding, she folded up the paper and began to dust.

Later that day Missus came into the kitchen to find Rachel petting Dinah, the black and white cat who lived in the kitchen, who was curled sleeping on the floor. She said sharply to Rachel, "You wash your hands before you touch anything else."

To Aunt Susy, she said, "Why do you keep that dirty animal in here?"

Aunt Susy said, "Ma'am, she catch mice, and we do have mice, 'cause we have flour and rice in here."

Missus said, "Get it away. You can take it out and drown it."

Aunt Susy said, "Yes, ma'am," and Missus walked away, her silk dress rustling, leaving behind the scent of lavender.

Rachel picked up Dinah and held her close to her chest. She felt Dinah's heart beat against her own, two beats to her one. She asked, "We aren't going to drown Dinah, are we?"

"Sugar, don't you worry. We're going to hide Dinah somewhere safe. Somewhere Missus will never find her."

"Aunt Susy?"

"Yes, sugar?"

"Why is Missus so mean to me?"

Aunt Susy looked troubled. "She ain't a happy woman. Now you help me hide Dinah."

Marse told Missus that she wasn't to beat the servants, but he didn't say anything about slaps or hard words. That Friday, Aunt Susy left Rachel to watch the Sabbath strudel and it burned. Aunt Susy returned to find Missus slapping Rachel's face with all her might. They both had to hear the words that were worse than the slaps. "*Neger*! *Affe*! You aren't fit to live in this house."

Afterwards, as Aunt Susy bathed her bruised cheeks, Rachel wept, so upset her "upstairs talk" deserted her. "Aunt Susy, what do I do so wrong?"

Aunt Susy hugged her. "It ain't you."

"What is it?"

Aunt Susy held her at arm's length and looked into her eyes. She touched one of the bruised cheeks. "She don't like black folks."

"I know that. But she hates me!"

Rachel was right. Aunt Susy sighed. "She never liked your mama."

"Why not? What did my mama do?"

"She was pretty, and kind, and Marse liked her. That was enough for Missus."

"Tell me again about my mama."

"She was darker than you. Her mama was from Africa. When you were a baby she sang you African songs her mama taught her."

"Do I look like her?"

"Of course you do."

Troubled, Rachel asked, "Aunt Susy, what happened to my mama?"

She had never seen Aunt Susy look so sad. "She passed on, sugar. The Lord took her when you were five. You know that."

Rachel never felt easy about reading in Adelaide's room, even though Adelaide assured her it was all right. Rachel said, "If your mama find out, she'll be mighty mad."

Adelaide said, "She won't."

They sat together on the bed, sharing the book between them, as Rachel spelled out the words and Adelaide helped her. Rachel heard the rustle of silk before Adelaide did. She looked up in fear. Missus stared at them both and said to Adelaide, "What are you doing?"

Defiantly, Adelaide said, "I'm reading Rachel a story."

"Don't lie to me. Was she reading?" She gestured at Rachel. "Did you teach her how to read?"

Adelaide's cheeks flamed. "We were looking at my book together."

Missus lost her temper and slapped Adelaide's face. Shaken, Adelaide put her hand on the reddened spot. Missus said, "Don't you know it's against the law to teach a slave to read? And don't you sass me, answering."

Adelaide dropped her eyes to the floor. "Yes, ma'am," she mumbled.

Missus turned to Rachel. "Slaves who read should be whipped. That's the law, too. You come with me."

Missus took Rachel into Marse's room, where Rachel had never set foot, since it was Ezra's task to look after Marse. Missus opened the clothes press and took out a leather belt that had a heavy silver buckle.

Missus raised her arm and raised her voice. "This is what happens to slaves who learn to read," she said. The buckle came down hard on Rachel's head. Missus cried out, "I'll sell you. I swear I'll make my husband sell you."

Rachel fell to the floor, covering her head with her hands. She was afraid that the buckle would catch her eye and blind her. "Missus, stop it, stop it!"

She heard the loud, angry voice before Marse burst into the room. "What is this?" He grabbed Missus and pulled her away. "What are you doing?" he shouted. "What in God's name do you think you are doing?"

Missus looked up. Anger blazed on her face. "She was reading. Adelaide taught her."

He ripped the belt from her hand. "You could have killed her."

Missus burst into tears. "Why is she in the house? I have to see her every day and remember. Sell her! I never want to see her again."

Rachel uncovered her head. Marse clenched the belt in his hand as though he wanted to use it beat someone. He glared at Missus. His voice was still loud and angry. "I'm not going to sell her."

"Send her out to work in the field. Not in the house. I can't bear it."

"I don't want her in the field. I want her in the house. And don't ask me again to sell her, because I won't."

Missus buried her face in her hands. "I hate you," she said, sobbing. "I hate her. I hate all of it."

Marse threw the belt on the floor. He slammed the door behind him as he left the room.

The buckle caught Rachel just above her right eyebrow. Aunt Susy said, "I'll do my best to heal it, but I'm afraid you'll have a scar."

A few weeks later, just before Adelaide's birthday, Rachel sat with Adelaide as she ate her supper. Adelaide's dining room wasn't really a room, but a space near the door, just big enough for a little pine table and four little pine ladderback chairs. In warm weather, when the door was propped open, she and Adelaide could see into the breezeway and almost into the kitchen.

Tonight Marse joined them. Rachel stood up, since it wasn't right for her to sit in the presence of her master. Marse bent down and said to Adelaide, "Well, young miss, what do you want for your birthday? Would you like a pony?"

"No, sir. I don't want a pony."

"What do you want?"

Adelaide had never said a word about the fight between her father and her mother, and she had never said a word about the cut above Rachel's eye, either. Now she looked into the face of her servant, then into the face of her father. "I want you to give me Rachel."

"I've given you Rachel! She's your maidservant."

She said stubbornly, "I want her to belong to me so that no one can sell her."

Marse frowned. "For that, young miss, you'll have to wait. You can't own property until you're twenty-one. Or until you're married."

On Adelaide's birthday, her father led her outside, where Sam, the coachman, stood beside a brown pony, harnessed to a new cart painted red, with a wooden seat big enough for two. Adelaide stared at her father. "I told you I didn't want a pony," she said, and turned to walk inside.

Adelaide stayed in her room and refused to eat. Her mother sent for the doctor, a young man with a clean-shaven, rosy face, who poked and prodded her and looked inside her mouth, as if he were buying a mule. He said, "There's nothing wrong with her."

Missus said, "Doesn't she need a tonic? Or castor oil?"

"She'd benefit from some fresh air. Perhaps a drive. It doesn't help her to stay in her room like this." He looked at Rachel. "Her servant is looking dull, too. Is she in here all day with her mistress?"

Missus said, "Of course she is. That's her duty."

"She can't do her duty if she gets sick. Let her have some fresh air, too."

Take care of young miss, Marse had said. Rachel thought about the pony and the cart.

A few days later, Rachel summoned her courage and went to see Sam at the stables. Sam was as important on the Mannheim place as Ezra, and Rachel had never dared to suggest anything to Ezra. The slaves on the place thought so highly of Sam that they called him "Mister Sam" among themselves.

Sam was a tall, lean man, very dark of skin, and he was as calm as a tree. People said that if the stable caught fire, a circumstance that made horses kick and scream with terror, Sam would be able to lead them to safety as peacefully as though they were going for a Sunday drive. Everyone and everything was calm around him. His fourteen-year-old son Ned, similarly dark and calm, helped him in the stables.

"Lil gal, what do you want?" he asked her.

Stammering a little, she explained the doctor's orders.

Sam said, "Let me feel the muscle in your arm." She held out her arm and Sam bent down to test the strength of her upper arm with his long fingers. He looked at Rachel's determined face and nodded. "Marse has to say yes."

They went to see Marse together.

Sam said, "It's good for the pony, and it's good for your gal, too. This little 'un is smart, and steady, and I know I can teach her."

Puzzled, Marse said, "Can't we spare Ned?"

"We could, but look at this li'l gal here. She's set on taking care of young miss."

Marse looked at her with surprise. She said softly, "Like you asked me, Massa."

He said to Sam, "You're sure I can trust her with the pony and the cart?"

"Yes, Massa."

Rachel had never seen Marse look like that. His look was almost tender. "All right. I'll allow it."

When she came to the stables for her first lesson, Sam said to her, "I don't want you yelling around the horses. Horses got sensitive ears, and nerves, and they don't like to be startled."

"I'll be quiet," Rachel said.

Marse had seven horses in the big stable that smelled of straw, fodder, and manure. Each horse turned its head as Sam and Rachel walked by. They stopped before the pony's stall. Sam said, "First, we got to introduce you."

"What's her name?"

"Brownie."

At the sound of her name, the pony turned her head. She had a brown coat with a white star on her nose. Her eyes were big and dark, with long lashes. The pony nosed Rachel's face, then her head. Rachel giggled. The soft nose tickled. "What's she doing?" she asked, her voice muffled.

"That's how she gets acquainted. Let her do it."

The pony nosed her shoulder, then her arm. "Can I touch her?"

"Touch her the way her hide grows."

As Rachel laid her arm across the horse's neck, she saw that her arm and the horse's coat were exactly the same color. Two brown gals together, she thought.

Sam taught Rachel how to hitch up the cart and harness the pony, making her practice until she didn't have to think about it to do it right. He watched her go around the stableyard, and trusted her to drive the length of the driveway to the road and back. Finally he said, "Now you ready to take her out."

She ran up the back stairs into Adelaide's room. "Adelaide! Sam says I can drive the pony cart! I can take you for a drive!"

Adelaide out down the book she was reading and grinned. "Can we go to Cassville?"

They stopped at the general store, where Mr. Stockton, the owner, greeted Adelaide and asked if Sam drove her.

Adelaide laughed and said, "Rachel drove me!"

Mr. Stockton grinned. "Are you the new coachman on the Mannheim place?"

Rachel knew he was making fun of her, but she smiled shyly and nodded.

Mr. Stockton gave Adelaide a peppermint candy and winked at Rachel. "You drive careful!" he said, laughing.

A few days later, when Rachel asked Adelaide if she'd like to go for a drive, Adelaide said bitterly, "Mama says I can't go driving."

Indignant, Rachel asked, "Why not?"

"She says I'm a young lady and I'm too old to act like a silly little girl. She says that people are laughing at me, letting my maidservant cart me around instead of going out in the carriage with Sam or Ned."

"That ain't true," Rachel said, so upset she forgot the proper talk that Adelaide had taught her. "Ain't no one laughing at us."

"Mama says that you belong in the house, not in the stables, and if you go there again, she'll beat you. I think she wants to sell you, even though Papa said no."

Rachel ran to the stables to see Brownie, so upset she was willing to defy Missus. Sam stopped her in the stableyard. He knelt to her eye level, not minding the muck, and put his hands on her shoulders. "Missus said you wasn't to be here."

"I want to see Brownie."

"I never saw a woman look so mad. I don't want her to find you here. I'm afraid that she'll hurt you if she whups you."

"Just let me see Brownie. One last time."

"You can't."

"Why not?"

"Marse sold Brownie."

There was more than one way to beat a slave. As Rachel walked back to the big house, she felt whipped in her spirit. She was heartsore that day, and for days afterwards.

Aunt Susy said, "You still pining for that horse?"

Rachel shook her head.

Bleakly, Aunt Susy said, "You learned the hardest way. As a slave, don't nothing belong to you. Not your food, not your dress, not your house. If you marry, not your husband, and if you have a baby, not your child. You lucky you broke your heart over a pony."

Several weeks later, a field hand named Livvy struck the overseer. The slaves, who knew the rest of the story, murmured it among themselves. The overseer had forced himself on her, and she had fought with him to save herself.

Livvy was put into the guardhouse while Marse decided what to do with her. Mordecai Mannheim rarely whipped a slave. If a slave was obstinate in the field, or disobedient with the overseer, he didn't bother to whip. He'd sell the slave, the way he'd sell a balky mule or a horse that had gone lame. A slave who displeased him would go into the next coffle bound for Mississippi, to be sold at a profit.

The slave dealers came from Cassville at midmorning, when Rachel was in the yard helping Aunt Susy with the weekly wash. Aunt Susy bent her head and plunged her arms into the washtub, but Rachel straightened up to watch as the overseer unlocked the guardhouse and led Livvy out. Her dress was dirty and torn, and her kerchief was spotted with blood where she had wiped her wounded face. Her feet were shackled together and she walked with difficulty. Her hands were bound behind her back with rope.

The slave dealer said to Marse, "Don't worry, I'll get a good price for her. She's young and strong, and they're paying good money for hands in Mississippi."

Into Marse's pocket to be sold away to Mississippi.

The dealer looked at Livvy with a lewd light in his face. He said, "Now that she's shackled up, I reckon she'll be more tractable."

To be forced along the way.

Rachel brooded about Livvy all day, and at the end of the day, when Charlie would be back from the field, she ran to his cabin to find him. Charlie was Aunt Susy's nephew and he was like a brother to Rachel. At fourteen, he did a grown man's work in the cotton fields, and she knew how tired he was at the end of a long day of hoeing and chopping. Today he looked even wearier than usual. He sat on the steps of his family's cabin nodded as she sat down.

"Livvy gone," she said.

"I heard."

"Sell her like a balky mule!" she said. "Beat her like a mule!" She couldn't say the rest. It bothered her too much.

Charlie said bitterly, "Did you ever see a mule shackled up?"

She burst into tears. "Marse sells people just like they were mules!" She sobbed and sobbed and couldn't stop.

Charlie sighed and put his arms around her. He said softly, "Hush, Rachel," gentling her until her sobs slowed.

Her voice choked, she said, "Someday I won't please him or I'll do wrong and he'll sell me to Mississippi like Livvy."

Charlie let her go. He said, "He'll never sell you."

"Why not?"

"Aunt Susy ain't told you?"

"No," she said, puzzled.

"You is old enough to know, and you should know."

"Know what?"

"Marse Mannheim is your daddy."

Chapter 2

The Only Israelite

Every year, Mordecai Mannheim had a frolic in May, when his planter neighbors and their slaves could take a brief respite from the cotton crop. He invited everyone in the county for a grand picnic, and let the slaves roast a pig to share with anyone who might miss it at a Jewish barbecue. There was always music. The Mannheims owned the best slave fiddlers in the county, a father and three sons, who could play a cotillion or a reel, and who could adapt Stephen Foster or Schumann for dancing. For the ladies, there was plenty of opportunity to gossip; for the girls, the chance to flirt; and for the men, Mordecai always brought out his birds for cockfights, accompanied by wagering and drinking.

The Mannheims were the only Jews in Cass County. For Adelaide, being a Jew meant keeping the "kosher laws," as every Mannheim servant called them, and going to synagogue in Savannah once a year. Adelaide, who was restless in her seat at Mickve Israel, had no religious feelings on the New Year or the Day of Atonement. She took note of the beautiful dresses of her mother's Savannah friends, and suffered the torment of Emilie Cohen, daughter of her mother's best friend in Savannah. Adelaide and Emilie were friends too, after a fashion, but Emilie was an expert pincher and tattletale.

Papa wasn't religious and he didn't mind. When a hill country man came up to him in the street in Cassville to say, "You're a Jew? You don't look different from anyone else!" her father grinned and said, "How should I look?" In the general store, when a pious lady said to him, "An Israelite! Just like in the Bible!" he laughed. And when his lawyer, a freethinker who went to church once a year, said, "I don't care what a man believes or whether he prays or not. That's his business, not mine," her father shook his hand and took the whiskey he offered.

Cass County was full of ambitious, rough-edged men, and her father fit in easily. His neighbors approved of a man who had prospered as a planter. Her father became known as a good host, a man who put on a grand frolic or barbecue or dance. He acquired fighting birds, and his cockfights entertained all the men of the county. Everyone acknowledged that he was a sharp man with a dollar, but no one said a word against his being a Jew.

It was harder for her mother, Adelaide knew. When Mr. Johnson bought the place next to her father's, Mrs. Johnson came to call. Drinking tea and nibbling at a sesame biscuit, she asked, "Who are your people, Mrs. Mannheim?"

Adelaide knew what she meant. Mrs. Johnson was asking about their relatives, thinking they might have acquaintance in common. But her mother froze as though she had forgotten the English. After a long pause, she said, "I don't think you'd know them, Mrs. Johnson. They live in Germany."

Mrs. Johnson's pretty face creased in dismay. "Is there no one nearby? No kin at all?"

Adelaide saw the pain in her mother's face and heard the effort she made to control her voice. "No, they're all far away, so far away I'm not likely to see them again."

Mrs. Johnson said awkwardly, "Mrs. Mannheim, surely the ladies of the county have made you feel welcome. Will we see you in church on Sunday? Do you attend the Methodist Church?"

Rosa shook her head. "We're Israelite, Mrs. Johnson. We don't go to church."

Mrs. Johnson looked at her with curiosity. "Where do you worship?"

"In Savannah."

"But that's so far away!"

Her mother wrote every week to her friends Mrs. Meyer and Mrs. Cohen, back in Savannah. "We'll go there once a year, for the High Holy Days."

"Once a year! However will you practice your religion?"

Her mother blinked back the tears. "At home," she said. "We observe our religion at home."

A few days before the frolic, at midday dinner, in Adelaide's hearing,

Rosa Mannheim talked to her husband as though Adelaide weren't there. "I'm worried about Adelaide at the frolic."

"There's no harm if she goes to the parties and barbecues and meets the boys, as long as she don't marry one."

Rosa shook her head. "I don't like it," she said.

Her father winked at Adelaide and laughed. "We can't refuse to associate with our neighbors."

The day of the frolic was pleasant for May, but Adelaide, newly laced into a corset, felt hot and a little faint. Rachel, still awkward with the new garment, had laced her too tight. She sat in the shade of the live oak trees with the Turners—Hattie, who was fifteen, and her brothers Ben Junior and Pierce, thirteen and eleven. The boys listened enviously to the sound of men cheering on the fighting birds. Ben said, "I'd like to wager, and I'd take a drink of whiskey, if I were offered." Hattie said, "No one would. You aren't old enough, and even if you were, drinking and wagering are sins."

Stung, Ben said, "And we aren't to flirt with Miss Adelaide, either, because she's to marry a rich Israelite in Savannah when she grows up."

Pierce said, "Ain't we good enough for her?" Pierce was a rough tease. He once pulled Adelaide's hair until tears came into her eyes. Now she wasn't sure whether he was teasing.

Ben said, "I guess not."

Irritated, Adelaide asked, "Who said that?"

Hattie, a telltale, said, "Mama did. She said your Mama told her."

Adelaide's corset pinched and itched. She looked at the Turner boys with scorn. "Both of you are the biggest fools I ever saw. I wouldn't marry either of you if someone held a gun to my head."

She got up and walked away. She didn't go far, since she couldn't breathe very deeply. She sank down onto the grass, in the shade—her mother would be mad if she stained her new dress, but she didn't care—and let the breeze blow over her.

Rachel, who was always pressed into kitchen duty at a frolic or a party or the Seder, hurried past her on the way to the kitchen. When she saw Adelaide she said, "Why are you setting alone? Are you all right?"

Adelaide said, "I'm so tired of being the only Israelite wherever I go."

Rachel said, "Can't do much about it."

"I could get up tomorrow and eat bacon for breakfast and go to the Baptist meeting."

Today Rachel was easy with her. She laughed. "Or you could go to Savannah." Last year Rachel had come to Savannah as her maidservant. "There are lots of Jews in Savannah."

Adelaide clasped her knees. "Mama wants to send me to Savannah to go to school. She said I could stay with the Cohens."

"Why don't you?"

"Papa won't have it. He said I could get finished just as well at the College in Cassville." She meant the Cassville Female College, newly opened that year. "He wants me to go there."

"That ain't so bad," Rachel said, smiling.

"Isn't so bad," Adelaide corrected, teasing, because she knew how well Rachel could talk when she felt like it. "If I go to Savannah, will you come with me?"

"Of course I will."

Adelaide, who had no sisters, had always envied the girls of the county who did. A slave wasn't a sister, but her affection would have to do. She hugged Rachel, and Rachel hugged her in return.

Before the fall term began at the college, Rosa went to see the headmaster, a courtly Methodist minister, to explain that as an Israelite, Adelaide needed special accommodation. She was to be excused from daily prayer, and she was not to eat ham or bacon at midday dinner. The Reverend Warren, eager to enroll the daughter of the one of the richest planters in the county at the College, nodded pleasantly and agreed.

The College offered young ladies a serious education. Adelaide studied science and mathematics in addition to Latin, Greek, philosophy, and history. The girls at the College came from all of the surrounding counties and towns— Macon, Marietta, Athens, and all of the rural places where their papas owned plantations and grew cotton.

Adelaide's classmates, pious like their mothers, worried about her. "Adelaide, where do you go to church? Where will you say your prayers?" Adelaide said, "I say them at home," which was a lie, because aside from the few words a week over the Sabbath candles, she said no prayers at all.

The dietary laws baffled the cook at the College, and Adelaide brought her midday dinner to school in a basket. It set her apart in a way that bothered her. She wished she could eat from the common table. But if she broke the "kosher laws," her mother would know.

Despite her oddity as the only Jew at the Female College, Adelaide made friends there. Her best friend, the one she giggled with and told secrets to, was Martha Edwards, whose family had a place near Marietta in Cobb County and forty slaves to work it. She was a gentle girl with clear gray eyes and a sweet voice. She was upset when she learned that Adelaide had no brothers and even more sadly, no sisters, and that all her cousins lived so far away in Germany that she had never met them. She said, "You must call me Mattie, and let me call you Addie, as a sister would."

The two girls became inseparable. Every day, they would sit on the sofa in the parlor of the College to do their lessons together, and when they tired of their studies, to whisper to each other. Mattie would say, "Oh, la, Addie, don't make me laugh so, my sides ache," but she would laugh until she had to wipe tears from her eyes. She would lean close to Adelaide, smiling to take the sting from her words, to ask, "Are all Israelites as wicked as you?"

They had been friends for six months when Mattie said, "You must come to stay with us, and meet my mama and my papa." Adelaide asked for permission at supper that night. Rosa said, "What if she has a brother? Or a cousin?" Mordecai said, "Rosa, we can't keep her locked up. It's just like at home. She can be pleasant to the boys without encouraging them."

When Mattie and Adelaide, accompanied by Rachel, arrived at the Edwards place on a cool day in February, Mattie flew into her mother's arms. "Mama! I've missed you so!" Her mother kissed her tenderly.

Mrs. Edwards reached out her hands to Adelaide and pressed them in her own. "So this is your dear friend from the College," she said, smiling. "Mattie tells me that you're an Israelite. I don't believe we've ever entertained an Israelite in our house."

"Mama, I should have written, but I didn't know how to tell you. Adelaide isn't to eat bacon or ham, because of her religion." Mrs. Edwards let go Adelaide's hands and looked at her guest in puzzlement. "My goodness," she said. "Whatever am I going to give you?"

When the two girls retired upstairs to change their traveling dresses, Rachel went with Adelaide, and Mattie's maidservant came to her room. "My servant's name is Polly," Mattie said to Adelaide. "Polly, say how do to my friend from the college, Miss Adelaide Mannheim."

Polly was thin and tall. She was very fair of skin, closer to ivory than to brown, and she had brown hair that fell in curls down her back. When she raised her head a little Adelaide saw that her eyes were hazel, and that she had a long, arched nose and narrow lips, like Mattie's.

Mattie said, "Polly, why do you look so unhappy? Ain't you glad that I'm home?"

Adelaide forced herself not to stare at the slave who looked just like her mistress. Polly's expression didn't change, but she nodded and said, "Yes, miss."

At dinner that day, Adelaide met Mattie's older brother James, who attended the University in Athens, where he was studying the law. He was a tall, gangly boy of seventeen, with the gray eyes and pleasant expression of all the Edwardses. Like Mattie, he was nicknamed at home. His mother and sister called him Jamie.

Jamie was soft-voiced, like his sister, and one of his first remarks to Adelaide was to ask what she liked to read. Adelaide was used to the boys of Cass County, loud and rough like their fathers, whose pleasures in life were hunting and cockfighting. None of them were readers, unless you counted the front page of the *Cassville Standard*, which advertised horses and slaves for sale. Adelaide knew only one man in Cass County who read for pleasure, and that was Reverend Warren of the College, who was a schoolteacher by profession. She was delighted to be asked. "I read my schoolbooks, as I should," she said, "but for pleasure, I like Sir Walter Scott."

"Do you read poetry?"

She hated to disappoint a boy with such a sweet expression. "A little," she lied.

Adelaide was having trouble with her dinner. The creamed peas were all right, and so was the biscuit, but if she ate them, she couldn't eat the chicken that had been set alongside the ham. She pushed the food around her plate, to make it look as though she'd been eating. She thought that she hated the kosher laws. She wondered if God would forgive her if she ate whatever was put before her.

After dinner, Jamie joined his mother and his sister in the parlor. Mattie said, "Jamie, read to us." She smiled at Adelaide—was that a cunning look on her innocent friend's face?—and said to her brother, "Read to us from that book of poetry you've been carrying around in your pocket."

Jamie blushed and took out the book. "William Wordsworth," he said, and as he read, he looked at Adelaide.

It was pleasant to be read to, even if the poem didn't make much sense to her, and when Jamie finished he asked, "May I read you another one, Mattie? Miss Adelaide?"

Every day of her visit, Jamie sat next to her at midday dinner and again at supper. Every day, the meals included something that Adelaide knew her mother would not want her to eat. Hungry, worried about offending, and tired of being set apart, she began to break the kosher laws. The chicken, cooked in butter. The cream sauce with it. Did God really care so much what a person put in her mouth? By the end of the week, she ate everything but bacon at breakfast and ham at dinner.

Jamie continued to read poetry to both girls after dinner. On the last night of her visit, as they walked from the dining room into the parlor, he smiled at her and said softly, "I write poetry myself."

"Like Wordsworth," Adelaide said, knowing it would make him blush.

"Not as fine as Wordsworth's." He stood very close to her, and she could smell the pomade he put on his hair. He said, "If I write you a poem, may I send it to you?"

Was this forbidden, too? She smiled at him and said, "My mama shouldn't know. Send it to Mattie and she'll give it to me."

Jamie blushed. "I promise," he said.

A few days after she returned home, her mother knocked hard on her bedroom door. Rosa was very pale, with a bright red spot on each cheek. Adelaide had never seen her mother look like that, unless she was scolding a slave.

Rosa held a letter in her hand. She said coldly, "Do you know what this is?"

Adelaide had been lounging in bed, reading, but she sat up straight. "No, Mama."

"Who is James Edwards?"

Adelaide began to feel cold. "That's Mattie's brother, Mama."

"Why is he writing to you?"

Adelaide stammered, "I didn't know—"

Rosa held the letter away from her, as though it were covered with manure. "It's a love letter! He wrote you a love poem!"

Oh, Lord. The foolish boy. He had sent the poem to her instead of to Mattie.

In a fury, Rosa said, "What did you do to encourage him? Did you let him hold your hand? Did you let him kiss you?"

Adelaide whispered, "Of course not."

Rosa tore the letter into pieces and let them flutter to the floor. "What possessed you?"

Adelaide shook her head.

Rosa grabbed her daughter by the shoulders. Adelaide turned her face away, but her mother clasped her face roughly between her hands. "Do you know what would happen if you fell in love with a boy who isn't a Jew? What would happen if you married outside our faith?"

"But I won't, Mama."

Rosa slapped her daughter hard. "It would be a disgrace. Do you hear me? A disgrace!"

Adelaide began to sob. "Mama, stop, you're hurting me."

Rosa slapped her again. "You're not to visit these girls from school ever again, do you hear me? Not to speak to their brothers or cousins ever again!"

Sobbing, Adelaide said, "Yes, Mama."

Rosa let her go. When she left the room she slammed the door.

A few days later, Mattie pulled her aside to sit in the parlor at the College in the few minutes between the end of morning instruction and midday dinner. Her sweet face was pale and pinched. She yanked Adelaide's hand to make her sit down on the sofa where they had shared so many confidences, and she said, "Your Mama wrote to mine. And my Mama wrote to me."

"Mattie, whatever is the matter?"

"My Mama said that she'd never had such a nasty letter from anyone. She said I wasn't to speak to you, not ever again. And she said if that's what Israelites are like, she'd never allow another one in her house, not as long as she lived." Mattie rose to go. Adelaide stretched out her hands, but Mattie turned and walked away without looking back.

Adelaide was doubly stunned, at the end of the friendship and the insult. She wasn't given to tears, but that night she cried herself to sleep for the loss of the girl she had loved like a sister. For nights afterwards, the tears came afresh.

After Mattie broke off their friendship, Adelaide grew quiet and spent a great deal of time by herself. She was polite to the girls at school, but at home she was either walking in the countryside, dressed in the old dress and boots she called her "rambling clothes," or she was reading in bed, propped up on her pillows. Her mother deplored both habits, telling her that neither was suitable for a young lady.

When the school year ended, and the round of frolics and barbecues began again, Adelaide felt lonelier than ever. Hattie Turner was a poor companion, and all of the local boys were forbidden to her. Adelaide had rarely cried, but now she found that tears came easily. On the morning of her father's frolic, which she had enjoyed only a year before, she got out of bed to sob. Rachel found her like that, sitting at her dressing table, her hands over her face.

Rachel set down the breakfast tray. Adelaide said mournfully, "I ain't the least bit hungry."

"I can take it away."

"No, stay for a moment." Adelaide gestured to the tray. "You eat it, if you want. It's a shame to waste it."

"I ain't hungry either, but I'll set."

She had confided in Rachel how much she had cared about Mattie, and Rachel knew, as her mother did not, how crushed she was when Mattie ended the friendship. Now she raised her tear-stained face and said, "I miss Mattie so."

Rachel nodded.

"Won't anyone call me Addie, not ever again." She sobbed afresh. "I never had a sister and now I never will."

Rachel handed Adelaide a handkerchief.

Adelaide wiped her face and blew her nose in the most unladylike way. She said, "If Papa wouldn't mind, I'd stay in bed to read instead of going to the frolic."

Rachel came to stand behind her and said, "Do you recall, when we visited Miss Mattie, she had a servant named Polly?"

"Of course I do." Uneasily, Adelaide recalled the girl's fair skin and hazel eyes.

"Didn't they look alike?"

Puzzled, Adelaide said, "I don't know."

"Look in the mirror," Rachel said.

Adelaide saw a familiar sight, Rachel's face and her own. She twisted around in her chair. "I don't understand."

Rachel's face was composed, but her face was the grayish color that reflected distress on a black skin. Adelaide stared at her servant. "Rachel, what's the matter?"

"Don't you see it?"

Adelaide shook her head. Rachel put her hands on Adelaide's shoulders. As Adelaide stared at their reflection in the mirror, she saw, for the first time, the similarity in the shape of their eyes and the curve of their lips. She thought again of Polly and Mattie, the same features on both faces, one white, one the palest brown.

Rachel said, very low, "As alike as sisters."

Adelaide whispered, "Can't be." She sat in stunned silence as Rachel dressed her for the frolic and combed her hair, as though nothing was different between them.

Later that morning, Adelaide sat alone under the live oaks, listening to the girls laugh and flirt with the county boys, listening to the men shout and cheer as they wagered on the fighting birds. She had no desire to get a plate of food, or chat with Hattie Turner, or to speak to anyone at all.

Behind her, she heard the voices of two ladies, the low tones of gossip. Everything they said carried in the soft spring air.

One said, "Did you hear what happened at the Taylor place? A lady who was visiting saw one of the slave gals nursing a baby and congratulated Mrs. Taylor on her newest. Only it weren't Mrs. Taylor's. It were the slave gal's." The speaker laughed. "White as a boll of cotton, and looked just like its daddy."

"Oh, la," said the other. "If that happened to me I'd make my husband sell her."

"Easier said than done." The voice dropped to a hiss. "Just ask Miss Rosa." A snort of laughter. "At least the gal looks like her ma."

Adelaide sat in the shade of the live oak, her face burning. She had always longed for a sister. Now she had one, in a way too shameful to admit to.

Chapter 3

Gentlemen of Savannah

Halfway through the Rosh Hashanah morning service, Adelaide shifted uncomfortably in her seat at Mickve Israel. Even though the synagogue sold tickets for "seats," they were wooden benches, like pews, on which the cushions did little to relieve the backside during a long day of prayer. The Mannheims came to Savannah every year for the High Holy Days, but this year, Rosa and Adelaide would remain after Mordecai went back to Cassville. Once her mother wrote to Louisa Cohen to say they'd be coming, Adelaide asked, "How long will we stay?"

Her father grinned. "Until we get you set up," he said, as though he were talking about one of his business dealings.

Rosa, who had tolerated Adelaide's education long enough, insisted that she end her schooling after she turned eighteen. Adelaide left her studies and her friends at the College with a sinking heart. She and her mother would go to Savannah and stay until she was engaged to be married.

In the synagogue, the Meyers sat to their right. Nathan Meyer, who owned Meyer's Dry Goods, had been her father's first employer in America. He was in his sixties, and his son Joe now ran the business. Last year Joe had come to Cassville as a possible suitor. He was twice her age. He had tactfully told her parents that he knew he was too old and dull for her, which saved the relationship between the two families. Adelaide was grateful to Joe, and she felt as easy with him as with a brother.

After Joe went home, her mother sniffed and said, "It's just as well. You can do better."

Her mother's friend Louisa Cohen sat with her family, which had bought more expensive seats a few rows ahead of them, closer to the pulpit. Cotton had been so high in the past few years that Mr. Cohen had become one of the richest factors in the city, dealing with planters as far away as Mississippi and Louisiana, and selling to brokers in Charleston, New Orleans, New York, and London. They were staying with the Cohens, as they always had. Despite the long friendship, her mother was now uneasy with Louisa Cohen. "She's become so grand," Rosa said, her awe tinged with sadness.

The Cohens had built a new house since the Mannheims' last visit. It was three and a half stories tall, and the architect must have thought of a castle, because it had a two turrets and first-floor windows that glittered with stained glass. When Adelaide and Rosa first arrived, Louisa Cohen came to meet them with her hands outstretched in greeting. Louisa had always been beautifully dressed, but now she was more gorgeous than ever. She wore a dress with a fitted bodice, made of striped silk that alternated light brown with dark, and a skirt that flared from the narrowest waist into a great bell of dark brown silk. Even when she stopped moving, her hoops continued to dance by themselves under the skirt. Her earbobs flashed as she moved her head and her fair hair shimmered in the late afternoon light.

Mrs. Cohen hugged her mother and stood back, smiling and clasping her hands. "Rosa, it's so good to see you! Are you well? You look peaked."

"We've been on the train since early this morning. We are a little tired."

Mrs. Cohen turned to Adelaide and looked her up and down. Adelaide had never felt such a penetrating stare. She thought, That's how Papa looks at a slave gal he wants to sell. Figuring what he can get for her.

"Adelaide." She reached for Adelaide's hands. As she grasped them, she said, "Whatever is that on your fingers?"

Adelaide looked at the strong, long-fingered hands that her mother despaired of. She said, "I write a lot of letters. It's ink."

"Goodness, you can't meet young men with your hands inkstained like a clerk's. We'll have to fix that."

Rosh Hashanah was late this year, at the end of September, but even in the cooler air of fall, it was hot inside the synagogue. Adelaide was dressed for modesty, not for the weather, and she felt unbearably hot. Her dress was lightweight wool, and underneath it she was laced too tight. She longed to do something that no lady should ever do. She wanted powerfully to scratch. She leaned over and whispered to her mother, "Mama, I need a breath of air. I'll be right back," and got up to go into the courtyard.

It was pleasanter there, and fanning herself, Adelaide offered up the only heartfelt thanks to God she had made that day. She was no better a Jew at Mickve Israel than she was at home.

"Adelaide!"

It was Emilie Cohen, who had grown into a beauty, with the blue eyes and blonde curls of a Southern girl. She was exquisitely dressed in a grown woman's silk, and she looked with scorn at Adelaide's girlish wool.

"What is it, Emilie?"

She bent close and whispered. "Do you see that gentleman talking to my brother Richard?"

All she could see was a top hat and a close-fitting frock coat. "He's dressed awfully fine," she said.

"That's Papa's new clerk. Just come from Charleston."

"Will I meet him?"

"You'll get introduced proper. He's to come to supper after the service is over."

The man turned and Adelaide caught a glimpse of a handsome, snub-nosed face, with dark hair under the glossy hat. He wasn't supposed to greet her, as they hadn't been introduced, but as she looked in his direction he smiled.

A few hours later, Adelaide stood before the mirror in her room as Emilie's maidservant, Annie, folded and pinned the neckline of one of Adelaide's new dresses to make her presentable to meet a gentleman of Savannah. Emilie, who watched, threw a glance at Rachel, who sat in the corner, mending one of Adelaide's petticoats. Emilie asked, "Did your maidservant make this dress?"

Adelaide said, "No, the modiste in Cassville made it."

"Is that what the girls are wearing in Cassville?"

"It's what the girls are wearing in New York. She took the patterns from Godey's."

Annie smothered a laugh. She was the color that slave traders called quadroon, ivory-skinned rather than brown, and she wore one of her mistress' cast-off muslin dresses. Emilie looked again at Rachel, in the new calico dress that had looked so neat in Cassville. "Where did you get her? Was she a field hand before you brought her into the house?"

Adelaide looked at Rachel in apology. Her mother had objected to bringing Rachel to Savannah, telling her that she'd be glad to buy her a proper ladies' maid once they arrived. "A girl who can sew, and properly arrange your hair. A bright girl." In Savannah, that meant "fair of skin."

Emilie looked admiringly at her own servant. "She was my eighteenth birthday present," she said. "Ain't she fine?"

Everything in this room was fine, brand new from England and made from dark, heavy wood. The bedstead was much too big for a girl, with a heavy wooden frame and a carved headboard. The clothes press was taller than a grown man, and the dressing table was just as big, with a mirror so large Adelaide could see most of herself in it. Just down the hall, she discovered, was the bathroom, with a porcelain tub big enough to sleep in. Or to drown in.

Annie pinned the bodice low enough to expose Adelaide's collarbone. Adelaide said impatiently, "You'd think I was getting married today, not having dinner with your papa's clerk."

Emilie laughed. "You wouldn't, if he were just a clerk," she said, and Adelaide could hear the old taunting tone in her voice. "He's a Pereira. Of the Charleston Pereiras. Benjamin Pereira's younger son."

Even Adelaide knew that the Pereiras, who were spread between Charleston and New Orleans, were one of the grandest Jewish families in the South. They were Sephardic immigrants from London who could trace their presence in the Carolinas to three generations before the Revolutionary War. At one time, they had grown indigo, sugar, and rice, but they made their fortune in brokerage and investment. Benjamin Pereira was a gentleman attorney who served the needs of well-to-do Charleston, Jewish and Gentile alike.

Stung, Adelaide said, "If he's so grand, why don't your mother want him for you?"

Emilie laughed. "My mama knows I can do better."

"Really? Is there a stray Rothschild in Savannah I don't know about?"

"There's a lot you don't know about," Emilie said, as she and her bright Savannah servant smiled at each other. Grown up, Emilie knew better ways to torment than to pinch.

When Emilie and Annie left, Adelaide sat before the dressing table with its enormous mirror to look at herself. Rachel fastened the moonstone necklace Emilie had lent Adelaide, and twined the silk flowers Annie had made in Adelaide's dark hair, which refused to lay flat in the damp air of Savannah. "Do I look all right?" she asked Rachel, fretting that she did not.

"You look fine."

Adelaide stared at the reflections in the mirror, hers and Rachel's. In this low light, with the curtains drawn and the gas lamps lit, the resemblance between them was strong. It showed in the eyes, the bridge of the nose, the set of the jaw. And the expression, too, the look they both got when they were thinking. Or worrying.

Rachel pressed her cheek to Adelaide's hair and put her arms around Adelaide's neck. Adelaide smiled and covered Rachel's hands with her own. "I'm as ready as I'll ever be," she said.

In the front parlor, which was full of more heavy furniture in the newest style, Adelaide was properly introduced to Mr. William Pereira. He was not tall, but he was graceful. His hand was slender, the skin very white, the fingers long and elegant. His eyes were a bright blue, startling in a man descended from Portuguese Jews. He was beautifully dressed in a suit of fine black wool, a snowy shirt, and boots that didn't show a speck of dirt, despite the filth of the Savannah streets. His dark hair was curled and he smelled of scent. "I'm pleased to make your acquaintance," he said, smiling at her.

Adelaide had been flattered before. It was strange to think that these attentions were all right, since they came from the son of a wealthy Jew of Charleston. "Likewise, Mr. Pereira."

"How are you finding Savannah?"

She said politely, "I enjoy it greatly."

"Have you traveled, Miss Mannheim?"

"Only a little, in Georgia. I've been to Marietta and Macon to visit my friends. Not far." She looked at him with interest. "Have you?"

"I lived in London for two years, when I was in my uncle's firm there. And I visited Paris, since it's as close to London as New Orleans is to Savannah."

She was truly interested, despite herself. "I've read about London. I wish I could see it."

"It's a wonder. I hope you can see it, someday." He inclined his head and asked, "What have you read about London, Miss Mannheim?"

"I've read all of Mr. Dickens' works. And Mr. Thackeray's. It makes me feel as though I know it, a little."

"Do you read poetry, Miss Mannheim?"

"Yes, I do. Do you?"

"Lord Byron," he said softly, turning his head a little, putting her in mind of the famous portrait.

The Cohens' dining room, for evening meals and for guests, had a table with room for twenty and enough chairs to match, all of them covered in red damask. It was so heavily paneled in mahogany that it needed gaslight, even on the brightest of midsummer evenings.

Louisa seated William Pereira to Adelaide's right at the dinner table to make him her partner in conversation throughout the meal. He leaned towards her and said softly, "I hear that you come from Cassville, Miss Mannheim. What is it like?"

Richard laughed and interrupted. "It's a godforsaken little place in northern Georgia!"

Adelaide said stoutly, "Begging your pardon, Mr. Richard, but it ain't. It's the county seat. We have two colleges, one for men and one for women, and they have chorales and theatricals and lectures all the time. We have our own newspaper, the *Standard*, and we have a bookseller who can get anything I want from New York and London."

William Pereira asked, "What else is there to do in Cassville? If I visited?"

She smiled at him and said, "We have all kinds of music. Some of our slaves are the best fiddlers in the county. You should hear them at our summer frolics. That's what we call our summer barbecues. The slaves roast a pig, and we have all kinds of food, and singing and dancing." She glanced at Richard and Emilie, who looked bored. Defiantly, she added, "We have cockfights, too."

Startled, Louisa said, "Blood sport?"

"My father has the best birds in the county. People come from all over, bringing their birds, to see them fight." Emilie made a face, what the girls at the College called a moue. Smiling, Adelaide said, "Girls ain't supposed to watch, but I have, and I've wagered on them, too!"

"Adelaide!" her mother said, in a warning voice, but William Pereira chuckled in his throat.

Smiling at Adelaide, as though she had heard a pleasantry, Louisa Cohen said, "I'm afraid you'll have to content yourself with teas and suppers and dances in Savannah."

William Pereira looked at her with interest. Adelaide made her face smooth and her voice sweet. She dropped her eyes—demure girls and slaves looked down—and just as Rachel would, she said to Louisa Cohen, "Yes, ma'am."

After dinner, in the parlor, William Pereira sat next to her again. His face was rosy from the wine he'd drunk. His eyes sparkled as he said, "So you have a passion for cockfighting."

"Don't let my mama hear you say so."

He laughed. "How much did you wager, Miss Mannheim?"

"I'll never hear the end of it," she said. "That I once risked a dime on two birds fighting."

"Did you win?" He was smiling.

"I did. I earned a dollar."

"Perhaps I might escort you to a cockfight."

She laughed. She hadn't know it would be pleasant to flirt, and under her mama's watchful eye, too. "La, Mr. Pereira, my mama would never allow it."

"Perhaps she would, if I asked her politely."

"Perhaps you might ask first about a tea or a supper."

His eyes sparkled. "Or a dance. Do you dance, Miss Mannheim?"

"If I have to."

"It don't sound like you enjoy it."

"I don't, usually."

"Perhaps you haven't had the right partner."

"Are we talking about dancing, Mr. Pereira? Or sparring?"

"Richard told me you were clever. He didn't tell me you were a wit."

Adelaide looked around the parlor and wondered if her mother could overhear them. She said, "A lady ain't supposed to be a wit."

He leaned close enough to whisper into her ear. "Better a wit than a lackwit."

His breath was warm, and her body seemed to warm with it, in sympathy. She should move away. But she did not. She turned her head to look at him. "Do you really think so?"

His mouth was beautifully shaped. She had had never looked so closely at a man's lips before. She thought—and now she felt a chill, atop the heat—of what it might be like to feel them on her own. She had never had such a thought. She moved away. "Mr. Pereira, didn't your mama tell you not to stare?"

He smiled—such a brilliant smile—and said, "I'm drinking you in, Miss Mannheim."

"Really? What is the taste, Mr. Pereira?"

"Sweet," he said softly. "Very sweet."

What was the famous quote about Lord Byron? That he was bad and dangerous to know? She said, "Don't bamboozle me, Mr. Pereira."

"May I call on you, Miss Mannheim?"

"You'll have to ask my mama about that, too."

"I already have," he said.

Mrs. Cohen's next day "at home" for callers was three days later. Adelaide found herself wanting to look pretty, and she asked Rachel to lace her into her best day dress, a taffeta in red and yellow plaid. She perched herself on the little striped settee in the Cohens' front parlor, which had room for two if a lady carefully arranged her skirt, and she and her mother waited for the man who was mad, bad, and dangerous to know.

Mr. Pereira came wearing a new frock coat. He asked her, "May I sit with you, Miss Mannheim?" and at the same time, cocked his head towards her mother, who was within earshot, to ask her permission. Rosa nodded and smiled, and Mr. Pereira sat.

He said to Adelaide, "I've brought you a book. A book of poetry."

"Is it Lord Byron?"

He smiled. He was very handsome when he smiled, and she was sure he knew it. "*Don Juan.*"

"I've read it, but I don't mind reading it again."

"You've had quite an education, Miss Mannheim."

"Really? Latin, and poetry, and science, along with drawing? Not so unusual."

"No embroidery? Or china painting? Or beadwork?"

She held up her hands. She had never gotten the inkstain from her middle finger. "I snarl every piece of needlework I touch, and the last time I tried to paint on china I broke the dish."

He laughed. "I can see you riding through the Georgia countryside with your hair flying. You're too vigorous for Savannah!"

"Why take half measures? I could wear a bloomer costume and scandalize everyone as I stride through the streets."

"You have a wild heart in your breast, Miss Mannheim."

Why did she feel hot and cold at the same time? Why did he seem to radiate his own heat? She blushed—she could tell it wasn't a dainty flush, but a deep red embarrassment—and she said, "I never thought so."

He reached to stroke the top of her hand. His fingers were surprisingly soft. Startled at herself, she turned her hand over to clasp his. He smiled at her and leaned closer to speak low. "I think you do, Miss Mannheim."

Rosa watched from her chaperone's chair and smiled at them both. When it was time to leave, he asked if could call again—the request was for her mother as well as for her—and both of them nodded yes.

In Savannah, which had hot afternoons well into autumn, it was the custom to nap after midday dinner. Adelaide rarely slept. She liked being awake in the dim and the hush. She put on her wrapper—blessed relief!— and sat on the bed to read, the habit her mother deplored. She picked up the copy of *Don Juan* that Mr. Pereira had lent her. The story of a rakehell was a peculiar thing to give to an unmarried girl, no matter how literary she was.

There was a tap on the door. "Adelaide?"

"Come in, Mama."

Rosa shook her head as she came into the room. "Reading in bed," she said. But her voice was gentler than usual. She sat on the edge of the bed and she said, "I want to give you a mother's advice."

Adelaide put down the book and sat up. "You want me to marry Mr. Pereira."

Her mother put out her hand. To Adelaide's surprise, she smoothed Adelaide's thick curly hair. "Do you care for him?"

Adelaide was startled into the truth. "I don't know."

Rosa touched her cheek. "It's a grand connection," she said. "They'd set you up very well."

"I know, Mama."

Still touching her cheek, her mother said softly, "A house in Charleston or in Savannah. The chance to live in London. Wouldn't you like that?"

"He hasn't asked for me yet, Mama."

Rosa patted her cheek again. "He will," she said, unusually tender. "I'm sure he will."

"Mama? How did you know you wanted to marry Papa?"

"I didn't. My mama and papa arranged it for me."

A few days later, all of them went back to Mickve Israel for the Yom Kippur service. Adelaide was old enough to fast all day, but by mid-morning her stomach was empty and her head was pounding. It was shameful to be in a house of worship on the most solemn day of the Jewish year, and to pray so hard for a cup of coffee. She slipped out to spend a few moments in the courtyard. She could hear the cantor's voice through the open door. It was overcast today, but it was never cool in the damp air of Savannah.

"Miss Mannheim?" William Pereira stood before her. "Are you having an easy fast?"

She sighed. "I wish I were," she said. "Why did God make it so hard to be a Jew?"

He laughed softly. "Better minds than mine have puzzled over that," he said. He reached for her hand. "Only a few hours until dinner. Can you manage?"

The courtyard was full of fellow worshippers and fellow sufferers. In the manner of close-knit, loose-tongued Savannah Jewry, they were watching. She moved her hand and said, "Mr. Pereira, we ain't alone here."

He pressed her fingers between his own. "Do it bother you? That they might know?" His blue gaze was very soft.

"Know what, Mr. Pereira?"

He said, smiling, "That I like you."

She said, "Are you flattering me? On God's Day of Atonement?"

He laughed and let go her hand. "I'd best get back inside. Before I do anything more I'll need to atone for."

After Yom Kippur, Louisa Cohen invited her fellow Israelites to the house for a dance, and immediately began to fuss. Over the guest list—only thirty guests, but the best people, meaning the richest. The menu, which bedeviled the cook for days. Adelaide's dress, which meant more work for Annie, who cut it like the other, to make it lower in the neckline and tighter in the waist and bosom.

The next time Mr. Pereira called, he said, "Miss Mannheim, why are you looking so downcast?"

"I've been invited to a dance."

He smiled. "I know. I pressed Mrs. Cohen to have it."

"You know how I feel about dancing."

"Have you waltzed, Miss Mannheim?"

She knew how to dance the cotillion, which was an old-fashioned country dance. The waltz was too scandalous for Cassville. "Whatever the dance, I have two left feet."

He laughed. "That's easily remedied. I can teach you." He gave Rosa and Louisa his brilliant smile. "Could we give Miss Mannheim a dancing lesson?"

Rosa smiled indulgently. Louisa said, "The ballroom isn't ready for a party, but there's room to take a turn. I'll get the key."

When Rosa and Louisa were settled in their chairs, William led Adelaide into the middle of the expanse of polished floor. He said, "It isn't like the cotillion. You have to come closer. Let me show you." He held out his left arm. "You clasp my hand with your right," he said. "Now put your left arm on my shoulder."

She felt the heat of his skin through his jacket. He said, "Now I put my left hand on your waist."

She could feel his touch through her corset. It made her cheeks hot, too. "Now I'll show you what to do with your feet. Watch me, and follow what I do." She nodded. "We'll start slowly, until you get the rhythm of it."

She concentrated on the toes of his shining boots and mirrored him. When she made a misstep, he stopped and said gently, "Let's try again."

Then she made a blunder, as she knew she would, and tripped over his boot. He caught her before she fell. Her face flaming, her skin hot everywhere his arms and hands held her, she said, "I told you how clumsy I am."

Smiling, he held onto her for a moment, then righted her. "You need more practice. Let's try again. Remember, you follow after me."

They practiced for a while, until she could follow him without a mistake. Still holding her for the dance, he said, "You have a natural grace, Miss Mannheim."

"I do not. You have a natural talent for flattery, Mr. Pereira."

"It ain't flattery to make a girl feel pleased. Now let's try it a little faster."

Maybe tripping over a man's feet was the way to learn how to dance. She no longer had trouble following him. He hastened the pace until they were whirling around the floor. She felt dizzy. She was sweating under her corset, and it itched up a storm, but she didn't mind. There was heat in her face, and heat—could that be right?—in her belly. Below her belly. In the place that her mother distastefully called "down there."

When they finally stopped, she was breathing hard in her corseted chest. He chuckled. "Did that give you pleasure, Miss Mannheim?"

"If being dizzy is a pleasure."

Still holding her in the waltz's embrace, he said, "I look forward to making you dizzy. I want to dance with you, over and over."

Mad. Bad. Dangerous to know.

Rachel had been coming to Savannah with Adelaide since they were both thirteen. She knew the Cohen servants, and she had learned the ways of the Cohen house. The Cohens were stricter about the kosher laws than the Mannheims, and they had always set a grander table and had a grander set of visitors. In the old house, the kitchen and the back stairs and the attic room where she slept had all become familiar. She knew Moses, the butler, and Cleo, the cook, but with the new house came new servants. There was the housekeeper, Augusta, thin and stern and light-complected, who sniffed when she met Rachel, as though she didn't think much of anyone who came from Cassville. Both of the servants to the younger Cohens were new. Cleo, who was dark-complected as well as bad-tempered, said to Rachel, "When young Marse and young Miss grew up they wanted smart new slaves. That Annie is too smart for her own good." Rachel agreed. Cleo added, "And so is that Octavian."

Octavian was even finer than Annie. He was broad-shouldered and slender, and he wore a beautiful suit of light brown wool. She would later learn that he received castoff clothes from young Marse Cohen, but they fit him as though they had been made for him. His skin was the palest brown, cream with a hint of coffee, and he had almond-shaped eyes with heavy lids. His nose was like a white man's, narrow and finely cut. His hair was like a white man's too, not wiry or woolly, but in soft black curls all over his head. His lips were full and soft, pink with a tinge of brown, and of all the new faces in this house, he was the only one to smile at her. When they met, he extended his hand to her. Startled at this city courtesy, she took it. His fingers were long and tapering, and his touch was soft. "Welcome, little country gal," he said.

Augusta, new to a Jewish household, took the kosher laws more seriously than many a Savannah Jew. On her first day, Rachel, tired and distracted, didn't watch what she was doing as she put the dinner dishes away. Augusta was quick to scold her. "Don't you put a meat dish in the milk dish cupboard! Don't your Marse and Missus keep the kosher laws at all?"

Rachel knew better, but she lost her temper. "I know the kosher laws just fine!" she flared. "I've been keeping a kosher kitchen since I was five years old."

Augusta slapped Rachel on both cheeks and put the dishes away herself.

Rachel stood in the pantry with her hands pressed to her stinging face. "Hey, little country gal," said a soft voice. Octavian looked a little tired, but the smudges beneath his eyes didn't take away his beauty. He put his hand on her shoulder. "Ain't they treating you right?"

"I ain't smart enough for Savannah," she said, surprised at the tears in her voice.

"Of course are you."

"Or bright enough, either."

"Don't cry," he said, and he touched her smarting cheeks with the tips of his fingers. She looked up in astonishment. No one had ever touched her with such sweetness.

He cupped her chin in his soft palm. "You're like the Song of Songs they say on Friday nights. Black but comely." Before she could protest, he kissed her with the softest touch of his lips. Then he said, "Marse needs me," and slipped away.

She put her fingers to her lips, as though she could capture the kiss and keep it there. The tears stopped.

Adelaide had dresses that needed mending, and she ran lightly up the back stairs to Adelaide's room. It was summer, and still full light at eight in the evening; she wouldn't need to strain her eyes by candlelight.

She caught a glimpse of her reflection in the huge carved mirror above the dressing table, and she lingered to look at herself. She was surprised by what she saw. Next to so many bright-skinned people, she had felt anything but comely, but her skin was a glowing shade of brown, and her eyes were black and sparkling. She smiled at her reflection and was startled to see the dimples in her cheeks. People had told her all her life that she had the Mannheim dimples, and now she saw them clearly.

Her new dress, made to fit her, showed off a woman's shape. Since she turned sixteen, she had grown what Aunt Susy called "bosoms." Her waist wasn't tiny, but it was slender for a girl who wasn't wearing a corset. She tried to see her own backside. White ladies wore hoopskirts to look bigger, but her bottom was high and round all by itself. She held out her arms to admire them. They were rounded and strong. Her hands were a little burned and scarred from kitchen work, but they were plump and shapely. She looked herself over, up and down and she laughed with delight. Octavian thought she was pretty, and she thought so too.

Octavian asked her to go walking with him on Sunday afternoon, when the Cohens gave their slaves a few hours to themselves. She wore her new dress, which he admired. They walked through the streets of Savannah, taking their time and going where they pleased, just as if they were free. The gutters were full of horse manure and the street smelled like a barn that hadn't been mucked out for weeks, but it also smelled like the magnolia blossoms that were still in full bloom on the trees. When they stopped to rest Octavian took money from his pocket—how had he come by it?—and bought her an ice to eat.

When they returned to the Cohens' house, they lingered in the butler's pantry. "That was fine," Rachel said, smiling at him in her delight. He leaned forward, and she came to meet him. He put his arms around her and kissed her. The touch of his brown-tinged lips made her so weak in the knees that she would have fallen if her back were not pressed firmly against the wall.

When Aunt Susy killed a chicken, she severed its head with a hatchet, and the headless body continued to run around wildly while the head lay far away on the ground. After that day, around Octavian, Rachel's body did all kinds of crazy things that she couldn't stop, and her head was somewhere else, unable to control it.

They came together whenever they could, in the pantry late at night, on the back stairs when no one was coming, or in the attic corridor during the day. Because of the possibility of discovery, their embraces were urgent and swift and incomplete. He would press her against the wall, kiss her with those brown-tinged lips, and quickly reach for any part of her he could caress without unbuttoning. He didn't fumble. His hands were very sure, wherever they moved on her body. He pressed himself against her, and the pressure of what Aunt Susy would call his "manly part" sent the headless chicken running. They had never had enough time, or enough privacy, to finish the frenzy they started.

On a warm October afternoon, they ducked into a space between two houses, and realized that it was as private—at least as private as the back stairs. He pulled her close. The space they stood in was only a few feet wide, about the width of the attic corridor, and it was dark with shade. It was close to someone's kitchen midden, too. As they kissed and caressed, as he hardened and she shuddered, she could smell rotting kitchen scraps and nightsoil.

He whispered, "Let me love you all over."

It wasn't right. If she were home, she would find them a clearing in the piney woods, and they would spread a blanket on a bed of pine needles and look up at the sky as they lay together. They would hear the crickets sing, and the cicadas buzz, and the mockingbirds call. If she were home, they would lie face to face, touch each other's cheeks, and murmur words of love, and caress each other with leisurely tenderness. If she were home, the preacher would bless their union, and everyone on the place would celebrate with her, and they would go into their own cabin and give themselves over to love.

Not here. Not to grab, and fumble, and lie together in a dark, smelly place. Not to make a baby with a bright face that would go back to be born in Cass County, another Mannheim slave. Through her heat she felt a chill.

They both heard a noise—was someone coming into the alley?—and they broke apart, hot and unsatisfied. They straightened their clothes. He said, "They'll be needing us in the house," and they walked uncomfortably to the house together.

A few days later, she lingered over the washing up, and he told Moses that he'd close up the house that night. When everyone was in bed, and the house was still, they went into the butler's pantry. For the first time, they lay on the floor. Moonlight came through the kitchen windows, and they could see each other plainly. When he kissed her, she felt the familiar craziness come over her. I can't stop, she thought. And I don't care. He hiked her skirt up to her belly, and put his finger inside her. He stroked her in a spot that sent waves of pleasure throughout her body. He unbuttoned himself and helped her curl her hand around him. The shaft was hot and velvety, and the tip was as soft as a baby's cheek.

Too late, they heard footsteps, then a voice.

It was Annie, in her nightdress, holding a candle. They sprang apart, knowing what she'd seen. She grinned and whispered, "You'd best be quiet. I came because Augusta thought she heard a noise," then she turned and walked lightly up all the stairs to the attic.

Rachel yanked down her skirt and sat up. She had never felt so ashamed, and her head was clear—and attached to her body—for the first time in weeks.

Octavian reached for her arm. He lay on his side. He was still unbuttoned, and he smiled at her with a spark of desire in those heavy-lidded eyes. "Where are you going?" he asked lazily. "We weren't done."

Rachel said, "I'm done, for tonight," and she stood up.

He held out his hand. "Just a little kiss before you go?"

"I'll go up first," she said curtly. "You wait a few minutes."

He stood up and tried to pull her close. "A little kiss goodnight."

She pulled away. "Do you want Augusta down here, asking us why we're making a ruckus?"

A few days later, Octavian caught Rachel alone in the attic at midday. Even in October, the attic hallway was stifling. The corridor was so narrow that two people couldn't pass in it. As the two of them stood there, they were close together.

He kissed her, holding her face in her hands. He pressed his body against hers, chest to chest, belly to belly, thigh to thigh. He said, "Let me love you."

Her head stayed attached. "I can't."

"Ain't nothing to be afraid of." His lips grazed her ear. His voice was tender.

"Yes, there is."

"Are you afraid of having a baby? Ain't no shame in that."

Don't nothing belong to you, Aunt Susy had told her. She hated the thought. The fear of it was stronger than the frenzy in her body. "Afraid of having a baby born into slavery."

He pushed her away, a little too hard. Her head hit the wall with a thud. He said angrily, "That's the damnedest excuse I ever heard from a gal."

"It's not an excuse."

His eyes narrowed and his lips curled in disgust. It was the only time she had ever seen him look ugly. "There are plenty of gals in Savannah. Gals who are willing. I don't need to spend another moment talking to you."

He ran down the stairs, escaping. She stood in the attic hallway, where it was so stuffy that it was hard to breathe, and rubbed the back of her head. Just a bruise. She'd mend. She put her hand on her chest, just over her heart, and she crumpled to the floor to sob.

On the day of the Cohens' dance, Rachel and Annie fluttered around Adelaide, smoothing her dress, arranging her hair, and fastening the clasp on her necklace. She had never looked forward to a dance before, and the unaccustomed feeling made her sharp. "Stop it, both of you. You put me in mind of two wasps buzzing around a sugar bowl." Annie nodded. "I'll go tend to Miss Emilie." She left Rachel and Adelaide alone. Adelaide was ready, and Rachel had nothing left to do.

Rachel said, "Don't fret. This dance will be over before you know it."

"I might actually enjoy it."

"Ain't like you."

"Mr. Pereira taught me how to dance the waltz."

"Did he."

Adelaide turned from the mirror to look Rachel in the eye. "He made me feel dizzy," she said.

Rachel's skin was too dark to show a blush, but Adelaide had learned to read embarrassment on her face. Adelaide said, "Oh, no. You, too? Who made you feel dizzy?"

"Hate to say."

"Not Marse Richard!"

Rachel shook her head. "Marse's man. Octavian."

It was all right. They were girls together, sisters who happened to be mistress and slave. "What happened?"

"Tried to toy with me and I told him no. Men can be fools, too."

Adelaide smiled. "I'll remember that," she said, and she rose to go downstairs to join the dancing, and the man who taught her to dance.

William gave her five dances in a row, including a waltz, until other young men—Richard Cohen, and some distant Cohen cousin, a boy her age, a clumsy but enthusiastic dancer—good-naturedly asked for her and took their turns.

Finally out of breath, she told the Cohen boy that she needed to sit down. "May I bring you some punch, Miss Mannheim?"

"No, thank you."

She settled herself into one of the chairs along the wall, not realizing that she was within earshot of the punch bowl, where the young men gathered, fetching for young ladies, or lingering to drink for themselves. She heard the voices but didn't recognize them.

"Who's the girl in the blue dress?"

"Miss Mannheim. Mordecai Mannheim's daughter."

"Mannheim? Doesn't he broker cotton and deal in slaves?"

"That's right. Tight with a dollar. Even among us Israelites, he's known as an old screw."

"She's promised to Pereira, I hear."

A laugh. "Close enough. Seems to have happened overnight."

"What does she have?"

"Three thousand acres, fifty slaves, a thousand bales of upland cotton last year. It's decent, but it's not a great fortune."

"It should be enough to hold Pereira."

"Have you seen him at the gaming table? I doubt it."

"So that's why he's in such a hurry."

Promised to him? The gossips of Savannah had been busy, already inviting themselves to her wedding. A grand connection, and a fistful of notes from the gaming table. Troubled, she recalled from her study of literature at the College that Lord Byron had been a man deep in debt.

Rachel sat with the other maidservants sat in the kitchen, all of them waiting to attend to a lady who had torn a hem, or burst a lace, or needed her smelling salts. She was too tired to be polite to another set of haughty Savannah slaves. She needed some air. She left the room, looking for the back door. As she put her hand on the doorknob she felt a man tap her on the shoulder. Octavian. Without turning, she said, "I told you I was done with you."

"Who did you think I was?"

She turned and put her hand over her mouth. "Marse Pereira, I'm so sorry."

"A lot of sass from a gal I haven't even started with." His cravat had loosened and his hair was disheveled. He was more than a little drunk.

"Marse Pereira, can I bring you anything? A drink of water?"

He leaned forward, and before she could step away, he had grabbed her to pull her tightly against him. "I don't want any water," he said, his face very close to hers. He smelled of sweat underneath the scent he had put on his hair. When she tried to pull away, he grabbed her tighter. He put his hand behind her head and pulled on her hair, so hard that her kerchief fell to the floor. He kissed her roughly, laughing when she tried to squirm away. He let her go. "That's what I want," he said.

After he left, she wiped her mouth and bent down to pick up her kerchief, which was dirtied by the mud and filth on the landing by the back steps. She turned it inside out to hide the dirt. With trembling fingers, she put it back on her head and tried to tie it neatly at the nape of her neck. She could not. Shaking, she stood in the doorway, holding her sullied kerchief. When the dancing paused, Adelaide would need her.

For days after the dance, Adelaide worried over what she had heard. Girls weren't supposed to know or care about money, but she was the daughter of a man who talked about money all the time. It was no secret to her that gentlemen wagered, from the rough country men who spent a dime on a cockfight to the swells of Savannah, who wagered at cards.

How much money did William Pereira risk at the gaming table? Her father must know. He was a cotton factor and a land dealer as well as a planter, and he knew all about debt. Certainly he would protect her property, just as her mother wanted to protect her virtue.

She was sure that William Pereira would ask her to marry him, and she doubted that he loved her. Did he treasure her? Or was he greedy for her portion, since he was in debt?

No planter's daughter could have the life she wished for—a life of reading books and writing until her fingers were stained with ink. A planter's daughter had to marry and become someone's wife. She couldn't help but be swayed by the weight of the Pereira name, and the glitter of the Pereira family. She thought of her friends who had become engaged, giddy and flushed and anxious and pleased. None of them had admitted to doubt.

A week after the dance, when Rachel brought up her breakfast, Adelaide asked, "Rachel, would you like to stay in Savannah?"

"That ain't a question about Savannah."

It was the servant's way of putting it, but Adelaide suddenly needed a sister's advice. Adelaide said, "I think Mr. Pereira will ask me to marry him." She turned to look at Rachel. "Should I say yes?"

Rachel, who had long ago become accustomed to looking Adelaide in the face, dropped her eyes. Like any slave, she said, "I don't know."

Adelaide pressed her. "You've seen him," she said. "You know what people say about him. What do you think?"

"Ain't my business."

"Look at me." Rachel raised her head. Adelaide had never seen her look so uncomfortable. "Of course it is. If I marry him you'll come with me." Adelaide said, "I think I love him, and I think he loves me. If he asks, should I say yes?"

"Ain't my place to say."

"Rachel, what's the matter?"

Rachel gave her a look of pure misery.

"Rachel, won't you help me? I don't know what to do."

Rachel met her eyes and her look was full of fear. "Wish I could," she said. "Don't know how I can."

A few days later, at breakfast, Emilie said to Adelaide, "Mama wants to buy another maidservant. There's an auction downtown. Let's take a look to see if there's anything that will suit."

Richard said, "Adelaide, do you want to come along?"

Slaves were always coming and going on her father's place, but Adelaide preferred not to think how they got there, or where they went. She had never been to a slave auction. But she wanted to be obliging, and a slave auction sounded more interesting than another visit to the milliner's. "All right. Should I bring my servant Rachel?"

Smiling, Emilie said, "Not unless you're thinking of selling her."

"Of course not!" Adelaide said tartly.

When they arrived, they walked into the building where the slaves were displayed. Emilie picked up an auction list, scanned it, and fanned herself with it. "It ain't a big auction," she said.

Richard said, "Let's look around and see what they've got on offer."

The slaves stood, either alone or in small groups, corresponding to the lots on the list. All of them, save babes in their mothers' arms, were hobbled by manacles on their ankles.

Emilie stopped before a little girl. She was younger than twelve—Rachel's age when she became Adelaide's servant—and she was a little slip of a thing. She was all alone, and her dark-complected face was smeared with tears.

Emilie said, "She wouldn't do. Mama won't want a baby who blubbers. She'll want a grown girl with a good disposition."

Richard said, "There are some grown gals over here."

They walked over to look at them. One had a baby in her arms, and another had two young children tugging on her skirts. The woman with the baby kept her eyes down, but the other looked up and said to Emilie, "Young miss, is you wanting a house servant? I can cook, I can sew, and I can do the wash." She gestured to the little girl at her side. "My little'un can help me in the kitchen."

Emilie said to Richard, "She might do, if they'll break up the lots."

Richard said, "It's too much trouble. There must be a gal by herself around here."

Emilie said, "This one."

She was listed as eighteen, Adelaide's own age, and she was very bright of skin, even fairer than Annie's quadroon. Her hair fell down her back in long curls. She wore a dress of crisp new calico, which showed a womanly shape, and even though her legs were shackled, she was not barefoot.

Richard said, "Now there's a likely gal."

Emilie looked at her list. "House servant, good seamstress. She might do."

"She won't go cheap. Not with that bright skin. And look at the rest of her."

Emilie looked at her brother with scorn. "We ain't buying her for you."

The girl raised her head, even though it was impudent, and she looked at Adelaide. There was no plea in her deep green eyes. No sadness. She knew that her looks added to her price, and to her peril.

Adelaide fanned herself with the auction list.

Emilie said, "Well, there ain't much here, and I don't see anything that Mama would want. Let's go." She looked curiously at Adelaide. "Are you all right?"

Adelaide looked at the girl, who was for sale to the highest bidder. Chilled in the pleasant fall air, Adelaide thought, So am I.

A few days later, as Adelaide sat in the parlor with her mother, William Pereira came in. He asked Rosa, "May I speak to Miss Mannheim in private for a moment?"

Adelaide's heart began to pound. Rosa smiled at Adelaide and nodded at William. "Of course," she said, and left the room in a rustle of silk.

Adelaide knew what he was going to say. All of Jewish Savannah knew.

He sat beside her on the little settee, close enough to crush her dress, and said, "Miss Mannheim, I could make you a pretty speech about how highly I regard you, and how fond I feel about you, and how I hope you feel the same about me. But you're too clever a gal to believe any of it." He reached for both of her hands. He was smiling and his eyes were brightly blue. "I'll say it plain. I like you a lot, Miss Mannheim. I like how smart and impudent you are. I think we could have a grand time together. A house in Savannah, where you'd never be bored, and a visit to London, to see all the sights there are to see." He pressed her hands in his own. "I hear they have bang-up cockfights in London."

She was too wrought up to smile. "Is it true that you're in debt?"

"It's a trifle," he said. "I lost a little at cards. I wrote to your papa, and he knows all about it. He'll write to my papa, and they'll take care of it before the wedding."

"If you were in any kind of trouble, would you tell me?"

"Of course I would, if I were." He grinned. "But I ain't!"

"What did my papa say when you wrote to him?"

"He said that he'd say yes if you would. So it's up to you."

She didn't reply. She was pondering, as Rachel would say.

He said, "Adelaide, if a man's going to dance, he needs a partner."

She looked up. He pulled her to her feet. "I know a better dance than the waltz," he said. He put his arms around her waist—she could feel their warmth through her dress and corset and her chemise—and he pulled her close. "Do you really not know?" he said, very low, his lips brushing her cheek.

She didn't reply. He pulled her closer and kissed her, his lips very soft against hers, just as she had imagined the first time she met him. She put her arms around his neck, and felt the warm band of flesh between his collar and the ends of his hair. He kissed her more deeply, parting his lips. How did she know to follow? His hands moved on her back, and she twined her hands in the soft silk of his hair. He pressed himself against her so that she could feel the length of him, his chest against hers, his belly against hers, some unfamiliar part of him against the fiery warmth "down there."

He let her go. "Better than the waltz?"

"Better than the waltz."

"Miss Mannheim, will you marry me?"

Her legs were trembling. She was hot and wet everywhere. She was hungry for something she had never tasted. Whether it was sweet or bitter, she wanted to try it. "I believe I will, Mr. Pereira."

On the Sabbath after Adelaide said yes to William Pereira, the Cohens took her and her mother to Mickve Israel to show her off. After the service, the Jewish women of Savannah, the settled wives and the girls still hopeful of marriage, all came to take her arm and kiss her cheek and welcome her into their midst.

The men stood in the foyer in clusters, talking. Religious Jews didn't talk about business on the Sabbath, but the Israelite men of Savannah weren't particularly religious. She heard snatches of conversation about the price of cotton, about deals in land or goods, and about slaves recently purchased and sold. As she walked by, she overheard a conversation. She couldn't see the speakers and she didn't recognize their voices.

"So the country mouse from Cassville caught Pereira."

"Maybe he'll be able to honor the notes and pay me what he owes me."

"How much does he owe you?"

"Nearly a thousand dollar. That's just me. I bet he owes half the men at Mickve Israel for the sums he's lost at cards."

A snort. "I bet he runs through her fortune in a year."

"Have you met her papa? He'll tie up her portion so tight he'll have to beg for a nickel to buy a cigar."

Another voice, equally derisive. "That should be a happy marriage."

"What difference does it make? When a man marries a plantation, to get himself out of a fix, he'll take the girl along with it."

"And the slave, too. Have you seen her? She's a juicy gal."

Another snort. "He do like a slave gal. Ask Benjamin Pereira."

Her face flamed. Did everyone know? That she had been sold to the highest bidder, who was deep in debt when he bought her? Who wanted her fortune, and her plantation, and her servant as part of the bargain?

A few days later, Adelaide walked into Meyer's to find Joe standing at his customary place behind the counter. She must have looked as troubled as she felt, because Joe said right away, "Miss Adelaide, what's the matter?"

"Joe, may I talk to you in private?"

It was wrong for an unmarried girl to sit alone with a man. But Joe, who was as kind and familiar with her as a brother, understood, and he led her into a small room in back, where a big desk, heaped with letters and scraps of cloth, filled the room. The air smelled of wool and felt itchy in the damp air. Joe gestured to her to sit. The room was so cramped that her skirt, filled out by her hoops, crushed against his trouser leg when he sat at the desk.

He asked, "What is it, Adelaide?"

"It's about Mr. Pereira. Something I heard at Mickve Israel last Sabbath."

"Gossip, no doubt," Joe said disapprovingly.

"I need to know if it's true." She knotted her hands in her lap. "Is he in debt?" Joe shook his head. "Is he in debt to you?"

She reached to grasp his hands, as a sister would. "Joe, you helped me when you didn't ask for me last year. Help me now."

He struggled with himself, and at last he said, "God help me if my father finds out I told you. He hasn't paid our bills in over a year. His father stopped honoring his notes."

"Why? Ain't they one of the richest families in Charleston?"

"He's in disgrace."

"Why? Don't most men drink and wager? Don't some lose money at it?"

Joe's face was full of distress. "It ain't fit for your ears."

"If it's about my happiness, I should hear it."

"He interfered with so many of maidservants in Charleston that his father got disgusted with him. Ben Pereira said that if he saw one more yaller slave child in his house, he'd stop paying his son's debts."

It happened in house after house, but no one ever spoke of it. It had happened in her own family. Her mother had never recovered from it. "I'm glad you told me," she said.

"You can't tell anyone how you found out."

She rose, her skirts rustling. She felt clammy and sick, but she smiled, as though this had been an ordinary visit to chat about the newest ribbons and the newest baby. "I can be closemouthed, too," she said.

She had to break the engagement. She decided to write to her father. She sat before the dressing table, where she could see all of herself in the mirror, and struggled to begin. It had never been so difficult to put pen to paper. She tried over and over, always hesitating over the phrase "interferes with the slaves." In the end she wrote about the subject that would goad her father without shaming him.

> Dearest Papa,
> It is very hard to write to you, but I must. Before I marry Mr. Pereira, you should know about his financial condition. He is deep in debt. I can't tell you how I found out, because it would be indiscreet.
> Will you make inquiries, to be sure? If he is in as much difficulty as people say, I shouldn't marry him. We must break off the engagement.
> Your affectionate daughter,
> Adelaide

Several days later, her mother came to see her just after breakfast, when the first letters of the day came to the house. She was pale and pinched. She said to Rachel, who was laying out Adelaide's dress, "You go on. Leave us alone. And don't stand at the door listening."

"What is it, Mama?"

"I've just seen the letter you wrote to your father." Her mother was coldly angry, a condition that Adelaide feared more than heat. "Do you really think that your father would let you marry a man who would ruin us? Of course he's made inquiries."

Adelaide whispered, "I didn't know."

"You foolish, foolish girl. It's the best connection you could ever hope to make. There's no question of breaking off the engagement. I won't hear of it."

Adelaide was silent. Her mother continued, "Don't say anything to Mr. Pereira. It ain't your business. Your father will be here in a few days, and he'll take care of things."

Adelaide raised her eyes to her mother's angry face. "Mama, I don't know if I can care for him."

"It's too late for that now," her mother said. "You're engaged to him, and you'll marry him."

Shortly after her talk with her mother, her father stopped at the Cohens' for a few days, and just before midday dinner, he called her into the library.

Adelaide sat with her father in the unfamiliar room, which was painted in dark red and paneled in dark oak. The leather chairs were so big that her father fit into his easily. She felt swallowed up in hers. She took a deep breath and said, "Papa, I have to talk to you about Mr. Pereira."

"I know," her father said. He had never sounded so indulgent. "Your mama tells me you're worried about marrying him."

"He's in debt."

Her father waved the words away. "I know all about his financial condition. I've written to his father. It's all taken care of."

"He gambles."

"So do I. That's nothing to worry about."

Every one of the words she needed was too shameful to say. She could not say them to a man whose interference had given her a slave sister. "I'm not sure I can be happy with him, Papa." She hoped that he would hear her desperation and be able to guess what troubled her.

But he laughed instead. "All gals get the jitters when it's time to get married. We'll have a fine wedding in Charleston and you'll forget all about it. Then I'll settle both of you back in Cass County and everything will be all right."

Louisa Cohen, pleased at her matchmaking success, invited William Pereira to dine with the Cohens for a small celebration of the engagement. Adelaide sat through the preparations without enthusiasm. She looked at her dressed and primped self in the mirror and said to Rachel, "After being turned out like this, what a shock he'll have, seeing me first thing in the morning in my dishabille."

Rachel said wearily, "Are you all right?"

She looked in the mirror and saw their two faces reflected, both equally disquiet. "Are you?"

Rachel said, "Doesn't matter about me."

"Will you be serving at dinner?"

"I'll be in the kitchen. Close by."

Before they sat down to dinner, William drew Adelaide into a shadow in the back hallway. He said, "You ain't still mad at me, are you? For being in debt?"

"Mad?" Adelaide said. "If I were really mad, you'd know it."

He pulled her close, so close she could feel how heated he was. He cupped her face in his hands, an ungentle embrace, and in a low voice, thick with passion, he said, "Would I?"

How could she have such terror in her heart and such heat between her legs? "You told me I was wild," she said, breathing hard. "I'll show you."

He said, "I can't wait to be married to you." He kissed her as he had when he asked for her, a foretaste of the marriage bed, and she cursed her body, which wanted something that her heart and her mind knew were wrong.

The guests toasted the new couple with champagne, and she lost count of how many glasses she drank. When the guests got up—the ladies to the parlor, the men to the library—she was tipsy, and she had an urge to use the chamberpot. She didn't want to ascend the grand staircase to her room. There was a back way that Rachel had shown her once. But she took a wrong turn and found herself in an unfamiliar hallway.

After two months in the Cohen house, Rachel could still lose her way. When she came downstairs, she stood in the back hallway, unsure of how to get back to the kitchen. As she tried to get her bearings, a soft masculine voice whispered, "Are you lost?"

"No, Marse Pereira. Just going. Cleo needs me in the kitchen."

He put his hands on the wall behind her, trapping her. "She can wait."

"No, sir, I'll be in trouble if I linger."

He leaned close and there was no escaping him. His breath smelled of drink. He said, "One kiss and I'll let you go."

She put a pleading tone in her voice, one she had never used on the Mannheim place. "Please, sir."

"I'm as good as married to your mistress," he said.

She didn't move. His hand slipped to her neck. To her collarbone. To the top of her breast.

If she refused, if she screamed, if she fled, he would find a way to hurt her. If not now, then after the wedding.

He squeezed her breast and moved closer. Close enough to kiss her. She said, "Marse Pereira, what if someone sees us?"

"I don't care," he said, and he put his hand down the bodice of her dress, right against her skin, to pinch her nipple. She gasped with the hurt of it.

He slid his free hand up her skirt, to the spot that Octavian had touched with such passion, but he wasn't gentle there either. He pressed his fingers inside her, so hard it caused her pain. She cried out, "Marse Pereira!"

He pressed against her and she felt his manly part, hard as a broom handle against her belly. Lord help me, she thought. A baby born in slavery, by a man she couldn't say no to. A man who would come after her again and again after the wedding.

In the dark passage were two figures pressed together, a man and a woman. Adelaide saw the back of the man's head and recognized the curls. When she heard the woman cry out, "Marse Pereira!" she was too shocked to move or speak. It was Rachel.

She called out, in a low voice that managed not to shake. "Mr. Pereira?"

At the sound of Adelaide's voice he let Rachel go. "Adelaide!" he said. The dark hid his face and Adelaide couldn't tell if he was embarrassed or not.

She stepped close to him, the man who had grabbed her in a dark hallway not an hour before, and said in a voice that was like a growl, "Are you interfering with my servant?"

He turned to face her and his expression was so intemperate that Adelaide thought he might strike her. "After we're married, she'll be my servant," he said.

Adelaide put out her hand and said, "Rachel, come with me. I need you." Rachel took her hand. Both of them were trembling. Under her bravery Adelaide was terrified. Mistress and slave walked hand in hand from the dark hallway.

Once in her room, Adelaide sank into the chair before the dressing table. "What did you do? To make him act like that?"

"Nothing," Rachel whispered. "Nothing."

Her voice rose. She heard her mother's anger in it. "You must have done something—to make him think—to let him do that to you that—"

Rachel's face was full of fear. "No. Miss Adelaide, I swear it. I didn't even raise my eyes to him."

"How could he?"

Rachel stared at her sister.

"Did you know something? Did you hear something?"

Rachel shook her head.

"No? Or can't say?"

Very low, Rachel said, "Can't say."

Adelaide raised her voice. "You knew he was like this and you didn't tell me?"

"How could I?"

"How could you do that? Let me marry a man like that?"

Rachel said, "Wasn't ever mine to say. Or to tell. Or to decide."

"Rachel, I don't know what to do." Adelaide covered her face with her hands, thinking of a future where both of them, mistress and slave, would be bound to a husband with no regard for either. She began to sob. Rachel put her arms around Adelaide and whispered, "Neither do I."

After Rachel left her, Adelaide sat before her dressing table, unable to sleep. It was the way of the world, in Savannah and in Cass County, she knew.

She was an unmarried girl, but she had been raised on a plantation where roosters fertilized hens, where boars mated with sows, and where stallions covered mares. She knew how animals rutted. Her affianced, who could kiss her with such passion, had enough lust left over to rut with her servant.

William Pereira would grab Rachel in the back hallway of their fine house in Savannah, and force himself on her, and rut with her in the rhythm of a stallion mounting a mare. He would use her servant and her sister to shame her.

She would become her mother, bound to a man who would give her children slave brothers and sisters. She would share her husband with a slave mistress, and she would see the evidence of her husband's preference in the faces of the children brought up in the house.

A white wife, and a slave mistress. For the first time, she understood her mother's bitterness.

Two days later, they all waited for her in the parlor: Mrs. Cohen, in a splendid dress that was finer than Adelaide's own, and Emilie, a diamond necklace sparkling on her white bosom, and weary Mr. Cohen, flanked by a smiling Richard. Mrs. Pereira was there, dressed quietly in gray silk, leaning on the arm of the tall and elegant husband who was disgusted by his son. William, dressed in a new black suit—was Joe still extending him credit?— stood next to his father.

William came to stand at her side and curled his hand possessively around her waist. He could touch her now, and use her now, as he pleased. The thought steeled her resolve for what she was about to do.

Her father said, "I want to wish William and Adelaide every happiness, and to hope for friendship and harmony between our two families."

Before William's father could speak, Adelaide said, "There's something I'd like to say."

Her father turned to her. Was that an indulgent smile? He said, "We'll allow the bride her piece."

She turned to William, as though they were standing under the wedding canopy, and said, "I can't marry you, Mr. Pereira."

No one spoke. She gathered strength, and she pitched her voice low to hide her fear. "You lied to me. You're in debt, so deep in debt that you can't pay your bills or honor your notes. And you've been interfering with the servants here. After we marry, will you interfere with my servant?"

The room fell into shocked silence. William recovered first. He grabbed her shoulders. "Who told you?"

She thought of herself, and of Rachel, and even though her mother would be furious with her, she thought of her mother, too. "I can't say. It was told to me in confidence."

He began to shake her. His hands were rough. "Who told you?"

She shook her head. Her heart was pounding and she couldn't catch her breath. She was laced too tight.

He raised his hand to hit her, and it was her red-faced, countrified father, not an elegant gentleman of Savannah, who pulled William roughly away, growling in a deep low voice, "Take your hands off my daughter." She was too shaky to stand. Her father's words were the last thing she heard before she crumpled to the floor in a faint.

Afterwards, when the hubbub subsided—after she was brought up to her bed, after the doctor was called for and sent home, after the engagement was formally broken by the heads of the two families—Augusta swept into her room.

As she lay there, too weary to move, Rachel sat worriedly by her bedside. Augusta said coldly, "Miss Adelaide will be leaving when she's well enough to travel. You'll start to pack her things tomorrow."

"Yes, ma'am."

When Augusta left, Rachel did something she had never done before. She undressed down to her chemise and crawled under the covers with her sister. Adelaide turned so that they could put their arms around each other. They lay clasped together as they fell into an uneasy sleep.

Chapter 4

Charlie

Mordecai Mannheim stayed in Savannah on business, and Rosa chaperoned Adelaide home. Adelaide and Rachel sat in silence on the railway seat, facing a silent and furious Rosa. Adelaide stared at her hands, which were folded in her lap, and Rachel stared bleakly out the window.

The silence at home was worse than any reprimand. The Mannheims ate in silence—Rachel served them at dinner, so she knew—and they moved through the house in silence. Adelaide let Rachel lace her and dress her hair in silence. When Rachel asked nervously, "Adelaide? Are you all right?" Adelaide didn't reply. She stared into her reflection in the dressing table mirror in silence.

Rachel sat at the kitchen table with Aunt Susy a week after they'd returned from Savannah. She said, "I wish they'd scold her. Or yell at her. Not talking is the worst thing I ever saw them do."

Aunt Susy said, "I don't think they know what to say."

Rachel didn't know what to say either. She knew that Adelaide had wrecked her chances of marrying anyone in Savannah, and had hurt her chances of marrying into any Jewish family in the South. Only a crazy woman would have said what she said in public to her fiancé and his family. If it was hard to marry off a country mouse, it would be well-nigh impossible to marry off a woman who was crazy.

Rachel said, "I thought she'd marry someone in Savannah, and that I'd stay there with her. Now I don't know what she'll do, and I don't know what will happen to me either."

Aunt Susy sighed. "You just got to wait. Wait until the shame wears off, wait until she looks for a husband again, wait until she makes up her mind. Or her mama and daddy make up their minds for her. Until then, you wait."

Adelaide spent most of her time in her room, reading and writing letters. Her hands were inkstained again. She put on her rambling clothes and walked across her father's holdings, not minding the chill or the damp of a Piedmont winter. She called on her old friends in the county, the girls who were her age and still unmarried. They didn't turn her away. They didn't pry, either. Mrs. Turner, the arbiter of social life among the planters of Cass County, said sympathetically to Adelaide, "Maybe breaking that engagement scandalized those folks in Savannah, but we aren't in Savannah."

Adelaide resumed the life she'd led after she left the College, as though she had never been away. She attended lectures and musicales at the College, she went into Cassville to look at the new books at the bookseller's, and despite Rosa's objections, she even went to visit some of her old friends from the College, who were now married and living near places like Macon, Marietta, and Augusta.

She was dull. Rachel could tell. She looked tired and pale, and she didn't tease as she used to. Nothing cheered her, not a new book, or Aunt Susy's best sponge cake, or the promise of a visit to her College friends. She told Rachel that she didn't feel right—not sick, but not well either. She was too restless to stay in bed or even to stay indoors. Her long rambles didn't cheer her, either.

On a dark gray day in January, Rachel tapped on Adelaide's door and stepped in to the room. Adelaide lay in bed, which was unlike her, and she had drawn the curtains against the feeble winter light.

"Adelaide?" she called softly. She opened the curtain.

A low voice came from the bed. "Leave the curtain. I have such a headache that the light hurts my eyes."

Aunt Susy had a remedy for headache. "Do you want some birchbark tea?"

Adelaide whispered, "Hush. Any sound makes it worse."

Alarmed, Rachel put her hand on Adelaide's forehead. She was sweaty and clammy at the same time. She thought, We can't have yellow jack up here. Remembering to whisper, she said, "We'll call for the doctor."

Dr. Roswell examined Adelaide and said, "It isn't fever. Just a bad headache. A sick headache." He left a vial of laudanum, saying in caution, "Just a drop in a glass of water. It's very strong."

The sick headache came back every week, and every few weeks it was bad enough for a drop of laudanum. Rachel knew that Adelaide wasn't sick. She was sick at heart.

Rosa began to remind Adelaide that she had to think about being courted and getting married. The needling was for Mordecai, too. With a spark of her old sass, Adelaide looked from her mother to her father at the table one night and said, "Maybe I shouldn't marry. Maybe I should stay a spinster, and a bluestocking, and teach at the College."

Rosa said sharply, "You'll do no such thing. A girl needs to get married."

"Or I could marry Ben Turner Junior. Ain't his father the second-best planter in the county?"

Mordecai said, "I'd disown you."

"Papa! You're joking!"

Her father's face grew very red and he threw his napkin violently onto the table. "No, I ain't."

Later that evening, Adelaide sat before her dressing table and stared into the mirror as Rachel brushed her hair. She said plaintively, "Rachel, what will become of me?"

Rachel put her arms around Adelaide's neck and pressed her cheek to her sister's hair. "Your mama and papa still want you to marry a Jew."

"I can't imagine how they're going to find one who will forgive my disgrace."

Rachel felt dull, too. Like Adelaide, she resumed the life she led before Savannah. She was busy all the time—baking bread, cutting up vegetables for dinner, dusting the parlor and the study, beating carpets, helping with the weekly wash, and trying to cheer Adelaide. But nothing held her attention. Every task irritated her and distracted her. She didn't feel right. Her back ached and her head ached, and when she asked Aunt Susy for birchbark tea for herself for the second time in a week, Aunt Susy looked at her darkly and threatened to give her a dose of castor oil instead.

Rachel still read the newspaper in secret, although she was no longer drawn by the glittering world of Savannah. She did see, in passing, that William Pereira had married Emilie Cohen, and that they had gone to live in London, where the groom had joined his family's English banking house. Good riddance, she thought. For the most part, she read about darker things. She read about the war of words over slavery in the Senate, where Charles Sumner so enraged his colleagues that one of them beat him senseless with a cane. She followed the stories about Kansas, where people had stopped debating about slavery and were fighting over it. Guns, not words, would decide whether Kansas would enter the Union as a slave state or a free one. She read the notices about runaways with bitterness in her heart. She hoped that every slave with a scarred back and an "R" branded on the cheek would follow the drinking gourd to freedom.

She hated the thoughts that came to her all the time, her anger over Adelaide twined around the affection like bindweed around the useful plants in the garden. Bindweed could choke and kill the plant you wanted, but the thoughts kept coming back, over and over. She couldn't help it, and she didn't know how to feel better.

She needed a darker frame of mind to match her own. She left the house for the field hands' cabins to see Charlie.

As a young, unmarried man, he had moved out of his parents' cabin, and he now shared quarters with three other "bachelors" on the place. This one, like all the slaves' cabins, was a rough pine building, about fourteen feet square, with whitewash inside and out, and oilpaper over the windows. Inside, the four bachelors used the fireplace to bake sweet potatoes and cornpone, and they slept on straw pallets on the floor. No one stayed indoors to sit or visit. In the summer, even at night, it was too hot. The steps were made of pine boards, and they were big enough for two people to sit on.

When Rachel came to see Charlie, he was sitting on the front steps, leaning back, resting. He wore a cotton shirt, sweat-streaked from a day's work, and cotton trousers stained with dirt at the knees. Like all of the field hands, Charlie had few clothes. His two field shirts had to last him all week.

When he saw her he smiled, sat up, and made room for her on the step. She sat, and as she had since she was a little girl, she leaned against his chest, wanting him to cradle her.

He said ruefully, "Rachel, you don't want to nestle against me. I haven't had time to wash and I don't smell sweet."

"I don't either," she said, laying her head on his shoulder. He sighed and put his arm around her. He had always been sturdy, but now his shoulders and his arms were thick with muscle. He stroked her back. He said, "You look weary."

"I am weary."

"How is Miss Adelaide?"

"No worse and no better."

"Someday she'll want to marry again."

She sat up, startled. "If she does, I don't know what will become of me." She sounded as bleak as she felt, unable to hide it from Charlie.

He said, "Give me your hand." Her hands weren't small, but he could still cradle them in his. His palms were callused from plowing and the backs of his hands were scarred from picking cotton. Charlie used his hands with great care. She had seen him comfort a crying child, gentle an angry mule, and calm a fellow slave who wanted to run away.

He said, "It ain't up to you."

"Ain't nothing up to me," she said, reverting to kitchen talk.

He said, "You so sad, Rachel. You can't stay sad forever."

"Ain't nothing to be happy about. Not now, and maybe not ever."

He leaned back a little to get a good look at her. "Do you know how pretty you got while you were away?"

She remembered admiring her reflection in the Savannah mirror. "Doesn't matter now."

"Sure it does. You still pretty. Sad and pretty."

"Charlie, don't flirt with me."

"Ain't flirting to say what I see."

"Someone flirted with me in Savannah."

"Marse?" he asked, and worry and anger flickered over his face.

The way of the world. "No, Marse's man." She remembered Octavian and her madness in the back hallways with shame. She tried not to think of Marse Pereira. "Just as bad as Marse. Wanted to dally. Tried to, every chance he had."

"Did he hurt you?"

"Only my head."

"Your head? What did he do to you?"

"Threw me against a wall when I told him no."

Charlie tightened his grip on her hand—even angry, he didn't want to hurt her—and he said, "If that nigger were here, right now, I'd give him what he deserves."

She looked away. "I was such a fool," she said. "I should have told him no right away."

"Doesn't matter. Ain't no call to hurt a gal if she refuses."

"Charlie, did you dally while I was away?"

He laughed. "Dally? Too tired all the time, getting the crop in. Did try to kiss Lydia once, since she teased me so much. She said no, too."

"Didn't hurt your head, I hope."

"No, just my pride."

"Do you have your eye on anyone now?"

"Until the crop is in, I have my eye on a mule's backside," he said. "Ever since Marse made me a driver I worry about things I never used to think about. Dorcas is expecting and I can't press her hard. Lydia gets some ailment twice a week and can't work—ain't nothing wrong with her, I know it. Jim had too much corn whiskey last night and doesn't feel up to much. Whenever a mule balks I start to fret. Don't know how we're going to make a good crop, and if we don't it's all my fault."

"Marse likes you. Trusts you."

"Didn't know how it would aggravate me, being a driver. Give me a hoe, put me behind a plow, I'm fine. Worrying and fussing about everyone and everything else, it's a torment."

She put her arms around him and hugged him close. She knew Charlie. She knew every inch of his skin. When they were children, they were bathed together, and she still remembered how his shoulders set, how his thighs curved, how his bellybutton curled in. She had seen his manly part. As he grew, she had brought him water as he worked in the fields, stripped to the waist. She knew the smell of his sweat and the smell of his skin underneath it, like fresh-turned earth. Charlie's body was as familiar to her as her own.

He put his arms around her in a gesture of pure comfort. He knew how to gentle her, too.

The next time she came to see him, they sat on the steps for a while. Charlie said, "Let's walk under the trees, where it's cooler." They slipped into the woods behind the cabins. As dusk fell, the air began to cool. Beneath the trees, the earth smelled dry and sharp and piney. The night animals crept out—Charlie and Rachel could see them scurrying across the bed the pine needles made—and the night birds began to call. They heard owls hoot softly as the night's hunting began. The whippoorwills, who came out at night, trilled to each other, and the peewees sang out the call they were named for: Pee-wee! Pee-wee! Rachel listened to the crickets start their song, and the cricket frogs, who sounded like them, call back in response.

She said, "I missed this, in Savannah. There are so many buildings there, and so many people, that it's hard to look up at the sky and remember that you can see the same stars as you see here."

"Waxing moon," he said, and she looked upward too.

They stopped walking and faced each other. She knew Charlie so well that she had never considered his looks, but now she looked at him afresh. Aunt Susy had always said that Charlie looked more African than most people on the Mannheim place. He had prominent cheekbones, and what Aunt Susy called a proud nose: narrow at the bridge, flaring at the nostril. His lips were full and under the brown they had a purple stain, as though he'd been eating ripe blackberries and hadn't wiped off his mouth.

He took her hand and looked into her face with affection. He said, "If I tried to kiss you, would you say no?"

She smiled. "I say yes."

He cradled her face in his hands, and bent—only a little, since she was tall for a woman—to kiss her gently with his purple-stained lips. He didn't pull her close. He didn't press against her. Just the touch of lips together, with more tenderness than she thought possible in a kiss.

He stepped back and put his hands on her shoulders. "Miss Rachel, do you like me a little?"

"Like you!" she said. "I've loved you all my life."

It was true, but she hadn't realized how it would sound after they'd kissed. It brought a smile of pure joy to his face. He put his arms around her and hugged her, the familiar brotherly affection tinged with a manly urgency. When they broke apart he held out his hand to her, and they walked easily under the trees, without needing to speak.

She hadn't known how dark the world had become since she came back from Savannah. After Charlie kissed her, she could hope that there might be light again. Charlie's kiss was like seeing the first ray of sunrise through the darkness.

Charlie was still her friend. Tired as he was, he was always glad to see her. He always offered her his shoulder, and he never refused her his ear. Even if they had nothing cheering to say to each other, it comforted her to talk to him.

But he was also the man who took her hand and walked with her under the pine trees. As the moon rose, as the nightbirds began to call, as the cool breeze began to waft through the forest, they stopped under the canopy of the trees and kissed.

The kisses were still tender, but they became more and more passionate, and they found it natural to embrace and to inch closer together, until they were touching, breast to chest, thigh to thigh, belly to belly. In Charlie's embrace, she never felt the madness she'd felt with Octavian. She felt heat, and she felt joy.

On a night when the moon was full, and the moonlight filtered through the trees, he held her without kissing her. He stroked her cheek. He said, "Rachel, I love you more than I can tell you."

She nodded and smiled. He didn't have to tell her. Every time he touched her, she knew.

"It's more than sport. Sport's for a moment. This is different." His hand on her cheek, his eyes glowing with affection, he said, "Rachel, would you lie with me?"

Oh, Lord. She loved him and she hadn't thought ahead to this. If she loved Charlie with her body, there could be a baby. A baby born a slave. She turned away, unable to meet those eyes she knew so well.

He said, "Something's troubling you. I always know."

"I'm ashamed to say."

"Don't be."

"I'm not afraid," she said. "Not of anything we might do together. But I am afraid—so afraid—"

"Of what?"

"Not of having a baby, either. But of having a baby born into slavery. That would break my heart."

His hand slipped to her shoulder. He was pondering something. He said, "Not everyone who lies together has a baby."

"Most people do."

He said, "I ain't supposed to know, but I've heard the women whisper about it. Aunt Susy knows about these womanly things. She knows those roots. If you asked her, she'd tell you."

She looked at him in astonishment. "How not to have a baby?"

He was much too dark to show a blush, but she could read the embarrassment on his face. "I ain't supposed to know," he repeated.

It was surprisingly difficult to bring up the matter with Aunt Susy. Aunt Susy had bathed her as a little girl, had helped her when she got her monthlies, and had explained the mysteries of love to her. Now Rachel blushed with embarrassment at the thought of telling Aunt Susy that she loved Charlie but she didn't want a baby.

Aunt Susy was known on the place as a root doctor. Even though many of her medicines were from the leaves or the seeds of plants, everyone referred to them as "roots." She was best known for her skill in easing pregnancy and delivering babies. One day, after a woman had been in the kitchen asking for a root to help her conceive, Rachel asked, "If a woman doesn't want to have a baby, are there roots for that too?"

Aunt Susy said, "Is this about Charlie?"

She was hot with shame. She said, "Charlie loves me and I love him."

Aunt Susy smiled. "Wondered how long it would take you to say so," she said. "He's been here, mooning over you."

It was suddenly easier. "We aren't flighty, wanting just to sport," she said. "But a baby—another baby for Marse—"

Aunt Susy said, "I wouldn't want to stop a baby if you had one growing, but I don't mind giving you roots to keep from having a baby."

"Will the roots work?"

Aunt Susy said darkly, "If they don't, I'll risk my soul and give you the other roots to stop it."

Aunt Susy made her a tea. "You drink this every morning," she said. "Don't forget a day."

"What's in it?"

Aunt Susy was secretive about her roots. She preferred to keep them a mystery. "Never you mind. It will work."

"How does it taste?"

"I put in some spearmint to make it taste pleasant. Remember, every day."

That evening she went to see Charlie and pulled on his hand to go walking in the woods. When they were alone, away from listening ears, she clasped his hands and said, "Aunt Susy gave me roots."

He grinned. He said, "Now we find the right spot—has to be quiet, and private, and let us see the sky when we lie down. Then we come back with a blanket."

"Why a blanket?"

She had never seen him look so happy. "To lie on. Otherwise you'll get pine needles in your backside."

Aunt Susy gave her more guidance about the act of love—even though it was useful, it embarrassed her dreadfully to hear it—and she found an old blanket, which she stuffed into a big basket. Desire made her stealthy. She didn't go looking for Charlie on the steps of his cabin. They met in their kissing place under the trees.

"Charlie, is this private enough?"

"Come with me."

He led her deeper into the woods, to a spot she had never seen before. It was a little clearing, ringed by pines that grew slender and tall. The ground was covered with old pine needles, the color of rust. The air smelled of resin from the trees, and of green things that grew in the fields beyond the forest. "Here," he said.

They spread the blanket and lay down on it. He said, "Look at the sky."

They lay together, touching lightly at shoulder and hip. She looked at the moon, a waxing crescent tonight, and at the stars. She listened to the sound of the crickets, and the whippoorwills singing, and the owls calling. She thought, this is just as I imagined it, when I was in Savannah.

She rolled towards him and asked, smiling, "How should we do this?"

He smiled. "Slow," he said. "Sweet and slow."

Slowly, he caressed her face and her neck. Slowly, he unbuttoned her dress, laughing a little to find the chemise under it. Slowly, they eased out of their clothes.

She looked at him—all of him, the broad shoulders, the muscled chest, the strong thighs. She said, "Do you remember how Aunt Susy used to put us in that tub together, when we were babies?"

"You grew up," he said.

"So did you," she said.

He admired her body with his hands, slowly, cradling her breast, stroking the curve of her hip, resting his hand on her belly. He gently cupped her womanly part. She guided his fingers inside her. He laughed in his throat and touched her gently.

She reached for him and curled her hand around him. This skin, which never saw the sun, was silky in her hand. He said, "Let me love you."

"Yes," she said.

He moved to lie on her, asking, "I ain't crushing you?"

His weight was like an embrace. "No. It feels fine."

Slowly, he came inside her body. Aunt Susy had warned her about the pain that was likely the first time. Even though she expected it, she winced. Charlie said, "I'm hurting you, I can see it."

"It happens, the first time. Shouldn't last more than a moment." Aunt Susy had been right: the pain was brief, and in its place was a blissful friction.

Charlie's member, like his hands, was gentle. She caught his rhythm, and rose to meet him. Still careful with her, he moved faster. She wrapped her legs around his hips to admit him deeper into her body. He pressed into her, so deep that she no longer knew where her body left off and here his began. They moved together, harder and faster, one flesh.

The spasm started between her legs, but she felt it everywhere—in her belly, in her chest, in her limbs. She felt bliss in her body, and joy in her heart. He cried out, and she felt his spasm resonate through her, adding to her own.

Spent, he rested on her. She wrapped her arms around him, delighting in the strong muscles of his back. He propped himself on his elbows and said, "You're all right? I ain't crushing you?"

"I feel fine," she whispered, kissing his cheek, then his lips.

They lay together, listening to the sounds of the summer night, until he began to fade inside her. He shifted a little. She said, "No, you're all right."

He said ruefully, "I have to move, sugar. I itch something terrible."

She laughed. "You'd best move, then, if you want to scratch!"

They lay side by side, letting the night breeze flow over their bodies, their hands clasped together. They didn't talk. They didn't have to.

Rachel felt as though the sun had come out. On the surface, her life was the same, work in the house and the kitchen and Adelaide's room. But every night, there was the comfort and joy of Charlie. And every morning, there was the tea to drink. The taste was bitter—no spearmint could cover it—but the reminder was sweet.

During the harvest, when the field hands worked into the evening to pick the crop, Charlie was so tired that he fell onto his pallet at night, too tired to eat. She saw him on Sunday afternoons, when he was too tired to stay awake, let alone to rouse to love her. She let him fall asleep on her breast and kissed his cheek while he slept. After harvest, there would be time for rest and ease and love again.

Adelaide stayed the same. She was still dull and restless, and she got a sick headache about once a week. Rachel didn't think about the day when Adelaide would consider courting or getting married. It was far in the future, like next year's harvest when this one was just over. As long as Adelaide stayed unmarried at home, Rachel would have the continued pleasure of Charlie's listening ear, his gentle hands, and his blissful ease inside her body.

Throughout the winter, they met outside. They rolled themselves into a blanket and ignored the weather if it were chill or damp. In the months before plowing started, they often met in the afternoon, when they had the least to do. On a gray day in March, they lay in their blanket, in close embrace. Charlie kissed her lips, and said, "Rachel, do you ever think about getting married?"

If she thought about getting married, she'd have to think about Adelaide. What would happen if Adelaide got found a suitor. What would happen if Adelaide got married. She was bound to Adelaide, and she would go where Adelaide went, to share whatever life Adelaide would have. Charlie wouldn't. She was suddenly more miserable than she had been for nearly a year. She said, "You know as well as I do that it ain't up to me."

He stroked her cheek. "I do know. But we don't know what's going to happen, or when."

"Charlie, what if I married you and then had to leave you because Adelaide married someone in Charleston, or New Orleans, or Natchez? I couldn't bear it."

He said, "She's likely to marry someone who needs a cotton hand. Why couldn't I ask Marse to sell me, so I could be with you?"

"I wouldn't even ask Marse Mannheim such a thing. I know what he'd say."

"What would he say?"

"That he wouldn't do it. He couldn't afford to lose you."

"There are plenty of niggers who can pick cotton. He doesn't need me."

"You're the best driver he's ever had on the place. He won't sell you."

He said, "Might he oblige you?"

"He won't do a thing to oblige me. You know that, and you know why."

The joy had gone out of their embrace. The blanket felt clammy in the damp air. Rachel shivered. The sky was gray again, and she was afraid that the sun would never come back.

A few weeks later, on a Sunday afternoon, clean from his Saturday night bath, dressed in his Sunday best, Charlie walked resolutely to the main house. He had been in the kitchen many times, but he had never stood on the front steps of this house, and he had never walked through the front door. He wasn't sure what he should do. Should he knock? Should he ring the bell?

The butler, Ezra, saw him through the window. He opened the door and scolded him. "What are you doing here?"

"I want to see Marse Mannheim."

"About what?"

"It's business. My business."

"Come around the back. You field niggers are so ignorant. You don't even know you can't come in the front door."

Ezra brought him in the back door, and led him through the pantry. He said, "You wait here and I'll ask him if he wants to talk to you."

Charlie waited. He was increasingly uncomfortable. He knew he didn't belong here, and he felt it more keenly with every moment that he waited for Ezra's return.

Ezra came back. "All right. He says he'll see you. You follow me, and don't you get any dirt on them carpets."

"I cleaned my boots as best I could," Charlie said meekly.

Lord, this house unnerved him. I shouldn't be in here, he thought, even if I did clean my boots first.

Ezra led him to a big room at the back of the house, where Marse Mannheim sat in a big chair. He said, "Charlie, come in."

Charlie came in. He didn't sit, because he knew he wasn't supposed to. He didn't look up at Marse, because he knew he wasn't supposed to.

"What is it, Charlie? Trouble with the crop, or with the gang?"

"No, Marse Mannheim, everything's fine with the crop and the gang. That's not why I'm here."

"Then what is it?"

It was well-nigh impossible to talk about this while he was looking at the floor. "Marse, it's about Rachel."

Marse said, "I've heard a little gossip, Charlie. I hear that you and Rachel have been stepping out together."

"More than that, Massa. I love Rachel, and she loves me. We want to get married."

Marse Mannheim says, "That's all right, Charlie. That's between the two of you. You don't have to ask me."

He couldn't stand to say this while he was looking at his feet. He raised his head and said, "Massa, I know she's bound to Miss Adelaide, and Miss Adelaide is going to get married someday and leave here to be with her husband. If I married her, and I couldn't follow her to stay with her, it would break her heart."

"What do you want me to do, Charlie?"

"Massa, if you could promise to sell me to whoever Miss Adelaide marries, it would make me easier in my mind."

Marse Mannheim said, "I can't promise a thing like that. You know that, Charlie."

"It would make her easier, too. She doesn't want to marry me now if she'll have to leave me. That would break my heart, too."

"Charlie, I can't let you go anywhere. I need you here."

"Massa, I ain't the only hand on the place who can be a driver. You know that."

"You're the best driver on this place. I can't make the crop without you. I won't sell you, not to anyone."

"Massa, I know it's a lot to ask."

Marse Mannheim said, "You and Rachel can get married. That's between the two of you. But she'll go where Miss Adelaide goes, and I can't guarantee that you'll be able to follow."

"Massa—"

"That's all I have to say, Charlie. You can go."

His gaze fell back to the floor. "Yes, Massa," he said miserably.

As soon as he left the room, Ezra was there to show him out. Did he stand at the doors, listening? Ezra saw how crestfallen he was, and he said, much more gently than when Charlie had come in, "I'll take you out the back door, Charlie."

He walked slowly back to his cabin, too upset to stop for anyone who greeted him. He felt beaten in his soul. He felt broken. Rachel had been right. She would go with Adelaide and he would stay. Getting married was a way to guarantee heartbreak.

Later that day, he stopped at the kitchen to see if she was there. He said, "Can you walk with me?"

She wiped flour from her hands and took off her apron. "Aunt Susy, I'll be right back," she said.

They walked slowly to the place where they used to linger to kiss. He didn't take her hand. She could tell how miserable he was. They halted and didn't touch. She said, "What's wrong?"

"I went to see Marse." He couldn't look her in the face. He stared at his feet. He said, "You were right."

She said, "You thought I was being stubborn. Or foolish."

"Now I know."

She said, "What's worse? Heartbreak later, when Massa decides for us, or heartbreak now, that we choose for ourselves?"

He shook his head. It began to rain, a fine drizzle, scarcely more than a mist. They stood together, not touching, as the rain caught in their hair and moistened their faces. They stood in the rain long enough for the mist to gather on their cheeks and trickle down it like tears.

They couldn't avoid each other, but they made no effort to see each other or talk to each other. Rachel went back to her narrow bed in the attic room she shared with Aunt Susy. For weeks she lay awake at night, curled into a knot against the pain in her chest and her belly. There was no more comfort and no more joy in her life. The sun had set, and she felt as though it would never come up again.

Six months after Rachel and Charlie had parted, Charlie came to see her.

He said, "I wanted you to know before anyone else does. I'm going to get married. We'll wait until after the harvest."

"Who is she?"

"Becky. New field hand. Marse bought her just before we started this year's crop."

Rachel knew her by sight. She was a sturdy woman, with the high cheekbones and coppery skin of someone who was part Cherokee. She spoke little. Her expression was calm. Rachel said, "She'll suit you."

Charlie didn't move to go. He looked abashed. He said, "Rachel, I miss you."

She stiffened.

He said, "No, hear me out. I miss you coming to talk to me. I miss you coming to nestle on my shoulder. We were like brother and sister. I miss that."

She said, "It's not the same anymore."

"I know. But hear me out. I told Becky about us, that we've been close since we were babies. I told her I loved you. She knows about that."

She turned away.

"Rachel, listen. She knows what it's like to lose someone. She was sold away twice. Once from her mama and daddy, once from her husband and children."

Lord, don't tell me about it.

He said, "She said that it's foolish to lose someone you love. It wouldn't trouble her if we were still friends."

She couldn't look at him. She said, "Maybe someday. Not yet."

He said, "I'll wait. I'll be here."

Ain't up to you.

He said softly, "You'll come to the wedding?"

Her eyes were full of tears, but she looked up at him. "Wouldn't be right to stay away."

When Charlie left her, she felt worse than she had for months. That day, Rachel found a quiet spot and cried until her eyes ached with the salt.

Chapter 5

A Jew in Georgia

Henry Kaltenbach had been working as a clerk in Meyer's Dry Goods in Savannah for more than two years when a portly gentleman with red cheeks and a double chin walked into the shop. Lightweight wool, he thought. A full suit. Three yards. He didn't want to look dull with a customer at the counter, but he felt dull. Savannah wasn't Dresden, but one Jewish-owned dry goods store was very like another. He had traveled a long way to feel that he was still behind the counter of his father's shop in Germany.

But the portly man surprised him. He didn't want lightweight wool. He said, "I'm looking for lengths for dresses." He had a heavy German accent. "My wife knows what she wants—she wrote it down for me—but I don't know what to buy for my daughter."

"Is she a girl? Or is she a young lady?"

"A young woman, but unmarried. She hasn't felt well, and now that she's better, she needs new dresses."

"I'm sorry to hear that she was ill. What is her coloring?"

"Brown hair, brown eyes," the man said.

Henry said, "I think I have some lengths that will suit."

They looked at muslins and cottons for day and at silks for evening. "Either the bright blue or the dark red will do, I think," said Henry.

"I think so," the man said. "The dressmaker knows how much she'll need. She can stop to tell you. Put it all on account. Mr. Meyer knows me.

Mordecai Mannheim. He has the address—we're in the country, and we get our mail in Cassville."

Henry held out his hand. "Henry Kaltenbach."

Mordecai Mannheim gathered up his hat. "Tell Nathan Meyer I was here. I'm sorry to miss him. Tell him that Adelaide is better."

"I'll do that, sir."

After Mordecai Mannheim left, Henry wondered if Miss Mannheim, the dark-eyed daughter who hadn't been well, was pretty.

Henry Kaltenbach, born Heinrich, was eighteen when the Revolution of 1848 began, bringing the hope for freedom to Jews as well as to their German neighbors. When the Revolution came to Dresden in 1849, Henry felt so strongly about it that he argued with his amiable father.

Henry said stubbornly, "It's about freedom, Papa. For everyone. Even for us."

His father shook his head. "It's never good for the Jews when Germans fight in the streets," he said.

"We're German, too," Henry said, thinking of the poet Heinrich Heine, born a Jew, his poems now beloved by his countrymen.

His father said sadly, "When you can go to the University, when you can have a profession, when you can be a citizen, without becoming a Christian first, you'll be a German."

In Dresden, the Revolution was crushed with particular violence. Prussian troops shot the revolutionaries in the streets. Henry, who had been on fire with the revolution's ideals, was so badly disappointed that he wanted to join the stream of "Forty-Eighters" bound for America.

When he told his parents how much he wanted to leave for America, his mother reached up to kiss him. She was short and round, and she always smelled pleasantly of cinnamon, as though she'd been making the strudel her son liked so much. "*Liebchen*," she said, as though he were still a little boy. "It hurts me to think of you so far away, and never to come home again." Henry looked from his father's kindly face to his mother's worried one, and agreed to stay in Germany. Finally his father wrote to the Meyers, distant cousins who had settled in Savannah in Georgia, and four years after the Revolution ended, Henry left Dresden for Bremen, and boarded a ship bound for the United States.

Henry marveled at the freedom he saw in Savannah. Even the Jews of Savannah were free to live where they pleased, work as they pleased, and if they'd lived in Georgia long enough, vote for any candidate they pleased. At Meyer's, he waited on men who had come from Ireland or Germany, as humble as himself when they arrived, who had made their fortunes. They had plantations along the coast and grand houses in town. Henry waited on their wives and daughters, who bought length after length of silk, the fabric whispering softly of money as he cut it from the bolt.

In this free country, the streets of Savannah were full of slaves, from the brightest of house servants to the field hands from the coast, who spoke a language indistinguishable from an African tongue. Many arrivals from Germany feared and disliked the sight of black slaves, but Henry was fascinated by them. They were part of the human family, even if they were different from any people he had ever seen.

Before coming to America, Henry had read about slavery. The ancients owned slaves, as did the modern Russians. But he was dismayed to see these sons and daughters of Africa, bound forever in slavery, in the streets of a country that was the world's beacon for democracy and freedom.

The Israelites of Savannah, rich and not so rich, were just like their Gentile neighbors in owning slaves. On his first Passover in America, exulting in his own freedom, he watched the Meyers' slave cook help her mistress make *haroses*, the wine and apple relish that reminded Jews of their hard labor in Egypt. As the dark hands chopped apples and mixed in cinnamon and wine, Henry was bothered by the thought that the people who had once been slaves in Egypt now owned slaves in Georgia.

The greatest freedom in America was the freedom to get rich. But in Georgia, no one made a fortune selling lengths of cotton cloth. Men made their fortunes growing cotton. Meyer's was close to Factors Row, and Henry went to see Richard Cohen, whose father's firm financed the wealthiest planters in Georgia, South Carolina and Louisiana.

Cohen told him, "You'd need land, about five hundred acres, and slaves. Five to start. Mules. Implements. Seed. It would cost you close to ten thousand dollars."

It was a ruinous amount of debt. Dry-mouthed, he said, "How would I ever pay it back?"

"You could, if the crop came in at a bale an acre, and the price held at ten cents a pound or higher."

"And if it didn't?"

"You'd be bankrupt."

When Mr. Mannheim returned a month later, Henry immediately

recognized him. "How is your daughter, Mr. Mannheim? Did she like the new dresses?"

Mannheim was surprised that he remembered. "Yes, she did. The new dresses cheered her greatly."

Henry said, "Will she come to Savannah herself? To pick out lengths that she likes?"

A shadow passed over Mannheim's face. "She doesn't care for Savannah," he said.

Too late, he remembered the scandal. Adelaide Mannheim was the girl who refused William Pereira because he interfered with his slaves. Henry, schooled in tact, said, "Let me bring you some pretty cottons to look at."

Mannheim didn't need to look at the lengths very long. "All of these will suit," he said. "You have a good eye."

Henry said, "My father owns a dry goods shop in Dresden and I grew up behind the counter."

"You're likely. Do you want to own a shop yourself?"

Henry laughed. "I didn't come all the way to America to open a dry goods shop."

Mannheim laughed too. "I didn't either. That's where I started, but not where I ended up."

"May I ask, sir, what your business is?"

"I have three thousand acres in cotton in Cass County. I broker cotton for my neighbors, and I make some from that, too. I have more than fifty niggers."

"And you started behind a dry goods counter."

Mannheim said, "Let me stand you to a dinner tonight. Do you keep the dietary laws?"

"I don't care for pork, but I eat anything else that's put before me."

"I'll come back at closing and I'll call for you."

Mannheim took him to an eating house where the clerks at Meyer's ate once a month, a pleasure they allotted themselves carefully, like their visits to the bawdy house. They were Jewish drunkards. Between the three of them, a single bottle of wine flushed their cheeks, made them laugh, and caused them to forget their English.

Mannheim said, "I like the beefsteak here, and the fried potatoes. We'll have a bottle of claret, and if that isn't enough, we can order another."

The wine came first, and emboldened by the initial glass, Henry asked Mannheim, "I'm grateful that you asked me here, sir, but why did you ask me?"

"I like to see an ambitious young man. It reminds me of myself when I first got here, back in '32. What's your ambition? How do you want to make your fortune?"

He didn't watch his words. "The real fortunes here are in cotton."

"Would you like to buy a place of your own?"

"I've thought about it," he said. "I made some inquiries."

"Who did you go to? Cohen?" Henry nodded. "I bet he wouldn't stake you a nickel."

"He told me I'd need ten thousand dollars."

Mannheim snorted. "Lowland place? Long-staple cotton?"

"He didn't say."

"If you look at an upland place, you can do better. Close to the hill country. You can grow short-staple cotton there just fine, if you're smart about it."

Henry said, "I didn't think to ask."

"Cass County's upland. I buy and sell land, too. I can keep my eyes open for you and let you know if I see anything that might suit."

Henry was suddenly wary. "Why would you do me such a favor?"

Mannheim said, "I ain't planning to give you anything. I'd lend you the money for land and slaves."

"What if I went bankrupt?"

"Do you gamble?"

"No," Henry said.

"I can tell you don't drink much. Save your money?"

"As much as I can. Why?"

"You've got sober habits. I'd trust you to borrow money until you make the crop to pay it back."

It was a risk to grow cotton. You could make a fortune. Or you could go bust. But if he didn't try, he'd never know.

The next day, Joe asked, "I heard you dined with Mannheim. What did he want?"

Suddenly sly, Henry said, "To thank us for dress lengths that made his daughter happy."

Joe shook his head. "I've never heard Mannheim thank anyone. And I've never known him to do anything unless there was profit in it. I'd be careful around him, if I were you."

I've been warned, Henry thought.

After his dinner with Mannheim, Henry covered scraps of paper with figures, one column for costs, another for profits. The sums were still staggering. Even if Mannheim could help him buy discounted land, even if he could furnish the place more cheaply, he would be thousands of dollars in debt, and his creditor would be a man that Joe Meyer, a good judge of character, didn't trust.

He stared at the figures again. If he made a good crop the first year he'd be out of debt. If he made three good crops in a row he'd have a start on a fortune.

Mannheim wrote to him, telling him that he'd found a likely place, and that he and the seller would be in Savannah in a few weeks.

The three of them met at the same eating house where Mannheim had beguiled him with the thought of owning his own cotton plantation. Mr. Johnson, who was selling, was a short, round, blond man with a rosy face. He said, "Just the land. I'm taking the hands with me."

"Where are you going?" Henry asked.

"I bought a bigger place in Mississippi. Delta land. Richest soil you ever saw."

"You did well there?"

"Well enough to quadruple my holdings."

Mannheim said, "It's five hundred acres."

Johnson said, "I had two hundred in cotton and a hundred in corn. The rest was fallow."

"Tell him how many bales," Mannheim said.

"I made a bale an acre."

In his head, Henry did the catechism he had learned over the past month: Two hundred bales. Five hundred pounds to a bale. Ten cents a pound. Ten thousand dollars. "How many slaves did you have to work it?"

"Five, including my housekeeper, who never worked in the fields."

Henry pressed his hands against the edge of the table, because they were shaking. "Did you ever have a bad year?"

"Sure," Mr. Johnson said. "We had a drought—when was that, Mannheim?"

Mannheim said, "But you made up for it the next season. I recall, because I factored you."

He wished that he knew more about buying a farm. "What is your asking price?"

Johnson said, "I need to sell in a hurry because I need the money for the Mississippi place. I'm asking two thousand for the land, the barn, and the house. It's a good house. You can move right into it."

After Johnson left, Mannheim ordered another bottle of wine and asked, "How are you inclined?"

"It sounds like a good place. But it's a lot of money, even for a bargain. I want to think it over for a day or two."

"You're still interested? You haven't wasted our time, looking and not buying?"

Henry knew when he was being pressed. He said, "If I were selling you a dry goods business, wouldn't you want to think it over?"

Mannheim laughed. "Of course I would."

"Two thousand for the property," Henry said. "How much for the slaves?"

"We'll watch for an auction. Distressed planters are always selling their niggers cheap. We'll find a bargain there, too." He poured Henry another glass of claret. "No reason to look downcast! Let's drink to your fortune."

Henry debated with himself for several troubled days and sleepless nights. He wanted very badly to make a fortune. He knew he shouldn't trust Mordecai Mannheim to help him do it. Greed overwhelmed good sense, and later that week, Henry signed two contracts. One was a title deed to a five-hundred acre parcel of property in Cass County. The other was a promissory note that obliged Henry Kaltenbach to repay Mordecai Mannheim the sum of two thousand dollars, plus commission for the sale, and interest.

The next time Mannheim came to Savannah, he told Henry, "You're in luck. There's a big slave auction at the fairgrounds next week. Over four hundred slaves. Two big plantations, all in the same family."

"What went wrong? Why are they selling?"

"Busted up for debt, I reckon," Mordecai said. "Who knows whether they speculated it away or gambled it away." Mordecai shrugged. "Let's go. They'll have an auction list, and we can take a look at what's being offered."

The auction fell on a day rainy, windy, and unusually cold for January in Savannah. There were so many slaves to sell that the pens had been set up at the fairgrounds on the site of the racecourse. The sheds were open to the weather, and the wind and the rain drove into the makeshift shelters, wetting and chilling everyone. Henry was cold in his heaviest wool coat. The slaves, who wore clothes of lightweight cotton, better suited to the coastal summer than to the day's wet and chill, were shivering.

The auctioneer had advertised the seller's desire to keep families together, and there were many groups that looked to be families. But Henry also saw people of all ages alone. As they walked through the shed, Henry saw a man by himself, sitting on the ground, his arms wrapped around himself against the chill, staring vacantly before him. Henry said to Mordecai, "What's the matter with him?"

"He's moody. You don't want a hand who's moody. Won't work hard."

Off to the side, under a corrugated tin roof, was a crush of people—white men, in warm coats—and a hubbub. The smell of cigar smoke was strong. "Would you like a drink?" Mordecai asked. "Warm you up in this weather." Henry shook his head. Mordecai took out his catalog and marked it with a pencil. "I see some likely lots for you."

The place was crowded with buyers. Henry watched as a man in a plaid wool suit—his eyes attuned to the quality of wool, Henry knew how cheap it was—stopped before a group, a man, a woman, and two children of less than ten. The man opened the slave woman's mouth to check her teeth. He squeezed the children's arms, testing the strength of their muscles. The slave man watched, his face impassive. The buyer turned to the slave man and said, "Bend over so I can see if you've got a rupture." The man didn't reply. He bent over.

A young slave man caught Henry's eye, and forced his face into a pleasant expression. He said, "Young Marse, are you looking for a good hand?"

Henry stopped. The young man said, "I'm a good hand. Grow rice, grow cotton, and I work hard. I'm healthy. Good teeth." He bared them. "Nothing wrong with me." Henry listened. The slave man warmed to him. "See that gal over there?" He pointed to a group not far away. "That's my sweetheart. Daisy. She strong, a good worker, and if we get married we have lots of babies for you. Increase. Will you buy us both, young Marse?"

Mordecai looked the catalog. "Daisy?" he said. "She's with her family. They ain't breaking up families. Six people, including young'uns. You can't afford to buy seven slaves. Don't waste your time here. Come on, I have other lots to show you."

The young man's face fell as they walked on.

Mordecai looked at the catalog. "There's a man with two boys," he said. "He sounds likely. Let's look at him."

They stopped before the man with two sons. The man in the plaid suit had gotten there first, and he was saying to the slave man, "Walk up and down for me. I want to make sure you ain't lame."

"I ain't lame," the man said politely. "My two boys are sound, and they're good workers, too."

Henry stopped before the man. He was a medium brown, and he was probably in his mid-thirties, although he was weatherbeaten, and it was hard to tell. He was sturdy, not very tall, and he was a little bowlegged. He had an obliging look. "What's your name?" Henry asked.

"Zeke, sir."

His name and his skill as a hand were on the list, but Henry wanted to talk to him. He asked, "What did you work at?"

Zeke said, "I've been a cotton hand all my life, but I can carpenter, too. My boys are half-grown, but they're good strong workers, like grown men. Luke—he's fourteen—he's a good cotton hand, and he helps me with the carpentering. Tom—he's twelve—he's good with livestock. Horses, mules, even cows, he can take care of just fine."

Mordecai said to Henry, "We aren't here to chat. We're here to spend your money wisely."

"I know."

As they walked away, Mordecai said, "They're likely. All of them. But you aren't here to make friends. You're here to invest in hands."

Henry nearly missed seeing her. She was seated on the ground, and she was so small that he thought she was a child. She had wrapped her arms around her knees, and she rested her cheek on her arm. Only when she stood up did he realize that she was a full-grown woman and that she had been weeping. She was very dark, an African black, and she had huge wide eyes in her small dark face. So much of her eye whites showed that Henry knew she was terrified.

He said gently, "What's your name?"

Her voice was pitched low with fear. "Minnie."

"What did you do on your last place?"

"I was a cook. I kept house, too."

Thinking of the young man's plea, he asked, "Is there anyone here with you?"

"No," she said. "I'm all alone."

Mordecai grabbed him by the arm and said, "You don't buy hands because you feel sorry for them. She ain't right. We keep looking." He looked at the catalog. "You want a big strapping gal to cook and keep your house for you. I can find you one."

Henry said stubbornly, "I like Minnie."

Mordecai stopped before a sturdy young woman. "What's your name, gal?" he asked.

"Bess, Massa. I'm a cook. Good cook. Strong. Carry a flour barrel by myself. Do the wash, too." She flexed her arm. "You can see for yourself."

Mordecai said to Henry, "That's what I mean."

"I'm going to bid on Minnie."

"You'd better get her cheap," Mordecai said.

The auction block was in the open, outside the shed. The merchandise walked up two steps, and stood before the crowd, so the buyers could see what they were bidding on. When the auction began, the buyers deserted the bar. They came into the rain and the cold to see the bidding. They opened their catalogs and got their pencils ready.

The bidding went swiftly. Henry was surprised that anyone could buy a human being with so little deliberation. Mordecai said, "Pay attention. Zeke and his boys are coming up."

"What should I bid?"

Mordecai, a seasoned slaveowner, said, "I wouldn't give more than two thousand for all of them. Half-grown boys."

Henry watched them, all three of them, walk up the steps to the platform. Zeke put his arm protectively on the slighter boy's shoulder. Tom, his name was. When all three of them stood on the block together, Zeke put an arm around each of the boys. The auctioneer pulled them apart. "Let them see you," he said impatiently.

The bidding swiftly ran up to eighteen hundred dollars. Someone was bidding against him. As Henry bid, he saw the boy Tom looking at him. Smiling. Hoping for Henry as his new Massa. When Henry's opponent bid higher, Tom's face clouded. The bidding reached two thousand. Tom looked as though he would cry. Henry bid, was outbid, and bid again. Henry paid twenty-two hundred dollars, but Zeke and the boys were his. At his victory all three broke into smiles, and Zeke hugged his sons.

Mordecai said, "Shouldn't have gotten carried away."

Minnie went cheap. The other buyers had shared Mordecai's thought. It was done. God help him, he was now a slaveowner.

Chapter 6

A Crop and a Courtship

Adelaide left the booksellers', where they had nothing new to show her, and walked down the street to the dry goods store. Mr. Levy and his family had recently come to Cassville, and now the Mannheims were no longer the only Jews in Cass County.

Levy's was set up the same as Meyer's in Savannah, with the bolts arranged by cloth and color on the shelves, and the ribbons and laces in the case. Adelaide wrinkled her nose as she pushed open the door. Meyer's had smelled of the lavender that ladies used for sachets, but Levy's smelled of camphor, a rougher way to repel moths.

The shop was full of people. At the counter, his back to her, stood a slight man with curly hair. With him were four slaves, a woman, a man and two boys. The slaves stood in a tight little group, not speaking, their eyes on the floor.

Mr. Levy said, "You'll want Osnaburg for their clothes."

"Oh, no," the master said, in a pleasant, German-accented voice. "Not Osnaburg, it won't stand up to wear. Show me some cottons, for shirts and chemises. Nankeen, for trousers, and fustian, for jackets. And a sturdy lightweight wool for a dress."

"You know your cloth," said Mr. Levy.

The man said, "I used to work in dry goods myself, before I came here."

Mr. Levy said, "You must be the man who bought the Johnson place. Mr.

Kaltenbach, is it? Mr. Mannheim was here last week and told me to expect you."

They shook hands. Mr. Levy looked at Adelaide, and said to Mr. Kaltenbach, "Have you met Miss Mannheim?"

He turned. He had a pleasant face to go with his pleasant voice, dark eyes and a mobile mouth. So this was Joe Meyer's clerk from Savannah, come to Cassville to grow cotton with her father's help.

Introductions were made. Adelaide smiled and gestured towards the slaves, who had not said a word. "I never knew a planter to dress his slaves so generously."

He flushed a little under her scrutiny. "Is it wrong, Miss Mannheim?"

"No," she said, "just peculiar. And costly!" Still smiling, she said, "Mama and I are at home on Wednesday afternoons. You must come to see us."

He smiled in return. "When the place allows it, I will," he said.

In the weeks after Adelaide met Mr. Kaltenbach at Levy's, the gossip made the round of the county, and now everyone knew that he had bought all five hundred acres of the Johnson place, and that he was come from Savannah but born in Germany, and that he was unmarried and an Israelite, like the Mannheims and the Levys. Adelaide knew that Mrs. Turner and Mrs. Levy were too polite to say so in her presence, but she knew what they were thinking. They suspected that Mordecai Mannheim had encouraged Henry Kaltenbach to come to Cass County so that he could put the young man in the way of his daughter.

Adelaide walked around the countryside in all but the worst of weather, and on a warm day in March, she put on her rambling clothes and went for a walk. She hadn't intended to stop at the Kaltenbach place, but her walk took her through the stand of pines at its edge. She stopped at the edge of a cotton field, where she saw the men working, angling their plows as they urged their mules to move slowly down the rows. If his slaves were here, he would be nearby, overseeing. She stood at the edge of the field to watch the men. All four of them were all dressed alike in nankeen trousers and dark blue jackets, straw hats on their heads against the early spring sun. She heard one of them call out, "Tom? Luke? You all right?" Then he called out, "Massa? Are you all right?"

A muffled, German-accented voice called back, "I'm all right, Zeke."

"You get tired, Massa, you stop."

The straggler tugged on the reins to slow the mule. "How is the row, Zeke? Does it look even?"

Zeke turned his head to look. "You getting better, Massa," he said, then he added, "Listen to me, driving my own Massa."

Henry Kaltenbach replied, "That's all right, Zeke, since you know how to plow, and I don't."

So Mr. Kaltenbach worked alongside his slaves. A man with less than five hands wasn't really a planter, even though the previous owner, Mr. Johnson, had thought of himself that way, and had done the work of an overseer rather than a farmer. There were numerous cotton farmers in Cass County. Her father did business with them, lending them money or selling their cotton, and he invited them to his frolics and wagered with them at cockfights. But he had never invited them to dine, or asked her mother to admit their wives to tea, and before her trip to Savannah, he would have darkened in fury if she had fallen in love with one.

She sat on the ground, since her rambling clothes were so old and worn that a little dirt wouldn't make them any shabbier, and waited for master and slaves to stop for a rest. When they left the field to drink from the dipper in the bucket of water at the field's edge, Henry looked up, not recognizing her in the old calico dress. Then he laughed and said, "Miss Mannheim! I didn't expect you."

"I didn't intend to stop. But I walked by and saw you."

He smiled and said, "Zeke is teaching me how to grow cotton." He held up his hands and she could see that they were calloused and rough. "I can plow a straight row. Nearly two acres a day." Did he know what he was saying? "Almost as well as a prime field hand."

Startled, she said, "Most people in the county would have a conniption if they heard you say so."

He laughed. Was he teasing her? "Miss Mannheim, plowing and hoeing are a farmer's work, whether he lives in Germany or Georgia."

She laughed too. "The whole county is talking about you. They didn't say that you have such dangerous ideas!"

"I had no idea it was so dangerous to plow a straight row." He straightened up—he was bent from plowing, like his slaves—and asked her, "Would you like to see the place?"

"I would."

"There isn't much to see yet, but I hope to have two hundred acres in cotton, and a hundred in corn." They walked past the barn. "The cow and the horse are out, grazing, and the mules are in the field with us." He said, "I can show you the house."

She appraised it. It was a one-story, low-slung house, built of whitewashed pine, but it had glass windows, and along the front stretched a shaded piazza with enough room for several chairs. No outbuildings. She wondered where the kitchen was. "Where do your people live?"

"We all live right here. Together."

A farmer with so few servants wouldn't need to build them cabins to live in. He said, "I know it ain't as grand as your father's. But it's my start on a cotton fortune."

She felt a little ashamed. Could he read her snobbery so easily? "For your sake, Mr. Kaltenbach, I hope so."

The pigs on the place were free to roam, and one of them came up to him to butt his leg with its snout. Without looking down, he scratched the animal between the ears. It grunted with pleasure and nosed her dress, hoping for another scratch. She laughed outright. "You're on good terms with our forbidden friends."

He said, "I've come to like them. I'll feel bad when Zeke slaughters them in the fall." He slapped the pig on its black, bristled rump and it ran away.

"I know this ain't a formal call, but it would be good to see you, Mr. Kaltenbach."

"As soon as I can leave the crop, I will."

It was odd to think that a Jewish dry goods clerk from Meyer's stood opposite her, his shirt stained with sweat, his hands rough from plowing, his heart full of hope to be a planter. She said, "Even a cotton farmer needs a respite, Mr. Kaltenbach."

When she came home she told Rachel that she'd met their new neighbor. Rachel looked up from the dress she was mending and said, "What is he like?"

"He was in the field with his slaves, plowing."

"Four hands," Rachel said reflectively.

"I ain't a ninny, Rachel. I know why Papa encouraged him to buy the Johnson place." Adelaide sighed. "He's a Jew. And I'm in disgrace."

A few weeks later, Henry was startled to get a note from Mordecai Mannheim inviting him to the Passover Seder. Was it Passover? As a solitary Jew, without other Jews to remind him, he'd lost track of the holidays.

91

The following Monday, on Passover eve, he arrived at the Mannheim place and let Mannheim show him the plantation. After three months on his own place, Mannheim's looked big and prosperous to Henry. He admired the cotton and the corn, the barn and the chicken coop, the smokehouse and the kitchen, the cotton gin and the cotton press. When Manheim boasted, "I have fifty-seven slaves now, counting the new crop of babies," he found himself envious. Mannheim only set foot in the fields to talk to his overseer. His drivers and their gangs labored for him.

In the house, he met Mrs. Mannheim, and politely reminded Adelaide of how they'd been introduced at Levy's. When he took her hand, she smiled and said, "It's good to see you again, Mr. Kaltenbach."

He caught her lighthearted tone and replied, "Likewise, Miss Mannheim."

As her parents watched, she asked him, "How is the crop?"

"Coming along."

"And our forbidden friends?"

"Flourishing."

"Spoken like a true farmer, Mr. Kaltenbach."

He laughed. "I never thought I'd entertain an Israelite lady by talking about pigs and plowing."

She was laughing too. "I never thought I'd be entertained to hear about it."

Her father said, "You two seem awfully familiar for people who spoke for a moment in Levy's."

Henry said, "Miss Mannheim stopped at my place on one of her walks, and we conversed for a bit while I showed her around."

Her mother said in warning, "Adelaide!" but her father laughed and said, "Up to your old tricks, are you, missy? Taking matters into your own hands."

As a boy, Henry had loved the Passover story, and in 1848, the year of freedom, it had resonated for him anew. Since he settled in Cass County, he hadn't thought of the irony of Jews, who still remembered their liberation from slavery, coming to America to own slaves. In Cass County, in 1858, slavery was not a story from long ago. It was the bedrock for Mordecai Mannheim's fortune, and if he were lucky, for his own as well.

As Mordecai read the words, "*Avadim hayinu b'erez mizrayim*, we were slaves in the land of Egypt," Henry looked around the Mannheim dining room. The Mannheim servants—no, the Mannheim slaves—stood against the wall, forbidden to sit down, waiting for the break in the Seder to bring in the dishes for the Passover meal. In a sidelong glance he saw Ezra, the butler, and a young woman. Had they heard these words all their lives, as he had?

At the Seder, Jews ate the bread of affliction, and the bitter herbs, and *haroses*, to remind themselves of the mortar they had been denied in making bricks for the Egyptians. How could they remember slavery in Egypt, and turn a blind eye to it in Georgia? He was glad of the four glasses of wine that were customary with the Seder meal. The claret drowned the refrain in his head, even as the enslaved Ezra filled his glass.

After dinner, when Adelaide's mother retreated to the parlor and her father went off to his study, she lingered in the dining room.

She asked, "How did you like our Seder?"

Henry said, with feeling, "It's always seemed strange to me that we Jews remember so well the story of our bondage and our freedom."

"Oh, la, Mr. Kaltenbach, it's just a story, from Bible times."

"Perhaps it means more to me," he said. "I lived through a time in 1848 when freedom was within reach, even for Jews in Germany."

"What happened?"

"Our hopes were dashed," he said sadly.

"But you're here now," she said. "A free man!"

"Miss Mannheim, does it ever strike you as strange that we Jews who were slaves in Egypt now own slaves in America?"

"What a peculiar notion. I've never thought of it that way."

He looked at Rachel, who was clearing the last of the dishes from the table. "What do your servants think, hearing this story? The old story, from Bible times?"

Adelaide waited until her servant was out of the room. "What would they think? They had better not get any ideas!" She looked at Henry with curiosity. "You ain't an Abolitionist, I hope."

Henry shook his head. "I can't afford to be," he said.

After he left Adelaide, he joined Mannheim in his study, where Mannheim offered him brandy.

Groggy with the Seder wine, he let Mannheim pour him brandy. Mannheim said, "You seemed to get along all right with my gal Adelaide."

Henry, still thinking of the Passover story, had to force himself to turn his thoughts to Adelaide. "She's very pleasant."

Mannheim, untroubled by the words of the Haggadah or the four glasses he'd drunk, said, "She's a likely gal."

Henry said slowly, "I don't know her yet, sir."

"Well, come back as often as you please. When she decides to marry, I'll do something for her. Keep that in mind, while you're visiting."

His head cleared a little. He remembered Joe Meyer's warning, that Mannheim never did anything without profit to himself. "Let me get settled first, and let me see how this year's crop comes in."

"You're short a hand. Maybe two. I thought you would be."

"We're doing all right."

"You've been out in the field yourself. Not just helping out. You've been plowing and chopping. Working yourself like a nigger." Mannheim took a long pull on his brandy, and said, "I don't mind selling you a few hands."

Henry said stubbornly, "I don't want to go any deeper in debt. Not until the crop comes in. After that, I'll see."

"You're a fool to do the work yourself. That's why you buy hands. But it's your place, and it's up to you." He drank again. "The fields look good. Crop looks good. You did right, buying Zeke and his boys. They'll bring in that crop for you."

On a warm day in May, as they were all chopping in the cotton field, Mannheim appeared beside the field, greeted him, and said, "How do."

Without thinking, Henry took off his hat and wiped his forehead with his forearm, a gesture familiar to every field hand. He said, "It's good to see you. What brings you here?"

Mannheim said, "I'm having a frolic at my place this Saturday next. You can meet all of the people in the county. Bring your niggers. We'll have a barbecue, and music, and dancing. They'll like it." He added, "I've asked some of the men to bring their birds, and we'll have cockfights, too."

The Jewish swells of Savannah wagered on horse races and boxing matches, but they considered cockfighting a low form of amusement. Henry had no taste for blood sport, but he was a Cass County man now. He and his slaves would go to be neighborly.

The day of the frolic was a taste of summer in May. The sun rose into a cloudless sky, and the air was warm enough that the men shed their jackets. The women who protected their complexions unfurled their parasols, and even the slaves, who had no such worry for their faces, put on their hats and bandannas.

At the Mannheim place, the front garden, well-tended by a slave gardener and his boy, was lush with dogwood, honeysuckle, and magnolia in bloom, and bright with blossoming flowers. The planters' party had been laid on out the front lawn. The barbecue pit for the slaves' dinner had been dug behind the slave quarters, and the smell of roasting pig strove with the sweet scent of magnolia. The notes of "Oh, Susannah!" filled the air.

Adelaide sat with Mrs. Turner, Mrs. Levy, and with Mrs. Payne, the pretty young lawyer's wife who was Adelaide's age, and full of sass. Mrs. Turner asked Adelaide if Mr. Kaltenbach had come to call on her yet.

Adelaide said, "He says the crop keeps him."

"He hasn't come to call on my Hattie, either."

Mrs. Payne said, "Oh, la, Mrs. Turner, I know you have a gal to marry off, but Mr. Kaltenbach didn't come here to court Miss Hattie." She poked Adelaide in the ribs, as though they were both schoolgirls.

"I believe that Mr. Kaltenbach is free to court any girl he likes," Mrs. Turner said coolly.

Mrs. Levy, in her German accent, observed, "His family would want him to marry a girl who's an Israelite, like himself."

"It seems the Israelites are peculiar about who they marry," Mrs. Turner said, looking at Adelaide. "As they're peculiar about what they eat."

Adelaide listened and thought irritably, It's no different from what the slaves say when I'm not there to hear. She wished that she could sass Mrs. Turner and say, "That's all right. He hasn't asked for me yet."

She felt weary of the close society of Cass County and of her own straitened circumstances, even though they were her own doing. She said, "I'm going to sit quiet by myself for a while," and left the group to sit alone under the big old live oak. The cockfights had begun, and the sound of the men cheering around the cockpit made her more irritable still. The marriage talk was blood sport for ladies, she thought: sharpening their teeth for the unmarried men of the county.

As she sat, looking into her lap and wishing she could be elsewhere, doing something else—even though she didn't know what—a familiar, pleasant, German-accented voice said, "Miss Mannheim!"

It was Henry Kaltenbach, dressed in his frock coat, looking more uncomfortable than he did when he worked in the field. She smiled at him. "It's good to see you."

He smiled too. "That's a pretty dress," he said. "Is it new?"

She laughed. "Mr. Levy's finest muslin," she said. "You should lose the habit of dry goods, Mr. Kaltenbach."

"As soon as I gain the habit of cotton."

They both heard the crowd roar around the cockpit, and she was seized with a wicked impulse. "Mr. Kaltenbach, will you go with me to lay a wager?"

Surprised, he said, "I thought ladies didn't wager on birds fighting."

"What could be the harm? A quarter on my papa's best bird? Come with me." And with more spark than she had felt for a long time, she rose to her feet and took his hand. More surprised than ever, he said, "Miss Mannheim, are you sure?" She held his hand tight. "Yes, I'm sure," she said. "Come with me."

They made their way to the cockpit, a wooden ring eight feet across, big enough to let three dozen men stand shoulder to shoulder around it. The handlers brought out the birds: her father's black rooster, and its opponent, a barred brown cock. As the birds caught sight of each other, they struggled against their handlers. Their feathers had been trimmed and their spurs had been sharpened to make the fight more lethal.

Adelaide and Henry found Zeke and his boys, who let them squeeze in. Henry said, "Zeke, this is Miss Mannheim," and Zeke politely replied, "How do, ma'am."

Mr. Stockton, who ran the general store in Cassville, stood on Henry's other side. He asked, "Would you like to lay a wager?"

Henry asked, "What's customary?"

Adelaide said, "A dollar if you're feeling flush, and a quarter if you ain't."

Henry fished four quarters from his pocket. He said to Luke, "I'll wager if you'll choose for me."

"The black one," Luke said decisively.

Adelaide raised her hand and her voice. She called out, loud enough for her father to know that she was there and that she was wagering, "A dollar on your bird, Papa!"

"Miss Adelaide's made her bet!" someone said, and the men laughed. Pierce Turner, who was now old enough to drink and to wager and well used to both, yelled out, "I'll change my wager to Miss Adelaide's favorite. Ten dollars on Mannheim's bird!"

A jug of whiskey began to make its way around the circle. Masters and slaves crowded together as the handlers released the birds into the ring. The birds rushed each other, landing blows on neck and head. The crowd whooped. The whiskey jug made another round, and the crowd grew louder. The black rooster drew blood, which streaked the barred brown feathers of the other. The men shouted and cheered.

Adelaide watched Henry, who was doing his best to follow the birds as they tore at each other and bloodied each other. She asked, "What are our chances, Mr. Kaltenbach?"

But the answer was lost in the tumult. Her father's bird caught the neck of the barred one under his wing, and pecked hard at the captive bird's head. Blood soaked the bird's feathers. The barred rooster sagged to the ground. As the loser died in the ring, the men whacked each other on the shoulder, in joy or grief, depending on their wagers. Pierce Turner cried out, "Miss Adelaide's favorite won! I won!"

Stockton said happily to Henry, "You won your bet."

Henry said, "I think I've had enough for one day."

"Don't you want your money?"

Henry said pleasantly to Stockton, "I want Zeke to have my winnings," and turned to walk away from the ring.

Adelaide followed him. "What do you think of our amusements?" she asked.

"I feel sorry for the birds, Miss Mannheim."

He looked pale. "You have a tender heart for a Cass County man, Mr. Kaltenbach."

"Is that a failing?" he asked.

She put her hand on his arm. "No, but it's bound to make your life harder in a place like Cass County."

"I'll keep that in mind."

She said, "Do come back to call, once you get the corn planted." She was teasing him, but she sounded just like her father.

Henry walked back to the house, where the tables were filled with platters of chicken fried in a crisp crust, dishes full of the corn pudding that Minnie called pone, and relishes of all kinds, tomato and corn and pickle. As the guests ate, the Mannheim servants carried away the dirty dishes and replenished the food on the table.

Henry poured himself a glass of water. He went into the shade to drink it, and downed it right away. A slave's voice said, "If you'd like another glass of water, I can bring the pitcher, sir." It was the young woman who had served at the Seder.

"No, don't trouble yourself. I can fetch it, if I want some."

Her face was filmed with sweat and there were circles of fatigue under her eyes. "Ain't no trouble, sir."

He thought of Minnie, who worked so hard to cook and wash and garden for their small household. He asked, "What's your name?"

"Rachel."

"How long have you been here?"

"All my life, sir. Born here, grew up here." Her speech was clear. She must have spent her life as a house servant.

She had a distracted look. He thought, when the masters take their ease, the servants work harder. "I won't keep you," he said.

"Thank you, sir," she said, and hurried away.

Several weeks later, when Henry sent a note to Rosa, asking if he could make a formal call, Rosa said to Adelaide, "Write back and encourage him to come to see you."

She said, "I like him well enough, Mama, but he ain't grand. A cotton farmer with four hands. He'll be lucky to make two hundred bales."

"You aren't in a position to be choosy."

Once Joe Meyer hadn't been good enough for her. Now Joe's former clerk was the best she could do for herself.

She remembered the fuss over getting ready to meet Mr. Pereira, and she refused to fuss this time. She asked Rachel to help her into the dress she'd worn at the frolic. Rachel insisted on smoothing lavender water into her hair. Despite the diminished circumstances, both of them remembered Savannah and Mr. Pereira, and before Adelaide went downstairs she hugged Rachel tightly, not minding that she rumpled her skirt. She whispered to Rachel, "Will you serve us tea? I want you to get a good look at him."

Downstairs, Adelaide arranged herself on the settee in the front parlor, where her mother was already sitting in the ladies' chair next to it. This room, which looked pleasantly onto the front gardens, was full of furniture in the newest English style. A green and white striped sofa faced the windows, flanked by wing chairs upholstered in green velvet. Little tables sat beside the chairs, and their surfaces, protected by lace doilies, were covered with small silver boxes, cloisonné vases, and miniature china shepherdesses from Henry's home of Dresden. On the floor was a Turkey carpet in a bright red pattern. The walls were newly papered in white and cream stripes, and on the two windowless walls hung large mirrors in ornate gilt frames.

Ezra showed Mr. Kaltenbach into the room. He wore a black frock coat and underneath it, a starched shirt, and he looked even more uncomfortable than he had at the frolic. Adelaide felt ill at ease, too. He was here as a suitor, and her mother was in the room to listen and to watch.

Adelaide fidgeted as Henry and her mother exchanged pleasantries about the weather, the beauty of the parlor, and the condition of the crop. Once he seated himself in the gentlemen's chair next to the settee, they were free to talk, but they were awkward, without the frolic's familiarity. She wished that they were out walking, where she could show him how the wildflowers grew, or tell him about the call of a bird. He surprised her when he said, "Your father tells me that you're a lover of books."

"I am," she said, surprised that her father, who had never cared what she read, had said so. And it was a subject that no mama, however vigilant, could object to. Had he placated anxious mamas at home in Germany?

He asked, "What are you reading now?"

"I'm reading the works of Mr. Dickens. The older ones, since he hasn't given us anything new. *Bleak House* and *Hard Times*."

"They're melancholy tales."

"When I feel melancholy, they suit me."

"Do you read the poets, too? Lord Byron? He's full of melancholy."

"Do you like Lord Byron?" She prayed that he did not.

"I like the German poets better. Goethe and Heine. Have you read Heine, Miss Mannheim?"

"No," she said, "but I know the Schumann lieder. We learned them at the College. I can sing the words, even if I don't understand them well."

He smiled. "I know the poems and the lieder, and I love them both," he said.

Under the sunburn of a cotton farmer was the heart of a bookish Jew. She felt better about having Henry Kaltenbach put in her way. "Would you like some refreshment, Mr. Kaltenbach? I can ask my servant to bring tea."

Rachel brought in the tray with the silver teapot and a plate of pastry. As she set them down, she watched Henry Kaltenbach, as servants did, without raising her eyes.

Henry looked at the plate and smiled. "Are these *schnecken*?" he asked Adelaide.

"Yes. Our cook knows how much I love them."

He took a bite. "They're just like my mother's. They remind me of home." He addressed Rachel. "Rachel, is it?

"Yes, sir."

"Please tell your cook how much I liked them."

"I will, sir."

When Rachel left the room, Adelaide asked, "How did you know my servant's name?"

He said, "I spoke to her for a moment at the frolic. She asked if I needed a glass of water, and she was in such a hurry that I told her not to trouble herself."

Adelaide hadn't realized that she had been holding her breath until she let it out. This was the attention of a man who was used to being generous to a servant, nothing more.

With undisguised appetite, he ate another pastry, and brushed the crumbs from his fingers. "Miss Mannheim, it's been a pleasure to see you, but I can't leave my hands alone in the field any longer. I have to go."

"Will you come back, Mr. Kaltenbach? To see us again?"

"That would also be a pleasure, Miss Mannheim," he said, and when he smiled a friendly warmth suffused his face. He rose, and said goodbye to Rosa, who gave him the smallest of smiles.

Later that day, when Rachel came to her room, Adelaide asked her, "Didn't know you were acquainted with him."

"Hardly acquainted. Spoke to him for a moment."

"What do you think of him?"

"Didn't expect him to say thank you to Aunt Susy. Was he kind to you?"

"Yes. He was."

"Do you like him?"

"I don't know, and I don't trust myself, after what happened in Savannah." She looked up. "He's the likeliest suitor I'll ever have, after Mr. Pereira, and if he ain't a brute or a fool, I'll consider marrying him."

He sent another note to ask if she would be "at home" again a week hence. She would be. Rachel laced her into her newest dress, a white muslin. White was for girls, but it was also for brides. She wondered if he would feel pressed, seeing her in it. She looked at Rachel. "Is he all right? I'm not making a mistake?"

"Can't answer for you. You know that."

Adelaide sighed and went downstairs to wait for Mr. Kaltenbach. He came in carrying a book in one hand and a bunch of flowers in the other. He smiled at her mother, then at her, and held the flowers out, saying, "These are for you. They're wildflowers, but they're pretty, and I thought you'd like them."

She took the flowers with both hands and laughed. "Do you know what these are?"

"No," he said.

"It's white wisteria. People around here call it 'bride's bower.'"

He blushed. "I didn't know," he said.

Her mother was listening, so she was careful in what she said. "It's a little early in our acquaintance for that, as much as everyone else wants it for us."

He surprised her again. "What do you want for yourself, Miss Mannheim?"

Her breath caught in her throat. Did he know how restless she felt? She could hardly say so, with her mother so close by. "What a peculiar question, Mr. Kaltenbach."

He said, "The philosophers can sometimes help us answer that, and so can the poets. I brought you this, too," and handed her the book.

"The poems of Heinrich Heine!" she said, truly pleased. "I'll read them, instead of singing them, and I'll think of you."

Over the summer, he came to see her every week. They alternated in their conversation, between poetry and the cotton harvest. Her encouragement about his cotton fortune made him smile, and his appreciation for literature pleased her. They moved from the parlor to the piazza, and the piazza to the grounds of the Mannheim place. She told him that she would like to walk, truly walk, not a genteel stroll under a parasol, but a ramble through the countryside under her old straw hat. He poked a little fun at her. "After working in the fields, a genteel stroll would suit me better." It was easy to oblige him. He was an obliging man.

On a gray, overcast day in July, when the air was so warm and wet that it was hard to breathe, he came to see her as a sick headache was brewing. He knew that something was bothering her.

Her mother, who knew how headache laid her low, had insisted that she come downstairs despite it. In her mother's presence, she did her best to deceive him about how bad she felt. "It's only a little headache. Not enough to fret over." She saw the bright spots before her eyes that presaged the pain and the sickness.

He glanced at Rosa. "Is there anything you take for it? Anything that will ease you?"

"Dr. Roswell gave me laudanum, but I'd rather not take it unless I really need it." The doctor had warned her against it, and she distrusted its pleasant warmth even more than she feared its potency.

"Laudanum is a strong drug. Not to be trifled with."

"Have you taken it, Mr. Kaltenbach?"

"No, but my sister took some after her baby died. She said it made her so stupid that she would rather be sensible, and suffer grief."

"She was brave. It's difficult to be brave when you feel grief."

"Miss Mannheim, I don't mean to cause you distress, but I heard about your engagement. If you felt grief, I'd hope that it would lift, and that your heart would be light again."

She lifted her eyes to his. "What did you hear about my engagement?"

"That it was a sorry business from start to finish."

"So you know about the scandal."

He said gently, "I always thought you were ill-used for refusing Mr. Pereira."

"It seems that everyone in Savannah knew that he was a spendthrift and a rakehell. Except for me."

Rosa shook her head, but said nothing.

He said earnestly, "Why should it be wrong to refuse a man like that? And why was the wrong all yours, and none of it his?"

When she was prone to headache she was also prone to tears. She raised her hand to her eyes, which were brimming. The tears roused him to pity, which was plain on his expressive face. He fumbled in his pocket and found his handkerchief. "Please take mine—I never use it—it's wrinkled but it's clean."

"Thank you." She wiped her eyes, and held it to her nose. She sniffed it. It smelled of eau-de-cologne, a pleasant smell, like Henry himself. Crumpling the handkerchief in her hand, she said, "You have a tender heart, Mr. Kaltenbach."

"If there's anything I can do to help you, you must tell me." Not minding that her mother saw, he reached for her hand and clasped it.

Despite the pain in her head, she smiled as they sat with their fingers gently laced together, and nodded.

After a summer of tea in the parlor, conversation on the piazza, and strolls through the garden, her doubts were laid to rest. She liked him. He was bookish and easy to tease, and above all, he was kind. He had been sympathetic about her disgrace, thoughtful about her headaches, and courteous to Rachel, in the distant way that a decent master should be kind to a servant.

He was safe as Pereira was not. He was as different from the bad Byronic boy of Charleston—the drinker, the gambler, and the despoiler of slaves—as a man could be. He was sober and ambitious, and his only gamble was to grow cotton. She felt none of the wild heat that she felt with Mr. Pereira. Mr. Kaltenbach gave off a pleasant warmth, scented with eau-de-cologne.

In Savannah, she had been led astray by passion, and she feared it. She felt no passion for Henry Kaltenbach. She felt friendship, and a little affection, but she didn't feel love. After William Pereira, love seemed too dangerous. She would marry without it.

For weeks, Henry was preoccupied with the question of asking Miss Adelaide Mannheim to marry him. He thought about it as he shaved at the backyard pump, as he ate, and as he wielded a hoe to chop the cotton again. He was so preoccupied that Zeke called to him, as they worked together in the field, "Massa! Watch out with that hoe! You nearly chopped your foot!"

If it were up to Mordecai Mannheim, Henry and Adelaide would have been married months ago. But it was up to Henry Kaltenbach, who worried over it.

If he thought about the dowry, keeping in mind that Adelaide's father was one of the richest men in Cass County, he knew that it was a good match that anyone would encourage him to make. If he thought about Adelaide herself—a young woman saddened and disgraced by her broken engagement—he was full of doubt.

Zeke said sternly, "Massa! If you don't put down that hoe, you'll chop your foot right off!"

Henry looked up, startled. Zeke went on, "Massa, you as bad as my boy Tom, always dreaming and mooning about something. Don't want you hurting yourself. Won't have it."

Henry straightened up and leaned on the hoe. He said, "Zeke, I'm going over to the Mannheim place this afternoon."

Zeke said, "You don't need to ask me, Massa."

"Should I ask Miss Mannheim to marry me?"

Zeke laughed. "How many hands will she bring over, Massa?"

"I'm going now, Zeke."

He put on a clean shirt and a cravat and told Minnie that he was going to the Mannheim place. She said, "You going to ask for Miss Mannheim, Massa?"

He felt as though he were choking. He pulled on his cravat, trying to loosen it. "What makes you think that?"

"Baths. Clean shirts. Flowers. Not hard to figure."

"Should I ask for her?"

"That's up to you, Massa."

"Minnie, when you got married, did you love your husband?"

Her face shadowed and her eyes became wary. "Who told you I was married?"

"Zeke did. When we were coming up to Cass County."

She looked away and her voice, when it came, was throaty with grief. "Don't ask me about it, Massa."

When Henry walked into the parlor, Adelaide could see that he was too restless to sit. He asked, "Could we walk a bit? In the garden?" He looked at Rosa, who said yes.

He'll ask for me today, Adelaide thought. Even though she expected it, her heart began to pound. "Have you been to our arbor?"

"I know we've been in the garden, but I don't recall the arbor."

She led him to a spot in the garden at the side of the house, which was sheltered by a tall live oak tree. Under the tree was a pergola, with four posts and a lattice top, about the size of a Jewish wedding canopy. A flowering vine enclosed the lattice. It was bride's bower, in glorious bloom.

He didn't draw close to her. He looked her in the face and said, "Miss Mannheim, I have no talent for flattery. All I know is how to speak plainly to you."

"Please do," she said.

"I know how much your parents would like us to be married."

"It's no secret," she said. "I know it too." Her eyes met his, and she said, "And you? How are you inclined, Mr. Kaltenbach?"

He reached for her hand and said, "I hope that we can be companions in life, and friends, and come to feel affection for one another."

"So do I."

"Love will come. I know it will." Still holding her hand, he asked, "Will you marry me, Adelaide?"

She thought, He's right, he doesn't have any flattery in him. She clasped his hand. "I will."

He put his hands on her shoulders and gently drew her towards him. He kissed her softly on the lips. His touch was so light that he barely touched her. Her head didn't swim and her knees didn't buckle. He was a kind man, and he wouldn't hurt her.

She would be married, much to her mother's relief, to a man her father was partial to. They would both get what they wanted: he would increase his fortune, and she would bury her disgrace. It wasn't love, but it would do.

That night, Rosa Mannheim hugged Henry, in a hiss of silk taffeta, and

Mordecai Mannheim toasted him as a new member of the family. Reckless, he drank two glasses of wine at the dinner table, and accepted a full glass of brandy in the study. "*Siman tov u'mazel tov,*" said his prospective father-in-law, lifting the glass. Henry nodded, and drank.

"You ain't turning into a drinker, now that you're going to be married?"

"No. Just celebrating."

"Terrified, more like it.

Henry laughed. "Not now."

"I need to talk to my lawyer in Savannah. Then we'll talk about the settlement."

Henry drank more brandy. "I need to get the crop in."

"I'll let Rosa and Adelaide get a start on all those doodads and flimflams that women seem to need when they get married."

He finished the glass. "A length of white satin."

"They can choose it. They don't need your help. You go pick and gin and bale that crop. When it's in, we'll talk."

By the middle of August, Zeke told him that the cotton fields planted earliest were nearly ready for picking. "We should start in a week or so," he said.

"How long will it take?"

"Depends on when the bolls are ready, and depends on how many hands are picking. Usually takes a few months."

"Will we have two hundred bales, Zeke?"

"Never know until it's weighed and ginned, Massa."

"Will it go faster if I work alongside you?"

Zeke looked uncomfortable. "Massa, it really ain't right for you to pick cotton."

As in the earliest days of their acquaintance, Henry said, "Why was it all right for me to plow and to chop, but it isn't all right for me to pick?"

"It was never right. Now that you about to marry Miss Mannheim, it really ain't right. It would shame Marse Mannheim to see his son-in-law working like a nigger."

"Marse Mannheim isn't here to know, and we need all the hands we have on this place to get the crop in." He looked down at his hands, callused and tanned from working in the fields for months. "Zeke, did you really think I'd gotten haughty from being engaged to Miss Mannheim?"

Zeke's face crinkled into a smile. "You, Massa? Course not."

They started picking on a day in late August, not long after sunrise, on a day that promised to be cloudless and hot. The cotton plants were about four feet tall, with woody stalks extending in all directions and at every height from the top of the stalk to the bottom. Henry was surprised at how pretty the cotton looked in full blossom. It reminded him of the first-fallen snow of a German winter.

Zeke gave him a canvas sack with a strap attached to the top and showed him how to sling the strap over his shoulder to keep the opening level with his chest. The mule Pretty waited at the edge of the field, hitched to the wagon. Zeke said, "When that sack is full, you bring it to the wagon. We weigh it, and then we take it to the gin at the end of the day."

He showed Henry a boll in full blossom, and another that was still budding. "Anything that ain't bloomed yet, we come back for later." He picked a boll, and said, "If it's ready, it come out easy. Watch for trash. Sticks, leaves, grit, all of it gets on the boll. Trash adds to weight, but it all gets ginned out. Pick the boll, not the trash."

Henry nodded. Zeke said, "Some bolls way low and others high up. You got to look all up and down the stalk. Otherwise you miss some. Don't want that." Henry nodded again. "You get tired, you stop. You get thirsty, you drink water. I tell my boys the same thing. Don't want anyone laid out flat, near dying."

"How much should I pick in a day?"

"I reckon you can do as much as Tom, once you get the rhythm of it. Two hundred pounds a day. Not at first. Don't fret if it's less than that at first." Zeke took a deep breath. "Listen to me driving you, Massa. Just like I'd drive my own boys. Ain't right."

"It is all right."

Henry started at the beginning of the row. The plants grew low enough that he had to stoop to look for the ripened bolls. The branches grew in all directions and it was hard to find the blossoms. He surveyed the stems, and began to reach for the bolls he could see. The stems were woody and spiny, and he cut his hands right away. He wondered if getting blood on the bolls diminished the value of the cotton.

Plowing had a rhythm and chopping had a rhythm. He couldn't find a rhythm for picking. He had to search for the bolls, reach for the bolls, and grasp the bolls to pick them. He moved down the row with agonizing slowness. The bag didn't seem to fill at all.

The sun rose, hot on his shoulders through his shirt, hot on his head, despite the broad-brimmed hat he wore. Even empty, the bag was heavy, and the strap pulled hard on his shoulder. He squatted for the lowest bolls, and stooped for the higher ones. He felt it in his back and in his legs. He knew from his experience plowing that he'd hurt at the end of the day.

Try to find a rhythm. Try to speed the pace. Try to find a way to stand and bend that didn't strain his back and legs too much. Try to get to the end of the row.

If he were a slave, he'd be whipped for being lazy.

He didn't try to match Zeke's pace, or even Tom's. He bent, and stooped, and searched for the bolls, and picked. By the end of the day, he had emptied his sack once to Tom's four times and to Zeke's six. He had picked a hundred pounds of cotton. His back ached, his legs ached, his shoulder ached from the strap of the sack, and his hands were cut and bleeding.

Zeke looked at the load in the wagon, and said, "Nearly full. Nearly a bale, I'd guess."

"Isn't it more than that?"

"Full weight, it's about twelve hundred pounds. Ginned, a little more than a third of that."

"That much trash?"

"Seed, Massa."

A bale! Looking at the wagon, Henry could have wept. All of that labor for a single bale.

Zeke said, "We store it today, and we gin and press it later."

They walked back to the house. It was still hot, and Henry's shirt stuck to his back. His hair was soaked with sweat under his hat.

Zeke said, "You'd best wash your hands. Get all the dirt off. You leave dirt in them cuts, they'll fester." He looked at his sons. "You too. Massa first."

Henry nodded. He ran water from the pump into the bucket they kept in the yard, and scrubbed the dirt from his hands as best he could.

Inside the house, Minnie greeted him with a cry. "Massa! Look at your hands!"

He looked. Cut and bruised. Cotton picking hands.

At the table he was too tired to taste what he ate. After supper he went directly to bed. A night's sleep didn't restore him. He hurt too much in every muscle to feel rested. When he pulled the sack over his shoulder, the next morning, he was already in pain.

There was something about picking that let him think, and in his fatigue, the thoughts were all dark. They would never finish this task. At a bale a day, they would have to pick for months to make two hundred bales. Mannheim had been right. They were short a hand, maybe two. They needed five prime hands who could each pick three hundred pounds a day, not a man, two boys, and a Jewish dry goods clerk from Dresden.

He got faster, because he could spot a boll quicker and reach for it quicker, but he never found a rhythm, as he had in plowing or chopping. As he speeded up, the sack got heavier, and he felt the strap drag hard against his shoulder. He tried switching it from side to side, but that only made both shoulders ache. Within two weeks, he could feel pain in every bone of his spine.

He had heard more than one slaveowner say, "Niggers don't mind picking cotton. They're used to working in the heat. They're used to stooping for those bolls. They're used to toting those sacks. They're used to working from sunup to sundown. They don't feel it like we would."

Henry knew when his slaves were tired and when they hurt. He saw how Zeke bent one way and another, trying to ease the pain in his back. He saw how Luke winced as he moved the strap of the sack from one shoulder to another. He saw how Tom's bright face grew ashen from the heat and the labor. His slaves were suffering, just as he was.

Anyone could plow or wield a hoe; that was any farmer's work, as he told Adelaide, in Germany or Georgia. But cotton picking was slavery. It was slavery's essence. Henry decided that the Israelites who were slaves in Egypt hadn't been set to hard labor making bricks. They had been set to picking cotton.

As the task wore on, he was so exhausted that it was hard to eat and hard to sleep. He had chosen this—he was a fool for doing so, as much by his own reckoning as anyone else's—but they had not. Next year, he would own enough hands to excuse himself from the cotton field. His slaves would continue to bend, and stoop, and drag the sacks, and cut their hands as they worked in the hot sun.

All week they picked, and on Sunday afternoon, when meeting was over, they ginned and pressed. The gin had to be fed by hand, and they worked together to do it. He felt despair as he watched twelve hundred pounds of lint, divested of trash and seeds, reduce to the equivalent of a single bale of clean cotton.

The bales increased at a pace that was painful to watch. A bale a day. Six bales a week. The bolls would die on the plant before they could pick enough to make two hundred bales.

After three weeks, Henry asked Zeke, "Should we put Minnie into the field with us?"

"She won't help us much in the field. She's a big help to us tending the garden and the kitchen. You decide, Massa. But I don't think so."

"Can we get more hands at this time of year?"

Zeke hesitated. "Won't like what I say, Massa."

"Tell me anyhow."

"They might have some people on the Mannheim place. I know you don't like to ask Marse Mannheim, Massa. But we short. Even a few hands would help."

"Would we buy them?"

"No, hire them by the day."

"It won't be cheap."

"Only way to make two hundred bales."

It galled him to ask. But the next day he asked Minnie to draw him a bath, so he could wash off the worst of the field's dirt and sweat, and he put on his Sabbath best. He was going to call on Mordecai Mannheim, admit that Mannheim had been right, and to beg for something for which he would owe money.

Mannheim was at his desk in the study, writing in his ledger as a gentleman planter should. He was smoking a cigar, which did not completely cover the odor of a recent fart. He got up to shake Henry's hand and said, "So you've been picking cotton. Not just helping out. Don't try to fool me, I can tell by the cuts on your hands."

Without being asked to sit, Henry sat. He said abruptly, "I need more hands."

"Came around, I see."

"I have two hundred bales on the stem. I need hands to pick it."

"How many do you want?"

"Two would help. Three would be better."

Mannheim said reflectively, "I can spare three."

Henry said grimly, "I know you'll charge me a ruinous rate for their hire. I don't care. I have to get the crop in."

"You've started to think like a planter. I'm glad to see it."

The next morning, three of Mannheim's seasoned cotton hands arrived at his place. Each of them swiftly and expertly picked two hundred pounds of cotton that day, and every day after. They went home at night to sleep in their own cabins, and they re-appeared at sunrise to start the day again.

Henry stayed in the field, pretending to oversee as he continued to pick. The Mannheim slaves didn't comment. He added his hundred pounds a day to the total. He still ached all over, and he was bone weary at the end of the day, but he had stopped worrying. Two hundred bales. Ten thousand dollars. He would clear the debt and have something left over.

Frost came late that year, and they worked into December to get the last of the crop off the stem. When they were done, when the Mannheim slaves went home, when they had ginned and pressed the last bale, he counted two hundred and three bales of cotton in the shed.

Zeke said, "We did good, Massa."

Henry looked at the weary faces around him, and he nodded. Zeke said, "It's a happy day, Massa. More than two hundred bales, and the crop is in. Now we rest, we have Christmas day, and after that, we pick and shuck that corn."

Mannheim took Henry into the study and closed the door. "Some brandy?" he asked, his hand on the decanter.

"No, thank you." If there was ever a time to be clear-headed, it was now.

At his ease, Mannheim poured himself a glass. He said, "I thought you'd like to know about the settlement."

"What about the crop?"

"What about it?"

"When will I know what we'll realize?"

"When we sell it. That's for next year. This is about the settlement."

"Can you give me an idea?"

"I wouldn't do that. I don't want to guess and be wrong. Now hear me out about the settlement."

Smarting a little, worried, Henry said, "Yes, sir."

"Adelaide's maid Rachel goes with her, so you'll get her. I'm going to give you Charlie. He's my best driver. I'll miss him, but he'll help you bring in the crop better than Zeke. Good hard worker. Good steady boy. You'll need more land. I have five hundred more acres in mind for you, next to the parcel you own now. You can't work a thousand acres with six hands. You need twelve or fifteen. I have some people in mind, for you too, all field hands. Three young men, Davey, Micah, and Freddy, all prime hands. And three gals, Lydia, Salley, and Harriet."

"Isn't Charlie married? Doesn't he have a family?"

"How would you know that?"

"Zeke is courting your gal Jenny. He knows all the people on your place."

"He has a family. What's that to you?"

"I want his wife and baby, too."

"I ain't sending him to Mississippi," Mannheim said. "It's only twenty minutes on foot."

"He'll be happier if his family is with him, on the same place. I want them to be together."

Mannheim shook his head. "Tender heart won't bring in the crop," he said. "Do you want Jenny, too? Since Zeke is sweet on her?"

"I didn't think of it, since they aren't married yet. Yes, I want Jenny too."

"All right. They'll work harder if they're together. I'm making up a list. Then there's the matter of the house. You can't take Adelaide to that tumbledown farmhouse you've been living in. You need a proper house, and a kitchen, and a bigger barn, and a smokehouse. Not to mention a row of cabins for the niggers to live in."

Henry began to feel warmly disposed towards his father-in-law. He hadn't realized how generous Mannheim would be. With five hundred acres, a new house, and eleven new slaves, he would no longer be a cotton farmer. He would truly be a planter. A thousand acres meant at least five hundred in cotton, and five hundred bales, at fifty dollars a bale, would bring in twenty-five thousand dollars. Even after the factor's commission and next year's supplies, that would be his start on a fortune. With the promise of twenty-five thousand dollars, he could come to feel warmly disposed toward Adelaide, too.

Mannheim said, "I'll lend you the money, of course."

Startled out of his reverie, Henry said, "For what?"

"Weren't you listening? For the land, the ten niggers, and the house."

"I thought it was a gift."

"Just Rachel and Charlie, and the trousseau. I'm selling you the rest."

Henry leaned forward, so angry that it was hard to get the words out. "I'm about to become your son-in-law! Have you no consideration? I'll be in debt to you for the rest of my life!"

"You'll clear five hundred bales next year, after the crop is in. That should take care of it."

Furious, he said, "What if I changed my mind? What if I decided to break off the engagement?"

Mannheim smiled. "Then I'd have to take you to court for a breach of promise."

Flabbergasted, Henry Kaltenbach agreed to marry Adelaide Mannheim, and went fifteen thousand dollars in debt to do it.

Rachel was surprised that Marse Mannheim wanted to talk to her. He said, "My girl is getting married."

"We're all glad, Massa."

"You'll be going with her."

She would never stop being afraid of hearing that he would sell her. But instead, he said, "You take good care of her. She needs it."

Her mistress and her sister. "I try my best, Massa."

He cleared his throat. He said gruffly, "I'll miss having you on the place." His red face got redder. "Who else will tell me what a bale is worth?"

In spite of herself, she laughed. "You don't need me for that, Massa."

"I'm proud of the way you've grown up. Smart gal. Good head for business." It was the closest he had ever come to admitting to their real relationship.

"Thank you, Massa."

A few days later, Charlie came into the kitchen. He rarely stopped by anymore, and he never lingered if she were there. Aunt Susy was in the dairy, churning butter, and the two of them had the kitchen to themselves.

"Don't rush away," he said. "I came to talk to you."

"I'm not going anywhere."

"I don't know if you heard, but I'm going over to the Kaltenbach place."

She shook her head and didn't speak. The silence was painful. They were both remembering the same thing. You can marry. That's your business. I can't guarantee you'd stay together.

He said, "Marse Mannheim wasn't going to include my family. Marse Kaltenbach insisted on buying Becky and the little one. Said he wanted to keep my family together."

I need you to bring in the crop. I won't sell you.

Charlie said, "You and I will be together on the new place. God knows, it ain't the way we hoped for."

Choose to break your heart now so Massa can't do it for you.

He said, "It's a small place. We'll see each other. I'd feel better knowing that we could be pleasant towards each other."

She said, "I never hated you, Charlie. Not for a moment. I just couldn't stand remembering."

He held out his hand, halfway between a handshake and a handclasp. "Can we mend things? Just a little?"

"It can't be the way it was."

He decided on a handclasp. "I know. Can't start afresh, either. But maybe we can start somewhere, and make it better than it is now."

"I'll try, Charlie."

"We can both try." He pressed her hand. Overcome with emotion, he remembered to be gentle.

"All right."

He let go her hand. He said, "Have you met Marse Kaltenbach? Do you know anything about him?"

She said, "I think he'll be a good Massa."

Charlie shook his head. "I feel beholden to him. Never even met him, and I already feel beholden to him. Don't care for it."

Chapter 7

A Jewish Wedding

Adelaide sat at breakfast in the dining room that pleased her father so much, and that she had thought was luxurious before she went to Savannah. The mahogany still gleamed and the silver still shone, but everything in the room seemed diminished to her. She had no appetite. She pushed her eggs and toast around her plate, pretending to eat.

"Mr. Mannheim," Rosa said to her husband at the breakfast table, "No one from Savannah or Charleston has agreed to come to Adelaide's wedding."

Her mother had always talked about the servants in their hearing as though they weren't there. Adelaide had never realized how they might dislike it until her mother spoke of her in the same way.

Rosa had sent out invitations to all of the Israelites of Savannah and Charleston. She hoped that enough time had elapsed to forgive what had happened in Savannah.

Everyone had refused. Rabbi Frankel had sent his regrets about not being able to conduct the wedding ceremony, and had referred them to an unknown rabbi who had just arrived in Macon to start a congregation there. Mrs. Cohen's reply had been particularly hurtful. She had returned the invitation to Rosa unopened. Only Joe Meyer, unable to attend because his wife was expecting a baby, had written a cordial letter, offering the bride and groom best wishes on their wedding day, and wishing them every happiness in their life together.

Her father shook his head. After the broken engagement, he had struggled to maintain his connections with the Jewish factors, brokers, financiers and merchants of Savannah and Charleston, and he was thankful that they would still do business with him. Their wives and daughters were a different story. They had closed their doors to the women of the Mannheim family.

He said, "I can't help it."

Rosa said bitterly, "How could she have brought this on herself?" As though she weren't at the table to hear.

Her father struck his hand against the edge of the table, startling her mother. "That's enough," he said sharply. "We'll have some kind of a wedding, God knows. I'll see what I can manage."

They invited their neighbors in the county, the planters like themselves and the professional men of Cassville, with their families, and all of them were pleased to accept. There would be about twenty people for the wedding and the wedding supper. Mordecai said, "We'll ask them to bring their niggers, and we'll have a frolic for them, too." It solved a problem for Aunt Susy: whoever might miss pig meat at a Jewish wedding could join the slaves at their barbecue.

Her mother wanted to fuss about the wedding supper, but Aunt Susy calmly laid out the menu for her. Fish in aspic to start. Then roast turkey and roast beef. A sweet potato pudding with egg and cinnamon, Aunt Susy's rendition of Jewish potato kugel. Relishes and pickles. For the wedding cake, a sponge. "I can make it special for a wedding."

Rosa said, "When I got married we had a honey cake with raisins."

Non-Jewish brides had fruitcake at their weddings. Interested, Aunt Susy said, "What's in that, besides honey?" She teased the ingredients from Rosa's memory. Flour. Sugar. Coffee. Oil—cottonseed oil would do. Orange rind and nutmeg to mask the flavor of oil. Sultanas rather than raisins, to be more festive, and slivers of orange peel to decorate the top. Aunt Susy could try making one, to see if she could get it right.

They would need everything to feed twenty at the table. Thinking about it made Rachel weary. When Rosa left, Rachel sighed. Aunt Susy said, "You sighing a lot lately."

Rachel was worried. Adelaide was quiet and moody as she'd been just after she returned from Savannah. She'd told Rachel that she didn't love Henry Kaltenbach, but that his was the only offer she'd ever have, and she'd make the best of things with him. Adelaide's practicality didn't fool her. Even a hard-headed girl wanted to be courted and cherished. Adelaide wouldn't say so, but she was full of doubt again.

Now that she knew where Adelaide was going, and where she would follow, she wondered what it would be like. She would spend most of her time with Minnie, and she wasn't yet sure about Minnie. Minnie was still proud of her connection with the Butler place. She was pleased with herself for knowing how to make French pastry. She was puzzled by the kosher laws. It wearied Rachel to think of instructing someone as sure of herself in the kitchen as Minnie.

She wondered most of all about Marse Kaltenbach, who had gone out of his way to keep Charlie's family together. She wasn't hopeful. She was still a slave. He was still Massa. But she was curious about having a new master who might consider her, too.

A few days before the wedding, Adelaide sat at her writing desk, writing one of the many letters to tell her friends that she was getting married. Her mother tapped on her bedroom door. She sighed at the thought of a long colloquy with her mother about the dress, or the trousseau, or the wedding supper, or the dancing afterwards.

Her mother looked drawn and tired. Since the refusals from Savannah, she had been sadder and bitterer than ever. She sat on the bed, the only piece of furniture that could accommodate her hoops, and gestured to Adelaide to sit next to her.

Her mother gave her an unusual embrace, and said, "I can't believe you're getting married." When she let Adelaide go, there were tears in her eyes.

Adelaide said, "Well, if I don't, a lot of people will be disappointed."

Her mother shook her head at the sass. She said, "Listen to me, Adelaide. Now that you're getting married, there are things you need to know. About your duties to your husband."

Her married friends had whispered to her about their wedding nights and marriage beds. One of them, her face flaming, had said, "If my husband hadn't been so kind, I never could have managed it." She wouldn't say more. What did an unmarried girl have to fear? Would gentle Henry Kaltenbach, who held her hand so softly, and worried when she had a headache, give her cause for fear?

Her mother struggled to speak. "About a married woman's duty." Rosa's pale face was bright pink with embarrassment. "The duty that makes children."

Adelaide blushed as bright as her mother, because she suddenly understood. "Is it different from the way the sows get piglets?"

Her mother's cheeks were still red with embarrassment. "Goodness, Adelaide, it's nothing to joke about. I did my duty all my married life, and I lost three children. Don't poke fun at it."

Her mother's dead children had shadowed her face and set it into bitterness. Adelaide had never thought about bearing children of her own, had never thought that her husband would give her children who might die, children who might kill her. After they were married, would Mr. Kaltenbach demand such a thing of her?

Her mother sighed. "To conceive children in pain, and to bear them in pain. That's a married woman's lot."

After her mother left, Adelaide sat unmoving on the edge of her bed. She knew that love brought pain, but she hadn't let her thoughts go as far as the marriage bed, or to childbirth. If marriage was so fearsome—so dolorous, and so dangerous—why would any intelligent girl get married?

Later that day, Rachel came to dress her and comb her hair. She said, "You look a sight."

"Mama told me all about my duty as a married woman. Marriage bed and childbed. Made it sound such a misery I don't know why anyone gets married."

Rachel sat heavily on the edge of the white bed that Adelaide had slept in since she was little girl. "Great day in the morning!" she said.

"Do you know different?"

"Yes."

"How? You haven't been married."

Rachel took a deep breath. "I ain't been married, but I've lain with a man."

So her sister was no longer innocent. Adelaide asked, "And you never told me! Who was it?"

"Doesn't matter."

"Did you want to marry him?"

Sadness passed over Rachel's face. "He married someone else."

"What was it like?"

Rachel looked down. "It's private."

Adelaide held out her hands. "I have to know."

Rachel looked up and took them. "What did your mama say to you?"

Adelaide said, "She said it would be my duty."

Rachel sighed. "Duty! Duty's doing the wash. When a man and a woman come together, if they're tender with one another, they feel joy."

Adelaide wished she could ask Rachel what happened, exactly, when a new wife lay down in bed with her new husband. She couldn't even find the words to stammer the question. Instead she asked, like a child, "Does it hurt?"

The sadness went away. Rachel said, smiling, "Only a little, the first time. You have to get used to it. Then it's the best feeling ever."

"Was he kind to you?"

Rachel stared at her in surprise. "Why would a gal lie with a man who wasn't?"

On the morning of his wedding day, Henry sat at the pine table for the last time with Zeke, Luke and Tom. Minnie had already gone to the Mannheim place, where she would be in the kitchen until late at night. She would not be in the room to see him stand under the wedding canopy or to smash the glass.

Zeke retrieved his jug of corn whiskey and set out four tin cups on the table. He said, "Before you go this morning, we toast you on getting married." He poured whiskey into Henry's cup. "Just a little," he said, "there's whiskey all day long at a wedding. You don't want to start fuddled." He gave Luke and Tom each a little. "Just a drop. You both too young to have more than a drop."

Zeke raised his cup. "To a happy wedding day, Marse Henry, and to a long and happy life with Miss Adelaide."

They all drank. Luke looked pleased to be treated as a grown man for the day. Tom made a face at the taste.

He looked around the table at the three of them. He would miss eating at this table with them, working in the fields with them, living in this house with them. He would miss hearing Luke and Tom bicker every night, and miss hearing Zeke say, "You hush and go to sleep." He had heard Zeke's voice every night for months, a comforting thing before he fell asleep.

Tomorrow, he would move into the new house, and they would move into their own cabin. These people, who had become as close to him as a family, would no longer be close by.

They all heard the sound of hooves on the dirt of the driveway. "Ned's here with the carriage!" Tom said, a smile lighting up his face. "Can I go to meet him, Massa?"

"You go on." Ned was here to drive him to the Mannheim place, where the wedding and the wedding supper would be held, and where he would spend his wedding night. Zeke and his sons, invited to the wedding and to the slave's frolic afterward, would walk there without him. Tom ran out the door and down the driveway.

As he had said on the day they baled the last of the cotton, Zeke said, "Happy day, Massa."

As he had felt on that day—but not said it, as he did today—Henry replied, "Bittersweet."

Zeke clasped one of his hands, and Luke clasped the other. Henry felt a lump form in his throat. He thought, It won't do to weep on my wedding day, any more than to drink too much. "You two go on."

They got up from the table, and walked quietly out the door, closing it behind them against the January chill. Henry sat at the table and looked around the house one last time. Then he stood up, tugged on his jacket, straightened his cravat, and went out to get into the carriage that would take him to the Mannheim place.

The rabbi who came from Macon was a young man, tall, rail-thin, and stooped, and clean-shaven in the American fashion. He was born in America, or had lived here since childhood, because he had the flat and slightly nasal twang of a Northerner from the Ohio Valley. He wasn't surprised that the guests were all non-Jews. He said that he'd gotten used to being the only Jew in the room, now that he lived in Macon. For these guests, used to the Book of Common Prayer, he'd be glad to translate and explain.

Henry had been to enough Jewish weddings to know a bridegroom's tasks. He had to put the ring on the bride's finger and get through the Hebrew blessing without stumbling. And at the end of the ceremony, he had to break the wedding glass, wrapped in a cloth against shards, with his right foot. The rabbi instructed him until he had the prayer by heart. As for the glass, he had to hope that it was fragile enough to shatter easily on the first try.

The ceremony was set for three in the afternoon, a moment when the day's light was already fading so early in January. It would take place in the parlor, where all of the fussy pieces of furniture had been removed, and twenty chairs had been set up in rows to face the fireplace, with a makeshift aisle between. The wedding canopy, a pretty piece of striped muslin attached to four posts, where he and Adelaide and the rabbi would stand for the ceremony, had been set up. There was already a fire in the fireplace, which Henry was glad of. The air was damp and chill, as it had been when he first came from Savannah to Cass County.

The guests began to arrive, and the house began to fill with the high-pitched laughter of women and the lower rumble of male conversation. Adelaide was upstairs, getting laced and buttoned into her dress. He would not see her until the ceremony.

Henry wandered through the house, unsure of what to do or where to sit. He felt in his pocket for the ring. He wished that he could go into the kitchen to find Minnie, or to the slaves' barbecue to find Zeke.

By the time the guests began to straggle into the parlor and settle themselves into the chairs, Henry, Adelaide, and the rabbi were already standing under the canopy, waiting for them. Mordecai and Rosa sat in the front row. Mordecai was flushed—he had been drinking to the new couple since noon—but Rosa was drawn and pale. The guests whispered and pointed at the canopy.

The rabbi addressed the guests. "It's good to see that the Mannheims have so many friends and neighbors to help them celebrate this occasion. I understand that none of you have been to a Jewish wedding before. We'll go slowly, and we'll explain a little as we go along, so it isn't so strange to you." He had the tone of an American reverend, alternatively sonorous and folksy. The people of Macon would feel at home with him.

He recited the first blessing of the service in Hebrew, the familiar one over the wine, and loosely translated it: "Blessed are you, God, who sanctifies wine." And the second: "Blessed are you, God, who has commanded us against forbidden unions, sanctified us with the laws of betrothal, and permitted us to marry according to your laws." He handed the Kiddush cup to Henry, who took only a sip, not wanting to be fuddled, and then said, "Now the bride." The Protestant crowd twittered in surprise: drinking during the service! What kind of religion was this?

"Do you have the ring?" the rabbi whispered to Henry.

He curled his hand around it in his pocket. "Yes." He took the ring out. The rabbi said to Adelaide, quietly, "The right hand." Adelaide held out her hand, and Henry put the ring on her index finger. She would move it to her left hand later, to wear it in the American fashion.

He was so deep in debt that it had seemed petty to care about the cost of the ring. It came from the best jeweler in Savannah, a rose-cut diamond surrounded by tiny sapphires, set in platinum, and it was pretty on Adelaide's long-fingered hand. Henry recited the Hebrew prayer, and surprised the rabbi by making the translation himself. "With this ring, you are consecrated to me as my wife, by the laws of Moses and Israel."

The rabbi addressed the crowd again. "Now we read the marriage contract, the *ketubah*. These days, we're more likely to draw up these documents in a lawyer's office than before a minister, but in ancient times, rabbis were lawyers and judges as well as ministers. A ketubah lays out how the husband will provide for his wife, while he's living and after he's gone, and it lays out the dowry she brings along." The rabbi began to read the ketubah, in its original tongue, not Hebrew but Aramaic. Henry knew a few words of Aramaic; it was the language of the Passover Seder. But the words of the ketubah were utterly unfamiliar.

Except for the sound of his name, the Jewish name he never used. On the ketubah, he was Hirsch Leib ben Meir, and his bride was Adah Leah bas Mordecai. Henry Kaltenbach and Adelaide Mannheim barely knew each other, but Hirsch Leib and Adah Leah were complete strangers.

As he listened to the rabbi read the ketubah, he thought of the contracts he had already signed, the ones that bound him according to the laws of the state of Georgia. As he had promised, he had signed titles to the land, the house, and the slaves, and he had signed a note for each. The total on the notes came to more than fifteen thousand dollars. He would need to make three hundred bales just to break even.

The rabbi began to recite the seven blessings that were the last part of the service. There was another blessing over wine, and another sip from the Kiddush cup. The crowd muttered again. They would think that Jews were allowed to be drunks in their synagogues. Henry was too nervous to listen. The breaking of the glass was next.

Before the rabbi handed him the glass, he explained to the guests that it symbolized the destruction of the Temple in Jerusalem, and that on every happy occasion, Jews liked to recall something sad, to make the occasion bittersweet. Henry, who rarely prayed, now prayed that he wouldn't disgrace himself. He took the glass from the rabbi and laid it carefully on the floor. He stood up, concentrated, and brought his heel down on the cloth-wrapped glass with uncharacteristic violence. To his relief, everyone heard the glass shatter.

It was done. They were married. He reached for Adelaide's hand, and she twined her fingers through his. Hand in hand, they walked slowly down the short, makeshift aisle between the chairs, stopping for teary hugs for the bride and heartfelt slaps on the back for the groom.

The slaves stood unobtrusively along the wall, watching. As Henry turned his head, he saw them, all of them, standing together and smiling: Zeke. Luke. Tom. Minnie. His people.

Through a haze, he heard the guests gossiping. One woman was saying to another: "What a peculiar service. Drinking! I tell you, I wouldn't feel married unless I'd said my wedding vows." He heard a voice—was it

Stockton's? "What was that business with busting a glass? Put me in mind of something else that gets busted on a wedding night!" There was a burst of nervous male laughter.

As the servants readied the table for the wedding supper, as the guests milled around the parlor—the women talking, the men drinking—Henry and Adelaide sat quietly in the back parlor. She looked very pale in her white dress. He hadn't realized that he would need to drink from the Kiddush cup, not once but twice, during the ceremony itself. He had lost count of how many sips of whiskey he had drunk just after the service, only one from each glass, but someone had handed him glass after glass. He felt lightheaded. He said, "Everyone is fussing over us today. And we're the people the least likely to enjoy it."

She nodded. "We're married," she said.

"How do you feel?" he asked.

"I feel dizzy."

He laughed. "So do I." He reached for her hand, and twined his fingers in hers. He asked, "May I kiss you?"

"Yes."

Very gently, he touched her face, cradling it with both hands. Then he slid his hands under her veil to cradle the back of her head. Her hair was thick and wiry under his fingers. He bent close to her, and touched his lips softly to her mouth. Her lips were cool under his, and she was trembling. He stepped back, and said, trying to make his voice as tender as his touch, "We'll have time later."

For Henry, the wedding supper went by in a blur. There was champagne on top of the whiskey, and every toast meant another glass. Henry was sorry that Aunt Susy had worked so hard in the kitchen, because he ate the food without tasting it. He needed something to soak up the alcohol. If it was a disgrace to be drunk in front of the guests, it would be a bigger disgrace to be drunk later, in the marriage bed.

Only the taste of the wedding cake penetrated Henry's daze. Like the strudel, it spoke of home. Aunt Susy had made his mother's honey cake, the cake that had graced every Jewish holiday of his life in Germany. Suddenly undone, he excused himself from the table and went outside to stand on the piazza.

His hair and his shirt were soaked with sweat, as though he'd been chopping cotton instead of drinking champagne. He took off his jacket and let the cold air flow over him. From here, he could hear the sound of fiddle music, and smell the roasted pig from the barbecue. The slaves deserved their pleasure. He knew, in his hands and his muscles and his bones, how hard they would be working again, once plowing started in February.

They would be missing him at the table. He still had a few hours of drink and conviviality before he was alone with Adelaide. The sweat had dried on his skin and he shivered in the winter air. He put his jacket back on and went inside.

Rachel spent Adelaide's wedding day in the kitchen. She, Aunt Susy, and Minnie had been preparing the meal since early in the day. They were all grateful that the wedding was in January, when it was not unpleasant to stand before the hot stove and the blazing hearth. All of them had cooked for parties in June and August, when standing in the kitchen meant sweating harder than a hand in the field.

They were joined by sisters Salley and Harriet, who would go with Rachel to the Kaltenbach place, and by a little girl named Lizzie. All of them would help with setting the table and washing up. Twenty guests would dirty every dish in the house, including the crystal glasses, which needed special care, and the servants would be boiling water all night to wash the dishes.

At mid-afternoon, Minnie asked Aunt Susy, "May I slip out for a few minutes to see Marse Henry get married?"

"I don't see why not," Aunt Susy said. "Everything's close to ready, and we can watch it. You'll be back in time to set everything up?"

"Of course I will." Minnie took off her apron. "Rachel, do you want to see Miss Adelaide get married?"

Rachel's head ached and her back ached. I wish I could take a drop of laudanum, like Adelaide, she thought darkly. "Aunt Susy will need me."

Minnie said, "Ain't you happy to see your young miss get married?"

Rachel said sharply, "I'm too tired. Ask me sometime next week, when I'm rested. Then I'll be happy."

Once the meal started, everything was a blur, of putting things on plates and making sure that nothing got cold; of hearing Ezra, ordinarily haughty and refined, cuss at them because if they didn't hurry to get things onto the serving dishes, the food would be ruined; of boiling endless tubs of water for washing; of washing the dishes that came back, piles and piles of them; of putting everything away to make room for the next round of dirty plates.

Rachel found little Lizzie struggling to dry one of the fragile serving dishes.

She said, "Be careful of that dish! Don't you break anything!"

The little girl flinched as though Rachel had slapped her. She was so young, not much older than Rachel herself when she began to help Aunt Susy in the kitchen. Ashamed, Rachel sank to her knees so that she was eye to eye with Lizzie. She touched her shoulder and said repentantly, "Honey, I'm so sorry. I shouldn't have been sharp with you. I'm so tired. We're all so tired today."

"Yes, we are," Minnie said, looking at a clean dish to make sure that she put it with the meat dishes and not the milk ones. Rachel had been sharp with her too, saying, "The blue-edged ones are meat, and don't put them in the cupboard with the gold-edged ones for milk."

Rachel was too tired to stop the kitchen talk from slipping out. "I ain't done after these dishes are washed and put away," she said. "I'm going upstairs to get Miss Adelaide ready for her wedding night."

Minnie said, "Lay out her nightdress and brush her hair?"

Rachel said, "And calm her down, and remind her to love the man she married, and ease her fear about lying with a man for the first time." Surprised, Minnie said, "Where's her mama? Ain't she the one to do all that?"

Rachel said, "Her mama scared the daylights out of her."

Minnie said, "Still don't see why it's up to you to get her ready for her wedding night. You ain't her sister."

All of the women in the kitchen fell into an embarrassed silence. Everyone's eyes shifted around the room, settling on nothing and no one.

A few minutes later, when they were momentarily together in the pantry, Minnie touched Rachel's arm and said softly, "I beg your pardon for what I said."

Rachel said, "You didn't know."

Minnie said, "Now that I do, I'm doubly sorry that I said it."

When the wedding supper was over, Adelaide sat wearily on the bed, still in her wedding dress, not caring that she crushed the satin and rumpled the lace. She said to Rachel, "I hate this dress but I'm scared to take it off."

"You'll feel better when I unlace you."

"If I take it off I have to put on that nightdress. And go do my duty in it."

Rachel laughed. "Told you it wouldn't be a duty."

"What if it goes wrong? What if it hurts? What if I hate him?"

"Take it slow. Sweet and slow."

Adelaide made the strangest sound, a laugh that was close to a sob. Rachel said, "Won't he be sweet to you?"

"Don't know. Hope so."

Rachel said, "Let me help you."

Once the new nightdress was on—it was a marvel of fine lawn and lace—Rachel left the top few buttons undone. Adelaide's hands rose to her throat. "Should I do up the buttons? Or not?"

"Already showed him your collarbone in that wedding dress."

Adelaide made the same odd sound, half-laugh, half-sob, and unbuttoned the nightdress to open below her collarbone. "Is that all right?"

Rachel laughed too. "By the time you're done, he'll see everything you've got under your chemise and your petticoat!"

Adelaide took a deep breath. "I reckon I'm ready."

"Wait a minute," Rachel said. She found the bottle of lavender water. "Hold out your hands." She poured a little of the perfume on a handkerchief and dabbed it on Adelaide's wrists. "Now bend your head back a little." The same for the hollow of Adelaide's throat. Then she poured a little into her palms, and smoothed it over Adelaide's hair.

Rachel held Adelaide's head between her hands and kissed the part in the hair she had just perfumed. She said, "Now you'll smell sweet. He'll like that."

Adelaide reached up and held onto Rachel's arms. She began to shake, then to sob. Her voice came through a clot of tears. She whispered, "Rachel, what have I done?"

When Henry turned eighteen, his cousins took him to a house of pleasure in Dresden, where he was guided into manhood, and where he returned until he left for Savannah. In Savannah, people called them bawdy houses, and the young clerks who worked for Meyer's Dry Goods in Savannah went to them as often as their wages allowed. On Henry's first visit, the girl was African, as dainty as a doe, and so young that Henry lost his desire. He couldn't bed a frightened child. He touched her only to press the money into her palm.

After that, he never went to the same place twice in a row, or to the same woman. He went every month, but it was like taking senna leaves. He left feeling purged, but degraded and sad.

On his wedding night, Henry, who had been embracing women for a decade, was as nervous as he'd been at eighteen. Before he knocked on the door of his bride's bedroom, he washed his armpits and his groin. He smoothed eau-de-cologne on his face. He put on his new nightshirt. This last struck him as particularly odd. No one wore a nightshirt in a bawdy house.

Adelaide's parents had given them one of the guest rooms for their wedding night, and in it, she sat up in bed, her hair loose over her shoulders. Her nightdress, designed to button to the chin, exposed her upper chest. Her eyes were a little red. Had she been crying?

He got into bed and sat beside her. "Adelaide, what's the matter?"

She said, "I'm afraid."

Of course she was afraid. She was clever and knowing, but in the matter of congress between a man and a woman, she was ignorant. What had her mother told her? For all her sass while they were courting, now she was shaking with fear.

"Oh, Adelaide."

She said, "My best friend from the College told me that her husband was kind to her on their wedding night. Will you be kind to me?"

He had been kind to a stranger whom he had bought for his pleasure. Surely he could be tenderer than that with the woman he had just married. He looked into her worried eyes and said, "Of course I will."

She said, "I know it's my duty—I'll do my best to be a good wife to you—"

"It isn't a duty," he said. "It's a joy." He reached for her hand. "But it's sweetest when a man and a woman are friends."

She raised her eyes to his. There was nothing clever or knowing in her face. She was a frightened girl. "I thought we were friends."

Holding her hand, he said, "We scarcely know one another. Perhaps we should be friends first, and husband and wife later."

Adelaide, so glib of tongue, stammered as she said, "You won't ask me—you won't press me—"

Still holding her hand, he said, "I would never compel you."

Some of the fear left her face. "How should we begin?" she asked. "To be friends?"

"Slowly," he said, smiling. "We'll be married all our lives. We can start slowly."

Wondering, she said, "I didn't know."

"What, Adelaide?"

"That you'd be the same in your nightshirt as you were in your frock coat."

He laughed. "I'd hope so."

They sat side by side in the big bed, he in his nightshirt, she in her nightdress, holding hands. They smiled at each other. He felt hopeful. He would court her until she lost her fear and trusted him to embrace her.

He felt her body ease. He saw how tired she looked. He said tenderly, "Are you weary?"

She felt enough at her ease to nod. "Bone weary."

He said, "Will you lie down with me? May I cradle you?"

At the word childish word "cradle," her wariness slipped away. "Yes," she said.

He lay on his back and stretched out his arms to her. She hesitated, unsure of what to do. "Rest your head on my shoulder," he said, and she did. He put his arms around her waist and pressed his cheek to her hair. She nestled up to him. She smelled of lavender water, and through the nightdress he could feel the unfamiliar shape of her body—the swell of her bosom, the bones of her spine, the muscle of her thigh.

He didn't move to caress her. He listened to the rise and fall of her breath. They lay together, not speaking, and when he turned his head to look at her again, he saw that she had fallen asleep. In sleep, she looked guileless and very young. She was now his wife, and she was in his care. He would do his best to cherish her.

He laid her down like a child and kissed her brow. He repeated the nighttime words his mother had murmured to him when he was a little boy: "Sleep well, *liebchen*. Sweet dreams."

He slipped quietly from her room and returned to his own. In the unfamiliar room her parents had given him, in the unfamiliar bed, he found that he was too roused to sleep. As though he were still a bachelor, he gave himself release on his wedding night.

Part 2

Chapter 8

A Pair of Hands

As Sam turned the carriage into the driveway of the new place, Adelaide and Henry both leaned to look out the window. The gravel of the driveway had been raked, and magnolia and dogwood had been planted here. They were dormant now, but they would be pretty and fragrant in the spring.

The house was painted white, with a shaded piazza that ran its length. It was the kind of house that people called "four up and down," two stories tall and four rooms on each floor. Henry turned to Adelaide and smiled. "Very different from the old place," he said.

It wasn't a bad house. But she had been raised in the biggest house in the county, and she had briefly set her sights on the grandest houses of Savannah and Charleston. She had seen houses like this all over Cass County and all over Georgia. No matter how prosperous, its owner was a small planter, a man who owned less than twenty slaves.

She did her best to sound pleased, since it was mean to spoil Henry's pride in it. "Yes, it is," she said, smiling back at him, as her heart sank.

Henry got out of the carriage first and reached for her as Sam handed her out. He took her arm. She had walked alongside him before. He had seemed taller then. "Come into our new house," he said. He looked at Rachel, who stood behind her, and said "Welcome. This will be your place, too."

As Adelaide watched, Rachel dropped her eyes and murmured, "Thank you, Massa." Adelaide wondered if she would be always be watching to make sure that her husband's interest was kindly and her sister's interest was servile.

In the entryway stood a small woman, very black of skin, in a calico dress and a spotless apron. Henry said, "Minnie, this is your new mistress, Mrs. Kaltenbach."

Minnie bent her head. "How do, ma'am," she said softly.

"It's good to meet you, Minnie." Adelaide turned to her husband. "Where are the other servants?"

"For the house? There's Minnie and your servant, Rachel."

No butler. No housekeeper. No housemaids. No coachman. She said, "Just two servants to run the house? Your cook, and my maid?"

Henry looked puzzled. "Yes," he said. "Won't that be all right?"

Adelaide looked at her husband, equally puzzled. "I don't know," she said.

Inside, they walked through the four rooms on the first floor, which were already filled with furniture. Her parents had bought the latest from England for themselves, and had given her their castoffs. That's my punishment for disappointing them so, Adelaide thought. Everything borrowed, and nothing new.

They walked through the breezeway that separated the kitchen from the house. She looked around the kitchen. It was just like the kitchen on her father's place—the same cupboards and barrels and hearth—except that the stove was new. Why would she care about the kitchen? That would be Minnie's concern, not hers.

She put her hand to her mouth to stifle the impulse to yawn. She nodded to Rachel and said, "I feel a little tired. I'd like to rest for a while. Rachel, will you come upstairs and help me?"

In her room on the second floor, all of the furniture had been her mother's. It was strange to see the big carved bed, the dressing table, and the clothes press in a room that was hers now. The room was unadorned, with white walls and pine floors, and the coverlet on the ornate bed was plain and white as well.

She sat at the dressing table while Rachel unpacked her dresses, shaking out the wrinkles so she could fold them properly to put in the clothes press. She asked, "Does Mr. Kaltenbach really think that I'll be spending my time in the kitchen?"

"You're Missus. You'll run the house, the way that Marse runs the place."

Adelaide stared in the mirror. She thought she looked tired and drawn, not at all like a bride should look. "How are we going to manage? With just you and Minnie?"

Rachel said, "You'll tell us what you want, and keep an eye on us, so we do things as you like. Tomorrow you can school us, Minnie and me." She put her hand on her sister's shoulder. "We'll manage just fine."

Rachel sighed as she left Adelaide's room and walked into the central hallway. If this house were laid out like the Mannheim place, there were back stairs. Those were hers. She walked down the stairs and slipped out the back door into the breezeway, which would be a convenience in bad weather.

In the kitchen, Minnie sat at a big pine table, waiting for her. She would work with Minnie at this table, and they would eat here, too. She looked around with a more appraising eye than Adelaide's. Like the kitchen on the Mannheim place, this one had a brick hearth, big enough to roast a pig or a turkey. There was a cast iron stove, too, brand new. Next to the stove was a sink, big and deep, with a pump built in. No need to go into the yard. On the far wall, away from the danger of fire, stood two tall pine cupboards, and near them were covered barrels for flour, corn, and potatoes. In the corner was the drum of cottonseed oil.

The kitchen cat slept near the hearth, curled into a ball. She was black with a white nose, chest, and paws, like Dinah, the kitchen cat of Rachel's childhood. Rachel bent to pet the cat, which stirred a little but didn't wake. Rachel asked Minnie, "What do you call her?"

"Call her Matilda. Brought her from the old place. She a good mouser."

Both of them were ill at ease. This new house had no rhythm yet. Neither she nor Minnie knew what Marse and Missus wanted, and how to work together to give it to them.

Minnie said, "We didn't start right yesterday. I'm still sorry for what I said to you."

"Nothing was right yesterday. Don't mention it. Do you need me to help you get supper?"

"I will later. I'll show you upstairs first. You can see Marse Henry's room, since you'll be serving him."

Henry's room, across the hall from Adelaide's, was the same size as Adelaide's, but all of the furniture was bigger and darker, as befit a gentleman. The bed had once been Marse Mannheim's, as had the clothes press and the washstand. There was a damask coverlet on the bed and a dark red Turkey carpet on the floor. A leather dressing case sat on the washstand, next to the jug and basin. Next to the case was a little bottle with a blue and gold label. She asked Minnie, "Is it medicine?"

"No, it's scent."

"Can I smell it?"

"Don't spill it."

Rachel said, a little too sharply, "I been a house servant all my life, and I don't spill things or break things."

She opened the bottle. It had a light smell of flowers and a hint of something orange. Rachel had never served a man who wore scent. She wondered if she would smell it on him if she got close enough.

On the wall opposite the bed was a picture of a city, with buildings even older than Savannah's. She came close to read the caption. "A Scene of Dresden," it said.

Minnie said, "Brought that picture from the old place. Cherishes it. That's his home."

Next to the print were two daguerrotypes in gold frames. In one, a bearded man and a small, round woman sat side by side, their hands clasped. In another, two pretty young women, their hair in dark ringlets, twined their arms around each other's shoulders.

"His mama and papa, and his sisters before they got married."

"Did they ever visit?"

"They stay back home in Germany, but they write to him every week. He writes to them too. Misses them, especially his mama."

The coverlet had already been turned up, and there were no clothes lying on the chair. Minnie opened the clothes press to show her where she should put things away once they were clean. Everything was neatly put away where it belonged: cravats, socks, and shirts. The shirts had been folded so they wouldn't wrinkle.

"Did you tidy already?"

"No, Marse Henry is a tidy man," Minnie said. "He's easy to take care of. Easy to please, too."

Rachel had never seen a Massa who folded his own clothes and put them away. She asked, "Where do we sleep? Is it up in the attic?"

"We'll go up there while it's still light."

They went up the back stairs to the attic. The attic room ran the length of the house and was about half its width. The peak of the roof was higher than Rachel's head, and she could stand up in this room. There were two big windows to let in light, and in the summer they would pull a breeze through the room. Rachel's attic room in the Mannheim house had been stifling in summer. She was grateful for the windows.

Rachel recognized the dresser with four drawers and the washstand for the chamberpot. They had been in Adelaide's nursery. The two beds had plain, roughly-made bedsteads, plain white coverlets, and pillows. Next to the nearest bed was a rocking chair, and neatly folded over its arm was a red and gold paisley shawl, the loveliest thing in the room.

"That's a beautiful shawl," Rachel said.

"Marse gave it to me."

"Marse?" She thought of Marse Pereira.

Minnie must have been a house servant all her life, too. She read the thought. "No, he's just kindhearted. Gave to me last Christmas. Wanted me to be warm, and wanted me to have something pretty."

Rachel nodded. As Minnie showed her the rest of the house, she wondered about a Massa who thought not just of his servant's comfort, but of her happiness.

By the time that Minnie went back to the kitchen to start supper, the house was as dark and quiet as if it were empty. It seemed wrong to make any noise in this house. She should light a fire in the dining room. She should look for candles.

Were there still candles in the dining room sideboard, where the candlesticks had always sat? There were not. Someone had emptied it before moving it to the new place. She would try the study. She recalled seeing a sideboard there, too.

The room was dark, and the figure in the chair was so still that she was in the room before she realized that he was there.

"Massa?"

Startled, he said, "Rachel."

It wasn't the first time that she had thanked God for a skin too dark to show a blush. "Massa, would you like me to light some candles for you?"

"Yes, thank you."

She came into the room slowly. He said ruefully, "Everything is so new here that none of us can find what we want."

She said, "Let me look in the sideboard," which was where the brass candlesticks stood, and she pulled open the door and found candles and matches by feeling for them. She lit the candles and asked, "Is that better, Massa?"

A smile crept onto his face in the flickering light. "Yes, it is."

During the rush of the wedding day, she had been too busy to get more than a glimpse of her new master. Now she studied him, with a slave's sidelong glance. He was broad in the shoulder, but otherwise he was slight. Aunt Susy would want to fatten him up. Unlike Marse Mannheim, who was going bald, he had a full head of youthful, brown, curly hair. His eyes were brown, too—liquid, like some black people's eyes. For a slender man, he had a prominent nose. Because he was clean-shaven, his face showed his feelings, and right now, he looked like Adelaide, sad and tired.

"Would you like me to light you a fire, Massa?"

"No, it's all right. Don't trouble yourself."

As he had said to her at the frolic, when she was so hot and rushed. Why had she remembered that? She felt her cheeks flush again. "Ain't no trouble, Massa," she said, and her embarrassment stayed with her as she helped Minnie cook supper and ready the dining room.

The new Massa and Missus sat uncomfortably at the table the Mannheims had relinquished to them. Rachel stood against the dining room wall, waiting to serve and clear away the dishes. The newly-married couple spoke little. They had trouble meeting each other's eyes. They were husband and wife, but they were strangers to this house, and to each other.

The next morning, Rachel woke just after sunrise to find Minnie already dressed. Still groggy, Rachel said, "Give me a moment, I'll be up." She rose and swiftly dressed, and both women went quietly down the back stairs to the back door that led to the breezeway to the kitchen.

Minnie fed the banked fire in the big iron stove, and Rachel filled the kettle at the pump. "Let me have some of that for coffee," Minnie said.

"I need a pitcherful to bring to Missus Adelaide to wash her face."

"Jar and basin in the cupboard."

She realized that there was a Marse as well as a Missus to attend to. "What about Marse Henry? Does he want hot water or his coffee brought up?"

"Marse Henry?" Minnie smiled. "In the old house, he'd take a bucket and the razor out to the pump and holler to me to tell him if he cut himself."

They heard the back door open, and the sound of boots in the breezeway. It was Marse Henry, whose face was smooth, and whose shirt collar was damp. Minnie, who had been so stiff with Rachel, smiled warmly at her master. She looked him in the eye and said, "Marse Henry, tomorrow you let Rachel bring you up some hot water. You got a washtable with a marble top in your room, and a mirror, and you wash and shave your face up there like a gentleman should."

It was the most affectionate scolding. Marse Henry said, "Minnie has very clear ideas on what a gentleman should do."

"Now that you is one."

Henry bent down to pet the cat. Used to her master's touch, she stretched in her sleep but didn't wake. "How are you, Miss Matilda?" he said softly, in the tone of a man partial to cats. "Did you catch a mouse last night?" He looked up at Minnie. "Will you give her a dish of milk?"

"I always do, Marse Henry."

"Is there coffee yet?"

"In a minute. But you should drink it in the dining room. With your new bride."

Henry looked around the kitchen, with its new stove and castoff dishes. His gaze settled on the pine table. He said to Rachel, "In the old house all of us ate together at that table. I'll miss that, in this house."

Minnie said, "Now that you married, you got a young missus to keep you company."

Wistfully, he said, "Just a cup of coffee, Minnie. Then I'll go into the house and eat my breakfast like a gentleman should."

Rachel served the new couple at their proper breakfast in the dining room, where they were a little easier with one another. Adelaide passed her husband the biscuits, inquired if he wanted jam, and reminded Rachel to fill his cup with coffee. At the end of the meal, she dabbed her lips with a napkin and asked her husband, "What will you do today, Henry?"

"I'm going to meet the new hands and talk to Charlie about the place. What will you do?"

"I thought I'd write letters to my friends to let them know we've been married. Since we aren't going on a wedding journey."

Rachel knew what a sore spot the wedding journey was for Adelaide. Newly-married couples usually took a few months to visit their relatives. There were no relatives to visit, unless they went to Germany, and Adelaide's disgrace had barred her from the homes of her mother's former friends who stood in their stead in America. It hadn't cheered Adelaide that Henry had said, "I don't mind, Adelaide. A small planter can't really leave the place for two months."

Henry asked, "Won't you talk to Rachel and Minnie about how you're going to run the house?"

She flared. "Goodness, Henry, do you think I'll spend my days in the kitchen, baking bread and plucking chickens? Why on earth do we have servants?"

After breakfast, Henry left the house to meet his new people, talk to his new driver Charlie, and walk the fields to see how much work it would be to plow and plant. It wasn't far from the house to the cabins, but the distance between master and slave wasn't measured in feet. The day was chilly—he had been here long enough to feel cold in the mild Georgia winter—but the sun was out, casting a pale, watery light. The four cabins were set back from the path, and built in a row. Each cabin had room for gardens for vegetables behind, and flowers, if the occupants were inclined, in front. Behind the cabins was a stand of trees, and behind the trees were the cotton fields.

His new slaves stood in silence outside the cabins, waiting for him. They didn't look up at him, but he could feel their scrutiny. They were taking his measure, wondering if he were a good Massa or a brute. Would he whup for pleasure, or only because he had to? Was he steady and sober, likely to keep the place together, or would he gamble and drink and lose everything to debt? Would he vex them, or beat them, or force them? Or not?

They kept their eyes down. As with Zeke and Minnie, the first time he met them, the deference of these people was heavily tinged with fear.

Zeke stood with his arms protectively around his sons' shoulders. Next to him stood a tall, slender woman Henry didn't know. She had long limbs and delicate features. That must be Jenny. He spoke to Zeke first. "It's good to see you," he said, in a rush of emotion, as though it had been weeks, not days, since their last meeting. "You're settling in? You're all right?"

Zeke said, "Yes, Massa. We all fine. Massa, Jenny and I have joyful news. We want to get married."

"As soon as you like, Zeke." He hugged Zeke, who had been so kind to him on his wedding day. "It will be a happy day, and we'll all celebrate it with you."

The slaves murmured among themselves, not sure whether they should show joy or not.

Zeke introduced Charlie, his wife Becky, and their baby, Josey. Charlie was strong and quiet, and he had the gravity of a mature man. Henry wondered how old he was. Becky was a sturdy woman whose skin shone a coppery color. She kept her eyes on the child in her arms.

"How old is your little gal?" Henry asked Becky.

"Just a year old," Becky said, touching the soft head with its fine nap of dark hair. "Massa, we're grateful to you for keeping us together."

Embarrassed at her gratitude, Henry nodded.

There was Micah with a look of dignity, even though his head was lowered. There was Davey, tall and powerful. Henry recognized him as one of the hands hired out to bring in last year's crop. There was Freddy, who had a restless look on his face. There were Salley and Harriet, sisters, high brown, quiet and robust, also part of the group that came to Henry's rescue last year. Then there was Lydia, light-complected and pretty, who managed to put a beguiling look into a glance that didn't meet Henry's eyes.

Henry said, "Welcome, all of you. If there's anything you need, for your use or your convenience, you let me know."

There was a chorus of murmured voices. "Yes, Massa."

"Charlie, come with me, and talk to me while we take a look at the place."

"Yes, Massa."

The slaves watched as the new master and the new driver walked into the strip of pine woods to the fields beyond.

When they were in the fields, Henry asked Charlie to look him in the face. Charlie couldn't. He focused his eyes on the ground, which had been plowed under and bedded after last year's harvest. He said, "How many acres on this place, Massa?"

"A thousand."

"How many do you hope to plant in cotton, Massa?"

"Five hundred."

Still looking at the horizon, Charlie said, "Five hundred bales."

"Can we do it?"

Charlie said, "Let me see the place and study it."

They walked past a field that had been planted in corn the previous year. Charlie said, "How many bushels of corn last year, Massa?"

"A hundred and fifty."

"How many hogs on the place?"

"Five brood sows, a boar for stud, and thirty shoats. Why?"

"Trying to figure provision. What did you give your people last year?"

Henry said, "We all ate together. You should ask Minnie, who fed us. She could tell you better than I could."

Charlie said, "On the Mannheim place we got four pounds of side meat and a peck of corn each, every week, and Marse Mannheim allowed folks to grow their own gardens, and to keep their own chickens, and to hunt and fish."

"Zeke tells me the woods are full of game, and Luke caught fish and crawfish in the stream and the pond."

"If you don't mind folks hunting, we should be all right. Hate to buy meat if we can get it for ourselves."

Henry asked, "What about the ham and bacon?"

Charlie said, "That ain't for us."

Henry said, "Mrs. Kaltenbach and I won't eat it, because of the kosher laws. What did Mr. Mannheim do with it?"

"He sold it."

"Why don't we keep it for the people on the place?"

Charlie looked down. "Hate to naysay you, Massa."

"What is it, Charlie?"

Charlie looked over the cornfield with its brown and broken stalks. "Don't like to depend on cotton alone. A good year, we make a bale an acre, we do fine. A bad year, we don't. Good to have something else to sell. Almost always had a surplus of corn on the Mannheim place, and we sold it. Ham and bacon, we can sell that too. Just in case cotton disappoint us."

Henry, a great believer in morning coffee, had shared it with Minnie and Zeke and the boys at their communal table. This morning, feeling the chill in his bones, he said to Charlie, "Would people work better if they had coffee?"

Charlie hesitated. "What is it, Charlie?" Henry asked.

Carefully, Charlie said, "Adds to what we spend on supplies. Adds to what we pay off when the crop is in."

He tried to sound light. "That debt is my worry, not yours."

Charlie said, "Them five hundred bales is as much my worry as yours. How else are we going to pay off the debt?"

Zeke had taught him how to plant and grow cotton. Charlie would teach him how to make a profit from it.

After breakfast, Adelaide readied herself to talk to her servants as mistress of the house. As she walked through the breezeway to the kitchen, she felt apprehensive. She wished she could laugh at herself. Afraid of her nigger cook! She was missus, and her servants would have to obey her.

But her hand trembled as she pulled open the kitchen door.

Rachel and Minnie sat at the big pine table, waiting for her. When she came into the room, they rose. "Ma'am," Minnie murmured, her eyes properly cast down. Rachel, who also cast her eyes down, dipped her head in greeting.

Awkwardly, Adelaide said, "Good morning, Minnie. You too, Rachel." All three of them stood uneasily, Minnie and Rachel waiting to be spoken to, Adelaide unsure of what to say to them. Rachel raised her head—not her eyes, Minnie was there to see it, and to think it too familiar—and said softly, "Missus Adelaide, perhaps you'd allow Minnie to show you the kitchen."

"Yes," Adelaide said, in relief.

Minnie, proud of the kitchen, showed her everything in it—the bins for flour and cornmeal, the big barrel full of cottonseed oil, the cupboard with its two sets of dishes, and the pantry. Adelaide had never paid much attention to the kitchen on her father's place—she never went in there, save to beg a biscuit from Aunt Susy—but she knew that her mother carried a set of keys at her waist. She asked, "Shouldn't we lock up the pantry?"

Minnie said, "We never locked up the pantry in the old place. Marse didn't want it."

"This is my house, too," she said, sounding as shaky as she felt.

Minnie made her face smooth. "Ma'am, we can do whatever you want, but if the pantry locked, we trouble you every time we need something."

Her mother would know whether this was sass or not, and would know what to do. But Adelaide had never commanded anyone, except for Rachel. She gave Rachel an imploring look. But Rachel dropped her eyes and said nothing. Was she afraid to command Minnie, too?

Flushed, Adelaide stammered, "We'll leave it unlocked, for now."

"Thank you, ma'am," Minnie said. Her face was impassive and impossible to read, a servant's mask that could hide anything beneath. "Let me show you the barn."

They went outside, into the chill of a January day. In the yard, one of the pigs came up to Adelaide and snuffled at her dress, like the pig that wanted its ears scratched when she first visited Henry. Today she pushed away the bristly dark snout. She said to Minnie, "On the Mannheim place the pigs are penned up. Why are they allowed to roam?"

Minnie explained, "We can pen them, ma'am, but if they penned up, we have to tend them, and feed them, and clean out their pens. If they roam they tend to themselves. Less trouble for us."

Minnie was right, but Adelaide resented her saying so.

They walked into the barn, where the smell of hay and manure was strong. Adelaide stepped carefully, lifting her skirts from the muck on the floor. Minnie said, "Have two fine cows. Daisy and her gal, Cassie. Good milkers." Daisy turned her head and stretched out her neck. Adelaide reached out a tentative hand and the cow nosed it. Adelaide started at the soft wet touch.

Minnie said, "Show you the dairy next." The dairy was a small wooden building, cold inside, smelling strongly of milk. The churn sat in the middle of the floor. To the side was a big closet, where metal pans sat on shelves. "What's that?" Adelaide asked.

"Cheese. Cold enough to make good cheese. Ready soon."

Adelaide asked, "Why don't we buy cheese in town and save the trouble of making it ourselves?" Wouldn't Minnie agree to that?

Minnie hesitated. "Those cows are good milkers, ma'am. Plenty for butter and cheese. And whatever we make here, for our provision, we save having to buy in town."

As they walked back to the kitchen, Minnie said, "No washhouse to show you, not on this place." She opened the door to the kitchen, and the warmth from the stove was welcome after the chill in the yard and the barn. Minnie said, "Do the wash right in here, ma'am. Easiest place to boil water." Adelaide had never thought about the wash. On her father's place clean petticoats and sheets appeared with no effort on her part.

Minnie asked, "Ma'am, how often should we do the wash?"

Adelaide knew that Aunt Susy did the wash, but she had no idea how often it was done. She said, "Once a day, I'd think."

There was a long silence. Rachel said nothing. Minnie said, "Ma'am, we can do anything you want us to, but the wash is a big job, and it ain't usual to do it every day."

Adelaide flushed. "What's usual?" she asked. She looked at Rachel, hoping that she would say something, but she did not.

Minnie said, as politely as she knew how, "You do it more often if there's a baby or sickness in the house, but once a week is usual."

Adelaide said, "That don't seem right. What if I insisted on doing it every day?"

Minnie said, "Ma'am, we'll do whatever you ask, but if we do the wash every day, it will be harder to get other things done."

"Like what?" Adelaide asked. She didn't sound like her mother, severe and commanding. She sounded like a little girl.

"Getting the meals, ma'am. Or sweeping and dusting in the house. Or tending the garden, come summer. All them things you have to do every day." She looked at Adelaide's unhappy expression and asked, "How did your mama do it?"

I don't know, Adelaide thought. She felt her cheeks go hot with humiliation. She said sharply, "Do it matter?"

Minnie said softly, "No, ma'am. But whatever we do, however we do it, we do it to help you."

How could Minnie sound so servile, and seem so insolent? Her voice trembling, Adelaide said, "Minnie, are you sassing me?"

Minnie cast her eyes down. She drew in her shoulders. Small as she was, she seemed to shrink. Her voice almost inaudible, she murmured, "No, ma'am."

Adelaide was so upset that she was afraid she would burst into tears. "You'll do as I tell you," she said.

Minnie didn't raise her head or her voice. "Yes, ma'am," she said.

Adelaide couldn't bear to be in the kitchen anymore. She couldn't bear to think that Minnie would know how incapable she felt. She gathered her skirts in her hands, as though she were out rambling and had to brace herself to leap over a ditch, and walked quickly from the kitchen into the breezeway.

In the breezeway, she could hear Minnie perfectly well. In a tone that didn't hide her scorn, she said to Rachel, "Do the wash every day! New young missus. Don't know a thing."

"Hush," Rachel said. "She'll hear you."

Minnie said, "Just the two of us to do the work of five. Or ten. I know her daddy the biggest planter in the county. I heard she turn down a rich man in Savannah, don't know why. What did she expect, marrying a man with a dozen slaves?"

"Hush," Rachel said.

Adelaide stood in the breezeway, feeling the sting of Minnie's judgment. She thought of her mother, weeping and furious, telling her father that she wanted to beat or sell a slave for insolence. She thought of her father, who never laid a hand on the house servants, telling her mother not to be a fool.

At midday, Adelaide sat down to dinner with Henry. She was too embarrassed to tell him about Minnie's disrespect in the kitchen. Instead, she prattled about seeing the garden and the dairy and the barn. She told him about the pig that had wanted her to scratch its ears.

He looked at the wall behind her, as though he were thinking of something else, something that absorbed him and bothered him.

She was his wife now, and she asked him a wifely question. "Henry?" she asked. "Is there something troubling you?"

He shook his head. "I'm all right, Adelaide."

Even though he was not, and neither was she.

Throughout that week, Henry remained preoccupied. When she asked him if anything was wrong, he shook his head. "Nothing to trouble you," he said. He hadn't insisted on her marital duty, and she didn't know whether to be upset or relieved. They would be friends first, he had said, and she hoped so. If he was troubled, she wished she could help him. In this, as in everything else, she found she didn't know how.

All that week, the ladies of the county came to call on her. Gray-haired Mrs. Turner visited with her daughter Hattie, who was no longer in danger of ensnaring Henry. Mrs. Levy stopped by, and tried to cheer her with recipes for German dishes that were kosher and with reassurances that she'd soon have children to keep her company.

Pretty Mrs. Payne had promised to call, too. Aggie Payne was a chatterer who said whatever came into her head. Adelaide knew that Mrs. Levy was kinder, and Mrs. Turner was wiser, but Aggie made Adelaide laugh.

On the day Aggie came to visit, Rachel and Minnie were busy in the kitchen. Adelaide answered the door. Aggie said, "Adelaide, wherever are your servants?"

Adelaide flushed. "They're busy. Come in and sit in the parlor for a moment. I need to talk to Rachel."

Adelaide ran into the kitchen in a panic. "Mrs. Payne's come to visit! She'll want tea and refreshment. What do we have to give her?"

Rachel was kneading bread dough. She wiped her face and left a streak of flour on her cheek. It highlighted the dark smear of fatigue under her eye. "There's strudel left from yesterday," she said. "It ain't fresh."

"She won't like it."

Rachel said, "Can't help it."

When the strudel came—it was soggy, and not at all pleasant—Aggie said, "Adelaide, what is this sorry mess?"

Rachel, who had wiped her face and taken off her soiled apron, was in the room. Adelaide flushed. "We ain't quite set up yet."

Aggie cast a glance at Rachel and said to Adelaide, "Start out with soggy cake, and you'll end up with goodness knows what. You'll have to learn to manage your servants better than that." She set down the dish, cake uneaten, and asked, "How is your husband?" Such an innocent question, such a sly look.

"Busy with the place. Bothered about something."

"Oh, la, it's probably business. Don't let it worry you."

She let the question that really worried her bubble to the surface. It was somehow easy to ask it of Aggie. She said, "Do you like being married?"

Aggie said, "Oh, it's much better than being a girl at home. I like my house, and my servants, and my children, and my husband."

Adelaide thought of the question she had wanted to ask Rachel on her wedding night. She struggled to get the words out. "What about your duty?"

Aggie looked at Adelaide, and knew without asking what was bothering her. She laughed. "Oh, that!" She said, "A man is just like a little 'un who wants a sugar tit. It ain't so much of a bother, except for having a baby, and it's over in a moment, and afterwards he's so grateful for it."

Adelaide had never heard a lady speak so bluntly about the marital relation.

Aggie went on, "And if you say no, you can get him to do whatever you want. And then you say yes again." She laughed, as though this were any ordinary kind of teasing. "But you don't want to say no too long, or too often." She shot a look at Rachel, who stood near the door, her face impassive. "There's always a slave gal, somewhere."

The memory of William Pereira was like a cold touch on her cheek. She nodded.

Aggie said, "My husband thinks it's a secret. He pretends he doesn't know any of the people on his place, but he knows Lucy just fine. He went to see her every week the last time I was expecting. I don't know if she had a baby, and I don't know if it looks like him. I don't see it, and I don't know about it, so it don't bother me."

She looked at Adelaide. "Why do you look so upset? You grew up on a plantation, and you know how it is."

She did. As did her sister, silent in the corner of the room.

That evening she surprised Henry on the landing outside his bedroom door. She put her arms around his neck, as she had once embraced William Pereira, and looked into his eyes. "It's time for us to be husband and wife," she said, her voice low.

"You're sure? You're ready?"

"Yes." He pulled her close and kissed her, with more passion that he had ever allowed himself. She felt the merest shadow of the appetite she had felt in William Pereira's embrace, and that was enough to bother her. When they broke apart, he said gently, "I'll come to you tonight."

Tonight she knew to put lavender water on her throat and in her hair, and to unbutton the new nightdress to expose as much flesh as a gown for evening.

She knew to wait for him prettily reclined on the pillows. She knew to throw back the covers to welcome him when he came to her in his nightshirt.

He lay down beside her and invited her to lay down with him. He kissed her with even more passion than he had a few hours before. He tasted of the brandy he had drunk before he came to bed. Had he drunk it for courage?

"Blow out the candle," he whispered, which she did, and when she turned back to him she could no longer see him. All she had to know him was his voice and the unfamiliar feel of his hands on her skin.

He touched her neck and felt the bare flesh of her upper chest. He put his lips there, kissing her gently, searching for the forbidden flesh of her nipple. She was startled. Was this what husbands and wives did together?

He said softly, "Pull up your nightdress," which she did, and he ran his hand up the flesh of her thigh, a part of her body that no one had ever touched, save with a washcloth. He touched her on the part that had led her so badly astray with William Pereira. Scandalized, she said, "What are you doing?"

"Helping you." He whispered, "Open your legs a little."

His touch was gentle, but she was frightened. He said softly, "Adelaide, my love, I promise I won't hurt you." He had kept his promise last time. She let him touch her nether lips, first with his fingers, then with an unfamiliar part that she had never felt on a man's body.

He pressed inside her, and she discovered that both her mother and Rachel had been right. It hurt—surprisingly so, and she gasped to feel it—but it was soon over, replaced by a sensation of friction. He was moving inside her, down there, back and forth, in a rhythm.

She lay still, puzzled by what he was doing, worried that she would feel pain again. He continued to move, and she wondered when she would feel the joy that he and Rachel and talked about. Suddenly he cried out—was he in pain, too?—and thrust so deep inside her that she felt another stab of pain herself. Then he was still.

Still atop her, he raised himself on his elbows and kissed her mouth. In a pleased, husky voice, he said, "Now we are truly married."

It's over in a moment. He's so grateful afterwards. It ain't such a bother.

Where was the joy? Her eyes brimmed. As he lay beside her, spent, she turned her face to let her tears seep into the pillow.

Chastened, Adelaide wanted to do something to show Henry that she could be a good Jewish wife to him. A few days before the Sabbath, she walked from the main house through the breezeway and into the kitchen. Both of her servants wiped their hands on their aprons—aprons no longer spotless—and bent their heads, murmuring, "How do, Missus."

She was still uncomfortable in the kitchen, but she had learned to sit at the table, so they could too. She said, "I want to make a proper Shabbos."

Minnie looked at her blankly. Adelaide thought, I have never seen her at a loss. She asked, "Hasn't Mr. Kaltenbach been celebrating the Jewish Sabbath?"

Disconcerted, Minnie said, "We keep them kosher laws, ma'am, as best we can. But he's always gone to your family's place for his holidays."

Rachel addressed Minnie. "The Mannheims always had a nice supper on Friday nights, to start off their Sabbath."

Adelaide said, "Yes. Like at home." It surprised her to say it and to think that this house and this place were her home now.

Rachel asked, "What do you want for your Shabbos dinner, ma'am?"

Adelaide hadn't realized she'd been holding her breath until she let it out. "Like my mother does," she said. "A braided loaf. Fish in sweet and sour sauce. Stuffed breast of veal. A sponge for dessert. And wine to go with it. Rachel, you can show Minnie."

Minnie said, "Have to get wine and veal in town, ma'am."

"That's all right. Rachel, ask Susy or Ezra about it, they'll tell you where to get it."

Minnie said, "What can I do, ma'am?"

"Help Rachel, whatever she needs."

Later, Minnie sulked about the Shabbos dinner. "I can cook anything I set my mind to," she said. "Wish she'd asked me. What is this bread Missus want?"

Rachel said, "Got egg in it. Make a braid, three strands, like for hair, and brush it with egg before it go in the oven. Ain't hard." She laughed. "Easier than that French pastry you so good at."

On Friday night, Adelaide admired the dining room, glad to see that the table was set with the good dishes and the wine glasses, and that the candles stood ready in the silver candlesticks. The silver Kiddush cup sat beside Henry's place, and the claret, bought in town, had been poured into the crystal decanter. The hallah was on the table, under a cloth. She felt at peace for the first time since she moved into the new place. She would make a Jewish house, as her mother had, and bring the calm of the Sabbath for herself and her husband. And put to rest the memory of the disappointment in the marriage bed.

Henry came into the room. He said, "It looks beautiful, Adelaide."

She smiled. "I'm going to light the candles." She lit them and said the only prayer she regularly made to God, and when she finished, she smiled at her husband. They sat. She said, "Would you say the Kiddush?"

He said ruefully, "I believe my Hebrew is a little rusty."

"That's all right. I don't think God will mind."

He raised the cup and stammered the blessing. Blushing, he asked, "Was that all right?"

"Yes," she said, smiling. "Hand me the plate with the hallah on it." She uncovered the loaf and blessed it as well as she could from memory. Then she broke a piece from the loaf and handed to Henry. "A good Sabbath," she said to him.

He said softly, "I haven't seen you like this."

"Do you mind?"

"Not at all." He raised the Kiddush cup and said, "A good Sabbath, Adelaide."

A week later, as Adelaide walked past the study, she saw her husband sitting at his desk. His ledger was open before him, and he looked at it as though the mere sight of the columns of figures gave him a headache.

"Is something wrong?" she asked.

He gestured towards the bill that sat beside the ledger. "This came from Cassville."

"What is it?"

"Now I know what Shabbos dinner cost us."

Abashed, she said, "I thought it would please you. Did I do wrong?"

He looked worried and tired again. "I need you to be frugal, Adelaide."

Puzzled, she said, "Was it extravagant to buy veal and claret?"

He sighed. "I hate to spend money on anything that isn't necessary. We need coffee, and flour, and cottonseed oil, and the hands need lengths and shoes. I hate to deny you anything. But I can't stand to add to the debt."

She tried to cheer him. "Ain't all planters in debt?"

"It's nothing to joke about. I want to be out of debt at the end of this season. I need your help."

Was something wrong? Hadn't her father made him a generous settlement? She said, "I ain't planning to be frivolous, running to Levy's every week for laces and ribbons. But I hope we could eat veal and drink claret with our Shabbos dinner."

He sighed and shook his head. "I know you aren't used to running a household. Let Minnie and Rachel help you. They're capable."

She felt afresh the sting of Minnie's judgment. She shook her head.

"Charlie helps me," he said.

"I won't be commanded by a servant," she said. She rose and left the room.

Adelaide went for a walk, hoping to walk away the unhappiness that cloaked her, like the chill and the mist of the February weather. Despite the thickness of her manteau, she shivered in the winter air. Standing in the pine woods, a distance from the fields, she could hear her husband's slaves singing as they worked. The song was wordless, half melody and half groan. Were they sad, too? Did they grieve for whatever slaves grieved for?

Hidden in the pine thicket that separated her father's plantation from her husband's, she let the fog settle on her face, a mist finer than tears, and let her worst thoughts trouble her.

When she agreed to marry Henry Kaltenbach, she had never thought beyond the wedding ceremony. She had never thought about the wedding night or the marriage bed, and she had never thought about living with her husband day after day. She had never thought about being mistress of her own place, and she had never thought that being the mistress of a small place, with less than twenty slaves, would be different from living as a girl on a place with more than fifty.

She had never dreamed that her husband—and her servants—would expect her to work like a slave in the kitchen, the garden, and the dairy, and would be disappointed that she could not. And she had never expected to feel so roiled with anger and hurt that she failed at it, and that her servants thought so and said so.

She wished she could talk to Rachel, but Rachel was far away. She laced and buttoned and combed with her usual skill, but she was slow to answer when Adelaide talked to her, and her answers were cursory. She said, "Yes, ma'am," and "No, ma'am," as though it took too much effort to say more.

Adelaide missed the sister's good sense, and her wit, and the comfort of her touch on shoulder or hair. But Rachel was a slave, and expected to work like one. She was too busy, too burdened, and too tired these days to be a sister.

When Adelaide came home from her ramble, she found Rachel slumped in a chair in her room, deeply asleep, her mending in her lap. Adelaide said softly, "Rachel?" but she didn't wake. She bent down and touched her shoulder gently. "Rachel?"

Rachel opened her eyes. Groggy, she said, "I'm so sorry—I fell asleep—"

"Careful. You've stuck the needle in your finger."

Rachel lifted her hands away from the dress in her lap, not wanting to stain it. She pulled the needle out, wincing, and quickly put her finger in her mouth to catch the blood. "Oh, Rachel," Adelaide said, and she wetted a cloth. "Take this. Do we have any sticking plaster?"

Rachel took the cloth and wrapped it around her finger. "I'll tend to it," she said.

"This isn't like you. Dead asleep in the middle of the day. Are you all right?"

"Just a little tired, ma'am."

"Don't ma'am me. Minnie ain't here to know."

Rachel rested her bandaged hand in her lap. "Bone tired."

"Why? What's wrong?"

"I didn't want to say. Didn't want to grumble." She sighed and rubbed her uninjured hand over her face. "Two servants in the house, and work enough for ten."

Two servants and a mistress, who was useless as a pair of hands, and wasn't likely to be otherwise. Well, her mother had raised her to be a lady, and what would a lady think? That she was short a servant, maybe two. That she needed another. But on this place, every grown hand was needed for the crop, and there was no one to spare for the house. On her father's place, there was always a little girl in the cabins to put into the kitchen, but the children here were babies.

Her husband had chided her for spending money on luxuries. But a servant wasn't a luxury. Surely her husband could be persuaded to find a half-grown girl to help with the heaviest work in the kitchen and at the washtub.

That evening, she found Henry in the study. He sat in the wing chair that had suited her father and that was too big for him, a glass of whiskey on the little table at his elbow, staring at the fire as it flickered and crackled.

Without asking, she sat in the wing chair opposite—it was so big that it swallowed her up, too—and said gently, "You're drinking whiskey."

He shook her head. "Just a little," he said. "It's good on a cold day."

"Or a tiring one." She put a gentle hand on her husband's knee, an intimacy she had never tried before. "You look so worried all the time, Henry. What is it? Is there anything I can do?"

He said ruefully, "I think about the place too much." He sighed. "Always more to do than you expect, and more to worry over."

In a gentle tone to match her touch, she said, "I know. It's the same in the house."

He looked up. "But you're all right? You're managing?"

"There's too much for Rachel and Minnie. Henry, we need another servant."

He no longer looked worried. He looked aggravated. A less gentle man would been angry. "Adelaide, we can't spare anyone who's in the field."

"I know." She kept her hand on his knee, trying to placate him.

He said, "We don't have a dime for another slave."

"We're in debt, I know that. But can't we buy the things we need?"

He slumped in the chair. "We can barely afford the things we need. We don't have money for anything extra."

"But won't we be all right when you sell the crop?"

He says, "I hope so, and in the meantime, I'm damned if I'll go any deeper in debt to your father."

Startled by the bitterness in her husband's voice, she asked, "I thought he made a settlement when you asked for me."

He hesitated. He drank a sip of whiskey. When he put the glass down, he said, as calmly as he could, "It ain't a fit subject to discuss with a lady. I'm sorry I mentioned it."

She took her hand from his knee. "Why is it I'm a lady when it comes to matters of business, but not when it's a question of working like a nigger at the washtub?"

"Adelaide," he said, more sharply than she had ever heard him. "I can't afford to buy another slave. You'll have to make do without."

There would be no half-grown girl to relieve Rachel. Her kindhearted husband was stony on this subject. She would have to find some other way to manage.

Adelaide decided to visit the most-respected lady in the county, Mrs. Turner, whose husband, like Henry, owned less than twenty slaves. She had never seen Mrs. Turner unless she sat genteelly on a sofa, with lace mitts on her hands and a skirt belled out by her hoops. Perhaps Mrs. Turner, who had been kind to her since she came back from Savannah, would be able to advise her.

She was in such a rush to talk to Mrs. Turner that she went right away, not thinking about whether was Mrs. Turner's day "at home" to callers.

The maid who answered the door said, "She's in the side yard, ma'am." Adelaide walked into the side yard, where she saw two women, similarly dressed in old calico dresses and straw hats, with their bare arms in a washtub of soapy water. Hearing Adelaide's footsteps, they raised their heads.

One of them was a slave. The other was Mrs. Turner.

Mrs. Turner, her arms dripping, stammered, "Adelaide! I didn't expect any callers today." She raised her wet hands and stared at them as though they belonged to someone else. "If you wait I can dress and come to take tea with you in the parlor."

Seeing Mrs. Turner like this—without her hoops, bent over the washtub— was as shameful as finding her on the chamberpot. Mortified, Adelaide said, "No, ma'am, I don't mean to trouble you. I'll come back on a day you're 'at home.'"

Mrs. Turner, the county's most exemplary lady on her days 'at home', spent her time on her place dressed no better than one of her slaves, and working just as hard as they did. Adelaide now knew the reason for the lace mitts. They hid the hands reddened and coarsened by labor.

Adelaide slept badly that night, waking to think that she should be in the kitchen and at the washtub. Her hands had never been pretty, but she hated the thought that they would coarsen. In the morning, she said to Rachel, "Put out my oldest dress. The one that's too worn to ramble in. And no crinoline or hoops."

Rachel looked as though she hadn't slept well for a long time. "Are you going for a walk, ma'am?"

She said sadly, "Don't ma'am me," hoping that Rachel would smile, but she only nodded and took the shabby calico from its shelf in the clothes press. She did up the buttons, taking care not to tear the worn-out cloth, but she didn't speak.

As Rachel dressed her, Adelaide looked at her hands, which were stained with ink. She wondered if a soak in the washtub would remove the ink that her mother had always deplored so much.

In the kitchen, Minnie, like Rachel, asked if she were going for a walk.

"No, Minnie. I'm here to help you and Rachel."

Minnie had to work to control her expression, but Rachel said, "It's all right, Minnie."

They were making hallah, and Rachel put her to a task that a little slave girl of five would be asked to do. She let Adelaide knead the dough, and under Rachel's direction, braid the loaf and brush it with beaten egg. Rachel put the loaf into the oven and said, "Now you watch it. Make sure it don't burn." Kitchen talk. Whenever Rachel was tired or upset she returned to it. There were dark circles under her eyes, and her brown face had lost its glow and taken on a dull grayish cast.

"How will I know?"

Rachel leaned against the edge of the pine table, as though she were too weary to stand upright. Her voice hoarse, she said, "Open the oven door and look. When it brown enough, we take it out and tap it to see if it ready."

Adelaide sat on a stool near the oven and opened the door so often that Minnie said crossly, "Leave that alone or it won't stay hot. Don't want to feed more wood if I don't have to." Abashed, Adelaide sat at the kitchen table and watched as Rachel and Minnie cut up apples and mixed them with cinnamon for a strudel. The smell of cinnamon soothed her. It reminded her of the Sabbaths of her childhood, before her mother's face was set in bitterness.

Lulled by the pleasant odor of apple and cinnamon, Adelaide was startled when it was overpowered by something else altogether.

"Adelaide!" Rachel cried out, too upset to say "Missus." "The bread! It's burning!"

Adelaide rushed to open the oven door, and the smell of scorched bread billowed out. She bent to look at the loaf. It wasn't burned, but it was scorched too dark to eat.

Rachel took it from the oven and said, "Can't put it on the table." She sighed. "Put it out in the yard, and the pigs will eat it."

In a small voice, Adelaide asked, "Whatever are we going to do for bread?"

Rachel leaned against the edge of the table. Her skin was as gray as ash. She shook her head. "I'll make another loaf. You go back in the house and let us finish here."

As she walked through the breezeway she could hear Rachel perfectly well, her voice louder and angrier than Adelaide had ever known it. She stopped. She wanted to hear what Rachel had to say.

"When I was a little gal I burned the Sabbath strudel. Her mother slapped me so hard she bruised my face. Called me stupid and lazy into the bargain, too." There was fury in that voice, but there was a sound like a sob, too.

"Hush," said Minnie. "She'll hear you."

"Can't bear it anymore," Rachel said. "Work from sunup to sundown, with never a moment to rest, and scarcely a moment to eat." The sound was definitely a sob. "She a fool, trying to help, making it worse. Lazy and no-account! If she were a slave her own mama would have sold her long ago."

Rachel's judgment hurt much more than Minnie's. And she was right. Adelaide was of no account as the mistress of this place. Not in the kitchen or the garden, or the dairy. And not in the marriage bed, either.

In the privacy of her room, she sank down on the edge of the bed, too numb to weep. Her husband was far away, burdened by the place and the debt, and her sister was so tired from her burden of the kitchen and the dairy and the garden and the washtub that she had no comfort to offer. When she got married, Adelaide had never expected to feel like this. She had never felt so lonely in her life, not even after Mattie broke off their friendship and denied the bond of friends who loved each other like sisters.

Every week since the wedding, Adelaide had invited Henry to her room and submitted to the marital ritual. He was always kind, and he tried to rouse her. He teased her and he tickled her. He kissed her on the mouth, on the breast, and—she blushed to think of it—he touched her "down there", too. Nothing helped. Nothing he did gave her pleasure. She couldn't imagine allowing herself to feel passion with Henry. She had married him to put passion away forever.

She kept Aggie's advice firmly in mind. He's so grateful. It's over in a moment. Ain't such a bother.

Except for having a baby.

Six weeks after the wedding, Adelaide woke to feel a bad cramp in her belly, worse than her courses. She couldn't recall the last time she had her courses. When she used the chamberpot, she found a mess of blood in it.

Worried, she told Rachel. "That ain't right," said Rachel, alarmed. "I'll get Minnie."

"Why would you want Minnie?"

"She knows about helping women who are carrying or laboring."

Minnie looked into the chamberpot. She was matter-of-fact. "Would have been a baby, if it had stayed put."

Adelaide asked, "What happened?"

"Just didn't take root right in the womb, Missus. Don't know why."

Frightened, she asked, "Will it happen again?"

"Can't say. Sometimes it does, and sometimes the next one is just fine. We wait and see."

Adelaide felt stricken, and she must have looked it, because Minnie said, "I'm sorry, Missus." It was first time that Minnie had been pleasant to her.

Alone with Rachel, still in her nightdress, she sat down on the edge of the bed, and pressed her hands between her thighs like a frightened girl. She thought of her mother, who had suffered through miscarriage after miscarriage during her married life. She thought of darker things, of babies born dead, and of women who died in bearing them. She began to shiver.

Rachel sat beside her on the bed. For the first time in weeks, she pressed her cheek to Adelaide's and put her arms around her sister. "I'm so sorry, Adelaide," she whispered. Adelaide clung to her, too sorrowful and alone with her thoughts to take pleasure in the only comfort her sister had offered since she got married.

A few days later, on a cold night early in March, Henry lay beside Adelaide after he had spent. He rolled over to face her and said softly, "Adelaide."

She turned to face him. It was dark, but the moonlight slanted through the curtains and into the room. She could see him, the shape of his face, the way that his hair curled after a day in the field. He smelled faintly of eau-de-cologne, and the day's sweat, and the soap that Minnie and Rachel used to wash his nightshirts. She said, "What is it, Henry?"

He propped himself on one elbow. "Is this the marriage you hoped for?"

Tears rose to her eyes. "I don't know what I hoped for."

Chapter 9

In the Ashes

R achel hadn't been to meeting since she left the Mannheim place, and when she took her meeting dress from the nail where it hung, it still smelled of soap and starch from its last washing. She slipped the dress over her head and buttoned it. It was too loose on her—she hadn't realized she'd lost flesh in the past few months—but there was no time to take it in. She didn't have a mirror in the attic room she shared with Minnie, but she felt bedraggled. She would have to go to meeting looking that way.

Yesterday, putting Adelaide's dresses away, she had caught a glimpse of herself in Adelaide's dressing table mirror. She stared at her reflection, remembering the girl who had coquetted with herself before the mirror in Savannah. When she came home, Charlie had told her that she looked sad and pretty. Now there were dark smudges of fatigue under her eyes, and her skin had an ashy look. She looked sad and weary.

When she and Adelaide were girls, they read the story of Aschenputtel, whose stepsisters sent her into the kitchen to sit in the ashes by the hearth. Adelaide had wondered how the stepsisters could be so cruel. Rachel knew better.

Rachel never let herself think about the life she would lead after Adelaide married. Aunt Susy had told her, "Don't nothing belong to you." Her future, like her food, her dress, and her happiness, didn't belong to her and wasn't hers to hope for. She would go where Adelaide went, and share the circumstances of Adelaide's life, whether they gave Adelaide misery or joy.

Now she knew. Adelaide was married to a small planter, who was too deep in debt to buy a much-needed girl for the house, and Rachel did the work that three servants had done on the place where they both grew up. Whatever Adelaide intended for her, Rachel felt like Aschenputtel. She shook her head and sighed as she smoothed her skirt.

On the smaller places, slaves went to the same church as their masters, but a big place often had its own meeting for slaves. Marse Mannheim had never cared what his slaves did for their own religion, since the Mannheims, being Israelites, had to manage for themselves. The Mannheim slaves—and now the Kaltenbach slaves, too—had their meeting outdoors in the summertime, and in the winter, they used a little wooden building they had put up, about the size of two cabins, with oilpaper on the windows and rough pine benches to sit on. The slaves' meeting house was in the woods between the two places, to keep their singing and preaching far from white ears and eyes.

It was a cold day, and she shivered as she walked to the meeting house. The air smelled sharply of pine, a smell that always reminded her of Charlie. She hadn't seen him, except in passing, since they all went to the Kaltenbach place, and they hadn't spoken. Minnie, who gossiped with Jenny, knew all about Marse Henry's regard for him. That news came to her almost every day.

When she opened the door to the meeting house, the room was full of people, and there was an outcry when they saw her. Sam clasped her hands and said, "We've missed you, little gal." Aunt Susy hugged her close and felt how thin she was. "Oh, sugar, they working you to the bone," she said, and she put her hand to her eyes.

Charlie said, "How do," as though they were strangers. "I do all right," she said, and she greeted Becky, who held Josey in her arms. Rachel asked, "How old is she now?"

Becky smiled. "More than a year. Got a few teeth. Just figured out how to say 'mama.'" She kissed the little girl's head and Rachel felt a stab of envy.

Charlie said, "Got another one on the way." Becky's face glowed with pleasure and embarrassment. "Charlie, don't you tell her our private business." Charlie's face glowed too. "Baby come due right at harvest," he said, but he was smiling and looking at his wife with affection.

They had made the baby just after they moved into their cabin on the Kaltenbach place. Rachel pushed the thought away.

The little building, packed with people, was hot and stuffy, and even though the bench was hard against her backside, her lids drooped as Judah preached. She woke with a start when Aunt Susy, who sat next to her, put a hand on her shoulder and whispered, "We all been that tired, sugar."

After the service, when everyone lingered, Charlie put his hand on her elbow. He said, "How are they treating you in that big house?"

She tried to sound light. "We still settling in, all of us."

"You look bone weary," he said.

"I know," she said, and it didn't come out light at all. If she didn't watch herself she would start to blubber like a gal no older than his daughter Josey.

"Don't be such a stranger," he said, his hand still on her elbow.

She righted herself. She had come to meeting for a purpose. She said, "Charlie, could I come talk to you? Somewhere private?" At his look of surprise, she said, "No, it's all right, it's about the business of the place."

His voice low, he said, "Come see me after midday dinner. We find someplace to talk."

When she came to see him, later that day, he said, "I know where to go that's private." He led, and she followed him, and as they walked she recalled their love with such pain, and such regret, that she was sorry she had asked him to talk to her.

He took her to their old spot in the woods, the place where they had first kissed, and first admitted that they loved one another. The spot where they had broken apart. She said, "Do you recall the last time we were here?"

He looked startled, then saddened. "Hadn't thought of that way," he said. "This is the most private place I know of."

She shook her head. She wasn't sure that she could stand here, remembering. "Maybe we should sit on your steps and let everyone know what I have to say."

He put his hand on her shoulder, as he would to steady any of the hands he drove. "You settle down," he said, "and tell me about this business of the place."

She told him about the burden of the work, and the lack of hands to do it. He nodded and asked, "Have you talked to Missus Adelaide?"

"No."

"She have to say yes."

She said, "I know a few things I ain't supposed to know. That she asked Marse Kaltenbach to buy another servant, and he said no because he so worried about the debt. Didn't want to stir all that up again, asking her. Try to do it roundabout. Like Br'er Rabbit."

He nodded. He knew all about going roundabout. He said, "What was you thinking?"

"Wondering if you could spare one of the gals from the field to help us with the wash and the dairy. Ain't a full day's work or a full week's work. Just sometimes."

He said, "I believe we can. Don't need everyone to plow and chop. Picking time, it might be different, but picking's a long ways off. Marse Henry have to say yes, too."

She said, "I thought you could sway him, since he think so highly of you."

He looked embarrassed. "How do you know that?"

"Everyone know it. He own this place, but you run it."

He dropped his voice low. When they were lovers, that low tone was always for something sweet. He said, "I talk to him. We do it roundabout."

She reached to clasp his hands, and in that spot, full of so much feeling, their eyes met, and she saw the regret in his face, as he could see it in hers. They both felt uneasy at the same time. The handclasp became a handshake between two people who had conducted business. "Thank you," she said, as they let each other go.

Since that first morning on the new place, Henry had come into the field every day to confer with Charlie, and the Monday after meeting was no different. After they talked about the crop and the hands, Charlie said, "Massa, have something else to tell you today, if you don't mind."

"Of course I don't mind."

"Rachel came to me yesterday. We grew up together, she like my little sister. She tell me that everything go well in the house, but she and Minnie stretched a little thin. She had a clever notion, Massa. Won't cause any trouble in the field, and won't cost us anything extra."

"What is it, Charlie?"

"Asked if we could spare a gal from the field to help out a little in the house. Do the wash, churn the butter, maybe work in the kitchen garden. Not all the time. Sometimes."

"Can we?"

"I believe so, Massa."

Henry said, "Why didn't we think of it sooner?"

"It were Rachel's notion. She a good servant. Didn't want to be forward."

Henry said reflectively, "If you think we can spare someone, we can. Who would you choose?"

Charlie wished he could grin. "Not Salley or Harriet, since they always want to be together. Not Lydia, she flighty. Jenny. She work hard, she obliging."

"Not your own wife?"

"Don't want to seem partial."

Henry fell silent, and he looked upset. Charlie asked, "Massa? What's wrong?"

"My wife told me for weeks that they couldn't manage with only two servants in the house. I brushed it away." Henry rubbed his face. "Too worried about the crop to care about anything else on the place."

Charlie thought, He ain't the least bit bothered by our going roundabout. He bothered by his own tender heart, and that tender heart will be the ruin of him. He said, "Massa, the house is for Missus to worry about, like the crop is for you. Don't trouble yourself. I talk to Jenny today, and she go to work and help Rachel and Minnie ease their burden."

Later that day, when Rachel went into Adelaide's room to put away the clean wash, she found Adelaide sitting at her little table, writing a letter. Adelaide put down the pen—her hands were stained with ink—and she said, "My husband just told me that he's sending a field hand over to help with the wash. I wonder how that happened." It was her mocking tone, which she put on when she was upset and didn't want to betray it. "Did you talk to him? Persuade him, when I couldn't?"

Rachel said, "Of course not. Wouldn't be right."

"Why would he think of it?"

"It was Charlie. Charlie must have talked to him and swayed him."

Adelaide turned to look at her sister. "And who put it in mind for Charlie? Would you know?"

Rachel felt her weariness lift. For the first time in weeks, she felt cheerful. "Might have been Br'er Rabbit," she said.

After she left Adelaide, she went back to the kitchen, where Minnie was kneading bread and Henry was sitting at the pine table, eating a biscuit left over from breakfast. Henry teased Minnie, "Will you make hallah on Shabbos, Minnie?"

Minnie looked up and met her master's eyes without any difficulty.

Rachel had often wondered how she had come to feel so much at ease with Henry. "Rachel will, Massa. She good at it."

"But you'll make me a honeycake like my mother's. Like the one we had at my wedding." He finished his biscuit—in the kitchen, at his ease, he didn't mind his manners—and wiped his face with the cloth Minnie had left for him.

Minnie smiled. "Whenever you ask, Marse Henry."

Rachel had seen Minnie scold her master and indulge him. There were times that she acted more like a mama than a servant.

Henry said, "I came to find you, Rachel. I'd like to talk to you."

She nodded and said, "I come now, Massa."

"Don't hurry. When you're ready."

When he left, Minnie said, "Why do he have his eye on you today?"

Rachel said, "Don't know. Why do a master ever have his eye on a slave?"

Minnie gave her a sharp look. She had seen it before, in the big house on the Butler place that she still recollected so well.

Since her first days in this house, Rachel had been deferential and polite to her new master. She took care of him in the unobtrusive way of a good servant—bringing up his hot water, making his bed, doing his wash, folding his clothes, serving his meals. She kept Aggie Payne's wicked words in the forefront of her mind, too—"There's always a slave gal, somewhere." She had no desire to bring the specter of Marse Pereira into the house. She would not give Marse Kaltenbach cause for the wickedness that slave gals were supposed to provoke in their masters.

She walked into the study with trepidation. She stood quietly near the door, waiting to be commanded.

He sat in one of the wing chairs that faced the fireplace and gestured to the chair opposite him. "Come in, Rachel. Sit with me."

She sat tentatively at the edge of the chair.

He said, "My mother would say you that you could sit in that chair with more than one buttock. Make yourself more comfortable."

Despite herself, she stifled a smile and settled herself more easily in the chair.

"Please, look at me," he said, in a gentle voice.

She could feel his gaze, even if she didn't meet his eyes. She had been a house servant all her life, and she had long been used to looking Adelaide in the eye. But this was different. She had to struggle to do as he asked. She raised her head.

He said, "Charlie talked to me this morning, about sparing one of the hands to work in the house. He told me that it was a clever notion of yours, and he was right."

She looked behind him at the wall as he spoke. The slave's illusion, meeting the eye and not meeting the eye.

He said, "When I met all of the field hands I told them that they should let me know about anything they needed for their use or comfort. I should have done the same for you." His tone was kindly. She thought of his kindliness towards Minnie. Perhaps she had nothing to fear.

He said, "I didn't know how hard you were working in the house. I didn't know that we had overtaxed you."

Wasn't that a slave's lot? No reason for a master to trouble himself about it.

He said, "It was my fault not to see it. I'm sorry, Rachel."

She had never heard a slaveowner apologize to a slave. She stammered, "Massa, it ain't right for you to say sorry to me."

He gently contradicted her. "Of course it is, if I've done wrong."

As though he owed her the courtesy. She was so surprised that she had to struggle to give him a courteous reply. "Thank you, Massa."

He held out his hand to her in a gesture of forgiveness. She didn't know which was worse, the apology or the handclasp. She could chide him about the lapse of decorum. "Massa, I can't shake your hand. Wouldn't be right."

He took back his hand and shook his head. Ruefully, he said, "Now that ain't right, either, too. To deny you a common courtesy."

"But I thank you for considering me, Massa."

"That will have to do, then," he said. "You'll let me know? If there's anything I can do for your comfort?"

Uneasy again, she said, "Yes, Massa."

"Then I'll let you go." As she rose, he rose too, as a gentleman would for a lady.

When she left the study she leaned against the breezeway wall, flustered and bothered. Her master had apologized to her. The man who could beat her, sell her, or use her as he wished, who was never obliged to speak a kind word to her or consider her in any way, had begged her pardon for acting wrong to her.

He was a kindly man. Minnie said so, and she had seen proof of his kindness in the way he treated Minnie. She thought of the way he had looked at her as he begged her pardon. Was it just his consideration? Or was there more in it?

There's always a slave gal, somewhere. As there was always a master whose look and touch were fired by desire and not consideration. When she thought of being considered, she felt pleased through. She wished that it could be an unsullied thought, a gift to warm her, without the taint of her memory of Marse Pereira.

A few days later, Rachel heard Henry come through the back door, his boots making a heavy tread on the floor. She heard a thud, and some German cursing. She put down her feather duster and went into the back room to see what the trouble was.

Henry sat on the bench by the door, tugging on his boot, unable to budge it. His cheeks were flushed. She asked, "Massa? Should I fetch your bootjack?"

"I've mislaid it."

Marse Mannheim's valet took off his boots at the end of the day. Without thinking, she knelt down and said, "Let me help you."

"What a fool I feel," he said, straightening his leg so she could grasp the boot heel and tug.

She touched Adelaide all the time, to lace her or dress her, but she had never touched her master. It wasn't intimate to take off a boot—a man would do it for a drunken friend, or a mother would do it for a child—but as she pulled it off, she was aware of his leg underneath the leather, and his foot in the sock. He watched her, following the boot as she clasped it to her chest. He flushed an even deeper red, and she realized why. He was looking at the swell of her bosom beneath the calico of her dress.

Her own cheeks burned, and she was careful to drop her eyes as she pulled off the second boot. It came off easily in her hands and she sat back on her heels. He was still flushed with embarrassment, but he was now looking carefully at his own hands, pressed to the knees of his trousers.

She asked, "Do you want me to bring your slippers?"

He gazed somewhere behind her, just as a slave would do, too ill at ease to stare, and he said, "I'd think that was Missus Adelaide's task, not yours."

Her cheeks were hot again. Did wives fetch slippers, and bring whiskey, and take off boots for husbands in Germany? On the Mannheim place, those tasks were for the butler and valet, Ezra. "It's no trouble, Massa."

He looked at her, his face now its usual color. With his customary courtesy, he said, "It's all right, Rachel. I'm going to sit in the study, and I reckon I can walk through the house in my socks."

She rose. "There's a fire laid in the study," she said.

He rose too. "I'm going to sit before that fire to have a little whiskey," he said. "Would you come with me, Rachel, and talk to me?"

"I'll serve you, Massa, but I shouldn't sit."

"No, it's all right, Rachel."

She remembered Aunt Susy saying, "What they say, we do." She inclined her head. "Yes, Massa." In the study, she sat in one of the wing chairs that faced each other before the fire. It was odd, as it had been since he apologized to her, to feel warm towards him and wary with him, at the same time.

He said, "It's good to sit down. Charlie won't let me touch a plow or a hoe, but I'm there to see how things are going. Always something to take care of, Charlie tells me, and I fret about it along with him."

He sounded just like Charlie, vexed at everything that could go wrong on a cotton field. At the familiar refrain, she said, "Plowing done by now. They chopping?"

Like her, he seemed relieved to talk about the crop. "Just about. Plowing and chopping don't worry me. I know we'll be all right. Harvest worries me, even though it's months away."

She was Mordecai Mannheim's daughter and the question came easily to her. "How many bales are you hoping for, Massa?"

Startled, he asked, "How do you know to ask that?"

"Raised on the Mannheim place. We all knew how many bales Marse Mannheim hoped for."

"We planted five hundred acres in cotton."

"A bale an acre?"

"If all goes well."

She said, "Ever since I was a little gal, Marse Mannheim would say to me, 'Cotton is ten cents a pound. How much is that a bale?'"

Surprised again, he said, "Fifty dollars. I'd be pleased at fifty dollars."

"He'd say to me, 'If we make five hundred bales this year, how much will we clear?'"

"Twenty-five thousand dollars," he said. "That's the sum I pray for."

Her unease with him faded in reciting the familiar catechism of the cotton market.

He looked at her, more keenly than she liked. He said, "Every day, when my father came home, my mother would ask him, 'How is the business? How is the shop?' She didn't work in the shop—he didn't need her there—but she worried about it with him."

She asked, "Massa? How bad is the debt?"

"That ain't your worry," he said, but his face was shadowed.

"All of us worry about it. Like your mama worried about your daddy's business."

He hesitated, and pondered, like a man doing sums in his head. He said, "Three hundred bales would clear it."

She nodded.

"And five hundred would make me a good profit."

"Then we all hope and pray for five hundred," she said.

They both heard the sound of Adelaide's boots in the hallway. She put her head into the door. Her cheeks were pink, her hair was in a tangle, and there was mud on the hem of her dress. She'd been rambling. She said, "There you are, Rachel. Why are you sitting in the study with Mr. Kaltenbach?"

Henry said, "I asked her to sit with me, and we got to talking about the crop."

"Goodness, Henry, you could talk about the crop with my father, or with any of your friends in town. Why would you discuss it with your servant?"

"She was raised on the Mannheim place. She has a good head on her shoulders."

Adelaide said sharply, "Rachel, come upstairs with me, I want you to help me dress for dinner."

Rachel looked at Henry and said, "Begging your pardon, Massa."

Henry said, "Adelaide, let her linger for a moment."

"I need her. Rachel?"

Rachel felt them both tugging on her. It had nothing to do with her. They were tugging on each other. "Excuse me, Massa, I need to help Missus."

Henry did his best to compose himself. "You should go with your mistress."

As Rachel left the room with Adelaide, she looked behind her to see a slight figure, in a chair much too big for him, whiskey glass in his hand, studying the figured carpet at his feet. Forlorn. She knew that word in German, too. It meant "lost."

Adelaide pulled roughly on her arm. "Don't linger," she said, her voice unusually harsh. "Come along with me."

Chapter 10

Slaves in Egypt

Every day, Henry walked the fields with Charlie, and together they worried about the crop. They watched for rain and worried about too much rain. They inspected the plants to see how they grew, and rued the fact that the weeds grew with them. If Henry said, "The crop looks good, Charlie," Charlie would say, "Never know with cotton, Massa. Good one week, suffering the next." If Charlie said, "I do believe we'll manage those five hundred bales, Massa," Henry, echoing Charlie's caution, would say to him, "We won't know until it's harvested, Charlie."

Being a cotton planter brought a new set of worries that Henry had never known when he was a cotton farmer. Last year, Zeke had told his sons what to do, and his boys, obliging like himself, obeyed him. Zeke had told Henry what to do, and he did it without question, since Zeke knew how to plant and raise cotton, and Henry did not. This year, Henry owned eleven strangers, and a twelfth to drive them.

Early on, Henry asked Charlie if he used the whip.

"I don't like to," Charlie said. "Never made anyone work better, man, woman or mule. You don't whup a man because he's tired, or whup an expecting woman because she queasy, or whup a young 'un because he'd rather be playing than working. No, for all that, you act gentle and you coax. Sometimes you do whup, little as you like it."

"For what?" Henry asked.

"For fighting bad enough to hurt someone. Or for stealing. Or for running away. Then you whup. If you don't, the hands won't respect you as a Massa. They'll think they can fight, and steal, and try to run away. Can't have that. Can't run a place that way."

Henry said, "Have you whupped anyone?"

"On the Mannheim place, the overseer whupped. But I told him who to whup, and why." Charlie shook his head. "Hated doing it. Had to."

He and Charlie worried about the hands together. Charlie knew who he could rely on—Zeke and his family, still hardworking and obliging, and his own wife. He kept his eye on the "young 'uns," as he called the young unmarried hands. Salley and Harriet, who were sisters, steadied each other, and Harriet, who liked Davey, steadied him. Charlie fretted over Lydia, who was never inclined to work hard. She had told him that she wanted to be a house servant, but Charlie said to Henry, "I don't think that gal will work any better in the house than in the field. She balky like that mule Pretty. One day I put them together in the field and they can balk together." Lydia was the finest singer among his sweet-voiced slaves, with a pure soprano to rival anything Henry had heard in an opera house. When Lydia sang, all of the pout went out of her face.

Charlie worried more about Freddy, who was his cousin, and for whom he felt responsible. Freddy was eighteen, old enough to live with the bachelors, and he resisted Charlie's well-meaning efforts to take care of him. Charlie said, "He spend all his time with Micah, and follow after him like a pup. Try to drink as much as Micah, too. He a fool. He just a boy and Micah a grown man twice his size."

Micah, one of Mordecai Manheim's family of fiddlers, was even more talented than his father and brothers. He was in demand all over the county, and he had played at frolics and weddings as far away as Macon and Marietta, which made him worldlier than the other slaves. He could play a cotillion for country dancing, and he knew all of the Stephen Foster songs that Cass County loved, but he also knew serious music for the violin. Henry had heard him play Haydn and Mozart with great skill and great feeling. He had a prodigious musical memory and an uncanny ability to transpose any tune for the fiddle. Henry had once hummed him the melody of a Schumann song and he had immediately been able to play it.

Micah was paid for his playing, a dollar or two at a time, and he had saved enough money to buy himself an instrument. He kept it in its case when he wasn't playing, and treated it with great care. He had cuffed Tom just for touching it.

On a pleasant day in April, as the hands were chopping the cotton fields, Charlie said to Henry, "Need to talk to you, Massa." They walked away from the field, next to the trees that separated the fields from the house, where they were out of the hands' earshot. "Micah came to talk to me the other day. Asked me if he could hire out to fiddle on the Turner place at that frolic on Saturday. I ain't inclined to say yes."

Something was bothering Charlie. "Whatever you tell him, I won't naysay you, Charlie. But tell me why."

"Fiddling for pleasure. When Micah fiddle, he see his kin, he get a plate of barbecue, he flirt with all the gals from miles around, and he get a dollar or two to keep, all for pleasure."

"What's wrong with that, Charlie?"

"Wouldn't be a thing wrong if he worked hard enough to earn some pleasure. You've seen him." Micah could be tractable in the field, but after a Saturday of fiddling, he was slow and he was sulky. Charlie shook his head. "Won't reward him for dragging his feet. He work hard, he get to fiddle."

"He won't like it."

Charlie said darkly, "He play that fiddle just fine. But around here we don't need him to play the fiddle."

Early in April, Mordecai sent word to Henry that he wanted to see him about last year's crop. Henry hadn't been in Mordecai's house on business since he signed the papers that put him so deep in debt. In the study, Mordecai shook his hand, offered him a chair, and asked him if he wanted whiskey or brandy. They were gentlemen together. Mordecai didn't mind that he said no.

Mordecai said, "I sold your cotton for you. I thought you'd like to know what you cleared."

"Of course I would." As though he hadn't lain awake at night worrying about what cotton was bringing in Savannah, New Orleans, and London, since the day the last of the crop was baled.

"I've written it out for you and made a proper accounting of the sale. But I can tell you right now that you made a profit."

Henry was immediately wary. He said, "Spell it out for me."

"I got you sixty dollars a bale."

Over twelve thousand dollars. He waited to hear the rest.

"I took thirty percent in commission. Then you had some further expenses. The additional plows, the mules, and the supplies, since you needed corn and hog meat. And some lengths and shoes, I see. There was the charge for hiring three of my hands. All of that brings it down considerable."

"How much?"

"I'll give you the paper to show you. If you want to pay off the rest of the debt—that five thousand you owe me—you're left with about fifteen hundred."

All of that work, he thought. All of that worry. He looked at his hands, where he could still see the scars from picking cotton. Fifteen hundred dollars. Enough for next year's plows, mules, flour, coffee, and lengths and shoes for his new slaves.

"Don't look so downcast," Mordecai said genially. "You cleared the debt. You made a profit. You did all right."

Fifteen hundred dollars. And he was in debt for ten times that against this year's crop. "I suppose I did," he said slowly.

"You sure you don't want a drink?"

"I'm sure," he said. "Send over the account. I want to see it." He got up to leave and shook his father-in-law's hand.

When Rachel saw him—he took a glass of whiskey from her, and was glad of it—she said, "What did you hear from Marse Mannheim, Massa?"

"I found out how we did last year."

She was raised on the Mannheim place and she knew. She said ruefully, "Sixty dollars a bale, less Marse Mannheim's commission, and supplies, and whatever debt you had against the crop—what was left?"

"How did you know?"

She said, "Marse Mannheim use to quiz me every week about what we would realize. I knew it, growing up, like I knew the weather."

Rachel's face was round, with dimples that were prominent on her cheeks. The dimples reminded him of pretty girls he'd known in Germany. Since he first met her, he wondered how an African woman came to have dimples.

He shook his head. "Fifteen hundred dollars," he said, reminding himself. His start on a fortune.

She said, "If you grew up on the Mannheim place, you know Marse Mannheim for a man who looks to his own advantage. Not to anyone else's."

"Joe Meyer said so, too." He shook his head. "I should have known when he brought Mr. Johnson to Savannah to swear to me he made so much money he could buy that plantation in Mississippi."

She hesitated. He said, "Tell me what you know."

She took a deep breath. "Marse Johnson did all right on the place. Made some money there. But he didn't buy his place in Mississippi with the profit. He bought it with his inheritance."

Henry rarely got angry, but he was so angry that the room swam before his eyes in a red haze. The color rose high in his face. Rachel said, "I'm sorry, Massa."

She watched him pause, and breathe deeply, and cool himself. He said, "I asked you. I'm not angry with you."

"Massa, we still hope and pray for those five hundred bales. To clear the debt."

Still angry, Henry said, "Better than clear it. Make me a decent profit. Even if that buzzard sells it for me."

When he had time to reflect later, in the quiet of his room, he wondered how a house servant came to be so wise in the ways of the cotton market. She said that Marse Mannheim had quizzed her about it when she was growing up. Why would he do that for a slave girl who was his daughter's maid?

As a dry goods merchant's son, Henry had absorbed the dry goods trade. He knew how to judge a length by the way it felt in the hand, and could tell good cotton, silk or wool from inferior. He had learned how to bargain at a trade fair, and to get the best price so he could sell at a profit. He had learned how to beguile a customer to sell a length and the accoutrements that went with it: buttons and linen for a suit, lace and ribbons and trim for a dress. It had sunk into his bones.

What was Rachel to Mordecai Mannheim, that he had taught her to know the price of cotton, and to calculate the loss from commission and fees, and to understand the mechanism of debt and its shadow, financial ruin? Was he pleased to have a smart little slave who could figure the price of a bale, or was there a darker reason for him to encourage her to soak the business of cotton into her bones?

In Savannah, Henry had met the men of substance who had many slaves, and he had met the light-complected slaves who resembled them, who grew up in the house and knew the family secrets, and who learned to read and write because a tormented father couldn't deny them. He had heard about the masters who freed slave women and slave children in the wills that were read after they died. Everyone knew, but no one said, that the women were their wives, in fact if not in law, and the children were their flesh and blood.

Late that night, unable to sleep, Henry realized why Rachel's dimples looked so familiar. He had seen them earlier that day on a less lovely and much more corpulent face. They were Mordecai's.

As Passover approached, Rachel was the one who swept out the kitchen, took out the special plates, and explained the Passover rules to Minnie. Minnie groaned. "Not more of them kosher laws. No flour and no corn and no rice. Whatever will I give them?"

"Get matzah from Savannah. Eat it like biscuit and grind it up for meal. And taters. How many taters have we got left?"

Minnie glared at her. "A week of taters in plantation house. From vol-au-vent to pone to taters. Cook like a field hand, and eat like one, too."

"Reminds them. That they were slaves in Egypt."

A few days before the holiday, Henry watched Rachel make *haroses*, chopping the apples and walnuts, adding cinnamon and wine. She asked, "Do you want to taste it, Marse Henry? Tell me if it's right?"

"No, Rachel, I trust that it's right."

"You're sure? Want it to remind you of home."

Home, where Jews had every reason to remember their oppression in Egypt, and to be angry about their persecution in Germany. "I'm not sure I want to remember home on Passover."

"Ain't like you, Marse Henry. Don't you care for Passover?"

"I feel different about it. Now that I'm a cotton planter."

She had rarely looked troubled in his presence, but now she did. She asked, "Massa, why do Jews remember Egypt?"

"We have long memories."

She raised her eyes to his—he had never realized how much they were like Adelaide's—and said, "If you got free, why don't you glory in it? Forget that you were in slavery?"

Very low, he said, "Could you ever forget?"

She turned away. To his dismay, she put her hand to her face.

"Rachel," he said, troubled and tender, as he always was when someone was in pain.

She turned her face to his and her eyes glistened with tears. "Massa," she said, her voice choked. "Don't speak of it."

He would not. But he would think about it, and let her tears trouble him.

Later that day, as Henry and Charlie walked through the field together, Henry asked, "Did the hands take a rest on Passover on the Mannheim place?"

"No, Marse Henry. Why should they? They ain't Israelites."

"I'd like to give them the day. Just the first day of the holiday."

Charlie, who still had difficulty meeting his eyes, stared at him in astonishment. "Massa, if you give them the day, it will cause you all kinds of trouble."

"Taking a day of rest?"

"Remembering the Exodus from Egypt."

A day for them to think about their condition as slaves. Charlie was right. It would cause him all kinds of trouble. But his conscience troubled him so much that he said, "I want to do it."

Charlie said miserably, "Massa, I've never naysayed you, and I won't now. But I worry that you'll rue the moment you set your mind on this."

As the Kaltenbachs recited the words of the Seder, telling each other the familiar story of liberation from slavery in Egypt, Rachel, their slave and sister, leaned against the wall, waiting to serve the meal. Henry had asked Rachel if she wanted Minnie to serve in her place. She said no.

Henry suffered through the Seder. He had never been so relieved to say its closing words. But he looked at Rachel, whose tired face filled with emotion as she listened: "This year we are slaves. Next year we will be free. This year in exile. Next year in Jerusalem!"

For a slave, those words were not a metaphor.

He got up from the table and said curtly to Adelaide, "I need some air," and he quickly left the room to walk out the door and onto the piazza.

This late in April, the day's warmth had lingered into the night. The magnolia had been in full bloom for weeks now, and its fragrance filled the air. The frogs had woken from their winter sleep and they trilled and boomed from the wet places by the rivulets in the woods. The owls had woken too. Their hooting cries reminded him of his first night in the old place, and of Minnie's pleasure in their nests.

He could hear the sound of the fiddle from the slaves' cabins. He stopped, hidden behind the trees between the house and the cabins, and watched his slaves in the bright light cast by the moon.

Micah sat on the steps of his cabin, Lydia at his side and Freddy at his feet. Micah had put down his fiddle. Freddy passed him the whiskey jug and Micah took it and drank deeply from it.

Salley and Harriet sat on the steps of their cabin, Davey with them. All three looked tentative, not sure whether to enjoy the music.

As Henry watched, Charlie came out of his cabin and walked over the bachelors'.

Micah raised the jug and asked Charlie, "Some for you, man?"

Charlie stood at the foot of the steps, his arms crossed. He said, "You quit that ruckus. People trying to sleep."

Micah said, "Sleep tomorrow. Some people want a little pleasure tonight."

"Fiddling for pleasure after work is done."

"Why not some pleasure tonight? Since we free men for a day tomorrow, in honor of Passover?"

Charlie said, "You free to make a fool of yourself, any day."

"Special day! To remember the Israelites getting free from slavery in Egypt!" Micah laughed. In the dusk his eyes and his smile were very white. "Hope for the day when we niggers get free, too!"

Henry thought, This isn't for my ears or eyes. If he moved they would hear him and know he was there. He stood still.

Charlie said, "Don't even speak of it."

But Micah was drunk and he didn't care who knew it. "If I ever get free I'll go to New Orleans and I'll make a living playing the fiddle." He put his arm around Lydia and hugged her to him. "Take Lydia with me, see if she can make a living as a singer. She sings almost as pretty as I play." He grinned at Freddy. "You want to come with us? Be a free man in New Orleans with us?"

Charlie said, "You quit that."

"Don't people come from miles around to hear me play? Didn't they tell Marse Mannheim, 'That nigger of yours can play like Paganini!'" He snorted. "Paganini a virtuoso of the violin. And what am I? A virtuoso of the hoe."

Henry felt worse than he had during the Seder. What would it be like, to have Paganini's skill and Paganini's soul and to be a slave whose life would be an endless round of chopping and picking cotton? He stepped from his hiding place and walked to the cabins, where Micah could see him.

"Massa!" Micah called out, his tone mocking. "Massa here! I play something for you, Massa!"

He rose, walked down the steps, and faced Henry as though he were on the stage. He tucked the violin under his chin and picked up his bow. Henry had never realized how big Micah was. He stood a head taller than his master and he outweighed him, too. Henry thought, He could pick up a hoe and strike me dead the way Moses killed the taskmaster who beat a slave.

Micah played a Schumann lied that Henry had once hummed for him, Henry's favorite Schumann lied, set to Heine's poetry. The lovely music chilled Henry. It was the accompaniment to thoughts that made him sick at heart. Micah hates being a slave, he thought. He hates me for owning him. He sees into me because he hates me so much. Chilled to the bone, Henry wondered about his tractable slaves, like Salley, Harriet, and Davey. Do they hate me, too? He wondered about Charlie, who had always seemed to be his ally. Did Charlie hate him?

When Micah finished, he took a bow, as though he were waiting for his audience to applaud. Master and slaves alike were silent. Charlie strode up to Micah and said, "Frolic over now."

Micah spoke to Charlie, but he addressed the audience that was too frightened for applause. "Listen to you. You Marse Henry's dog, just like we are. You forget, because he give you a scrap and a bone and pet you on the head, that you a nigger and a slave, just like the rest of us."

Charlie said, "You act ungovernable, you know what we do."

Micah grinned. "Are you going to whup me? I thought we didn't whup around here." He looked insolently at Charlie, and even more insolently at his soft-hearted master.

Charlie rushed Micah, trying to grab the front of his shirt. Micah cried out, "The fiddle! Don't hurt the fiddle!"

Charlie had a fistful of Micah's shirt in his hands, and he was close enough to spit in Micah's face. He said, "Damn you and your fiddle."

Charlie would do it. He would wrest the fiddle from Micah and break it in two. Henry ran up to his struggling slaves, men much bigger and stronger than he was, and said, as masterfully as he could, "Charlie, don't break the damn fiddle. How ungovernable do you think he'll be after that?"

Abashed, Charlie let go Micah's shirt, and astonished, Micah stepped back, his fiddle and bow still in his hands.

Henry said curtly, "That's enough. All of you, go into your cabins and get some sleep."

Micah picked up the jug of whiskey. "Frolic over tonight," he said to Freddy, and both of them went into the bachelors' cabin.

The day of Passover rest was quiet, but the next day, when the hands went back to work, Micah began to sing. Micah sang, "Steal away, steal away, steal away to Jesus…Steal away, steal away home." Lydia didn't join them. But Freddy, who followed after Micah and imitated him whenever he could, sang in harmony with him.

Charlie laid down his hoe and said sharply to both of them, "Massa listening! You sing something else."

They stopped. Micah said, "Thought you wanted us to sing."

Charlie said, "What did I say to you? About not giving me reason?"

Micah put down his hoe. His body tensed and he seemed to grow even taller and broader. Charlie hit Micah across the face, not hard enough to hurt, but hard enough to shame. Micah tightened his jaw and thought about returning the blow, but he did not. Then Charlie turned to Freddy and slapped him hard enough to leave a mark on the light brown skin. "You do that again," he said, in the tone of an angry father, "and I'll hurt you worse than that." The other slaves put their heads down and hoed as though they had seen nothing and heard nothing.

Henry walked over to Charlie—he had never seen Charlie so badly shook up—and said, "Walk with me a little." When they were out of earshot of anyone in the field, Henry asked, "What was that about, Charlie?"

Charlie shook his head. He was afraid, and Henry had never seen him look afraid before. "Won't have them singing that."

"Why not?"

Charlie, who had just started to look him in the eye when they talked, dropped his eyes and began to mumble. "Can't say, Massa."

Henry, a reader of poetry, knew a metaphor when he heard one. He said slowly, "Is that song about running away? Are you worried that someone might run away?"

Charlie didn't look up. He couldn't say it, not even to a master as benevolent as Henry. And even as benevolent a master as Henry, now that he knew himself, couldn't help, either. There were problems that no amount of coaxing could fix. Master and taskmaster thought of the meaning of Passover and looked at each other in wordless worry.

That day Henry thought about things that gave him no peace. It didn't matter that slavery on the Kaltenbach place was benevolent, and that he himself was known to all the slaves as decent and kind. It was still slavery. And for his slaves—he suspected that Micah was the only one who said so, but they all felt so—freedom was better than the kindest form of slavery.

He couldn't free them. They were his main capital asset, and exploiting their labor was the only way that he would ever get out of debt. And if, God forbid, he couldn't get out of debt, they were the only thing he could sell to save himself from bankruptcy.

Slavery wasn't right. It gave him pain to own Minnie, and Zeke, and Charlie. It gave him pain to own all of his slaves. But as a slaveowner, he was bound himself—bound to the debt, bound to the crop, bound to the hands who would plant it and harvest it for him.

He wished that there were someone he could talk to, the way he talked to Rachel about the crop and the debt. How could he ask a slave if she wanted to be free?

When she came into the study to pour him a glass of whiskey, she asked, "Is there trouble, Massa?"

"Why do you ask?"

"Have a downcast look today, Massa."

He said, "Rachel, did anyone on the Mannheim place ever run away?"

She hesitated and said, "Not to my recollection, Massa."

"Why not? Surely not for love of Mr. Mannheim."

Mordecai's daughter wouldn't be drawn today. She said slowly, "Marse Mannheim sells slaves. Every so often he'd bring a coffle through, people he bought in Savannah, bound for Mississippi. Everyone on that place knew that if you ran, you'd be in the next coffle." She looked with worry on her face. "What's the trouble, Massa?" she asked, even though she knew.

He shook his head, and she knew what he meant—"I can't tell you." She said, "Shouldn't have asked you, Massa."

The day after Micah sang about stealing away, Charlie came to him first thing with a grim face that was the gray color of a dark face in deep distress. He said, "Freddy gone."

After all of their worry about Micah, it was Freddy who had stolen away. Henry had never suspected Freddy, who seemed so shy and so boyish. "What do we do?"

"Send out word. Let the patroller find him."

"Will they hurt him?"

"We tell them not to set the dogs to find him."

Two days later, the patroller, who was also the county sheriff, brought Freddy back. Freddy's shirt and trousers were filthy with coppery dust and dirt, and he'd lost his shoes. Even though he kept his eyes down, Henry could see that his face was bruised and bleeding as though he'd been roughly handled. His feet were shackled and he walked with difficulty. The patroller yanked on his arm to make him move faster. He found Henry at the edge of the cotton field, and as every slave on the place watched from the corners of their eyes, he shoved Freddy toward Henry and asked, "Is this your boy?"

Henry said, "He's my hand."

The patroller said, "Best lock him up until you punish him."

Charlie put his hand roughly on Freddy's shoulder. Without speaking, he pulled Freddy along with him and shoved him into his cabin. He said to

Henry, "We get Zeke to padlock that door. Shackles ain't enough to hold him."

Henry felt cold and sick. He said, "Do we whup?"

Charlie's face was set and gray. "For this we whup." At his master's stricken look, he said, "Otherwise they all think they can run away."

"Do you want me to do it?" Henry asked.

"No. Overseer does it. Up to me."

"How many lashes?"

"Ten."

Henry thought of how slight Freddy was and how fragile he seemed. He thought of how protective Charlie had always been. "We'll kill him."

Charlie shook his head. "Enough to scare the others. Enough to hurt. Ten strokes."

Later that day, Charlie asked Zeke to raise a post taller than a man. Charlie stretched his hands over his head to show Zeke how tall it needed to be. Henry forced himself to watch as Zeke built a whipping post for Freddy. As he worked, Zeke's pleasant, obliging face was grim and gray, like Charlie's.

The next day, the last day of Passover, all of the slaves, even Rachel and Minnie, were gathered to watch, and Adelaide came to join Henry, to show that Missus and Marse were of one mind about this punishment. Charlie led Freddy, whose feet were still shackled, to the post. Charlie stripped Freddy of his shirt—he still wore the shirt streaked with red dirt from his escape—and he pulled Freddy's hands around the post and tied them together with a rope. Everyone could see how tightly he pulled the rope.

Charlie took out the horsewhip. The sight of it made Henry blanch, because no one had ever used it on the horse. Charlie raised the whip and he brought it down on the slender light-brown back. The whip whistled through the air and landed on the flesh with a sickening thud. The first lash raised a welt. Freddy didn't pretend to be brave. He cried out in pain as the whip hit his skin. The second lash drew blood.

Charlie didn't spare Freddy. He put his own anger into Freddy's punishment. They all listened to the rhythm of the whip: the whistle, the thud, the blow, and the cry.

After the sixth lash, Freddy fainted. Charlie stopped and turned to Henry. "Should I revive him and finish up, Massa?"

Henry was appalled. "No. He's been punished enough." He looked at Charlie. "Cut him down and let Minnie tend to him."

Henry didn't linger on the faces of his slaves, but he saw the same expression on every face. No one dared to look him in the eye, and their downcast faces were ashy with anger and fear. On a place where benevolence had been the rule, ten lashes cut deeper than brutality every day.

He went into the house and sat heavily in the chair by the unlit hearth in his study. From his seat, he could see the trees that separated the house from the fields. On warm days, with the windows open, he could hear his slaves singing as they worked. Today, as they worked, they were silent.

Adelaide stepped quietly into the room. Instead of sitting in the opposite chair, she sank to her knees before him and reached to clasp his hands. "What's wrong, Henry?" she said, her face full of concern.

He said, "To own slaves is wrong."

She looked at him with puzzled eyes. "Without slaves, how could you grow cotton?"

Her solicitude was sweet, but it didn't lessen the bitterness of the day. "To punish a slave with a whip is wrong, too."

She pressed his hands with her own. "No master likes to use the whip. But they have to fear you, sometimes. Otherwise they'd all run away."

He shook his head.

"I'll ask Rachel to bring you something. Coffee and something to eat. You'll feel better."

When Rachel came in, carrying a tray, she set it down without speaking, and kept her eyes on the floor, as she had not done for weeks.

"Rachel," he said, pleading. "Please look at me."

She raised her eyes to his and he met them. They were so dark that the iris melted into the pupil, and they were blank and expressionless.

If she never teased him again, never laughed in his presence again, never looked him in the face again, he deserved it. He had abused every slave on the place.

After the whipping, Rachel brooded over how to act around Marse Henry. She had hoped for his kindness, and had been encouraged when he first became her master. When he whipped Freddy, she felt her early hope drain away. It was hard to speak to him and serve him, because she was so frightened, and so angry to be frightened. It was worse than Marse Mannheim, who had never considered her. Marse Henry had been kind to her. It bothered her greatly that he might be as heartless as any other master.

She wished that she could talk to Charlie as she had when they were children, before love and loss intervened in their friendship. She missed Charlie's broad shoulder more than she wanted to admit. But it was too hard to see him again and to remember the way that the Mannheims had stood in the way of their happiness.

On the Sunday after the whipping, she went to meeting, along with a group of chastened slaves. Afterwards, in the thinned crowd, she lingered to talk to Charlie. The air was sweet and the sun promised summer's warmth, but it cheered and warmed no one today.

"How is your wife?" she asked, since she hadn't come to meeting.

"Josey cutting a tooth. Fussed all night. Becky ain't feeling well herself. Queasy all the time now. So they stayed at home." He asked, "How are you? Look bothered."

"We all bothered by that whupping."

His face tightened the way it always did when he considered something difficult. "A bad business all around." He put his hand on her shoulder, his driver's gesture, for anyone who might be watching. "Walk home with me?"

They walked along the path worn through the pines by the slaves who knew the secret of the meeting house. They listened to the birds calling. It was the time of year for birds to mate and nest. He said, "Do you want to duck into the woods, so you can speak your piece private?"

Her eyes stung. "How did you know?"

"You always came to me when there was trouble in the big house. Different house, same kind of trouble."

They stood in a small space between two tall pines, where the branches filtered the summer's light and dappled his face. She said, "I thought he was a good Massa. Now I ain't so sure."

He faced her, too far away to touch her, and said, "Sometimes a good Massa has to whup."

"Did he order you? To whup?"

Charlie shook his head. "He was loath to do it. I had to goad him."

Surprised, she said, "It was you?"

"If it ease you, he didn't want to whup. And you saw that he didn't like it. Cut Freddy down after six strokes. Send Minnie to tend to him. Turn green, like white folks do when they sick, and go into the house to drink early in the day. Tender hearted."

"Why did he do it?"

Charlie's voice rose. "He kind. He decent. He tender hearted. And he want five hundred bales to take to market. Can't get five hundred bales unless everybody work. Sometimes they work because they want to and sometimes they work because they afraid not to."

"Charlie. You mad. Ain't like you to be mad."

"All of us mad. I'm mad at myself and they all mad at me." He sighed. "Easier to be mad at the nigger driver than at Massa."

She wanted to put her hand on his arm, a gesture that had always calmed him when he saw things at their darkest, but she didn't dare. She asked, "How they acting?"

"Freddy won't say a word to me. Micah call me Massa's pet dog."

"That's mean."

"I ain't his pet dog," he says. "Massa treat me like a mule, useful to him." He leaned forward a little, his face animated by strong feeling. "Now you a pet to Miss Adelaide. A pet ain't useful. A pet a plaything. She coddle you, and cuff you, for her own pleasure. Pet dog! Ain't right to treat a grown woman like a little dog that sets in your lap."

"Charlie, that ain't exactly fair," she said, upset.

He shook his head. "It's still bitter, what happened between you and me. And how them Mannheims stood in your way to take away your happiness."

Our happiness, she thought. "Don't even speak of it."

He looked at her stricken face and realized how he'd hurt her. He said, "I don't care much for Missus Adelaide, but I care about you. Always have. Still do."

She took a deep breath. It wouldn't do to cry. He couldn't comfort her, not even the way he used to, with a brotherly broad shoulder. She said, "It's over and done with, Charlie. You married, you settled, you happy with Becky. Don't know if I'll ever be settled or happy, but ain't up to me, and it certainly ain't up to you."

They walked back to the Kaltenbach place in silence, and parted—he to his cabin and she to her burden in the big house. She wasn't comforted. Charlie couldn't help her. He cloaked his disappointment with Marse Henry in anger. She wrapped hers in sadness.

In mid-July, the rain began with a storm. Unlike the winter rain, which came out of a gray sky, a storm descended from a sky variegated with black and green. The air turned heavy and dense and the temperature dropped by ten degrees. Lightning hit the ground in bolts so powerful that they singed the earth. Where it hit a stand of cotton, the smell of scorch lingered in the air. When the rain came, it was cold and drenching. The fields ran with water.

The storm passed, but it continued to rain. It rained steadily for two weeks, sometimes a drizzle, occasionally a downpour, but most often a steady rain. It stayed cool.

While it was still raining, Charlie and Henry walked the fields. The soil had turned to red mud that dirtied their boots and crusted the hems of their pants. Charlie picked up a handful of earth and let it run like soup through his fingers. He said, "I don't like this weather." He reached for a half-opened boll and touched the exposed fluff. He said, "Hope it stops raining. Hope it gets warm again." He found unopened buds and looked at those too.

"What are you looking for, Charlie?"

"Worried about boll rot, Massa."

"What's boll rot?"

"Bolls get wet and they don't dry out, they get mold, just like cloth does. Buds can mold, too. If the bolls get wet enough, lint locks up and seeds start to sprout right in the boll. It's all worrisome, Massa. Moldy boll, hardlocked boll, sprouted boll is ruined."

Henry looked up at the gray sky. "Can we fix it?"

"Pray for sunshine."

It rained for another week. At the beginning of August, a few weeks before harvest, the rain stopped, but the temperature didn't rise, and the sun didn't come out.

Charlie and Henry walked through the muddy fields to look at the bolls. Charlie checked a plant at random. His face was grim. "Look, Massa."

It was a full-formed boll that should have been ready for picking. But it was full of sprouted seeds, and at its base was an ugly clump of black mold.

Henry said, "Can we harvest that?"

Charlie felt the part of the boll that was white. "It's hardlocked, Massa. Never fluffed. Can't harvest it."

"What about the buds?"

Charlie looked for an unopened bud and found a cluster. "Look, Massa." The buds were streaked with mold.

"Will it flower?"

"Might. Won't be bright. Best you can hope for is stained cotton. Lower grade than middling white."

"What does that mean?"

"Less per pound, Massa."

Henry said, "We won't make five hundred bales."

"We'll lose some of the crop. Can't tell yet how much. Have to study it, look at more than a few plants, look at all the fields."

They walked up and down the rows, their boots squelching in the mud, looking at the cotton plants. Half the plants they touched had some kind of damage, whether it was mold, hardlock, or sprouting. Buds and bolls were equally affected. They walked through each of the fields, moving slowly along the rows. In each field, it was the same: about half of the plants were too badly damaged to harvest.

Henry said, "Charlie, what do you think? How much have we lost?"

"About half, Massa."

"How many bales, do you think?"

"Won't swear to it, but I think we'll be lucky to harvest two hundred and fifty. Might be a little more, could be a little less."

"And it will be lower grade than last year."

"Won't know for sure until it's picked, but I'd say it's likely, Massa."

Henry was wet through, and he felt cold and sick, as though he were coming down with a chill. Two hundred and fifty bales.

Charlie said, "Massa? Only one good thing about this."

"Whatever it is, it's cold comfort."

"It ain't black rot or armyworm. Black rot, gets the roots, gets into the soil and stays there. Armyworm, that can come back year after year." He looked at Henry's stricken face. "Boll rot don't come back next year. If we have good weather, we'll be all right."

"Next year." Another year of debt. Another year of borrowing against the crop. Another year bound to Mordecai Mannheim.

He walked slowly back from the field. He couldn't bear the thought of going into the house, the silent house that he had gone so heavily into debt to build for the wife who had never warmed to him. He walked into the kitchen instead, where Rachel and Minnie were eating pone and cowpeas for their lunch.

When Minnie saw him, she put down her fork and said, "Massa, you wet through."

He sat heavily in one of the pine chairs and said, "I'll be all right."

Minnie said, "You go in the house and change your clothes. Rachel can dry and brush those for you."

"In a moment."

Minnie said, "Massa, what's the matter?"

He took off his sodden hat and wiped his forehead with his sodden sleeve. He said, "The crop has boll rot."

Rachel had said little to him since Freddy's whipping. Now she asked matter-of-factly, "How bad is it, Massa?"

"Charlie thinks we'll lose about half."

Rachel said, "Two hundred and fifty bales."

Minnie's eyes went wide. She grabbed Rachel's arm. She said in alarm, "Massa, does that mean we'll be in debt? Will we get busted up for debt?"

Henry hesitated. Rachel answered for him. She said gently to Minnie, "Marse Mannheim doesn't want us to get busted up for debt. He'll let us carry the debt and pay it off when next year's crop comes in."

"Don't want to get busted up for debt," Minnie said, so upset that her eyes filled with tears.

Henry said, "I believe I will go inside and change my clothes. I'm soaked to the skin." He rose heavily, as though his joints hurt him, and went into the house.

Fifteen minutes later, Rachel found him sitting in his study, still in his wet clothes, staring at the hearth.

"Would you like a glass of whiskey, Massa?"

He shook his head. "Rachel, please sit with me and talk to me."

She obeyed him. She sat.

He said, "What you told Minnie—was that sugar to make her feel better, or is it true?"

This was cotton business, their common interest and their common bond. She took a deep breath. "Marse Mannheim wants his money back. Ain't no advantage to him to ruin you."

He said, "Charlie told me that whatever we harvest won't be middling white. Less per pound. How much less?"

The angry slave and the planter's daughter warred within her. She answered as a Mannheim. "Depends on the grade. You won't know until it's graded."

He rubbed his face with his hands. He said, "Two hundred and fifty bales of stained cotton."

"You ain't ruined," she said. "Just set back."

He groaned. "I'll be in debt to Mordecai Mannheim for the rest of my life," he said.

"Don't think so," said Mordecai Mannheim's daughter.

A few weeks after the whipping, Rachel found her mistress bent over the chamber pot, retching. Rachel poured her a glass of water and gave her a cloth. Adelaide rinsed out her mouth and wiped her face. She said, "Nothing tastes right going down, and it all comes back up. It's worst in the mornings, but I feel queasy all the time now."

Rachel had her own idea, but she called for Minnie. Minnie felt Adelaide's belly and asked, "How long since you last had your monthlies?"

"A few months," Adelaide said.

Minnie was pleased. "Baby took root this time. We still watch, and worry. But you about three months gone, and that's a good sign."

Adelaide put her hand on her still-flat belly and looked grave. "Will it be all right? Will I be all right?"

"Missus Adelaide, don't know what's up to God. But the rest, we do whatever we can to keep this baby where it belong. Until it ready to come out."

When Minnie left, Adelaide sat on the edge of her bed and shivered. "Rachel, I'm afraid," she said. "The first one—the one I lost—"

Rachel felt weary. But Adelaide needed her, and called to her as a sister and not a slave. Worry and envy warred in her as she put her arms around Adelaide.

Adelaide pressed her face against Rachel's chest like a child seeking comfort. "Will you help me?" she whispered. "Will you take care of me?"

Rachel laid her cheek against the top of Adelaide's head. Her sister's thick dark hair was soft against her skin. She sighed. "Of course I will," she promised.

That night, Adelaide asked Henry to come to her room, and when he lay beside her, she said, "I have something I need to tell you."

"What is it?"

What did her friends say? "I'm in a delicate condition," she said, glad of the dark that hid the embarrassment on her face.

Her husband, who had been fluent in English for years now, said in a puzzled tone, "What is it, Adelaide? Are you ill?"

It was hard to speak plain about this. "I'm expecting a baby," she said.

He laughed. She heard joy in it. "When will it come?"

"Minnie says in February."

"That's wonderful news!" He reached out his hand to stroke her cheek.

Suddenly she couldn't control the tears. She began to sob. He put his arms around her. His voice full of concern, he said, "What is it, *liebchen*? I know that women feel afraid, especially the first time—"

"I'm afraid I'll lose it."

He hugged her close. "We'll call for the doctor—you'll have Minnie to help you, and Rachel—"

"I lost the first one."

"The first one? When was that?"

"Two months after we were married."

Silence. Then a low, stunned voice. "Why didn't you tell me?"

"What good would it have done?"

"I could have helped you somehow—comforted you—"

She couldn't bear his embrace or his kindness. She pulled away and covered her face as she sobbed. "Leave me alone."

Chapter 11

People of the Book

When Rachel walked into Marse Henry's study, the newest *Savannah Republican* lay on the desk. It had already been opened, read, and re-folded. Even as neat a man as Marse Henry couldn't make the paper lay flat again. Since it was harvest, he was in the field with Charlie, and unlikely to return to the house until noontime. He would never know that she had unfolded it. She gave in to the temptation to sit at the desk and to read the news of the world, the bad with the good.

On the front page were the words "Insurrection at Harper's Ferry." She read, first with interest, then with fascination, then with horror, about the raid on the federal arsenal at Harper's Ferry in Virginia. John Brown, the firebrand of Bleeding Kansas, had organized a party of men to raid the arsenal, with the intention of arming the slaves of Virginia and inciting a revolt to end slavery. He had been captured by the Virginia militia and was now in prison, awaiting trial for treason.

Rachel stared out the window at the pine grove that separated the house from the cotton fields. This late in October, the sun was no longer summer-strong, but the air was still warm and sweet. She could hear the birds calling: Pee-wee! Pee-wee! She could hear the field hands, who looked forward to the corn harvest that would end the work year, singing: "Shuck that corn before you eat. . ."

She tried to imagine a revolt on this place, the shots ringing out, the house and fields in flames, death. . . The thought made her feel sick at her stomach. She could not. She re-read the newspaper report, making sure she hadn't missed anything, her hands trembling.

John Brown's war was a war to end slavery. Even if slaves didn't talk about being free—unless they were reckless or drunk, as Micah had been—they thought about it. They sang about it, stealthily, in the field and at meeting. They dreamed about it. They whispered among themselves about people who followed the drinking gourd to freedom. They spoke low about the news they heard from people who could read, about the debate over slavery in the North.

What would freedom look like? Beyond being free of the command of Marse and Missus?

She would be free every moment of every day, she thought. She would get up when she was ready. Even if she got up early, it would be because she wanted to. She would buy her own dresses, in silk and satin, not just in a slave's calico. She might even wear a corset, if she felt like it. She would eat marmalade every day.

Those were a child's dreams. What would a grown woman do with her freedom?

She would have her own house, and keep it as she liked. She would come and go as she pleased—to Savannah, or New Orleans, or New York, as far as the train would take her. She would make her way in the world—she didn't know how, but there would be a way—and be paid for it, money to keep. She would stop pretending that she couldn't read or write. She would buy books for her own, and she would have the leisure to read them. She would marry, if she met the right man, without fear that either of them would ever be parted by being sold away.

Freedom wouldn't guarantee her a life of wealth, or ease, or even happiness. But it would give her the power to choose, every day, how she would live her life. She closed her eyes, dizzy with the thought.

When she read the newspaper in Marse Mannheim's study, she had plenty of warning—Marse Mannheim had a heavy tread. Marse Henry's step was silent and he was in the room before she could lift her head from the pages and pretend she'd been dusting.

He didn't speak, and her heart began to pound, so fast she felt sickened. He could see that she'd been reading, and since he'd already seen the paper himself, he knew full well what she'd read in it.

She said, "I know it's against the law. Will you whup me for it?"

Sadness spread over his face. "Not for reading," he said. "Never for reading." When he spoke, his tone was one of gentle curiosity. "How did you learn to read?"

The relief was as sickening as the fear. She thought she might faint. She was still trembling when she said, "Missus Adelaide taught me when we were little girls together."

"And you got a beating for it."

"So did she."

"Yours worse than hers, I'd bet." Sympathy flickered over his face.

Rachel took a deep breath. She surveyed the back wall, which was full of bookshelves. "So many books," she said. "Have you read them all?"

"Most of them," he said. "These books were one thing I don't regret going into debt for."

"How much do books cost?"

"The Mannheim question," he said, teasing. "Less if they're bound in paper and more if they're bound in leather. I like the leather best. It feels better in your hands." He walked to the bookshelf behind the desk—the one he could reach if he moved the chair—and looked at the books. He was so close to her that she could smell the eau-de-cologne on his skin. He plucked a book from the shelf and handed it to her. She looked at the spine. "Charles Dickens. *A Christmas Carol*," she read.

"I read that to Zeke and Minnie last year at Christmas."

She handled the book, hefted it, brought it to her nose and smelled the leather. She kept the book between her hands, reluctant to let it go. She asked, "Did they like it?"

"Minnie wanted me to read her all of Charles Dickens."

She relinquished the book so he could put it back on the shelf.

He said, "We'll keep the reading a secret." He gestured toward the shelves.

She looked down at the desk, where the paper's headline was black and alarming enough to read at a distance. He reread it too. He said softly, "It's very troubling."

Wary again, she said, "Yes, Massa."

He gestured at the paper, his face full of distress, and said, "This isn't right, but neither is slavery."

She had never heard a slaveowner admit to such a thing. She had never thought that a master might hate slavery. In her astonishment, she felt as she did at the close of the Passover service, dizzy with the promise of freedom. She tried to compose herself, but when she spoke she was as reckless as he had been. "Massa, do you think that slavery will ever be over?"

She had never seen him look so sad. "I wish I knew," he said.

As soon as news of Adelaide's condition spread to the ladies of the county, they came to visit. Mrs. Turner, whose pregnancies were safely in the past, reassured her that she would have an easy time, and Mrs. Levy's face lit up as she talked about the joy her children had brought her. Rosa came, her face pale and worried, and held her daughter's hands as she recalled how sick she had felt and how frightened she had been. After each of these visits, Adelaide told Rachel, "If she weren't my mama, I'd tell her to stay home and leave me alone until it's born."

Rachel had to bite her lips to keep from saying something she shouldn't. She was full of regret again, and it galled her that Adelaide was expecting a baby. She forgot that she had refused Octavian in Savannah, and nearly refused Charlie, because of her fear of bearing a child that would be a slave. She brought the ladies of the county tea and cookies, and stood in the corner of the room, clenching her fists into the folds of her skirt as they fussed over Adelaide's "delicate condition".

Within a few weeks after Adelaide realized that she was expecting a baby, she began to feel sicker than she had ever felt in her life. It was the "indisposition"—her lady visitors were too polite to mention nausea and vomiting—and she was indisposed from her third month. Some ladies, her callers told her, felt better in the "delicate condition," but she did not. The headaches that plagued her after she returned from Savannah returned, worse than ever. There was laudanum for headaches, but she feared that it might not be good for a baby. When she was stricken, she lay flat, getting up only to be "indisposed" into the chamberpot.

By her fourth month every part of her body seemed to swell. Not just her middle, although that was bad enough, meaning that Rachel had to make her a corset designed for an expecting woman a little early, and let out all of her dresses to accommodate it. A few weeks later it didn't matter. Her fingers swelled so badly that she could no longer wear her wedding ring, and her feet enlarged so that the only thing that fit were her bedroom slippers.

Just before her sixth month, when ladies withdrew to lie down until confinement, she woke to find blood on her nightdress. Neither her callers, who were free with the details of the "delicate condition", nor Minnie, had said anything about bleeding. When Rachel came in that morning, to set down the breakfast tray, she asked Rachel to get Minnie.

Moments later, an alarmed Minnie flew into her room. She said, "If you bleeding, something ain't right. If you don't mind, ma'am, let me feel your belly."

Minnie put her hands on Adelaide's swollen middle and felt the child through her wrapper and her skin. She looked relieved. She said, "Baby ain't dropped. Riding high, just where it should be."

Adelaide asked, "What does that mean?"

Minnie said, "Baby ain't ready to come yet, and won't come early."

"Is that good?"

"It sure is, ma'am. Now you give me your hand. I want to see if it's swollen."

Adelaide extended her hand. Minnie laid it in her palm and looked at Adelaide's fingers. She asked, "Are your feet swollen, too, ma'am?"

Adelaide said, "Yes."

"Raise up your nightdress so I can see your legs." She looked at the swollen flesh of Adelaide's ankle. Both Adelaide and Rachel watched as Minnie pressed her finger into the flesh of Adelaide's calf and looked at the dent that didn't go away. Minnie frowned. "Ma'am, you holding water. You got dropsy."

"Is that bad?"

"For a carrying woman, it means you could lose the baby. You need to lie down, and stay in bed, until that baby's born."

She'd felt too sick to go out, or come downstairs much, but being confined to bed upset her. "Not get up at all?"

Minnie said, "Ma'am, you can sit upright to eat, or to read, and you can surely get out of bed to use the chamberpot. But otherwise, you need to stay in bed, with your feet resting on a heap of pillows to let that water drain off. Otherwise, it bad for you and bad for the baby."

Minnie's tone was matter-of-fact and concerned at the same time, but it frightened her. "How bad?"

"Ma'am, did your mama ever lose a baby when she was carrying?"

As she knew so well, since her mother had come here every week since she heard the news, reminding her and alarming her. "She lost two."

"You lie down and get those feet up. We do everything we can to make sure that baby come when it should. Not sooner."

After Minnie left, Adelaide sat heavily on the bed. Rachel said, "You should lie down, like Minnie told you. I can get some pillows to put under your legs."

Adelaide didn't move. She said, "Rachel, I'm afraid."

Rachel thought of her own mother, dead in childbed, and pushed the thought away. "Minnie will do everything she can," she said. "She's mighty stubborn. Don't think she'd take kindly to losing a fight over someone sick, even with God."

Adelaide tried to laugh, but the sound came out as a sob. Rachel sat heavily on the bed next to Adelaide and put her arm around her sister's shoulders. Adelaide began to sob in earnest. Rachel sighed. She put both her arms around her sister and held her close. She stroked the dark, wiry hair that would never stay smooth, no matter how much Rachel pomaded it and brushed it. "Hush," she said, in a comforting tone she hadn't used since Adelaide got married.

Adelaide whispered, "Will you help me?"

Rachel felt envy and pity war in her. Both felt as heavy as shackles. She whispered back, "Of course I will."

Adelaide had spent some of the pleasantest hours of her life in bed, reading a book, but now that she had been ordered into it, she was bored and dull. "I'm sick of books," she said to Rachel.

"Never thought I'd hear you say that," Rachel said.

"Don't we have anything new?"

Henry, hearing that she needed something to read, came to her room with a book in his hand. He kissed her forehead. Without the marital duty to weigh on them both, he was sweet again. "Walter Scott is diverting, and it's a long book. It should keep you occupied for a while."

"What is it?"

"*Ivanhoe*. It has a beautiful Jewess in it." He blushed, as he did when they were courting. "The fair Rebecca."

She read *Ivanhoe*, and *Rob Roy*, and the *Bride of Lammermoor*, trying to lose herself in the Scottish countryside and to forget her headache, her nausea, and her fear of the birth that came closer and closer. She felt peevish and acted like it. She installed a bell by her bedside that she used to summon Rachel. To bring her broth or toast or a coddled egg, the only foods she could bear to eat. To put a cool cloth on her forehead against the headache. She wished that she could ask Rachel for the comfort she really wanted.

Stay with me, she thought. Hold my hand and assure me that I won't die bearing this baby. Promise me you'll raise it, if I do.

Rachel grew to hate the sound of the bell. She ran up and down the stairs many times a day, fetching and carrying until her back ached and her mood turned dark.

Minnie saw it. She said, "You mighty vexed."

"As though I don't have enough to do in this house. Now I nurse her, too."

Minnie said, "She want you because you her sister."

"Ain't her sister in the parlor, or the dining room, or anywhere else people would know. Just in the sickroom." She repeated Charlie's words. "Feel like a dog when she ring that bell for me. A pet dog."

Minnie said, "You bitter."

"Will I marry? Will I have a baby of my own? Don't think so. Got to set in Miss Adelaide's lap, so she can pet me. Or cuff me. Or sell me. Whatever her whim."

Minnie said, "If you find a man to marry, she won't stop you."

"Could I live together with him on the same place? Marse Henry wouldn't sell me and he don't have a dime to buy a man I'd marry. That's a fine life, your family and your happiness up to someone else."

Minnie shook her head. "Can't decide if she your missus or your sister. Can't decide if you love her or you hate her. That eat out your heart. Not this nonsense about being sold away."

Not long after Minnie had needled her, Rachel brought a tray into Adelaide's room, a coddled egg and dry toast. Adelaide sighed. "I wish I could tolerate marmalade," she said. She had dark circles under her eyes, and except for the swell of her belly, she had lost flesh.

"Not too much longer," Rachel said, trying to soothe, although she felt almost as miserable as Adelaide.

"Months and months," Adelaide said, tired and petulant, more like a little girl than a grown woman expecting a baby.

Rachel tried a subject that might be cheering. "Have you thought about a nurse for the baby?" Since white ladies didn't nurse their own children, or take care of their own infants.

Adelaide said peevishly, "Ain't two of the hands nursing? Either one would do, I'd think."

"Doesn't matter so much for a wet nurse, as long as she's healthy. But you'll need a nursemaid later, when the baby's weaned."

"I can't think about it now. I feel too miserable. Surely we can decide later."

Rachel knew that the baby's nursemaid would spend more time with the baby than Adelaide would, not just suckling it, but caring for it. Adelaide would be Mama, who dandled her child once a day. The baby would need a mammy to lavish it with constant attention. It would be better if the attention was laced with tenderness.

She had to talk to Henry, but she would go roundabout. When she brought his nightly glass of whiskey, she said carefully, "Marse Henry, now that Missus Adelaide's coming closer to her time, we'll need to consider a nurse for the baby."

"What are you thinking?" He wasn't fooled by her tone. He asked as though her opinion mattered, and as though he trusted it.

As always, his consideration gladdened her and troubled her at the same time. She said, "Becky and Jenny are both nursing babies. I thought we might ask one of them to nurse Missus Adelaide's."

"They're both good women."

"They are. Good with children. But if I could say—" She stopped, feeling her cheeks flush. This wasn't her child, or her say.

"Of course you can."

"I'd say Becky. Nothing ever bothers her or flusters her. And I've never heard her say a mean word to her own child."

"She's very like Charlie in that. Patient and kind. They're well suited to one another."

The hurt flared again as she thought of Charlie and his happiness with Becky. She said, "People say that the two of them love each other like bread loves salt."

He said, "I've never heard that before. Where does it come from?"

Surprised, she said, "An old story. I've heard it told since I was a little girl. I thought everyone knew it."

"Tell it to me."

She said, "A long time ago, there was a king who had three daughters. He wanted to know who loved him best, so he asked them. The oldest said, 'Daddy, I love you more than all the silk and velvet in the world.' The second one said, 'I love you more than all the gold and jewels in the world.' The youngest said, 'I love you like bread loves salt.'

"He was so angry that he sent the youngest one away. He gave his kingdom to his two eldest daughters, and as soon as the kingdom was theirs, they sent him away too, and he had to wander the world as a beggar.

"After he wandered a long time he came to a big house, and he walked humbly into the kitchen and asked for a little bread. The kitchen maid recognized him, and she made him bread without salt.

"When he served he said, 'This bread isn't right.'"

"She said, 'Daddy, don't you know me? I'm your youngest daughter.'"

"He remembered what she had said, and he wept. His tears salted the bread. He tasted it, then he knew that she was the only one who ever truly loved him."

Henry smiled. "It's a wonderful story. It's just like King Lear, the story that Shakespeare wrote."

"Tell me about Shakespeare."

"He lived in England, a long time ago, and he wrote plays that were marvelous tales. When I lived in Savannah I went to the theater and saw the plays on the stage."

"Are they in a book? The plays?"

"Yes, they are."

In this room, under Henry's eye, her desire for books overwhelmed her. She gestured to the bookshelves behind the desk. "There's a whole world in those books," she said. "A whole world I don't know."

A few days later, Rachel stood in the library, broom in her hands. The lure of the books on the shelves was too strong today. She set the broom carefully against the wall and walked close to look at the books. She turned her head sideways to read the titles, stamped in gold on the spines, and touched the leather of the bindings, not minding that it rubbed off on her fingers. She let her hand linger on *A Christmas Carol*, the book that Henry had read to his slaves last year.

She carefully extricated the book from the shelf and let it rest in her hands. She savored the thought that she could read this book for herself. As with the newspaper, she was so absorbed by that thought that she didn't hear him slip into the room until he was beside her.

Her heart pounded. It was too hard to shake the old fear, that Rosa would sweep into the room and beat her for touching the books. Even though she knew better, she looked at her master with shame on her face. "I'm sorry," she said.

"No," he said, "it's quite all right."

"I'll put it back."

He looked at her sadly. He asked, "You've never had a book of your own?"

She raised startled eyes to his. Didn't he know that it was illegal for a slave to own a book? She asked, "How could I, Massa?"

After harvest, winter started in earnest. The weather got gray and raw.

Rain fell every day, the constant shower that boded well for next year's crop, but kept everyone indoors except for a quick rush to the barn or the henhouse to tend to the animals and their needs. In the cabins, everyone burned the wood chopped after the harvest, and sat by the fire to sew, whittle, or tell stories.

On a cold, gloomy morning early in December, Minnie asked, "Marse Henry, are we going to have Christmas this year?"

Henry was glad to hear the request. The memory of the whipping had receded enough for Minnie to speak to him, and even tease him again. "Of course we will. A celebration, a feast, and presents for everyone. Like last year, only more festive, since there are more of us."

"Ham," Minnie mused, "and roast chicken for them that doesn't eat ham—"

Henry said, "Why don't we butcher one of the shoats? And if Zeke doesn't mind hunting for a turkey, we'll have that too."

Minnie's face lit up. "And all kinds of vegetables," she said, "and pies."

Rachel said, "Minnie, can you make a potato pancake?"

"Massa, is that what your people eat for Christmas?"

Rachel said, "Jews have a December holiday too. They're for Hanukkah." She looked at Henry, who met her eyes. "We made them on the Mannheim place."

"What's in them, besides taters?" Minnie asked.

Rachel said, "Onion, and egg, and ground up crackers. You fry them. I'll show you." She asked Henry, "Would you like a roast goose, too? Like at home?"

A blush rose to his cheeks, and moisture came to his eyes. He was thinking of his family in Germany, so far away that they might never see the baby that was coming. "I think I would prefer the turkey, for my new home. Then we'll have something old and something new together." His eyes were bright. "And gifts, too. In Germany, we tell the children that Saint Nicholas brings them gifts on Christmas day. I think that Saint Nicholas can make a visit to a Jewish plantation in Cass County." He asked, "What should Saint Nicholas bring us?"

Rachel said, "When Missus Adelaide was a little girl, she always had an orange on Christmas Day."

"Was there one for you?"

"No, Massa," she said softly.

Later that day, as Rachel ran to the henhouse to gather eggs for dinner, she met Charlie in the yard, on his way to muck out the barn and to feed the animals. It wasn't raining, but it was chilly, and she shivered in her shawl. Charlie said, "I got something to tell you. Business of the place. Come into the barn, it's too cold to be out here."

The barn was pleasantly warm with the heat of the livestock. Charlie stood next to the mule Pretty, who nosed him for an apple, and said, "Marse Henry's tender heart will be the death of me."

"Why?"

"Asked me what the young'uns might want for a Christmas gift." He meant the young, unmarried hands—Micah, Davey, Freddy, Salley, Harriet, and Lydia. "Said he wanted to get them each something special, and asked me what it should be."

"Never heard of such a thing." Most masters gave all the slaves the same gift—lengths of cloth, or new shoes, or tobacco, or whiskey.

"Told him it would cause trouble if he was partial. And reminded him about adding to the debt."

She said, "Charlie. It's Christmas. He feels generous. Is that so wrong?"

Charlie shook his head. "He still feel bad about whupping Freddy. Ain't the way to fix it."

On Christmas day, it was still dark when she and Minnie walked into the kitchen. Minnie lit tallow candles in the candlestands, then stoked the fire to get it going. Both of them saw the two packages on the table, wrapped in cloth and tied with a bit of ribbon, one round, one small.

The door opened, and the familiar voice said cheerfully, "Saint Nicholas must have come last night."

Rachel said, "Massa, I didn't bring up your hot water—you haven't shaved—"

He rubbed his chin and said, "No matter. I had to see what Saint Nicholas brought you."

Minnie gestured at the packages. "These are for us?"

Henry sat at the table and they did too. He picked up the smaller package and said, "I believe Saint Nicholas wanted Minnie to have this," and when she reached out her hand he pressed it gently into her upturned palm.

Minnie, so deft in the kitchen, fumbled with the velvet ribbon that held the package closed. When she got it open, she was speechless. Five silver dollars, brand new, gleamed against the wrapping.

When she could get the words out, she said, "Massa, is this for me?"

Henry smiled and nodded. Minnie stared at the pile of bright silver. "I never saw so much money in my life," she said. "Massa, thank you."

"Rachel, open yours," he said affectionately.

Rachel, who was as deft with a needle as Minnie was with a paring knife, fumbled with the ribbon on her gift, too. When the wrapping fell away, she was too surprised to speak. Her master had given her the Christmas gift she had desired since she was a little girl in the Mannheim house. He had given her an orange.

Saint Nicholas visited each cabin, leaving the gifts that Marse had chosen with such care, and in each cabin, the gifts were opened to cries of surprise and thanks. A set of chisels for Zeke, to help him carpenter. A penknife for Luke, and fishhooks for Tom. New bonnets for Becky and Jenny to wear on meeting day. Lengths of sprigged calico for Lydia, Harriet, and Salley. For Charlie, a real pipe, and good cured tobacco to smoke in it. For the bachelors, some rum to celebrate the day. For little Josey, a wooden top, and for baby Ben, a wooden rattle.

After breakfast, Henry said, "Rachel, I'll be in the study this morning. Come to see me."

In the study, above the fireplace, the mantel was decorated with swags and rosettes of red velvet ribbon and pine boughs—Minnie's doing, because she had definite ideas about what Christmas should look like, even if her Israelite master and mistress didn't. The room smelled of the pine boughs and of the pine logs burning in the fireplace, the scent of winter in northern Georgia.

Rachel sat in her customary chair, opposite his. He said, "The orange was for the little girl. This is for grown woman." He handed her something square and heavy wrapped in brown paper.

She lifted it, trying to guess what it was, and prolonged the suspense by carefully pulling the paper away. Suddenly she couldn't bear to wait any longer, and she ripped the paper off and let it fall to the floor.

It was covered in dark red leather. A book. She turned it to look at the spine, where the author and title were stamped in gold. "*The Plays of William Shakespeare*," she read.

She hefted the volume in her hands before she opened it. The book's weight was deeply satisfying in her palms. She turned the book on its side, with the spine in her lap, and drew in her breath with surprise. The pages were edged in gold.

"Open it," Henry said. "See what's inside."

She opened it and carefully turned the pages to the table of contents. She saw the name she knew: "King Lear." And many others she didn't: "Romeo and Juliet." "The Tempest." "The Merchant of Venice." "Othello."

Henry said, "It isn't all of his plays, but it's the ones that are most beloved. The ones that I saw on stage in Savannah."

She closed the book and ran her finger over the gilt edge of the pages. "I never thought to own a book. And such a beautiful book! I will treasure this book as long as I live."

Smiling, he said, "I'm glad that it pleases you."

Emotion welled up in her, and her eyes filled with tears. The tears trickled down her face and wouldn't stop. He knew that she wouldn't care for a length of calico or a new pair of shoes. He knew that her proudest accomplishment in life was being able to read. His gift told her that she was as smart as anyone who had ever read this book, and that she deserved to read it, too.

Henry said, "Rachel. Take this." He reached into his pocket, and pulled out his handkerchief, which was rumpled but clean.

She wiped her eyes. When she spoke she had to struggle to control her voice. She said, "You added to the debt to buy this for me."

He laughed softly. "The Mannheim question." Smiling, he said, "I'm already deep in debt. As you know." He leaned forward. "Deep in your debt, too," he said, his eyes full of affection.

As she held the book in her lap, she realized that all of the other indulgent gifts were to disguise the feeling that had gone into this one.

After the holiday, the weather continued cold and raw. The sun never seemed to rise. Every day, Rachel opened the curtains for Adelaide, who sighed and said, "I'm so tired of lying here and waiting for this baby I feel like I'll die of boredom."

"Ain't nothing to joke about," Rachel said, even though she felt the same way.

Adelaide was sobered, as she always was when she mentioned death. "When it comes, will you stay with me?"

Now Rachel sighed. She held Adelaide's hands and promised her yes.

A few weeks later, when Adelaide rang the bell for Rachel, she ran up the stairs, ready for a request for broth or toast or a book. But she found Adelaide sitting up in bed, worry on her face. She said, "I think the baby's coming." She gasped and pressed her hand onto her belly. "It's like a cramp, only worse." At Rachel's look, she said, "I ain't shamming."

Abashed, Rachel said, "Didn't think you were." Rachel had helped Aunt Susy at a few births, and she knew to ask, "Did your water break yet?"

Adelaide knew what she meant. Minnie had been clear about this a few weeks ago, and Adelaide had blenched to hear it. "No," Adelaide said.

"Should we send for your mama?"

Adelaide shook her head. "I want you," she said.

"I'll get Minnie."

Adelaide lay back on the bed, her face drawn. "Stay with me," she said.

Rachel pulled the chair close to the bed and sat. "Do you want me to read to you?"

Adelaide closed her eyes. "Hold my hand."

Rachel said nothing and let Adelaide cling to her hand. Suddenly Adelaide groaned and tightened her grip.

"Rachel?" she asked.

"It's all right. I'm here. I ain't going anywhere."

How long until her water broke and the pains came swiftly? And after that, how long until it was over?

"Rachel?"

"What is it, sugar?" The endearment slipped out. It was for moments of love, between lovers, between mother and child. Between sisters.

"I'm afraid."

Rachel stroked the hand that gripped hers so tightly. "You'll be all right."

"I'm afraid that I'll die."

Rachel said, "Minnie won't allow it."

"Thought she said it was up to God."

"When it comes to birthing a baby, I'd wager on Minnie and not on God."

A weak laugh. Then another groan. "I want to stand up," Adelaide said.

"Let me boost you." She helped Adelaide up and they both saw the great wet stain on the bed. Adelaide cried out, "The water!" She mopped between her legs with her nightdress.

Rachel found a towel. "You use this," she said, "and I'll get Minnie."

She ran down the stairs and through the breezeway to tell Minnie. Minnie looked up from the pot she was scouring, washed her hands, and came upstairs.

Adelaide's pains were closer together, but when Minnie checked her, she said, "She ain't close yet. First baby, take its sweet time."

It was not a sweet time. Adelaide began to groan in real pain, and she clenched Rachel's hand so hard she bruised it. Rachel said anxiously, "How do you feel?"

Adelaide looked at her with unfocused eyes. She said, "My head aches so. Like being hit with a hammer."

"I'll get a cloth," Rachel said.

"Don't leave me," Adelaide pleaded.

"Only for a moment, to wet the cloth."

Adelaide pressed her hand to her belly and groaned again.

Rachel brought the cloth and the water pitcher, too. "Are you thirsty, sugar?"

"Yes."

Rachel held out the cup, but Adelaide was stricken with another pain. When it passed, Rachel lifted Adelaide's head and trickled the water into her mouth.

Why was the day so dark? Why did the minutes go by so slowly? Every pain seemed to last an eternity, yet the hand on the clock moved only a few minutes.

Rachel had helped Aunt Susy with more than one birth, but she had come in near the end, when the baby was coming. There had been plenty of ruckus and mess, but she had never sat for hours at a laboring woman's bedside, bathing her forehead, helping her drink water, holding her hand—Lord, Adelaide had a grip—and feeling the pain along with her.

When the pains came hard upon each other—when the reprieve from pain was too brief for the hands on the clock to measure it—Minnie said, "Now we getting closer."

How could a woman be in such pain and endure it?

Adelaide lay back on her pillows, her face filmed with sweat, her nightdress hoisted up to her hips so that Minnie could feel for the baby and pull on it when it crowned. She whispered, "Rachel, promise me."

"What, sugar?"

"If I die, will you say Kaddish for me?"

"Whatever it is, I'll say it," Rachel said. She bowed her head to hide the tears that rushed to her eyes. "Sugar, will you let me stand up? Just for a moment?"

"Don't go away."

"I won't."

She rose and walked to the window, where she could see the day's gray light fading through the pine trees. She pressed her face to the chill of the glass and let her tears wet it.

Minnie looked up. "What's the matter?"

Rachel turned, not caring that Minnie saw she'd been crying. "Is she going to die?"

Exasperated, Minnie said, "Baby's all right, pointed the right way, still quick. She's all right. Just having a bad time. Ain't nobody dying, not today. Sit with her, she want you."

Adelaide began to cry out, a piercing cry. Rachel winced. Every scream seemed to go right through her bones. She wondered what Marse Henry, holed up in his study, forbidden to come upstairs until it was over, was thinking. She wondered if the screams went through his bones, too.

"Adelaide," she said, too upset to care that she called her sister by her name in Minnie's earshot. "Oh, Adelaide."

Adelaide was too far gone to hear. Ordinarily prudish, she didn't care that Minnie had hoisted the nightdress somewhere above her waist. She didn't care that Minnie's hands were inside her body, trying to gauge when the baby would come out.

Minnie said, "God bless! That baby's coming!" To Adelaide, she said, "Do you feel it? Can you push that baby out? You push, and that baby will slide right out. Almost over."

Almost over. Adelaide roused herself. She pushed. Minnie said happily, "You doing fine. Almost there."

She pushed again, and cried out, this time with relief. The pain was over. Minnie said, "All the way out. You push one more time and we get that afterbirth." Minnie said happily, "You got a beautiful little boy. We clean him up for you and then you can see him."

Adelaide was too exhausted to lift up her head, and Rachel, still in the chair by the bedside, slumped with exhaustion, too. When Minnie brought the wriggling bundle, she put the baby on Adelaide's chest. Adelaide was too weary to put her arms around him. Rachel reached out to steady the baby, but Minnie said, "I hold him for you, ma'am, and you take a good look at him."

Adelaide opened her eyes and looked into her son's face. He was tiny. And red. And wrinkled. She reached out her hand to touch the cheek of the puckered little face. He began to cry. To scream, just as she had to get him into the world. She tried to smile at him, but instead tears came to her eyes and she sobbed in unison with her son.

Minnie said, "We bring him back after you get a chance to rest." She looked sharply at Rachel. "You go lay down. The last thing we need is two gals out flat."

In the hallway, Rachel leaned against the wall, but she wasn't ready to rest yet. She wanted to see the baby. She slipped into the room behind Adelaide's, which had been made into a nursery a few weeks before when Becky moved into the house, bringing her own baby, little Ben, with her. There were two cradles, one for the new arrival and one for Ben. Henry had put a bed in the room for Becky, and provided the rocking chair that every nursing woman needed. Becky sat there now, cradling her son, one hand on his bottom, the other on his back, while she watched the newcomer sleep.

It was fully dark, and the room was lit by a single candle, which flickered as Becky rocked back and forth, soothing her son. Charlie's son.

Rachel felt tears rise to her eyes. It had been too long and too wearing a day. She should take Minnie's advice and lie down. She could see the baby tomorrow.

Becky said, "How is Missus Adelaide?"

Rachel righted herself. "Worn out. She sleeping." She asked, "How is the baby?"

"Sleeping. He all worn out, too, getting into the world."

Rachel bent over the cradle to look at him. She reached into the cradle, and touched her finger to the baby's palm. He grasped it tightly with his tiny fist. She marveled at the grip of those little fingers. He opened his eyes and he gurgled and smiled at her. Her sister's son. Her nephew.

She heard Henry's step on the stairs, and his voice, very low, talking to Minnie outside Adelaide's door. He tapped on the nursery door and came in. He was haggard. It had been a hard day for him, too, listening to Adelaide's agony and not being able to do a thing to help. He nodded to Becky and whispered to Rachel, "How is he?"

"Come see."

He stood close enough for her to know that he smelled a little of brandy. That was all right, for a new father. He bent over the cradle and his head was close to hers. He looked at his son and smiled at the baby. Then at her. His brightest smile.

Softly, he asked Rachel, "May I hold him?"

"Of course, Massa."

He bent down and picked up the child as though he'd been handling babies all his life. He knew to put his hand behind the soft, fragile, downy head. He looked into the little face, still squashed from being born, and said joyfully, "Ain't he beautiful?"

The baby murmured, as though he were talking to his father. Henry looked into the unfocused eyes and smiled. "What are we going to call you, *liebchen*?" he asked.

Surprised, Rachel said, "Won't you name him after yourself?"

"No, we Jews don't do that. We honor the memory of someone who died. I'd like to name him after my uncle Menachem, if Adelaide doesn't mind."

Despite her fatigue, despite her sadness, Rachel laughed. "That's a mouthful of a name to give him."

Henry kissed the still-red little cheek. "We'll find a good American name that starts with the same letter."

It wasn't her say, but she said it. "Like Matthew."

Henry considered. He looked at the baby again. "Matthew is a good name," he said. "I'll ask Adelaide what she thinks." He asked, "Would you like to hold him?"

Unable to speak, she nodded.

He handed her the baby and she couldn't help herself. She pressed the child to her chest and kissed the top of his head. Then she lay her cheek against the soft bald pate and rocked him back and forth. He whimpered a little in protest. "You're all worn out," she whispered.

She gently laid the baby in his cradle, and bent over him as he wriggled a little and settled down to sleep. Henry bent beside her. He touched the tiny, red hand, as she had, which flexed at the touch of his finger. He looked at Rachel, smiling.

It hurt her so much to stand beside Henry and look at Adelaide's baby that she wished she could faint.

She stood up and smoothed her apron, the servant's gesture, reminding herself who she was and what she was. Later, upstairs in her attic room, she finally allowed herself the storm of tears she had been wanting to cry all day.

Rachel was better after a night's sleep, but Adelaide was not. She developed a fever. Minnie, who had not worried for a moment during Adelaide's difficult delivery, was now worried. "If it childbed fever, she in trouble," she said. "Don't send for that doctor, he'll bleed her, won't do any good. We watch. We do what we can. We wait."

Rachel, Minnie, Jenny and Becky took their turns sitting at Adelaide's bedside. As they watched and waited, Adelaide got sicker. Her fever rose, and she became delirious. She forgot where she was, and thought that her dreams were real. Rachel sat beside her on the day when she woke, her forehead slick with sweat, her eyes unfocused, and said, "I thought I was dead."

Rachel said, "No, it was just a bad dream."

Adelaide propped herself on her elbows. She looked at Rachel without seeing her. She said, "I heard you say Kaddish for me, and I watched my husband throw dirt on my coffin."

Rachel put a cool cloth on Adelaide's forehead and waited until she fell asleep again.

Whenever Adelaide woke, she asked for Rachel. Rachel spent hour after hour in the chair by Adelaide's bedside, bathing the fevered forehead, spooning birchbark tea between the cracked lips, trying to soothe away the mad thoughts that fever brought, thoughts of her own death.

As Rachel sat in Adelaide's sickroom, late winter turned into spring. The trees began to leaf out, the birds began to nest again, and the cotton seeds went into the ground to sprout and grow. The misery in the sickroom made a mockery of the sweetness in the air. Adelaide's room smelled of sweat and camphor, but the breeze that came through the opened windows smelled of magnolia blossom.

On a pleasant day late in March, as Adelaide slept, Rachel walked to the window and pressed her cheek against the glass. Today the pane was no longer chill as it had been on the day the baby was born. Rachel felt dizzy with weariness. If her sister had been a burden before she got sick, now she was even heavier. Lay my burden down, Rachel thought. Set me free of it.

Standing at the window, Rachel thought, If she dies, I'll be free of her.

Then she thought, If she dies, I'll never forgive myself for wishing it.

When Minnie came to relieve her, she said, "You look a sight. When was the last time you had anything to eat?"

She couldn't remember, since nothing she ate had any taste to it. To please Minnie, she went downstairs, but she didn't go into the kitchen. She walked into the study, where she kept Henry's Christmas gift, her Shakespeare book. She hadn't been able to read it in weeks. She hadn't even come into the room to take it off the shelf, hold it in her hands, and press it to her cheek.

Henry found her there, standing before the shelf that held the book, too dazed with weariness to touch it. He said gently, "How is she?"

She didn't know what Jews did for someone as sick as Adelaide, but she asked, "Should we send for the rabbi?"

Henry said, "We don't do that. The rabbi comes for the funeral." He winced, realizing what he had said.

She said, "Then we should write to him now." She felt too weary to stand. He said, "Let me help you," and he put his arm around her shoulders to guide her into the nearest chair, where she always sat when they talked about the crop and the place. She bent her head and laid her hands flat on her knees, as though the pressure would keep the tears at bay.

He looked down at her hands. They were strong and long-fingered, like Adelaide's, but there were kitchen scars—from the fire and the knife—on the dark skin. He leaned close enough so that she could smell the scent on his skin, and the brandy on his breath, and she did not move away.

He knelt before her. He said, "Of course you grieve for your sister."

She couldn't raise her head, but it was sorrow, not servility. She said, "Marse Henry, I don't know what to do, but I pray for her."

Irreligious, freethinking Henry said, "So do I."

On the tenderest spring day of the year so far, when the new birds sang and the trees smelled of new leaves and the air was fragrant with honeysuckle, Minnie ran into the kitchen, where Rachel stood listlessly at the stove, boiling water to wash the breakfast dishes. At the sound of Minnie's urgent steps she braced herself for the worst possible news.

"How is she? Is she—" Rachel couldn't bring herself to say the word "gone."

But there was a grin on Minnie's face. "No. Fever broke. She better. Sat up and asked me for a piece of toast with marmalade on it."

Rachel leaned against the edge of the sink and pressed her hand to her face. She began to sob and she couldn't stop. Minnie took the kettle off the stove and said, "You set down."

"I thought she was dead," Rachel said, sitting heavily, still sobbing.

"Well, she ain't. Wasn't her time."

Rachel thought of her dark thoughts at Adelaide's bedside. I'd be free. And I'd never forgive myself. She sobbed and sobbed.

Minnie said, "You weary through. So weary you ain't all right yourself. You go to bed and stay there. I'll take up the toast and finish them dishes."

The sobs slowed. "Does Marse Henry know?" she asked, her voice thick with tears.

"Told him first," Minnie said, smiling.

When the rabbi finally came, it was for a joyous occasion, the *bris milah*

and naming ceremony. From his slaves, Henry had learned to go roundabout. Before the rabbi arrived—the one from Macon, who had married them—Henry told Adelaide that he'd like to name the baby after his late uncle, and that he'd need an American name to go with the Jewish one.

She was still thin and pale, with dark circles under her eyes, but she was well enough to put on her wrapper and eat breakfast at the table. She helped herself to marmalade and smeared it on a biscuit. "He will."

"What do you think of Matthew?"

"I hadn't thought of it."

He flushed a little—it discomfited him to lie, even this little fib—and said, "I favor it."

She smiled. It was good to see her smile, even though she looked so drawn. "Then it's all right with me, too."

Everyone on the place was invited. The slaves who had come from the Mannheim plantation, otherwise versed in Judaic lore, had never seen a *bris milah*, since the Mannheims had only a daughter. Jews didn't make that kind of fuss for girl babies.

Assured that it was a festive occasion, everyone came to celebrate. They were flustered at what they saw. Men who butchered hogs and women who severed the necks of chickens blanched as they watched the ritual knife and the ritual surgery of circumcision. Afterwards, the men put their hands protectively on their lower bellies. If they hadn't been in polite company, they would have cradled their privates.

Charlie, who looked a little gray in the face, said to Rachel, "You said it would be like a frolic."

Rachel hadn't enjoyed it either. The sight of the beaming daddy and the proud mama had upset her more than she wanted to admit. "Thought it would be. Baked enough cake for it."

"Give a bitty baby wine to make him drunk, then cut on his tenderest parts. How did the Jews ever come up with such a thing?"

Henry, who was flushed and beaming, said to Charlie, "Happy day, Charlie! Have a little whiskey to toast the new arrival."

Charlie muttered to Rachel, "Take more than a little to feel better."

Rachel said irritably, "Have as much as you like. We celebrating today."

As Adelaide recovered, Rachel's sense of relief faded, and the familiar envy took its place. Adelaide was Mama, who drifted into the nursery when she felt like it and dandled the baby. Rachel, like any black woman who took care of a baby, was "aunty." Not aunt.

But Matt drew her. He was hers, in a way that no one could take from her. She went into the nursery as often as she could, even though it hurt her to think that Matt belonged to her only in secret. As Adelaide was her sister in secret.

She told Becky that she was glad to watch the babies as they slept. She rocked the cradles with an equal hand—robust brown Ben in one, slight Matt in the other. Becky called them "milk brothers." It was a brotherhood that wouldn't survive their earliest years. A little white boy of seven was a Massa in miniature. A little brown boy of seven was a slave.

Outside, the day was bright springtime. In a few weeks Marse Mannheim would hold his frolic, and everyone would go to his place to eat and drink and exclaim over his birds. The ladies would fuss over the new baby, and the girls would cast their eyes at the men—the white girls demure, to find husbands, and the slave girls bold, to make a baby with any man who pleased them.

She looked at the two babies in their cradles, Charlie's and Marse Henry's, and she couldn't push away the thoughts that troubled her most. No husband to make her happy. No child to give her cheer. Only the hearth, and the ashes, and the bonds of servitude, as long as she lived. Or as long as Adelaide did.

Henry tapped on the door. He smiled to see Rachel sitting by the cradle. He asked, "May I sit with you?"

"Won't ever deny you, Massa."

He sighed as he pulled the chair close, to the cradle and to her. Since Adelaide had recovered, Rachel had been distant again. He missed the woman who had sat and grieved with him as Adelaide listened to the call of the world beyond.

Since Matt's birth, he had seen how Rachel looked at the baby, with a hunger as great as her hunger for the book he had given her. Seeing the sadness on her face, he put his hand gently on her arm and asked, "Rachel, did you have a husband? Did you have a child?" God help him, if her heart was broken when Mannheim sold them away. He would listen to her tell him so.

She shook her head. "No, Massa. Never had a husband or a child, and I ain't likely to."

The bleakness in her voice startled him. In his kindest voice, he said, "Someday you'll find a man to make you happy."

She shook her head again. There was such sorrow in the curve of her shoulders that he wanted to gather her in his arms. Of course he could not. And he did not. Instead he offered his handkerchief.

She pressed it to her face and took in the smell of his scent. The eau-de-cologne. She breathed it in deeply, noticing the tang of orange in it, and tried to hold in the tears.

There was a tap at the door. It was Adelaide, still pale from her fever, but well enough to put on her wrapper, a task a lady could do for herself.

Startled, Henry said, "Adelaide, I thought you were resting."

"I'm well enough to be up. Henry, what are you doing?"

Henry said clumsily, "Rachel started to sneeze, so I gave her my handkerchief."

Adelaide remembered, as her husband did not, that he had been ready with his handkerchief during their courtship, when she wept over the ruin of her life in refusing William Pereira. Adelaide gave her sister a sharp look. "If she's catching cold, she shouldn't be near the baby."

Rachel, better at lying than Henry, said, "Ma'am, I was dusting today. It's nothing. I'm all right."

Adelaide said, "Let me hold the baby."

Henry said to Rachel, "We'll let Missus Adelaide have the rocking chair," and they both rose at the same time, giving Adelaide room to bend over the cradle. Rachel watched anxiously as Adelaide picked up the baby and settled into the rocking chair. Rachel fretted, "Keep your hand behind his head."

"I ain't planning to drop him, Rachel." Adelaide carefully supported the downy head. "I missed you so, when I was sick," she said. He made gurgling noises and blew a spit bubble. Adelaide cooed to her son, "What are you saying? Are you saying how do to mama?"

Unable to bear it, Rachel said, "Let me take him—"

Adelaide glared at Rachel over the baby's head. She said, "I reckon I can hold my own baby."

At the sound of an angry voice, Matt began to whimper. Rachel said, "He ain't used to you and you ain't used to him—"

Fully angry, Adelaide said, "I'm his mama. You ain't even his nurse." She gave Rachel a poisonous look. "Give my husband back his handkerchief."

Rachel made her face impassive. She pulled the handkerchief from her pocket and held it out to her master. When he took it from her, their fingers touched. Henry blushed as he crumpled the cloth in his palm. "Thank you, Rachel," he said.

Whenever Rachel came into the study, she stopped to look at her book. She never had time to read it, but if she had a moment to rest, she would put it in her lap and let its beauty remind her of a life beyond slavery. Marse Henry considered her more than a slave. She thought of him, and of his kindness to her, every time she touched the book's leather cover.

She was delighted by this book, but she was troubled by it. It was an extravagant gift to give a slave. It showed partiality, and it showed interest. The gift of the book didn't erase the memory of Freddy's whipping, but it took away its terror. She was still his slave. Henry was still Massa. But he was also a man who understood her in a way she had never expected. He knew what her soul craved. It craved a book.

She stood before the shelf, her hand on the book's spine, as she heard Adelaide's step in the hallway. Now that Adelaide was better, she took pleasure in reading again. It wasn't unusual to see her in the study, looking for a book. Rachel picked up the duster and went back to her dusting. Adelaide came into the room to find something to read.

Adelaide lingered before the shelf, taking her time, as happy before the books as most women were before a tray of ribbons at Levy's Drygoods. She pulled a volume from the shelf—bound in leather, the title stamped in gold—and said, "I don't believe I've seen this book before. It must be new."

Rachel said fiercely, "Don't take that one."

Adelaide held the book in her hands, surprised that Rachel would care what book she read. "Why ever not?"

Rachel was hot with indignation and trembling with fear that she would show it. "Because it's mine."

"Yours!" Adelaide said. "How do you figure that?"

"Marse Henry gave it to me for a Christmas gift."

Adelaide knew all of the books in the house, and she knew the worth of a book the way her father knew the value of a slave. She hefted the book in her hands, feeling the quality of the leather, and turned it sideways to look at the gilt on the edges of the page. "Really?" she said. "I'll have to ask him about it." She turned to go, and Rachel couldn't contain herself. She reached for the precious book and pleaded, "Don't take it away."

Adelaide held the book in her hand and stared at her sister. "Goodness, Rachel. It's only a book." As though she couldn't see the distress on her sister's face.

Later that day, Adelaide walked back into the study, the book in her hands, to talk to her husband. She held out the book and said, "Rachel told me you gave this to her."

Henry flushed bright red, as though she'd caught him out in a lie or a sin. "I gave all of our servants gifts at Christmas," he said.

She said, "I don't mind that Rachel reads, but what is this? It must be the most expensive volume in the house." She set the book on his desk before him. "Moroccan leather binding, silk bookmark, pages edged with gold. How much did that book cost you?"

Henry didn't reply.

"How much flour and coffee could we have bought, for what you paid for that book? How many lengths of cloth for our hands, and how many pairs of shoes?"

Henry was still flushed. He said, "Rachel is a loyal servant. When you were confined she did the work of two or three, without fuss or complaint. I wanted to give her something fine as a Christmas gift."

"A little too fine," Adelaide said, watching her husband.

He raised his voice. "Why can't you let her have anything for herself? It's only a book!"

Adelaide picked it up. "I'm going to take this back to my room," she said. "I haven't read Shakespeare for a while." She smiled at Henry, but she was trembling.

As she walked slowly up the stairs—since her recovery, emotion tired her, even more than exertion—she thought, It's not only a book. No one would get so angry, or feel so guilt-ridden, over a book.

In her room, she set the book on the night table next to her bed. The Moroccan leather and the gilt pages now tormented her. This gift spoke to her clearly, and as she listened to the tale it told, her cheeks burned.

In her mind, she could hear the wicked, mocking tones of Aggie Payne as she gossiped with the ladies of the county, leaning forward and laughing to tell them that upright Mr. Kaltenbach, who was so softhearted a master and had such doubts about slavery, had finally found himself a slave gal. She imagined the rougher tones of the men, gathered in town at Stockton's or at the cockpit on her father's place, jeering: "Gave her a present to win her favor, I hear. But it weren't a length of calico for a dress or baubles for her ears." She could hear them guffawing. "Damn fool, he gave her a book!"

Chapter 12

Neither Death Nor Distance

Adelaide kept Rachel's book in her room. She wished she could get rid of it, but it was too fine a thing to maltreat by burning in the fire or throwing down the well. The longer it stayed on her shelf, the more she doubted the passion that had prompted her to take it. Perhaps the fury, and the mocking voices that came with it, were a lingering result of fever. Perhaps she had been foolish to think that it was more than a book.

She told herself to put the book back in the study to let it lose its sting. She found she couldn't do it. The book bothered her, whether it was on the shelf or on the night table by her bed, and it would bother her on the shelf in the study, too.

On a pleasant morning in June, a few weeks after the Mannheim frolic, as Rachel brushed her hair, Adelaide said, "Minnie told me that I'm well enough to do my duty again."

Rachel had never gotten used to hearing love in the marriage bed called duty. She said, "Do you feel all right?"

Adelaide sighed. "I hate the thought of another baby," she said.

"Can't be helped, if you lie with your husband."

It had been nearly a year since Adelaide found out she was expecting and had closed her door to Henry, and that was too long to keep saying no. Aggie's wicked voice had never deserted her. The slave gal was close by, and her name and face were familiar. If Henry succumbed, she wouldn't be able to say, in Aggie's flippant way, that she didn't see it and it didn't bother her. It would be right before her eyes, to hurt worse than miscarriage or childbirth.

Henry was solicitous when she asked him to come to her. "Are you feeling well enough?" He was angry with her, too, but he was still a kind man.

She assured him that she was.

Getting ready was a little like getting ready for her wedding night again. Rachel helped her into the wedding nightdress, which was still her best. Tonight she unbuttoned the buttons herself. Rachel brushed her hair. Adelaide picked up the bottle of lavender water. She said, "Remember, on my wedding night? How you said it would make me smell sweet?"

Rachel took the little bottle from Adelaide and found that her hands were shaking. She twisted off the cap with sudden vehemence. "Yes," she said. She pushed away the thought of Adelaide in bed with her husband, and poured the lavender water into her palms to smooth it into the part of Adelaide's hair.

"Rachel, why are you so rough?" Adelaide asked.

"Be sweet to him," she said.

Adelaide turned to look at her servant. "Why wouldn't I be?"

"He was cut up when you were sick. Prayed for you. We both did."

Adelaide said, "The two of you got awfully familiar while I was sick." The ghost of William Pereira was in the room and both sisters felt it like an icy caress on the cheek.

Rachel shook her head. "You all right now," she said. "Go do that duty of yours."

Adelaide said sharply, "Make a wish for me."

"What?"

"That when we're done, I ain't in a delicate condition again."

It wasn't a wish to embrace on, or say a soothing word to. Rachel nodded as she left the room.

When Henry came to her, Adelaide was afraid that he would guess how little joy she felt in awaiting him. When he kissed her, she kissed him back to encourage him. When he embraced her, she pressed herself against him. He said, "Adelaide, what's gotten into you?"

"It's been a long time," she said softly.

"You were so ill."

"I'm all right now."

Impatient, she pulled up her nightdress for him. He said, "Slowly." He kissed her mouth, and her breast, and stroked her naked thigh. This was familiar, too. The detachment, and the yearning for it to be over.

He lay atop her and kissed her mouth again. Something wasn't right, and now she was experienced enough to know. His member was soft against her belly.

"Henry, what's the matter?"

"It happens to a man sometimes, if he's tired or burdened."

As much as she dreaded it, she wanted him to rouse and spend. She stroked his cheek, trying her best to be a solicitous wife. "What burdens you so?"

He looked away. "The crop. The debt."

"The crop is all right. Five hundred bales, I hear. You'll clear the debt. What is it, Henry?"

He didn't reply. She thought of the book, and felt full of alarm. "Is it about us?"

He looked up. "Why would you ask that?"

"Most people don't marry for love. They manage better than we do."

"You don't know that," he said.

Why did she think of Aggie and her husband, whose marriage was salved and plagued by Lucy? "I don't know what to do," she said softly. "To make it better."

"Neither do I."

"Should we try again?"

"Not now." He lay on his back, looking into the darkness.

She rolled away from him to lie on her back and stare at the ceiling, the pose of the wife doing her marital duty, except that her mind was full of thoughts that she couldn't mention to anyone. She could hear Aggie's voice, saying the things that no lady should ever speak of. "Why can't a man rouse to do his duty? If he don't care for his wife like he used to. Or if he's taking his pleasure elsewhere."

When Rachel left Adelaide, she didn't want to go upstairs to her room. Sometimes she could hear things in the attic that she didn't want to hear. Bedsprings. Sighs. Groans. She hated that a slave was considered deaf and blind when it came to things that would deeply embarrass a white person.

She sat in the kitchen, letting only the sliver of moon light the room. She yearned for the book that Adelaide had taken from her. Feeling it in her hands and in her lap put away the thought of the girl who sat in the ashes.

She sat until she felt cramped. She had promised Minnie she would make sure all the candles were snuffed and the front door was locked before she went to bed. The house was dark and the door of the study was open.

In the unlit room, her master slumped in his chair in an attitude that anyone would recognize as despair.

"Massa?"

He looked up. "Rachel! Why are you still up?"

"Closing up the house for the night. Do you want me to light a candle for you?"

"No, I'm going to bed soon, and I'll manage without."

He sounded so sad that she couldn't bear to leave him. She came into the room, moving easily in the dark, and sat in her customary chair, the one opposite his. She settled herself and asked, "What's wrong, Marse Henry?" She rarely used his name, even with the prefix of "Marse." It felt too familiar to her.

"How do you know?"

"The way you set. Like a man troubled."

He tried to straighten himself, but he was as bent as a man who had been dragging a cotton sack all day. "The debt," he said. "I worry all the time about the debt. I feel I'll never be free of it." He sounded bleak, and she recalled her own bleak moment, when she told him that she would never find a man to love her.

She said slowly, "I have a notion of something that might help. If you'd allow it." In the dark, her voice came out lower and sweeter than it would in daylight. "If you'd let me, I could take a look at your ledgers and your contracts. To see if there's anything you might do different. If it would help, Marse Henry." Her own tone startled her. Affectionate. Tender. Familiar. Much too familiar.

He sat up as though he'd been stung by a wasp. Pulled his dressing gown tight around him, even though she couldn't see anything in the dark. Put his hands in his lap. He said, with pain, "Thank you, but I doubt it."

Softly, she said, "If you say so, Marse Henry."

Just as softly—it came out tenderly—he said, "You go upstairs to bed. You need your rest."

She rose. "Good night, Marse Henry."

"Sleep well, Rachel. Sweet dreams."

Henry was tormented when he went to bed that night. The man who couldn't rouse to love his wife was roused from the moment that Rachel came into the room, when he couldn't see her face. All he had of her was the smell of her skin, woodsmoke mingled with sassafras. He hadn't been able to see her face, her darkness melting into the room's darkness. All he had of her was the white of her kerchief and the whites of her eyes and the sound of her voice, very low.

When she spoke to him in the dark, offering her clever notion, her voice was so caressing that he thought, What would it be like to hear that voice in the dark, beside me, every night? Mortified, he had thanked God for the darkness that hid the flush in his face and the shame beneath his dressing gown.

He and Adelaide had married for advantage, knowing they didn't love each other. His parents had found love after they married, and Henry saw it whenever they touched each other or smiled at each other. He had wanted a marriage like theirs for himself. He wanted a woman who would help him in life, listen to him when he was troubled, and show him sweetness at the dining table and in the marriage bed. He hoped that he and Adelaide would come to love each other. But they had not.

He thought back to the marriage ceremony, where the marriage contract had spelled out his obligations in the case of a divorce. In Germany, they could find a rabbi to grant them a divorce. No one divorced frivolously, but Jews could admit that a marriage had been a mistake, and could be free to find love with someone else.

But in America, he couldn't divorce Adelaide, even though Jewish law allowed it. Southern custom did not. They would never live down the shame. Adelaide would die a social death, and he would never drink or do business with another planter or factor anywhere in the South.

And he was bound to Mordecai by a bond even deeper than marriage. By Jewish law, he could divorce Adelaide, but by all the laws of Georgia, he would never be free of Mordecai until he paid off the debt.

Ever since Henry surprised Rachel in reading the newspaper, he had grown bolder in asking for her opinion on matters of the day, and she had grown bolder in offering them. A week after their conversation in the dark, when he found her with the *Savannah Republican* unfolded before her, he asked her who she favored in the presidential election.

Politics, like cotton, was an easier subject than the things that truly bothered them.

Without hesitating, she said, "Mr. Lincoln."

"So do I. Why do you like him?"

"I've always liked him, ever since he debated that Mr. Douglas."

Henry quoted, "A house divided against itself cannot stand."

She wished she could say the rest: Half slave and half free. Today's news, however contentious, was safer ground. She gestured toward the newspaper. "Nothing but talk of secession today."

"I know. If the South secedes, there may be war with the North."

She'd read the correspondence that came from the coast, where the owners of the great lowland places hated Mr. Lincoln even more than the Piedmont planters did. The *Republican* was full of talk about war, but it chilled her to hear someone say so. "If that happens, who will we sell our cotton to?"

He said, "There are people who swear English mills will buy our cotton."

"Why would they, if we go to war?"

"If they were only as wise as you."

She touched the flimsy newsprint. "Cotton is high this year."

He nodded. "I'm hoping that we'll have a good crop on the place."

"Have you signed your factoring contract with Marse Mannheim yet?" she asked.

"Not yet." He winced.

"Massa, let me look at the old contracts, like I asked you. The ledgers, too. To see what you agreed to last year." In daylight, he could see that she was talking about the business of the place. Not any private business between the two of them.

"I hate to look at it." But he wavered.

"I know. But if you get better terms, you can clear more, no matter what kind of a crop you have."

He said slowly, "To get out of debt."

"Yes," she said, meeting his eyes, with a sharp gaze like her father's. "To get out of debt."

A few days later Rachel took the pie from the oven, wiped her hands on her apron, and readied herself to look at her master's ledgers. She had fretted over this, even though she had insisted on it. Despite her reminder to herself, that it was about the business of the place, she recalled the exchange in the dark.

He sat behind his desk, looking apprehensive, but when she came in, his face brightened. He said, "You have a smudge of flour on your nose." Teasing and nervous.

"Do I." She rubbed her nose and her fingers came away floury.

He gestured for her to sit. "It's no pleasure to do this."

She said, "You'll be glad when it's done."

"I hope so."

She said, "Show me the ledgers first."

He handed her the ledgers. Marse Mannheim had great leather volumes that took up the surface of his desk, but Henry's ledgers were the size of ordinary books. She opened the topmost and read the date, January of 1859. The writing was German script, like Marse Mannheim's, only neater.

He watched her read. She read these pages easily, the way he read a book of poetry. He waited, increasingly uncomfortable, until she looked up and said, "You started five thousand dollars in debt. Did you borrow the money from Marse Mannheim?" She was all hardheaded Mannheim today.

"Yes," he said.

"And he gave you the promissory notes."

"He did."

"Then you bought some stock and supplies against the crop, and went into a little more debt in town. And you hired some hands from Marse Mannheim—was that to pick the crop?"

"It was."

"And then you cleared sixty dollars a bale on your two hundred-some bales. Twelve thousand four hundred dollars, less those expenses. After you paid off the debt, you had fifteen hundred dollars left."

"That's right."

"Then you got engaged. When did Marse Mannheim make the settlement?"

"December."

"He gave you two hands—me, and Charlie—but I don't see any settlement."

He said, "That was the settlement."

She stared at him in astonishment. "Great day in the morning! Do you mean to tell me that he sold you everything else? The hands, the stock, the land, the house?"

He felt the anger over again, remembering. "That's right."

She drew in her breath. "So that's why you've been so deep in debt."

"Yes." He felt his gut contract.

She said, "Can I see the notes?"

He found them and handed them to her. His hands were shaking.

She looked at them and said, "There's nothing wrong with these. He's charging you interest, but it's reasonable. But you realize, don't you, that he can call these in whenever he wants to? Doesn't have to wait until they're due?"

"No," he said, his mouth dry.

She sat with his financial records in her lap, her hands resting on the open ledgers the way most women's would rest on their needlework. She was angry, and she looked it. "I never saw such a bad bargain."

He thought of himself in Savannah, so dazzled by the idea of a cotton fortune that he didn't ask what he was signing. He hated the thought that he had been a fool and a gull, and he hated that she could see it. He struggled to find something—anything—to say to her.

She said, "I know you're mad. You should be. He took advantage of you at every turn. The debt. The commission. The settlement. God in heaven, what a settlement! He didn't give you his daughter. He sold her to you. And on the worst possible terms. You went fifteen thousand dollars in debt to marry Adelaide Mannheim." She had never let herself feel anger in his presence. But it was on his account. It was for Mordecai, who had ensnared him so badly.

He was now furious, a feeling he rarely allowed himself. He said, "That's a fine way for Mordecai Mannheim's other daughter to speak to me. How well your father provided for you! I never saw such a bad bargain."

She put the ledgers and papers on the desk and, against all the rules of decorum for a slave, stood to tower over him, and raised her voice. "Really? He could have sold me to a bawdy house in Savannah. Or a rice plantation in South Carolina. Or a sugar grower in Louisiana. Or put me in one of his coffles bound for Mississippi. Was it really such a bad bargain he made, giving me to you?" Her anger grew as she spoke, to flare into a fury equal to his.

He rose and came from behind the desk to stand and look her straight in the face. She had never seen him so angry before. He said, "To own you. Then to give you away. Like a mule! He gave me a mule, too!"

She let herself feel all of the outrage of her childhood. She wanted to let the words pour out, to tell him what it felt like to be considered the like of a mule in the custom of the country and the eyes of the law. It was dangerous for a slave to be this angry. It was doubly dangerous for her to forget, ever, that she was a slave. Their familiarity had made her reckless and stupid. She clenched her skirt with her fists and bit her lips to keep back the words that a slave should never say to a master.

"Rachel," he said, still hot.

She shook her head.

He reached for her hands, and when she refused to unclench her fists, he wrapped his fingers around her wrists. The gesture made her think of shackles and she pulled away. God help her, she would say it. If he forgot all their familiarity, if he beat her, if he sold her, she would say it. In a blaze of anger, she cried out, "I hate being a slave!"

He dropped her hands as though her skin burned him. He turned away. She was sure that she had finally pressed him too far. Her heart racing, her mind racing, she thought, How many lashes will he order? Will he do it himself, or will he ask Charlie to whip me?

When he could face her again, she saw pain mingled with the anger on his face. "I never meant to own another human being," he said, his voice low and choked. "It gives me pain to own Zeke, and Minnie, and Charlie, and everyone else on the place. But it gives me anguish to own you."

For the first time in her life, she didn't say, "Yes, Massa," and excuse herself. She ran from the room, ran from the house, and kept running, not knowing where she was headed. She could keep running. She could run away. She ran until her heart pounded so hard in her chest that she had to slow. Breathing hard, she thought, If I ran away they'd hunt me down, and bring me back in shackles, and whip my back raw, and brand an "R" on my face.

She slowed to a walk. She hadn't come through this part of the piney woods before, and she hadn't seen the house. It was bigger than a cabin, but only a story tall, and ramshackle. It must be the old house on the place, the one that he talked about so fondly.

She walked up the steps and unlatched the door. It was hot inside, and the floor was dusty with neglect, but it was quiet. Her legs suddenly buckled, and she sat heavily on the floor in the middle of the room.

She drew her knees to her chest and wrapped her arms around them. She was trembling all over, a powerful shudder like sobbing, but without tears. She gave herself up to the thought that pounded in her head the way that her heart pounded in her chest. I hate being a slave. I hate being a slave. I hate being a slave. It was as though Henry had set her free to think the worst thought she could imagine.

Like all fits, this one spent itself, and she suddenly felt weary to the marrow of her bones. She heard the door open, and she heard the tread of his boots on the planks of the floor. Henry sank to his knees before her and looked into her stricken face. Breathing hard, as though he'd run after her, he grasped her hands in his. Her work-scarred hands. He said, "We remember being slaves in Egypt. How can we own slaves in Georgia?"

She bent her head to hide the tears that rose to her eyes. He had seen into her heart and touched the deepest desire there. "I want to be free."

He whispered, "You should be."

He had opened the floodgates and she let her all her deepest desires flood out. "Free to read and to write. Free to look anyone in the face, and be called Miss Mannheim. Free to fall in love, and marry, and have babies of my own, and to stay together as long as we lived." The floodgates were open too wide. She thought of Charlie, her lost chance for happiness with Charlie, and she sobbed.

"Oh, Rachel," he whispered. She bent her head to hide the tears, and he reached for her hands, to clasp them and twine his fingers through hers.

She raised her eyes to his. He was so close that if he leaned forward, just a little, his lips would touch hers.

His look was full of tenderness, and it horrified her. She started and sat up. He let go her hands. He reached to brush her cheek with his fingers. "No," she said, her voice low and unsteady.

He sat back on his heels. His face was wet. He reached into his pocket and gave her his clean, crumpled handkerchief.

She took it and unashamedly wiped her face. "I need to set alone for a while," she said.

He wiped his face with his sleeve, not caring that he smeared it. He rose and walked quickly from the room, through the door, and down the steps.

For days afterward, Rachel was afraid. She thought of Eliza, the pretty, smiling mother who knew songs from Africa, who had died bearing Marse Mannheim a second child. She had never known whether Marse Mannheim cared for her mother, but she had lived with the consequence of his feeling all her life. There was nothing but pain and trouble when a master decided to favor a slave gal.

She was so bothered that she couldn't bear to be in the same room with him. If he came into the kitchen, she excused herself for a task in the garden or the dairy. If he asked her to sit with him in the study, she dropped her eyes and said, "I'm sorry, Massa, Missus Adelaide wants me and I can't linger."

He watched her go with sadness, but he didn't command her. One day, as she left the kitchen, a scrap of conversation drifted into the breezeway before she shut the door. Minnie, who had watched him become familiar with Rachel, now asked him, "Do you know what's bothering that gal?"

Like one of his slaves, Henry said to the woman whose eyes were as wise and sharp as an owl's: "I can't say, Minnie."

That Sunday, Minnie insisted that Rachel come to meeting, even though she didn't want to. "Someone you should meet," she said.

"Who? Is Mr. Abraham Lincoln come to pay us a visit?"

Even Minnie, who couldn't read, knew that Mr. Lincoln was campaigning to be president. She said, "The stuff you read in that newspaper make you crazy. Put on your meeting dress and come along with me."

Her dress fit again, now that she ate enough and slept enough, but she didn't feel pretty. She felt dull and weary from the burden of worrying over Marse Henry.

As soon as she and Minnie came to the meeting house, and saw the people gathered outside, she knew why Minnie had insisted so hard.

"This is Jim," she said.

Jim was the newest man on the Mannheim place, a pleasant-looking man with a skin lighter than hers. "I work under Mr. Ezra, and I serve Marse Mannheim," he told her.

"I'm on the Kaltenbach place now, but I grew up on the Mannheim place."

"Marse Mannheim gave me Sunday afternoon for myself," he said. "Would you come for a stroll with me?"

If she said no, she would never hear the end of it from Minnie. As everyone watched, she accepted Jim's invitation.

That afternoon they went walking in the woods, where the pines cooled the air a little. In the heat, the smell of resin was sharp and pungent. He told her about himself. He had been a house servant all his life, as she had. "My mama wouldn't say who my daddy was, but I suspect he was the overseer," he said. His mother was dead, but he had left behind brothers and sisters when he was recently sold away to cover his master's losses on the cotton crop. Marse Mannheim had bought him to sell, but kept him for himself. "Can't tell if that's bad or good," he said.

"Everything Marse Mannheim does is for his own advantage," Rachel said.

"So I'd best be careful."

He hadn't been married, but he'd left a sweetheart behind, and the memory was raw for him. "Doted on her. Sweetest gal. Name of Janey."

"I'm sorry."

He said, "You know what we say when we get married. Til death or distance do us part."

She nodded. He was a nice-looking man, and not a bad-hearted one. But her attention was elsewhere.

"When Miss Minnie tell me about you, I thought we might suit." She nodded. He asked, "Might we stroll together again? Find out?"

It would keep Minnie from needling her. "Yes. Next week, after meeting."

Minnie knew better than to pester her or to sing Jim's praises. She nodded when Rachel told her that they would take another stroll.

The next week, Jim gave her a bunch of wildflowers he'd gathered. "Wish I had something better for you."

"It's a kindly thought."

"I believe Marse Mannheim favor me. Promise me a gift of a cravat. Tell me that if I'm to serve a gentleman I should dress like one."

"Be careful. Don't forget, he looks to his own advantage."

"I won't."

They walked through the pines until they could see the outline of a house, weathered and silvery, through the trees. "Who live there?" Jim asked.

"My Massa used to, before he built his new house."

"Anyone there now?"

"No, it's empty."

"Would you like to set on the stairs and rest for a bit?"

She remembered running up these stairs, full of rage at her condition in life. She recalled Henry's face as he said, "Slavery is wrong." She shook her head. "Don't mind setting on the grass," she said.

"Miss Rachel, there's something on your mind, and it ain't me."

She couldn't find the words to tell the polite lie she owed him. He said, "Your heart is set on someone else, ain't it?"

Surprised, she couldn't reply. He put a friendly hand on her arm. "Wouldn't suit me at all to step out with a gal in love with someone else," he said.

She said, "You ain't mad at me? Or at Minnie?"

"My heart's set on someone else, too. Still think about Janey. Maybe I won't, someday."

A few days later, Henry, who sat behind his desk, the ledger open before him, asked her to stay to talk to him in the study. She said, "Massa, I shouldn't—"

"Just for a moment, Rachel. It shouldn't be anything to trouble you."

She didn't feel enough at ease to sit. She remained standing.

Upset, he said, "I heard there's a man on the Mannheim place who's been courting you."

"Hardly courting, Marse Henry. Went for a stroll with him after meeting."

"Is he kind to you?" He rubbed his face with his hand, a sign of distress. "He's a fool if he doesn't treasure you."

He sounded just like Charlie, jealous of anyone who might cause her pain. "It ain't like that, Massa."

"Do you care for him? I swear I'll buy him so that you can be together."

She gestured toward the ledger. "Don't go into deeper into debt on my account, Massa."

He said, "I would, if it gave you happiness."

His tenderness was worse than the rough pull of Marse Pereira's hands, and more perilous. "Don't trouble yourself, Massa. We didn't suit each other. I ain't getting married any time soon."

For weeks after he grasped Rachel's hands and wished for her freedom, Henry thought about setting her free. He had never considered manumitting a slave before, and he had no idea whether he could. Henry went to see Cat Payne, in his capacity as Cassville's junior lawyer. He and Cat had become friends. Cat told him, "I don't have many law cases, but I have a heap of books." He had offered Henry the freedom to borrow any book he pleased.

Now they sat in Cat's pleasant little office and his man Marcus brought them coffee. "Can I free my slaves?" he asked Cat.

"After you're dead."

"What do you mean?"

"Can't free a slave while you're living, not according to the law in Georgia. Write it into your will, and you can free anyone you like." Marcus stood in the corner of the room. Without turning his head, he was listening carefully.

Henry asked. "There's nothing I can do? While I'm still alive?"

"You could try going North. Even then, you'd have trouble, because of that Dred Scott decision. They'd be fugitives. Anyone could snatch them up and bring them back into slavery."

Henry shook his head.

Cat said, "Why would you want to free your slaves? You need them to run your place."

Henry's cheeks went red with embarrassment. Cat saw it and his face broke into a grin. "We lawyers see this all the time," he said. "You're fond of one of your slave gals. Does she have children?"

Henry was stunned into silence.

"It's nothing to be ashamed of."

Henry stammered, "It isn't like that."

"Whenever Aggie's indisposed or confined, I go out to my place to see Lucy. She has two young'uns that are mine, and one of them looks like me. I give her a little something for herself and those babies, but I ain't planning to free her." Marcus stood against the wall of the office, his face impassive as he heard every word Cat said.

Henry was still blushing. Cat said, "No reason to have such a tender conscience. Just don't rub Adelaide's nose in it."

Rachel sat with Henry in the study a few weeks before Rosh Hashanah, watching him drink a little whiskey. They were still awkward with one another, unless they talked about the crop. But all the dull detail of picking and weighing cotton, of harvesting and shucking corn, couldn't disguise the deep disquiet they felt. They each knew the other's deepest desire, and no amount of servility on her part or decorum on his could take that away.

He said, "Rachel, I'm going to Savannah for Yom Kippur."

"Will Missus Adelaide go with you?"

"I'll ask her." He said, "Have you been to the service?"

"No, but Missus Adelaide told me you fast, and think about your sins, and ask to be forgiven."

"We do. And we ask for ourselves to be inscribed in the Book of Life for good this year, not for evil."

"What's the Book of Life? Is it like a ledger, with the debts on one side, and the credits on the other?"

They both thought of the ledger that had made them open their hearts to each other. He said ruefully, "You would see it like that."

She looked perturbed. "Didn't mean to mock something holy."

He said, "No, you're right. That's just what it is. God keeps a ledger, just like any planter does."

She gestured to his desk. "How do you think you'll come out?"

He looked into her face, and she had to turn her gaze away, because she could feel how much he wanted to touch her. "I don't know."

Later that day, as Rachel served her master and mistress their supper, Henry asked Adelaide if she'd like to go to Savannah for the Yom Kippur service at Mickve Israel. Adelaide said, "They still remember my broken engagement in Savannah. I don't think I want to go to Mickve Israel, even to save my soul." She looked at her husband. "Why do you feel so repentant this year, Henry?"

Rachel felt her face turn to stone. Henry didn't look at her as he said to Adelaide, "It's good to ask for forgiveness. We should do it every year."

Henry went to Savannah by himself. He would stay with Joe Meyer and his growing family. The Meyers bought an extra seat in the synagogue and he was welcome to use it.

In Savannah, it was good to see Joe, and to meet his wife Dorothea, affectionately known in the family as Dortchen. She was a clever, teasing, warm-hearted Jewish girl, whose family owned a dry goods business back in Germany. There was already one child, a little boy of two, and she was expecting her second. Joe and Dortchen were happy together. He could see it in the way she smiled at him, in the way he put his arm tenderly around her waist, in the way they embraced at the end of the day.

All of the tender things he had hoped that Adelaide would do, once they were married.

That night, after the Kol Nidrei service, he lay sleepless in an unfamiliar bed in the Meyer house, thinking of Rachel. He thought of her eyes, the almond shape like and so unlike Adelaide's, the iris so dark that it melted into the pupil. Her cheeks, with their lovely sculpts of bone above her dimples. Her lips, brown tinged with pink, fuller than Adelaide's. Of the sound of her voice, even if all she said was, "Yes, Marse Henry." He rarely heard it these days, but he cherished her laugh. It was a deep rich sound in her throat, and it reminded him of the taste of coffee and chocolate. He thought of her body in her faded calico dress, the lovely swell of bosom and belly and thigh.

He woke from a dream that Adelaide sold Rachel while he was gone, with his face drenched in tears and his nightshirt wet with seed. Before he left his room he tried to scrub out the stain himself, doubly shamed—that the servant would know, and that it happened on Yom Kippur night.

In the synagogue, Henry's attention wandered. As a boy, pressed to go to the Yom Kippur service with his father, pressed to fast, he had ignored the prayer and instead thought all day of how hungry he was. Mickve Israel used the new book of prayer, which translated the Hebrew liturgy into English. All his life, he had repeated the long list of sins that Jews repented of, but he had never understood what the words meant. Lying in all its forms, stealing, violence and lawlessness were all there. But slaveholding was not. To his surprise, neither was adultery.

During breaks in the day-long service, the men of Mickve Israel, whose interest in worldly things never flagged, talked about the presidential election. Henry, his attention fogged by fasting, heard snatches of their conversation. "Don't like that Abraham Lincoln." "Won't be on the ballot in Georgia." "If he wins the South won't tolerate it." "We'll secede." "South Carolina first, and we'll be right behind them." "Secession? Bad for business."

He heard a familiar voice calling out, "Mr. Kaltenbach!"

It was the former Emilie Cohen, beautifully dressed, with her husband William Pereira, also beautifully dressed, by her side. She said, "I wanted so to see my family for the High Holidays that I made William leave his business to visit from London."

Pereira said, "Emilie, don't you recall that Mr. Kaltenbach married Miss Mannheim after she returned to Cass County?"

"I do recall," said Emilie, smiling in that Savannah way, so polite and so scornful.

Pereira asked, "Miss Mannheim—excuse me, Mrs. Kaltenbach—is she well? I heard that she had a child."

Henry felt dizzy. "Yes, a little boy," he says. "We're all well, thank you."

Pereira said, "Whatever happened to her servant? Rachel, I think her name was."

The world seemed to swim before Henry's eyes. "She's with us. Also well."

When the service was over, Henry and Joe went back to Joe's comfortable house, where Dortchen had made a festive meal to break the fast. The soup with dumplings, the stuffed breast of veal, and the honey cake were all familiar. They spoke of a Jewish life in Dresden, where the memory of slavery had contemporary currency in the way that German Jews were oppressed and wronged. It was hard to eat. He thought of Adelaide and of Rachel. His day of repentance had done him no good. He was still guilty of betraying them both.

Dortchen went upstairs to settle her children for the night, and he and Joe sat in the parlor. Joe, who rarely drank, poured him a glass of whiskey and watched as he drank it, then asked for another. Joe said, "Henry, what's the matter?"

"Do you love your wife?"

Joe never looked surprised. He said, "I was lucky. Our families arranged for us to meet, but we liked each other, and we suited each other."

"I didn't marry for love," he said. "I married for advantage. For Mordecai Mannheim's advantage, it turns out."

Joe waited. His silence had netted him many a confession. Henry said, "I don't love her, and she doesn't love me, and there's nothing I can do about it. I'm deep in debt. Even if I could divorce her, I wouldn't be free of Mordecai. Because of the debt."

Joe was too tactful to say, I warned you. But Henry remembered that he had said it.

Joe watched Henry drink and look miserably at the Brussels carpet. He spoke in German, as though their native tongue were better for telling secrets than English. "What's wrong, Heinrich?"

"I've fallen in love," he said.

Softly, Joe said, "Is she married to someone else?"

"No." Full of whiskey, full of repentance, he said, "But she's forbidden to me."

Joe had lived in the South long enough to guess what he meant. He was quiet for a long time. "Heinrich, it's a *shande*." He used the Jewish dialect word that meant "shame" and "disgrace." He said, "Whoever she is—don't tell me who she is—it's a disgrace for you, and shame in betraying Adelaide." He sighed. "Put it aside, Heinrich."

"I can't," he said.

While Henry was gone, Adelaide told Rachel that she wanted to walk to town. "Come with me. You don't need to carry a basket. If we buy anything we'll have it sent to us."

It was late September, and the summer's warmth held an undertone of the winter chill to come. It was a bright, cloudless day, the sky a blue dome above their heads. Hawks flew above, looking for the mice and squirrels attracted by kernels falling from ripened corn. The leaves on the live oaks had just begun to turn, a hint of brown along the dark green. September was full cotton harvest, and as they walked past the cotton fields onto the main road, they saw the field hands bending to pick the bolls, dragging the heavy sacks slung over their shoulders. They weren't really singing, since it was hard to sing as you stooped and bent. The song was a holler, part grunt and part moan.

They walked along the dirt road that went into town, well tamped down by horse and mule and cart, and Adelaide took Rachel's arm, as though they were schoolgirls together instead of mistress and slave.

She said, "Why do you think my husband was so eager to go to synagogue in Savannah?"

Rachel thought, I'll tell as much as I can that's true. "I reckon he wanted to see his old friends in Savannah. He did ask you to go along."

"Yom Kippur ain't a frolic of a holiday. You fast, and you sit in the synagogue all day, and you confess your sins and ask God to forgive you."

"Can't set in a meeting chair all day long. Get up, wander about, say how do to your friends. And there must be a bit of a frolic afterwards, to make up for not eating all day."

Adelaide stopped, pulling a little on Rachel's arm to make her stop, too. She looked into her sister's eyes. "What does he have on his conscience?"

It took all of her slave's self-control to keep her face composed. She told a truth God wouldn't hate her for. "All this talk about slavery and secession has him bothered, I think."

"How would you know?"

"He doesn't mind that I read the newspaper, and we talk about the news of the day."

"Don't tell me he agrees with those Abolitionists up North."

She felt it too strongly to keep it tamped down, and it came out more emphatic than she intended. "He's troubled by owning slaves."

"That's awfully tender-minded, for a slaveowner," Adelaide said.

"He's a tender man. As you know."

Adelaide looked searchingly into Rachel's face and tightened her grip on Rachel's arm. She said, "I don't recall that anyone repents of owning slaves on Yom Kippur. Just the ordinary sins. Lying, cheating, stealing, adultery. Has he been up to any of those?"

Rachel drew in her breath. She said, "Can't say, ma'am."

"Can't? Or won't?"

"I wish you wouldn't press me so, ma'am." She pulled away a little, to break free, but Adelaide held her fast. They walked into town that way, and by the time they reached Cassville, Rachel had a bruise on her upper arm.

When Henry sat down to midday dinner at home, Adelaide wanted to know about the people she'd known in Savannah. He said, "I saw Miss Emilie Cohen. Mrs. William Pereira, now. She was staying with her people in Savannah for the holidays."

Adelaide drew in her breath and held it. Rachel, her face impassive, pressed her back against the dining room wall. "And Mr. Pereira?" Adelaide asked.

"I saw him, too. He asked after you. And after Rachel."

Spots of color appeared on Adelaide's cheeks, but Rachel's face went gray. Adelaide picked up her knife and cut her chicken as though she hated it. "I hope he goes swiftly back to London," she said.

Henry spent a restless night, falling in a shallow sleep and starting awake. In the morning, he slipped into the kitchen early, where he found Rachel alone. He said, very low, "Come to see me in the old place after breakfast."

She met his gaze, her dark eyes asking the question the discretion kept from her lips. He said, still low, "No. Later."

Over the breakfast table he watched the wife to whom he was married by all the laws of Israel, and thought of the shame and disgrace that he would bring to her. Rachel served the meal and cleared the table, but he kept his eyes away, seeing only her hands, as he had the first time she served him when he was courting Adelaide.

After the meal, he went upstairs and tapped on Adelaide's bedroom door. There was no answer, and he opened the door to slip inside. He had rarely been in this room in daylight, except when Adelaide was confined.

He found what he was looking for. It was too big to put into his pocket. He hid it under his jacket and secured it with his arm. He walked resolutely down the stairs and from the house.

It was a ripe day in October, still warm and sunny, good weather for picking cotton. He heard the field hands singing the holler that was so well suited to the bending and stooping to reach for the bolls.

In the bright light, the old house looked worn and neglected. The steps sighed as he took them, and the door creaked as he pushed it open. He had forgotten how small this room was. How plain. It was a good place to speak plain.

He thought of the sin he'd been unable to repent of in Savannah. That he loved a woman who was not his wife. That he loved a woman who was his wife's sister. That he loved a woman who was a slave.

He let go the object he'd been holding under his arm, and rested it in his hands as he waited for her.

He heard the steps sigh for her, too, and she came quietly into the room to stand close enough so that he could touch her.

He held it out and said softly, "This is yours."

She said nothing. She took it, feeling the leather in her palms, as she looked at him with eyes liquid with surprise and sadness.

He said, "It should always be in your hands."

"Did she give it back to you?"

He shook his head. "It belongs to you," he said.

The sun illuminated her face, and he saw her afresh. How beautiful she was. How beloved. He brushed her cheek with his fingers, and said, very low, "I love you."

She still held the book in her palms. She shook her head. Was it a refusal? Or was she unable to reply?

He said, "I want to cherish you and to honor you. I love you as a husband loves a wife, the wife of his heart."

No word from her. Not a sweet one, and not a teasing one. No word at all, just the surprised look of those dark eyes, so much like her sister's.

He said, "I won't be father to a child as Mordecai Mannheim was to you. If you love me, if you come to me, I'll do what I can so that no child of ours will be born a slave."

Did those dark eyes moisten with tears? Still no word.

He took his hand away. He said, "If you say no, I'll abide by it. But I'll grieve for it."

She found her voice. "Let me go."

"Now? Or forever?"

"For now."

"Of course. I won't hurry you."

She handed him the book. He said, "No. It's yours, forever."

She nodded. "Keep it here for me. Hide it."

He took it from her hands. She turned to go and he didn't try to recall her. He watched, and then listened, as her quick, resolute step carried her from the house.

A few days later, when no one—neither Minnie, nor Adelaide, nor Henry—needed her for any reason, Rachel took off her apron and slipped away to the old house. It was cool for October, a damp gray day that reminded her of winter, and she wished she'd worn her shawl. Rain came down in a drizzle that temporarily halted picking. The steps of the house were wet, and the air inside was damp. The light that came through the rain-wet windows was so dark that she wished that she had a candle against it.

She sat on the rough floor of the house that had given Henry such happiness, and hugged her knees to her chest as she pondered what he had said.

I love you.

He had always known what her soul craved. Consideration, when she first came to the new house as Adelaide's maid. Kindliness, to ask what she needed for her comfort. An orange, to heal the hurt of a childhood when Christmas belonged to her Israelite mistress and not to her.

A book, bound in leather and edged in gold, full of tales spun by someone who knew the story of how bread loves salt. He had retrieved it from Adelaide's grasp and returned it to her. It belonged to her. He had said so, his eyes glistening with feeling. He was willing to defy the woman he had married to mend the wound that Adelaide had rent in her. She pressed her head to her knees and wept.

I love you.

There were masters who would take a slave woman without saying a thing. Without asking. She remembered Marse Pereira and wept afresh. There were masters who would mouth words of love, whether they meant it or not. She was grown, and old enough, and wise enough, to understand that Marse Mannheim had likely said those words to her mother. And there were men whose minds were open, and whose hearts were full, who said those words with such meaning that the Lord heard them, and blessed them for saying so.

I love you.

Lovers said so. Sisters might, as well.

She sat up, her face smeared with tears. Could she feel that way about Adelaide? Did Adelaide feel that way about her?

Since she was a little girl, she had been Adelaide's companion. Her helpmeet. Her servant. Her pet dog. Oh, Charlie, she thought, her sore eyes stinging. I rue the day you said so. Did Adelaide feel anything more for her? Did Adelaide care for her? Worry for her? Did Adelaide know anything her soul craved?

Everything hurtful and dark came to her, as she sat in the deepening dusk. Adelaide had thrown away her own life to save her sister. Adelaide had refused William Pereira, who would have married Adelaide for her fortune and debased Rachel for her body.

Was it a lady's fury at being used and shamed? Or a sister's love? Or both?

The thought checked her tears. There were slaves who owed a mistress nothing but a false face as they laced up a corset. She felt anguish as she contemplated whether she owed Adelaide more than that.

Did she? What of the woman who had never imagined that she might want a husband of her own, or a child of her own? What of the woman whose spite kept her from her nephew's cradle, and whose distrust saw every courtesy of her husband's as a danger to the promise he had made to his wife?

It was perilous to anger the woman whose mother's marriage had been defiled by her father's slave mistress. If she angered Adelaide, she could swiftly find herself in a coffle bound for Mississippi, her wrists manacled together, her feet bound by shackles that slowed her walk to a shuffle. Was Henry's love such a prize that it outweighed the peril of Adelaide's discovery, and Adelaide's wrath?

He had given her the freedom to choose. To say yes or no, as she decided for herself. He had urged her, as no one ever had, to search her own soul to ask, what do you crave most?

To love you.

She shook as she understood it, as though she had caught the ague. To look you in the eye. To call you by name. To delight you when we lie together. To help you in life, and to let you help me, as much as you can.

To be free.

She shivered with the fear and the wonder of it, worse than the ague. Someday, somehow, she would be free. He hadn't promised it. He could not. But she could see it, the way she could see the light of summer glimmering faintly behind the bleakness of winter.

This year we are slaves. Next year we will be free.

She rose, cramped and sore from sitting and weeping so long, and dusted off her skirt. She straightened herself and took a last look around the humble place where Henry had felt at home. She wiped her face and readied herself to walk back to the house that was now his, and Adelaide's. To face her life there, whatever it brought. And to say, I love you.

She came unbidden into his study, and unbidden, she shut the door. She looked into his familiar face: the dark, kind, liquid eyes, the prominent nose, the expression open as a book was open, for anyone to read. For the first time since she had met him, she didn't say, "Massa." Or "Marse Henry." She said simply, "Henry."

He touched her cheek and caressed it with such sweetness that her eyes filled. She said, "We ain't free to do this. Neither of us."

"No, we're not. We're bound together." He took her hands. "I will love you forever."

She looked into his eyes and said the words of the marriage vow she knew so well. "To have and to hold, to love and to cherish, for better or for worse."

He said the rest, as well as he remembered it. "Only death will part us."

"Death or distance," she said, making the vow that slaves made.

"Neither death nor distance. Forever, beyond both."

She touched his cheek, as gently as he had touched hers. "Yes," she said, so low that she thought he might not hear her.

He looked into her eyes, his brown liquid eyes meeting her inky irises, and he pulled her to him. He whispered, "Beloved," and he kissed her, his lips opening to hers, and hers to his. She felt his heart beating against hers, one beat in rhythm to her own.

Chapter 13

Steal Away

After they made their vows to each other, Henry and Rachel met in their hiding place to plot when they could be together. As they sat cross-legged on the floor, Henry took her hands in his. He said, "We could slip away at night."

"All kinds of folks are out at night. Micah and Lydia slip away together all the time. It they saw us, they'd know."

"When, beloved?"

"After midday dinner. When Adelaide lies down to rest, and when I could be anywhere on the place."

"Charlie expects to see me after dinner."

"Tell him you want to sit in the study and write in your ledger. Or that you need to go into town."

His face shadowed. "Yes," he said, making a new set of vows that bound them together in deception.

Rachel was glad of Henry's promise about preventing a baby. But a baby, and not having a baby, was a womanly secret. She asked Minnie if she knew a root for it.

Minnie said, "I don't like to give that root to anyone."

"That ain't so. Didn't you help Lydia?"

"Tell me you're stepping out with someone on the Mannheim place, and I'll be inclined to help you."

Rachel said, "I reckon you know why I'm asking."

Minnie said darkly, "I don't trust myself to reckon."

"Do you want Marse Henry's blood kin to grow up in slavery?"

Minnie put her hand to her face. When she looked up she was furious, but her eyes were wet. "Ain't a root. It's a seed. Queen Anne's lace. If you chew it the morning after you sport, you won't have a baby."

"What does it taste like?"

"Taste? Bitter. No one eats it for the taste."

When Rachel and Henry fixed the day for their first time together, she trembled. He embraced her. "Beloved, are you afraid?"

She said, "Only of being found out."

He didn't say, "There's nothing to be afraid of," because there was.

The next day, after the midday dinner dishes were scraped and stacked and washed, Rachel prepared herself to lie with Henry for the first time. If she were a lady, she would bathe, and perfume herself, and put on a silk wrapper trimmed with lace. Instead, she smoothed her hair and smoothed her skirt and stuffed a blanket into the biggest basket she dared to carry over her arm. If she met anyone she would say she was hunting wild plants in the woods for Minnie.

It was near November, harvest time, when the early bolls had been picked, and the green of the cotton plants had begun to wither. The chill in the air dampened the resinous scent of the pines, and the live oaks had begun to fade for winter. The birds that called during the day sang out their names: chick-a-dee-dee-dee! Pee-wee, pee-wee! Phoe-be, phoe-be! As she slipped into the woods she heard the tapping noise of woodpeckers, who liked the bugs that lived in dying pine trees. She heard the small noises of small animals. Mice and squirrels, like pigs, favored pinecones and pine nuts. The pine woods, cool even in summer, were beginning to feel wintry.

Today, in daylight, the house's grayed boards looked silvery. When she stepped onto the piazza the planks sighed a little underfoot. She pushed open the door and stepped inside.

Alone, waiting, she lingered in the main room, really seeing it for the first time. Used to a grand house, now living in a substantial one, this place looked small and humble to her. She took in the whitewashed walls, the plain pine floor, and the old-fashioned stone hearth. Some men, like Marse Mannheim, enjoyed the grandeur of a big house. Henry didn't. This modest place had pleased him.

She heard a light step on the piazza—it sighed for him, too—and a light hand on the door. He closed the door behind him. As if he were going into the fields, he had put on a hat against the sun, and unbuttoned his jacket. He smiled and stretched out his hand to her. Hand in hand, they went slowly into his old room.

She set down the basket and lay the blanket on the floor. She was trembling again. When she straightened up, he caught both her hands in his own, and held them gently. He asked, "Is this your first time?"

She decided that it was best to be truthful. "No, it isn't." Would it disappoint him that she wasn't pure, as his wife had been? "When I was eighteen I loved a man, and we lay together in love for a year."

He looked at her for a long time, reading her face. "You look so sad," he said. "What happened?"

She couldn't tell him the whole truth, but she wouldn't lie, either. "He fell in love with someone else and married her."

He didn't speak, but his touch on her face was as light as a breath of air. It didn't bother him that she'd been sullied. It bothered him that she'd been hurt. She looked up and said, "The ending was bitter, but the loving was sweet. The first time, and always."

He gathered her into his arms and kissed her, very gently, on the lips. "Lie down with me."

They lay down on the blanket, side by side. He cradled her head, touching her hair. "Your hair is so soft," he whispered. He kissed one cheekbone, then the other, and then kissed her mouth. She returned the kiss, parting her lips to give it passion. He laughed a little—it wasn't easy, to laugh and kiss at the same time—and at the familiar sound, her fear melted away. She said, "Let's take it slow. It's sweeter if it's slow."

He said, "I am dying for you, but I want to look at you, and touch you, and savor all of you."

He touched her everywhere through her dress, letting his hands curve around her hips and buttocks. She stroked the muscles of his shoulders and his back. He was slighter than Charlie—she was a little ashamed to think so— but he was wiry. As he looked. He moved a little away from her, and touched her throat. Her collarbones. Her chest. He curved his hand around her breast, looking into her eyes, and said, "How I have longed for this."

She said, "I want to feel you against my skin." She reached to unbutton her dress, but her hands were shaking. He covered her hands with his own. "Let me help you." He had trouble with the buttons, but she liked seeing that. He wasn't used to undressing a woman. Together, they slid the dress over her hips and down her legs. He looked at her in her chemise and petticoat, smiling, then reached for the buttons on the chemise. Unbuttoned it. Pulled it off. With her help, pulled off her petticoat. She lay beside him, naked except for God's glory, and he propped himself on his elbow to admire her. He said, "You are so beautiful—so beautiful—"

"Black but comely."

"Just beautiful." He reached for his jacket, to take it off, but his hands betrayed him. She said, "Now let me help you." She knew how to undress a person, even if her hands were unsteady. She undid the buttons on his shirt. On his trousers. Laughed to see the drawers underneath. She had been washing them and putting them away for months, but she had never seen them on. "Don't tell me these have buttons, too."

He laughed. "Let me take my boots off."

"No, let me," she said. It was the first wifely thing she had ever done for him, and he watched her as she did it now, at ease in her bare skin. "White folks wear more clothes than black folks do."

Naked at last, smiling, he said, "Part of our general foolishness."

The teasing tone was familiar, even if his body was not. She murmured, "Let me look at you." Kneeling at his side, she touched as she looked. His nipples, which were small and hard and tinged with brown, like a fair-complected black man's. The whorls of hair around them, darker and coarser than the hair on his head. His ribs. She laid a gentle finger on him, to trace one of the prominent bones, and he said, "If you're gentle with me there you'll find out how ticklish I am." She couldn't resist. He began to wriggle, and to laugh, telling her, "When my sisters found out how ticklish I was they tormented me."

She stopped tormenting him. She stroked him with a firm hand, smiling. "I can feel every one of your rib bones. If Minnie saw you without your shirt she would cry. All that effort to fatten you up. All for nought."

She continued to move her gaze and her hand over him, savoring the sight of him and the feel of him. His hipbones, nearly as prominent as his ribs. His flat belly, where a stripe of dark hair pointed to his privates. His long thigh, covered with dark hair, finer and softer to the touch than the hair on his chest. His member, eager for her, hard against his belly. She cradled him in her hand. She said, "So that's what a grown man who's had a *bris milah* looks like."

"Now you know." He reached out his arms and she lay down beside him. He embraced her, holding her head between his hands, kissing her with parted lips. She chuckled. "Slow," she said. "Sweet and slow."

He breathed deeply. He eased. He lay beside her, exploring her as she had explored him. Her breast, with the soft brown nipple that hardened beneath his fingers. The curve of her hip. The slight mound of her belly. The soft black hair on her mound of Venus. She sighed with pleasure when he laid his hand there. Her nether lips, which were wet. He parted them with his fingers—she helped him, opening her thighs to make it easier for him—and found the wet little pearl of flesh inside. "Oh, that's good," she said, arching her back as he touched her. Her desire fueled his own, and he caressed her until she spasmed and cried out with pleasure.

He bent down to kiss her belly, letting his lips travel from her navel down to her hand. Still at her ease, she said, "What are you up to?"

He moved her hand away. He found what he was looking for and put his tongue on it. She began to laugh, and to writhe, and by the time he was finished her entire body had arched in a spasm that made her moan and laugh at the same time. He said, "How was that?"

Still laughing, she said, "Never tried such a thing before, but I liked it!"

He rolled over and reached for his trousers, taking something from the pocket. "What is that?" she asked.

"It's a rubber sheath. It keeps the seed from the womb. So there won't be a baby."

She watched as he put it on. She chuckled again—he liked the sound of it, it was throaty with desire—and said, "That's a mighty funny looking thing."

He pretended to take offense. "Are you laughing at me?"

"I ain't laughing at you. I'm laughing at that rubber overcoat you've got on your privates."

"Hush," he said affectionately. "Let me lie atop you." She lay on her back and opened her arms to him. "Yes," she said, her eyes shining, her legs parted wide to welcome him, and he slowly entered her. "Am I hurting you?" he asked.

Charlie had asked her that, as he eased his sturdy, muscled body atop hers. She felt disloyal, remembering Charlie as she ran her hands over Henry's slender frame and felt his lean body cover hers. For all his heft, Charlie had never hurt her, and finely-made Henry wouldn't, either.

"No. Feels fine. Just take it slow."

He covered her, and eased inside her, and she welcomed him into her body. She opened to him like a flower, blooming. She opened her legs to let him in and arched her hips to pull him in deeper. He eased inside her, so deep that she couldn't tell where he left off and she began. She wrapped her legs around his hips and they rocked together in the entwined rhythm of one flesh, until they both cried out in simultaneous joy.

Slick with sweat, cross-eyed with pleasure, spent, he lay on her breast. When he spoke, he said, "*Gott im Himmel.*"

She laughed. "I never addled a man so bad he couldn't speak English."

He kissed her collarbone. "I never felt so good."

They lay together for a long time, without moving. She asked, "You're all right? You don't itch?"

He murmured, "No. I want to stay inside you. It is the best place in the world. I hate to leave it."

"You're always welcome back," she said, smiling.

He turned to look at her. "Am I? You'll steal away with me again?"

She touched his face and said, "We say 'slip away' for sporting. 'Steal away' is for running."

"I know. Not very far, beloved. Only to this place. Maybe farther than that, someday."

"Next year in Jerusalem," she murmured.

"Yes," he whispered, his lips against hers. "Next year in Jerusalem."

The book of Shakespeare's plays was gone.

How long had it been missing? Adelaide didn't know. As much as it troubled her, she had gotten so used to its presence that she had stopped looking at it.

Perhaps Henry had taken it, without telling her, to put back in the study. She went to look while he was in the field, so she could search for it at her leisure, but she couldn't find it on the shelf. Uneasy, worried, she moved the papers on his desk and opened all the desk's drawers, finding nothing but the ledgers, with their columns of figures that gave him so much grief.

Adelaide went up the back stairs, which she never used, to the attic room that Rachel shared with Minnie.

Even on a cool day, it was warm in the attic, and the open windows didn't freshen the air enough. The sparse furniture—the narrow beds, the two chairs, and the washstand—didn't fill the space. She had never realized how little a slave had for her own use. Rachel's good calico dress hung on a nail in the wall. On the washstand was a slop jar and a basin, and on its rail hung a clean rag, Rachel's washcloth. Next to it was a cracked china dish with a horn comb, missing a few teeth, and some hairpins.

Adelaide opened the drawer of the washstand, but it held only a chemise and a petticoat. Disappointed, Adelaide knelt to look under Rachel's bed, but all she saw were great balls of dust, the sign of a servant who was too weary to sweep for herself. She heard steps on the staircase and quickly rose, brushing the dust from the front of her skirt.

Rachel stopped in the doorway. Too startled to contain herself, she cried out, "What are you doing in my room?"

Adelaide said, "I'm looking for that book of Shakespeare's plays." Letting her hear the accusal.

"It ain't here," Rachel said, too flustered to talk properly. "Didn't you look in the study?"

"It isn't in the study."

Rachel said, "Maybe Marse Henry had a desire to read it."

Adelaide said, "You go into his room and look for it."

Rachel said indignantly, "I don't touch his things, except to put away the wash." Reminding Adelaide that she was not a thief. "Why don't you ask him for it?"

Suddenly Adelaide couldn't bear the thought of asking Henry about the book, only to see him flush bright red, a sure sign that he was lying. She glared at Rachel. "If that book is gone—"

Rachel glared back at her. And interrupted her. "It ain't."

That night, Rachel dreamed that she was back in the Mannheim house, about to be beaten. She saw the belt with its heavy buckle and she was full of fear, because the person who held it was angry enough to blind her with it. She heard the belt whistle through the air, and heard a furious voice cry out, "I swear I'll sell you!" She woke in a sweat of guilt and fear, with an ache over her eye where the cut had healed years ago. The voice was Adelaide's.

A few days later, as Adelaide walked into the breezeway to talk to Minnie about midday dinner, she saw Rachel and Henry standing together outside the kitchen door. Rachel had a basket over her arm, the one she used to gather eggs in. The two of them stood close together, at ease with each other. As Adelaide watched, Rachel leaned close to Henry and put her hand on his arm. A wifely gesture. Henry covered her hand with his own, and smiled with a happiness she had rarely seen on his face.

In the still-pleasant air of late fall, Adelaide felt cold, then hot, as though suspicion were a kind of fever. She turned and ran up the stairs to her room and sank into her chair, tormented more by her thoughts than what she'd seen. It is. It can't be.

Rachel came into her room and she said sharply, "What are you doing here?"

"Doing the wash today, ma'am. Collecting your dirty things."

She didn't say, "Don't ma'am me," because she was too angry to allow her sister anything but servitude. Had Rachel been deceiving her? She could deceive too. She said, "Of course I'm all right. Why would you think any different?"

After midday dinner, unable to rest, Adelaide went to look for Rachel. She stopped in the nursery, where Becky sat to rock Matt in his cradle. "Becky, have you seen Rachel? I need her."

Becky had never been easy with her, but today she dropped her eyes and mumbled, "No, ma'am, I ain't seen her."

Adelaide left the house to walk into the kitchen, but she didn't see Rachel or Minnie. Minnie might be in the barn or the dairy or the garden, and Rachel might be with her, or elsewhere. As she went outside she met Minnie, who was coming from the dairy. Now that the days had cooled, she was making cheese again.

"Minnie, where's Rachel? Is she helping you?"

Minnie dropped her eyes. "No, ma'am."

"Where is she? I need her."

"Sent her out to gather some roots for me."

"Why didn't you go?"

"I need to watch this cheese. She know what I want."

"Minnie, is everything all right?"

Minnie had never been easy with her, unless she was sick or near dying. "Yes, ma'am. Everything just fine. I tell Rachel to go to you when she get back."

Why would Minnie be uneasy? "Where is Mr. Kaltenbach?"

Minnie looked surprised. "He's usually in the field with Charlie after dinner, ma'am. If you want him, you should look for him there."

She walked over to the cabins, where she found Charlie, who was sitting on the steps of his cabin. He jumped up to see her. She asked, "Have you seen Mr. Kaltenbach?"

Charlie said, "No, ma'am, but I thought he might have gone into town this afternoon. He go all the time to Stockton's, or to that man who sells books. Sometimes to visit his friend Marse Payne."

When she didn't reply, Charlie added, "Sometimes he come late into the field because he lie down after dinner and fall asleep. Might be sleeping."

"Charlie, when he tells you where he's been, does he flush red?"

Charlie hesitated. "Hard to tell. This cold weather do chap a man's face."

Henry never slept during the day. Adelaide went into the house, more bothered than she'd been before. Where was her husband? Where was Rachel?

She went into her own room and sat in the chair by the window. Suspicion and good sense warred in her. Rachel is gathering roots, she thought. Henry walked into Cassville to go to Stockton's.

Or they were somewhere, the two of them, hidden away, together.

She thought of the way they had stood together in the yard, with the ease of people intimate with each other. She leaned back in her chair, sick with a memory that had nothing to do with the tender touch she'd seen. She was in a dark hallway in the Cohen house in Savannah, seeing the back of a head of curly brown hair, hearing a low, frightened voice cry out, "Marse Pereira!"

A few days after Abraham Lincoln became president, when the *Savannah Republican* was full of clamor for secession, Adelaide went upstairs to her room at the hour when she could find neither Rachel nor Henry, to brood over what she had seen and what she suspected. Her head ached. She felt hot, as she had when she was feverish after Matt's birth. She got up to stand at the window and to press her face against the chill of the windowpane. It was dark and gloomy these days, damp even when it wasn't raining. She looked out on the side yard, and the garden, and the pine woods behind.

She saw Rachel emerge from the kitchen, her shawl over her shoulders and her basket over her arm. Roots for Minnie, Adelaide thought.

Or perhaps not. Rachel looked around her—what was she expecting? A bear, or a mountain cat?—and walked quickly through the stand of live oaks on the other side of the house. The Mannheim place was in the opposite direction, through the pines and behind the cabins. Where was she going?

Adelaide didn't move, as though Rachel might know that she lurked, and be startled if she made a sound. She watched until her sister disappeared into the uncleared thicket of trees that grew beyond the live oaks.

The side door opened, and Henry walked out. He wore his jacket and his hat, as though he were going to join Charlie in the field, but he didn't walk in the direction of the cabins or the fields. He followed the path that Rachel had taken, past the live oaks into the pine forest, and like Rachel, he disappeared into the woods.

She leaned against the windowpane. Jealousy flared in her, hot and cold like yellow fever. Aggie had said, If I don't see it, I don't know, but Adelaide was not like Aggie. Tomorrow she would be ready to follow them and to find out where they went together.

The next day, after midday dinner, she went upstairs to her room. With some difficulty, she took off her good muslin dress by herself, and put on her rambling dress and her boots. If anyone asked, she was going for a ramble, even though it was foolish to walk outdoors when it was so damp and chill.

She slipped outside. She would hide in the stand of trees beyond the live oaks, and wait.

It wasn't long. Rachel came through the live oaks, her basket over her arm. Adelaide listened until her footfalls faded away, and she waited for Henry.

He came too, not as quiet as Rachel, not as furtive. When he was still in sight, but far enough to miss her if he looked behind him, Adelaide followed him through the trees. Someone had worn a path here. She wondered if they had worn it, or if it had always been there.

The trees opened to a clearing, where she recognized the small, weathered house. The old house on the place, the one that Henry had apologized for when she rambled by, before they were married. She watched as Henry walked up the steps. His own step was light and eager. She was sorry she couldn't see his face. She wanted to know if he was smiling.

Once he was inside, she slipped quietly around the side of the house where another clump of trees grew. They were pines, which never lost their protective greenery, and their branches poked and scratched her as she tried to find a vantage point where she could look unseen into the window.

In daylight, she could easily look into the house, and clearly see into the room. As she watched, Henry embraced Rachel with a lover's passion. As she watched, Rachel kissed Henry with a lover's hunger. As she watched, her husband and her sister lay down on the floor together, laughing and crying out, and as she lingered, they betrayed her.

Chapter 14

To Preserve the Union

When the *Savannah Republican* arrived, just after the presidential election, Rachel and Henry were so eager for the news that they postponed their embrace until they had read about Abraham Lincoln's victory. "Hallelujah," Rachel said, tears in her eyes, and Henry hugged her with all his strength. "Don't care if you bust my ribs doing that," she gasped. "I'm so glad."

In the coming weeks, their mood turned to dismay as they read about Georgia's rush toward secession from the Union. Within a week, leading Georgians were calling on the Georgia Assembly to consider secession. A week later, the Assembly voted to authorize a convention to vote on Georgia's secession from the Union, and charged each county with holding an election for convention delegates. Too keyed up for love, too agitated even to undress, Henry sat on the floor with Rachel and said, "I'm going to put myself forward as a delegate."

This late in November, the days were cool. The chill seeped in through the closed windows and under the closed door. Rachel shivered a little despite her shawl. She asked him, "Why?"

The daylight that came through the window was watery and gray. "Someone should be there to vote against it."

She gripped both his arms tightly. "The Assembly approved a million dollars for a militia last week. They're getting ready to raise an army, sugar. They're getting ready to go to war."

"You're mighty upset. You're gripping me tight enough to bruise me. Hold my hands." She let go and took his hands, a looser grip, and he said, "I don't think we Union men can stop Georgia from seceding. Or from going to war. But I know I'd never forgive myself if I didn't go to raise my voice against it."

"Would you go to fight?"

He pressed her hands with his own and met her eyes. She had never seen him so resolute. "I wouldn't fight for secession from the Union. And I wouldn't fight for slavery."

She looked away, too troubled to meet his gaze. He reached out and put his arms around her. "We don't know what's going to happen, beloved. We can't fret about the future we can't see."

She pressed her face against his chest and said in a muffled voice, "You worry about everything you can't see. Listen to you, trying to cheer me."

He stroked her hair and kissed her head. "It's only right. You've carried me more than once."

She sat up straight. He leaned forward and gently kissed her lips. She smiled a little. "How are you going to get yourself elected?"

He kissed her again. "I'm going to talk to Mordecai. He has friends all over the county. If he vouches for me, it should help. And I'm going to talk to Cat, too. He ran for the Assembly once. He'll be able to advise me."

He went to see Mordecai the next day, and told him what he was planning to do. Mordecai said, "I need to know how you're intending to vote."

"That's a matter of serving the people who elect me. And of serving my own conscience."

"That's the trouble. I don't trust that tender conscience of yours." He looked sharply at Henry. "In my mind, a good politician stays bought after you buy him."

"I'm in debt to you. I didn't sell myself to you."

"What do you need? Money?"

"A good word," Henry said.

Henry, who assumed that support for the Union meant opposition to slavery, was worried that his Union sympathy would cost him votes. His friend Cat explained to him why Cass County was likely to be pro-Union. Most of the county's voters had been Whigs before the Whig Party broke up to become the Republican Party in the North. Henry said, "I thought the Republicans were against slavery."

"The Northerners are," Cat said. "But the Whigs agreed to be quiet on the subject. You could be a slaveholder and support everything the Whigs cared about—everything that a strong federal government could give you. Railroads, and commerce, internal improvements and a national bank."

"It doesn't make sense to me."

"Most people in Cass County aren't for secession. They don't like being forced to choose between slavery and Union. Being a Union man won't hurt you in Cass County."

Henry's support for the Union was a thin veil over his feeling against slavery. He thought that the voters of Cass County would see through it. They did not. In January of 1861, they elected three delegates to go to Milledgeville to vote on secession: Benjamin Pierce Turner, veteran of the Mexican War, who already represented Cass County in the Georgia Assembly; the lawyer, Cat; and Henry, as a small planter with strong pro-Union sympathies.

Rachel, watching the election, said to Henry, "If Georgia secedes, maybe Cass County can secede from Georgia."

Henry wasn't sure how long he'd be gone, and he prepared as though he'd be absent for months. He talked to Charlie about getting ready to plow, even though plowing was a month away. He talked to Minnie to make sure that she had everything she needed for the house. And he asked Rachel to write to him while he was gone, to let him know how the plantation was faring. They met every day in their hiding place, but they spent more time talking than dallying. They were both too apprehensive for it. "I'll write to you," he said, as they sat together, a blanket wrapped around them both, against the winter chill.

"How will we keep it a secret?" Even though the postmaster never opened a letter, he knew every piece of correspondence that came to Cass County.

"Any letter to you I'll address to 'Miss Mannheim', and I'll tell the postmaster to hold them until you come for the mail."

Under the heavy blanket, Rachel shivered. He put his arms around her. "I won't be gone long," he said.

"I know. I ain't worried about that." Whenever she was worried or upset she reverted to kitchen talk. "Worried about the convention, and what comes after it."

He kissed her. "One thing at a time." He kissed her again, with more passion. "Send me off with a little joy, beloved."

She smiled a little, despite herself. "We'll give it a try, sugar."

Milledgeville, Sunday, January 20, 1861

> *Dearest Rachel,*
> *It's done. The convention approved the ordinance of secession yesterday. We Cassville men all voted against it, but we're in the minority. Next week the convention will form a government and arrange to write a constitution. There's likely to be another convention for that purpose. I don't know if we opponents will be asked to attend as delegates or not.*
> *As I listened to the speeches, and heard the ordinance read, my heart sank. It is about slavery. It is about the preservation of slavery. It is about the sovereignty of slavery. It's no longer possible to pretend otherwise. Any Georgian who is in rebellion is for slavery.*
> *You're right. It will come to war. How can I go to war to support slavery? God help me and God help all of us.*
> *As soon as I know when we'll adjourn I'll write to tell you. I miss you terribly, even in these few days. Kiss Matt for me, and hug Minnie. I'll be home in a few days.*
> *Your Henry*

They had close quarters in Milledgeville, which was so crowded that men doubled up in every room in the hotels and in the boarding houses. He and Cat shared a bed, something that he had not done since his earliest years as a poor clerk. Both of them, married men used to comfort, bickered and complained like boys, about who snored, and who stole the covers, and whose bare feet were the nastiest. Neither of them had privacy, and when he wrote to Rachel, Cat asked him who he was writing to.

Henry covered up the letter with his sleeve. "My wife."

"Did she change her name to Rachel?"

Irritated, Henry said, "A man can't spit, or fart, or write a letter here without someone putting his nose into it."

Cat said, "There's only one Rachel I know of on your place. Mannheim's slave gal that he gave to you."

"Why would I write to her? She can't read."

Cat said, "Mannheim used to bring her to my partner's office when she was just a little slip of a thing. She'd sit at my desk and pretend not to read the papers on it. Did you know that she can read upside down?"

"Don't tell anyone."

"I won't. My man Marcus can read and write and no one's supposed to know."

On the eve of their return to Cassville, the three Cass County delegates sat at table in a Milledgeville eating house, dining on beefsteak and drinking claret in a shared mood of dismay. Cat's conduct at the convention—spirited in defense of what he cared about—was no surprise. Henry knew that Cat would be loyal to whatever cause he embraced.

Henry had known Ben Turner only slightly before coming to the convention. People in the county knew Turner, called Captain Turner because of his Mexican War service, as the local Representative to the Assembly. He was from a family with antecedents in Virginia and South Carolina, courtly in manner and cultivated as well as educated. He was delighted that Cat's full name was Catullus, and addressed him in Latin when all three of them breakfasted together. He was a slaveowner—he called his slaves "servants"—and he was affectionate towards his house servants and kindly towards his field hands. Early in their acquaintance, he said to Henry, "I find that servants need a firm hand. They're like children. I try to be like a father to them."

Henry disagreed, but he didn't know how to say it as politely as Turner deserved to hear. He liked Turner. Turner never raised his voice, but he had the strength of conviction. He supported the Union in vote after vote. It was easy to follow his lead. To his surprise, Turner liked him. After the secession vote, he said quietly to Henry, "I like to see a young man who isn't a hothead."

"I never have been, sir."

Turner had deep-set blue-gray eyes that saw things keenly. He said, "You're considerate, too. Not everyone would be polite to the woman who runs the boardinghouse. And kind-hearted. I heard you inquiring after her little boy, who's been ill."

Henry said, "My father-in-law thinks that kindness is a flaw in my character."

"Mannheim? He's a hard man. I disagree. Kindness is a virtue."

"Thank you, sir."

After being seduced by Mordecai Mannheim, Henry distrusted his affection for Turner. He reminded himself that this man, whom he liked so well, owned ten Africans and had no tenderness of conscience about it.

Now Cass County's three Union men worried about the future. Cat said, "Captain Turner, do you think it will come to war?"

"Yes," Turner said quietly.

"Where will your loyalty be?"

"To Georgia," he said, "although it's bitter for a Union man to have to say so."

Cat asked, "Henry? What do you think?"

Henry said, "War is a terrible thing. As a very young man I saw the streets run red with blood in Germany after the Revolution of 1848. I think that my loyalty will always be toward peace."

Turner said, "I think we're past that, now."

Henry came home in despair, which even Adelaide could see. When they sat down to dinner, Adelaide asked, "Why are you so downcast, Henry?"

He said, "We go to Savannah in March and write a constitution to govern us."

Adelaide said lightly, "That ain't so bad."

"To write a constitution that says that slavery is right, and just, and should be the law of the land forever? That's about the worst thing I can think of."

Adelaide looked sharply at Rachel, who was taking the soup tureen from the table. She said to her husband, "It ain't exactly the moment to tell everyone how much you hate slavery."

Later that day Rachel told him, "Marse Mannheim is here and he wants to see you."

Henry said wearily, "Did he say why?"

"No."

"Didn't sell the crop while I was gone?"

Rachel shook her head.

They sat in the study. Mordecai said, "I hear you voted against secession at the convention."

Henry wondered how he knew. "We all did, we Cass County men. We all voted for the Union."

"I don't understand it," Mordecai said. "All of you own slaves. Ain't your interests with the South?"

"None of us wanted to break up the Union, sir. Or to rush to war with the North."

"Is this one of your damn fool twinges of conscience?"

Henry thought of gentlemanly Captain Turner. "Principle enters into it. But so does self-interest."

"Tell me how a cotton planter can be interested in supporting a government that wants to tear his slaves from him. How in God's name will you grow cotton?"

Henry said, "If they were free, you could pay them to grow cotton. Just like the Northern mills pay people to make cotton cloth."

"Are you mad?"

"I don't think so."

"Do you want a whole troop of John Browns down here, stirring up your slaves? Encouraging them to rise up in insurrection?"

"Insurrection?" Henry said, puzzled.

"Do you think your niggers love you the way you love them? They'd just as soon murder you and burn your place to the ground. Don't you know what happened in San Domingo?"

Henry had met people from Charleston who still remembered the slave insurrection in the West Indies. He had never thought that Mordecai was haunted by it. "How would going to war with the North be any better?"

Mordecai looked at him with contempt. "If you can't see that a cotton planter, a slaveowner, should support the South, should support secession, then God help you."

After Adelaide found Rachel and Henry together, she continued to deceive both of them. She didn't say a word to Henry, even though her heart was sore with anger, and whenever Rachel asked, "Are you all right, ma'am?" she smiled and lied, "Of course I'm all right." She grew up watching her mother weep and beg her father to sell Rachel, who reminded all of them of the ill-fated Eliza. She heard her father refuse, over and over. She would not humiliate herself by going to Henry to make the same plea. She knew that he would refuse, too.

Henry was deep in debt to her father, and until the debt was discharged, her father held Henry in thrall to it. She would go to her father. She would be like Br'er Rabbit, who tricked Br'er Fox into doing his bidding. She would be subtle with her father. His own outrage would do the rest.

After Henry left for the constitutional convention in Savannah, Adelaide asked Tom to drive her to the Mannheim place. On the way, she opened the carriage windows to let in the March air, warm and springlike, scented with the first blossom of honeysuckle and magnolia. She breathed as deeply as she could, savoring it.

To disguise her purpose, she sat with her mother in the morning parlor, talking about Matt, and whether he'd recovered from his cold, and if they'd called for the doctor. Rosa said, "You shouldn't let that slave woman of yours doctor him." Rosa asked whether her slaves were working hard, and Adelaide was momentarily silenced. I haven't come here to tell Mama, she thought. Ezra brought tea and sesame seed cookies, which she pretended to eat, taking a bite and crumbling the rest into the saucer.

"I'd like to talk to Papa," she said. "Where is he?"

Her mother gave her an odd look. "He's in the study."

Her father sat behind his big desk, looking at the window at the cotton fields, watching the slaves work. Even as a grown woman, she had rarely been in this room. It still smelled strongly of cigars, an odor that she had never liked. He said, "Well, missy, what brings you here? Do you have some business to transact?"

As though she were still a little girl. "Yes, I do."

He gave her an odd look, as her mother had. "What kind of business, missy?"

It was hard to speak. She remembered choking on her news about William Pereira and Rachel with her father. She clenched her hands in her lap. "It's a bad business."

"Is it your husband?"

She nodded.

He said, "Well, he don't drink, or gamble, or beat you, unless he's picked up some bad habits I haven't heard about. What is it?"

She dropped her voice very low. "There's a slave he favors, who favors him."

Her father laughed. How could he laugh? "Oh, that's nothing," he said. "He'll get over it. Who is it? That hussy Lydia?"

Adelaide raised her eyes from her lap. "He says he loves her," she said, so low her father had to lean forward to hear her.

He frowned. He was remembering, and he was bothered. "He's a damn fool," he said. "Who is it?"

She shook her head. Tears rose to her eyes. "It's so shameful—I can barely say it—"

Her father said impatiently, "Don't choke on it, Adelaide. Tell me."

The tears stopped. "It's Rachel."

Her father's red face turned pale. He looked away. When he spoke, his voice was low, like a bear's growl. "How do you know?"

I saw them, she thought, but she couldn't say such a thing to her father. "A wife knows."

"Make him sell her."

She looked at her father with a sharp gaze, like Rachel's. "Do you think he would?"

He balled his big hand into a fist and pressed it hard against the edge of his desk, as though he were angry enough to hit someone in the face. Whether he was angrier at Henry or at Rachel, she didn't care. It was her father's burden now, not hers.

⁓

When the constitutional convention ended, Cat stayed in Savannah to visit people he knew, but Henry didn't linger. On the train home, he stared out the window. In April, the countryside was beautiful, full of lush green growth and flowering trees, and if you grew cotton and corn, the sight of the new crop brought joy to the heart, too. Henry watched the lovely, peaceable sight of the lowland landscape as it gave way to the Piedmont, and thought of the conflict with the North that secession would bring. This beautiful place would be a battlefield. The fields would be trampled into mud, and the pretty creeks would run red, as the gutters of Dresden had in 1849. Henry shivered in the warm spring air. Georgia would go to war to defend slavery, and he knew he could not follow.

The Abolitionists were right. Slavery was evil. He loved a woman who was a slave, but that was only the beginning of his own trouble. He was a Union man who hated slavery with all his heart and soul, and he had the misfortune to be a slaveowner in Georgia on the eve of war.

Early in April, Captain Turner began to enlist the signatures of men who wanted to raise a Cass County regiment. Cat signed up and accepted a lieutenant's commission. He said to Henry, "Why are you hesitating?"

He wished that he could talk to Cat about his doubts. But he knew what Cat thought about slaves, and slavery.

Henry loved Rachel. He couldn't marry her. He couldn't free her. Now he was going home to try to explain to everyone he knew—to all of the men who wanted to rush headlong into war—that he could not fight for the cause they embraced.

How could he tell Cat? He could not.

The news of the bombardment of Fort Sumter flew to Cassville. The shooting was over on April 13ᵗʰ. The next day, everyone in Cassville knew. War had begun. The men were jubilant, the women were fearful, and the slaves kept their eyes down and their opinions to themselves.

Whatever he needed to do, Henry wanted to settle the debt first. He went to see Mordecai.

Mordecai said, "Why are you in a hurry to sell?"

Henry thought, I've been crazy to sell since the moment I knew I have five hundred and sixty bales. "I'd like to be able to pay you what I owe you."

Mordecai said lazily, "War will drive the price up. It's already at fifteen cents a pound. If we wait, I can do better for you."

"I don't want to wait. Sell now. Fifteen cents is fine with me."

"I won't do it. It's going to go a lot higher. I couldn't stand to cheat you like that."

Henry said, "Is something wrong? I've never known you to refuse a man's money before."

Mordecai knew perfectly well how badly Henry wanted to be free of the debt. Now he looked pleased to say, "I've speculated on cotton more than once. I want to hold the crop back. You'll be surprised at how well we can do once war breaks out."

Later, as Henry and Rachel held each other, once again too upset to undress or kiss, he said to her, "It doesn't make sense to me. We may not be able to sell at all once war breaks out. Why won't he sell now?"

Troubled, she said, "He wants to keep you in debt."

"Why?"

"To keep a hold over you."

"He already has a hold over me. Why is he tormenting me like this?"

Rachel sat up and wrapped her arms around her knees, trying to control how she trembled. "I don't know."

The next day, Rachel came to find Henry, who was sitting in his study, writing in his ledger. "What is it, Rachel?"

"Your father-in-law is here to see you."

Mordecai never came here. "Tell him to come in."

Mordecai came into the room and immediately settled himself into the chair she had once claimed as hers. He said, "Rachel, pour us some brandy," as though he were in his own house.

"Yes, Massa," she said, and filled two glasses from the decanter, serving Mordecai, then Henry.

Mordecai said, "You stay. This concerns you, too."

Rachel felt chilled, as she had the night before. Henry said sharply, "Aren't you going to ask her to sit?"

"She's a servant. She can stand."

"In this house, we consider everyone's comfort. Even the servants'."

Rachel cast her eyes down and said, "Marse Henry, I can sit on the footstool."

"She's considered her own comfort."

Rachel carried the footstool to the far wall of the room, where she would be nearest the door. The footstool was very near to the ground, and as she sat on it she felt as though she were crouching to ward off a blow.

Mordecai said, "This business about supporting the Union has gone far enough."

"You know I voted against secession at the Convention. With the rest of the Cass County delegates."

"Now I hear you're telling people you're refusing to join the Confederate Army."

"Why would I? As a supporter of the Union?" And, Rachel knew, a man who hated slavery. "How could I do such a thing in good conscience?"

"This fight isn't about principles, or honor, or conscience. It's about cotton and the money that comes from cotton. To grow cotton you need slavery. I don't care what your conscience tells you. If you're a cotton planter, you should be supporting the Confederacy."

"Mr. Mannheim, you don't command my conscience."

"Don't I? Let me spell it out for you. How much money do you owe me?"

Henry said, "You know better than I do."

Mordecai repeated, "How much? You tell me."

"Thirteen thousand five hundred dollars."

"Say I wanted to call in the debt early."

Henry felt as though he were drowning. He said, "Some of that is the land, and it's mortgaged for ten years."

"The land's a trifle. There's plenty left, for the house, the stock, and the slaves. Ten thousand. Say I called in the notes. How would you raise the money?"

"Sell the crop," Henry said. "You can sell the crop, any time you want." He raised his voice. "I've begged you to sell the crop."

"I'm going to hold the crop. Cotton's going up, and I'm planning to make my profit. But I want to call in the notes now. How would you raise the money?"

Rachel began to feel the fear that had haunted her childhood.

Mordecai said, "How many of them niggers do you own free and clear?" When Henry hesitated, he answered his own question. "There's that woman who cooks for you, and that man who married the gal from my place, and his two half-grown sons. And the two I gave you. Charlie. And Rachel." He threw a glance at Rachel, huddled on the footstool by the door. He chuckled and said, "I reckon they'd bring about six thousand dollars at auction in Savannah. That would be enough to satisfy me."

He could still sell her.

Stunned, Henry said, "I can't sell them."

"Why not? Do you love them so much? You're in debt. They're valuable property. What's the difficulty?"

"I can't bring in the crop without Charlie, or run the house without Rachel and Minnie."

"You'd manage. I'd send over McKinley to oversee. And I'm sure there's another nigger woman who could cook for you."

Still stunned, Henry said, "Do I understand you right? If I sign up to fight, and put myself in the way of a Union bullet, you'll leave my place alone. If I stay here, as my conscience tells me to, you'll force me to sell the servants I care about."

"That's your difficulty," Mordecai said, taking a long pull at his brandy. "They ain't to care about, any more than you care about mules."

"If I go, will you leave the place alone?"

Mordecai said, "I might send you an overseer to keep things running while you were gone. But I'd leave your property alone."

"The stock and the slaves?"

"Your property."

His mouth dry, Henry said, "Give me some time to consider it."

"Ain't much to consider," Mordecai said. "I hear that Turner is raising a regiment. You could go talk to him about enlisting." Mordecai held up his glass. "Rachel, pour me another, and we'll drink to the health of the Confederacy's newest soldier."

After Mordecai left the room, Adelaide walked into the study. She looked at Rachel, crouching and abashed on her footstool by the door, and Henry, slumped in his chair. Henry raised a stricken face. "How did he know?" he asked.

Look at them, she thought. Both of them. "I told him."

Henry said nothing.

Adelaide gestured toward Rachel, who was still crouched low on the footstool by the door. "I knew you'd never sell her, so I didn't bother to ask."

Henry found his voice. He sounded hoarse. "Sell her?" he asked. "You would sell your sister?"

Adelaide let herself feel all of the anger she'd been hiding for weeks. "That's a fine thing for you to say," she said to Henry. "After you've betrayed me."

She said to Rachel, as coldly as she could, "Come upstairs with me. I need you."

Rachel rose as though she was in pain and followed Adelaide up the stairs to her room. Adelaide sat before her dressing table and looked in the mirror instead of at Rachel. She said, "How long have you been lying to me?"

Rachel stared at Adelaide's reflection instead of her face. "Doesn't matter now, ma'am."

"How could you do such a thing?"

"We fell in love."

Adelaide wasn't angry and her calm was more frightening than anger. "Do you really think he loves you? Your master, who can use you as he pleases, and sell you when he tires of you?"

God help her, she would tell Adelaide the truth, as she had once told Henry the truth. "I know he loves me. He wants to free me."

Adelaide laughed. "Oh, that's fine! He wants to divorce me, too. Do you think he can oblige either of us, by the laws of the state of Georgia?"

Rachel stared at their reflection in the mirror. Her face was as gray as ash. She had wounded Adelaide to the marrow of her bones. In return, her sister had found a way to hurt her worse than to sell her.

Later that day, Henry caught Rachel outside the kitchen and whispered, "Tonight."

She said, "How can we?"

He said, "She knows. Does it matter, now?"

That night, she wrapped herself in her shawl and hurried through the dark and chill to be with Henry. She had been out at night before but tonight the sky was overcast and moonless. Every small sound in the woods startled her, even though she knew the small sounds were birds and mice, the little creatures that the great owls hunted, to capture and tear limb from limb as they ate them.

When Henry came into their hiding place, they put their arms around each other and held each other, unable to speak. Rachel began to shudder. Henry's embrace couldn't stop her or soothe her. "He hates that we love each other. He hates it so much that he'd sell me and kill you by sending you off to war to keep us apart. She hates us too. She told him so he could hurt us."

Henry stroked the muscles of her back, trying to stop her from trembling. He said softly, "Oh, beloved."

"What are we going to do?"

"I can't figure it," he said. "Can't free you. Can't marry you. Can't pay off the debt. Can't refuse to enlist. Can't bear any of it."

"We should steal away. Two fugitives together."

He held her tighter. He said, "Even if we got away, what about everyone else here? What would happen to them? He'd sell them all. Put them up at auction and make up the next coffle for Mississippi."

She groaned. He said, "Rachel. Beloved. I can't see any other way to save you, and the rest of the people here, and the place. I can't fight Mordecai on this and win. I have to join the Confederate Army."

She groaned again, as in deep pain. "And I have to stay here to bear it."

"Put your arms around me."

She was still shaking, but as she held him, the shaking subsided. He kissed her gently on the lips. She said, "I'm so heartsick I don't think I can rouse to kiss you."

He said, "I can't bear to feel you tremble like that. Nestle with me. Just nestle with me."

He felt her body ease against him, and he kissed her again. She said, "I'm still heartsick."

"I know. So am I. But I love you, heartsick or not."

This time she kissed him back, a tentative kiss, and said, "If you go, what will happen to us?"

"I'll love you forever," he said, renewing the promise he made when he first told her he loved her.

She said, "Until death or distance do us part."

He reminded her, "Nothing will part us. Not even death."

She began to tremble again. War brought death too close. Not even love could drive it away.

The next day, Henry saddled his horse, which he rarely did, and rode the five miles to the Turner place to see the Captain. He found Turner sitting in his study, writing with an old-fashioned quill pen. The room was full of books. He had the Latin historians and poets, and he had many books on the law. The furniture was simple and restrained, like the man himself. The weather couldn't decide whether it was winter or summer, and today the windows were closed against chill, and a fire burned pleasantly in the grate. Turner invited him to sit and offered him a glass of whiskey. From Turner, he didn't mind accepting the glass. He drank a little and said, "Captain Turner, I hear you're raising a Cass County regiment."

"I am. I thought you weren't going to volunteer."

"I wasn't."

"What persuaded you?"

What if he told the truth? That Mordecai would rather see him dead in battle than alive to love his slave daughter? He said, "I owe my father-in-law a great deal of money. He has very strong feelings about secession. He threatened to call in my notes, and ruin me, if I didn't sign up."

Turner said, "That's very hard of him."

"You know him, sir. You know he's a hard man."

Turner looked at him with his keen, sad eyes that were blue and gray at once. He said, "You know it ain't an adventure to go to war."

"I do know. This ain't for my pleasure, sir."

Turner said, "If you do sign up I can see about getting you a commission as a lieutenant."

"I hate fighting, sir. I don't think I'd make much of an officer."

"We have plenty of hotheads who are eager to get killed for glory. If we want to win this war, we need decent men who think clearly and don't care for bloodshed." He held out his hand. "I'd be glad to have you in my regiment, Mr. Kaltenbach."

Henry went home to realize that he had to swiftly decide how to run his place while he was gone. He cursed himself in thinking he'd never enlist and not realizing that he'd need to make provision for running his place while he was gone. Mordecai was the obvious man to keep eye on the place. Henry wanted someone to keep an eye on Mordecai.

That afternoon, just after dinner, Henry found Rachel in the kitchen, and asked her to come into the study. She came into the room tentatively, as though she had never been there. He sat in his customary chair and invited her to sit in the chair that she had once thought of as hers.

He told her what was bothering him. They sat in silence for a while. Rachel said, "I have a notion."

He said, "Rachel, it won't help now to act the slave, just tell me."

"Make Charlie your overseer."

Henry nodded.

"He's been your overseer since you bought the place. Tell Marse Mannheim you'll send Charlie over every week to report on how things are going. Ask Marse Mannheim to write to you to let you know if there's anything that needs to be decided, or signed."

"How will I know if he's taking advantage of me?"

She said, "I'll be writing to you, too."

It was unusual, but not unheard of, to put a trusted driver in charge as an overseer. Mordecai would draft the factoring agreements and make the major purchases, but Charlie would be the day-to-day overseer of the crop and the place. Rachel knew, even better than he did, that Mordecai's regard for Charlie would make the arrangement tolerable.

To Henry's surprise, Mordecai didn't object. He said, "Charlie's a good boy. His hands work hard. Send him over every week to talk to me, and I'll write to you."

He's gotten what he wants, Henry thought bitterly, as he left. He can afford to be cordial.

Charlie was in the field. Henry waved to him and Charlie came over to Henry, taking off his hat and wiping his brow with his sleeve. "What is it, Marse Henry?" Looking him right in the eye.

Henry said, "I've just enlisted in the army and I'll be leaving in a few days. Before I go I wanted to talk to you about managing the place while I'm gone."

Charlie said, "Didn't figure you for a Confederate, Marse Henry."

"Ask Marse Mannheim about that."

Charlie shook his head. "How long will you be gone, Marse Henry?"

"I signed up for two years. Maybe the war will be over sooner. I wish I knew."

"Will Marse Mannheim send his overseer?"

"He's already asked me. I told him no. I don't trust McKinley and I know you don't either. I told him I want you to oversee the place while I'm gone."

"It's one thing to guide the crop for a few weeks. It's another to oversee. You know that."

"Of course I know that. If Marse Mannheim wants me to get shot at by the Union Army he'll have to put up with you overseeing."

Charlie, ever-tactful, was having difficulty hiding his surprise. He looked dubiously at his master. "Marse Henry, I'll do whatever you ask me to, you know that. But I have my worry about how we'll manage."

"I know it ain't usual. I don't trust Marse Mannheim to look after my interest. But I do trust you."

Charlie looked his master straight in the eye again. "All right, Marse Henry. I'll do my best."

Henry said, "Thank you. It takes such a load from my mind to think of you running the place for me." Henry put out his hand. Charlie stared at him. Henry said, "You won't shake on it?"

"I ain't a gentleman, Marse Henry."

Henry shook his head. Charlie was one of nature's gentlemen, but he, a planter who was going away to fight to defend slavery, was a fool today. "I know you'll do fine without me, Charlie."

After her father talked to Henry, Adelaide felt the satisfaction of someone who had fought a duel. Now she was afraid for what she had done. Rachel served her in ashen silence. Henry couldn't look at her or speak to her. Her anger had raged, and now it had cooled, and she regarded the wreckage with remorse and dismay.

She went to see Henry in his study. He sat at the desk, turning over the pages of his ledger. His eyes were red and his face was pale, as though he hadn't been able to sleep. As though he had wept in the hours that he lay awake. The past week had aged him. She saw the first strands of gray in his hair.

He didn't invite her to sit and she remained standing. Like a supplicant, or a servant.

She said, "When I told Papa about you and Rachel I never thought it would come to this."

Her husband looked up. "Well, it's done," he said curtly.

She clenched her hands and pressed them into the folds of her skirt. "Take care of yourself," she said. "And write to me."

He laughed bitterly. "As long as I'm in one piece, I'll write to you," he said, and at the distress in her face, he added, "You can't sell Rachel while I'm gone. You can't sign a contract. And don't ask your father to sell her, either."

She leaned over the desk and reached out her hands to him. "I'm so sorry, Henry."

He shook his head. "It's too late for that," he said. He shut the ledger. "As soon as I'm situated I'll write to you."

Before he left, Henry found a flag, the Stars and Stripes that so recently had been the flag of the United States. He said to Rachel, "Stockton had it in back and he gave it to me. He thinks I'm crazy for wanting it."

She said, "What are you planning to do with it?"

"Raise it and fly it."

She looked at him in astonishment. "You are crazy."

"I ain't. Ask Tom and Luke to help me put it up."

The afternoon before he left, Luke, who was smart about building, figured out how to mount the flag and raise it. He said worriedly, "Massa, it's the Union flag. Is it all right?"

Henry thought of how angry Mordecai would be to see the Stars and Stripes flying over the Kaltenbach place. "Don't worry, Luke. It's all right." He stood back and admired the flag as it rippled in the spring breeze. "You keep that flag flying while I'm gone."

Tom and Luke gave him a look that he recognized from his earliest childhood. His mother, hearkening back to the Jewish dialect of her childhood, used to call damn foolishness *goyische kop*. Gentile brains. He had them now. His slaves thought so.

Luke said, "Yes, Massa. We keep it flying, Massa."

Tom, always the more emotional of the two, said, "Massa, are you going to be all right in the war?"

He put his arm around Tom's shoulders. "I hope so." Luke, suddenly stricken with strong emotion himself, put his arm around Henry's shoulders, and the three of them stood beneath the Union flag in awkward embrace.

That night, Rachel and Henry stole away to their hiding place to spend their last hours together. Henry, always talkative, was quiet tonight. They didn't speak as they lay down on the rough blanket that had seen them through so much joy. They held out their arms to each other and took refuge there in silence.

He kissed her, and she returned the kiss. It was desire, but it was desperation, too. He was going away to fight, and neither of them knew if he would come back. He wasn't gentle with her tonight. He was fierce, gathering strength for the hard battle and the long separation ahead. She met him, fierce herself, admitting him so deep inside her that he seemed to touch the very core of her body. Tonight's love would have to last. Tomorrow, he would be gone.

In the morning, all of the people on the place came to say goodbye to Marse Henry as he left to join his regiment in Cassville. It was a heartbreakingly beautiful spring day, pleasant and cloudless, the air scented with the sap of every new and green thing, from the ornament of magnolia to the usefulness of new cotton and pine. All of them, men and women, grown folks and children, stood at the gate as he rode by and waved to them, pretending to be jaunty about going off to be a soldier.

After everyone else had gone back to the kitchen or the field, Rachel watched, and listened, until Henry and his horse were out of sight and out of earshot. She felt an unfamiliar twinge in her belly and she rested her hand there. For a long time she stayed there, her hand on her belly, looking at the Union flag waving gently in the April breeze.

Part 3

Chapter 15

Eliza

A delaide went into Cassville, where she would stop at the post office for letters and look at the new books, even though she didn't have a dime to buy one. The post office was full of ladies who had come to retrieve letters from their absent men. Mrs. Turner was there, doubly deserted, since both of the Turner boys had joined the regiment their father commanded. Aggie was there, shaking her head over the letter she'd been too eager to wait to open. Even Mrs. Levy was there for her letters, since Sam Levy had gone too, following the army as a sutler in Richmond.

The postmaster had gone away to fight, and his replacement, who wasn't a Cassville man, was still learning the people of the county. He asked Adelaide who she was, and as he bent to retrieve her letters, he said, "I have a passel of letters for the Kaltenbach place, for you and Miss Mannheim. Is she staying with you? Will she come for her own letters?"

Aggie looked up. "Who is Miss Mannheim, Adelaide? Is she a cousin to you? Will we meet her?"

All of the letters were in Henry's hand. "There's no such person," Adelaide said, flushing. "I believe my husband is having a little joke with me."

On the way home, she pulled out the letters addressed to Miss Mannheim and hefted them as though she could guess their contents by their weight. One letter a day, and long letters, too. It was wrong to open a letter addressed to someone else, but she sat at the roadside, tore open the envelope and smoothed the paper to read it.

"Dearest Rachel," she read, and the words swam before her eyes. Her head began to ache so fiercely that she dropped the pages into her lap. I should tear these letters to bits, she thought. I should burn them in the parlor fireplace. But first she would read them.

A few hours later she went looking for Rachel, who was in the kitchen garden, kneeling to weed the vegetable patch. She said coldly, "Come inside and talk to me in the parlor."

Rachel rose and wiped her hands on her apron, turning the cloth the color of red clay. "Yes, ma'am." She followed Adelaide inside.

Adelaide threw the letters on the parlor table. Too upset to use the letter opener, she had ripped them open with her fingers. "He's been writing to you."

Rachel said, "You opened the letters?"

"I read them, too. All of them."

Rachel's face flickered a little. "Those are for me."

"No, they ain't. Nothing in this house is for you." Adelaide's voice rose. "By rights, you shouldn't be able to read them. You shouldn't be able to read at all."

Rachel didn't speak. She let her dark gaze do its insolent work, staring at the sister who had taught her to read and write.

"I should burn these."

Rachel didn't reply. Those dark eyes, iris melting into the pupil, shaped so much like her own.

She could burn every letter that Henry wrote to Miss Mannheim. She couldn't do a thing about the feeling that burned in his heart as he wrote to her. She said, "I'm going to read every letter he writes to you before you do."

Rachel said, "Why would you torment yourself so?"

Adelaide sat heavily in the nearest chair, a dainty thing not suited for strong emotion. "Go away," she said. "You can have these after I'm done with them."

April 30, 1861

Dearest Rachel,

If war were like this, it wouldn't be so bad. All of us officers have gone to Camp Brown, just outside Smyrna, where we set up on the church camp ground. We live in tents, and we're learning how to soldier. We drill and drill and drill some more, and you would be surprised at me, since I can now clean and load a rifle, and to hold it to shoot at someone else, not at my own foot. The country boys, who have been shooting squirrels out of trees since they were old enough to hold a musket, have stopped snickering at me.

I share a tent with Cat, and we've set up housekeeping with the help of his servant Marcus. Cat has brought a trunk full of things that he and Marcus believe a gentleman needs. I can't imagine how they'll manage once we join the battlefront, unless Cat has his own supply wagon. Marcus offers to brush my coat or polish my boots—he thinks I'm a sorry sight as an officer, as Minnie used to think I was a sorry sight as a planter—and he looks at me ruefully when I refuse.

We eat well, but I'm the only Israelite in the company, and every day I hope that God forgives me for breaking the kosher laws.

I miss you terribly. I keep your letters in my tunic pocket close to my heart. Kiss Matt for me, and reassure Minnie as best you can.

Your Henry

Since Henry left, Adelaide had time to reflect on what she'd done in sending him to war. The jaunty tone of this letter reassured her. And his love for Rachel reminded her why she'd done it.

After Henry left, Rachel was so angry at Adelaide that it was a relief to put on the slave's mask again, to keep her eyes on the ground, and to say little more than "Yes, ma'am." She thought of the recent trial that had horrified every slaveowner in Georgia—of a trusted housekeeper and cook accused of poisoning her master. Delia Willis had been found guilty of murder and executed by hanging. That was a slave's punishment for unbridled anger.

She felt tired all the time, so tired that she wanted to lie down every afternoon and sleep through the hottest part of the day. She never slept well at night, when she missed Henry with every bone in her body. Sometimes she rose from her bed in the attic to slip out to their old hiding place, where she had left one of his unwashed shirts. She pressed it to her face and breathed in his smell, eau de cologne and laundry soap and the faint tang of sweat, and curled up with the agony of missing him.

She didn't pay much attention to missing a monthly—she was too distracted, and too tired, to notice—but on the day that the smell of frying side meat, usually savory, turned her stomach, she suspected that it wasn't an upset or the flux. Over the next weeks, the smell of bacon became equally disgusting, and a walk past the smokehouse made her retch. When she missed a second monthly—too nauseated by pig meat to eat anything but eggs and greens—she knew. She was carrying, and the baby was half a Jew.

When she couldn't hide the nausea from Minnie any longer—she got up from the kitchen table to lose her breakfast outside—Minnie knew too. When Rachel came back, ashen and shaking a little and wiping her mouth with distaste, Minnie said, "How far along are you?"

"About two months."

Minnie said, "Still time to stop it."

She put her hands protectively over her still-flat belly. "No," she said miserably. "I can't do that."

After all their care and planning—the rubber sheaths, that he had gone to such lengths to buy, and the seeds, which she had been so faithful about taking, until that last frantic week before he left—something had gone wrong. His promise to her, and her promise to herself, about never bearing a baby into slavery, had been broken by distraction and nature's caprice. It wasn't like that, but she felt like any other slave gal, carrying another little slave for Massa.

Since Henry left, Charlie came to talk to Rachel daily about the crop and the hands. Did Charlie know about her and Henry? She knew how slaves gossiped—everything in the main house was of interest to them—but Charlie had never said a word to her. She didn't know whether it was ignorance or tact. She felt a wave of nausea, and thought, There's going to be a reckoning with Charlie, too, when he finds out.

It became Charlie's habit to come into the kitchen at the end of the day and to wash his face at the kitchen pump, as Henry used to, before sitting down to tell Rachel about the crop and the hands. Minnie offered him a glass of buttermilk, which he gratefully accepted, and it became the preface to his daily report, as Henry's whiskey had once been to his. How everything was growing, now that it was summer. How many rows they had chopped. How the mules were faring, and how many visits to the blacksmith there had been lately. The ongoing problems with keeping everyone working and steady. Three of the "young'uns," Micah, Lydia, and Freddy, tested his patience every day.

She and Charlie were cordial with one another, even if they were no longer close. She was too miserable to miss their earliest relationship as brother and sister, and too heartsick to miss their year as lovers. They had business to transact, she and Charlie, he to bring in the crop, and she to keep an eye on Marse Mannheim. She owed it to Henry to do her part. She hated the thought of distracting Charlie from his.

It was hard to pay attention to Charlie's reports, between her nausea, her fatigue, and her worry over how he would take the news when he found out. One day he said, "Rachel, you ain't listening to a thing I'm saying."

"It's too hot in the kitchen." It was; they'd been baking bread that day. "Let's go outside for some air."

They walked toward the pine trees that separated the house from the fields and she suddenly felt the nausea overcome her. She said, "Excuse me," and managed to turn away before she bent over and vomited up everything she'd eaten that day.

He said, "Are you all right?"

Shaking, embarrassed, she said, "I ain't sick, if that's what you mean."

"Let me get you a dipperful of water." He was gone a while, fetching it from the kitchen. She rinsed out her mouth with the first sip and drank the rest, slowly, hoping it wouldn't come back up.

He said, "Are you carrying?"

"Yes."

He put his hand gently on her shoulder—the driver's gesture—and said, "We sit down in the shade for a while."

To her shame, the water she had drunk came back up before they settled under the nearest tree. He waited until she sat, then sat beside her. "How far along are you?"

"Three months now."

"When Marse Henry left."

She flared. "Why would you say such a thing?"

He sighed deeply. "I know. We all do."

She stared at him, her face hot with shame. "Lord help me. Do they know on the Mannheim place?"

He said, "You know how everyone talk. I reckon they know all over the county."

She buried her hands in her face and sobbed. When she raised her head she said huskily, "It ain't what you think."

"Don't know what to think. I thought better of Marse Henry."

"Never meant for this to happen."

Charlie put his arm around her shoulders. "No one ever do. But it does."

She turned her face to him and sobbed against his broad chest. He enfolded her and held her close. He let her weep herself out. Very low, he said, "Don't care about any of those folks in that house. I care about you."

She pulled back. Wiped her eyes with her apron. Tried to reclaim her dignity. "We got work to do together. Bring in the crop. Keep an eye on Marse Mannheim. We got to do that, regardless."

He said, "You always was proud and stubborn and you ain't changed a bit. All right. We do it."

A few days later, Adelaide came into the kitchen. She stared at Rachel, who was making a batch of pone, and asked her curtly, "Where's Minnie?"

They were mistress and maid again, but they had little to say to each other. Now, in her best servile tone, Rachel said, "She ain't here, ma'am."

"Well, go find her. I need her."

Rachel had enough warning to pull out the chamberpot she kept in the kitchen, for this very purpose, to retch into it and not make a mess on the floor. Adelaide said with distaste, "What's wrong with you? Are you sick?"

"No, ma'am." In a few weeks she would start to show, and it was better to tell the truth now than to let Adelaide surmise it later. "It isn't a sickness to be expecting."

Adelaide, like everyone else, asked, "How far along?"

"A little over three months."

"Conceived in April."

If Rachel dared, she'd say, "April 17th," which was the date of Henry's last night before he left for Camp Brown with his regiment. "I believe so, ma'am."

Adelaide stared at her sister and the betrayal hung in the air between them. She said, "If that child looks like him I'll sell it."

Rachel laughed. It was an awful but idle threat. A baby was worthless on the slave market.

Camp McDonald, Big Shanty, Georgia
July 25, 1861

> *Dearest Rachel,*
>
> *Hearing that you're expecting a child, I'm torn in two. I'm full of joy that we'll have a child together. I'm full of despair that our child, despite all our hopes to the contrary, will be born into slavery.*
>
> *Since we left, I've been pestering Cat to draft a will for me. It's bitter to think that the best I can do for you is die in battle, since I can manumit you and the child after I'm gone. I never knew that Cat is, as his manservant Marcus says, "flighty." Or perhaps it bothers him to think that any of us might*

die, and that we'd need to arrange for it before we march away. I should ask Marcus to help me. I suspect that Marcus does half of Cat's lawyering, since he is calm, and orderly, and can read Latin as well as English, and has a better copperplate hand than many a lawyer.

We got the news of the victory at Manassas a few days ago. Many of the men are jubilant. They think that the Confederacy will win the war. You know, as well as I do, that it's wishful thinking. If I were prone to wager—which I'm not, except for growing cotton—I know where I'd put my money. Who has the manufacture for rifles and cannon? Who has the food and supplies? Who has the trade with the rest of the world? As proud as we are of cotton and slavery, I don't see how it will help us win the war.

My own men are mostly farm boys from Cass and neighboring counties. They have a boy's sense of adventure. Most of them have never been away from home, and this is a grand undertaking for them. They seem fearless. I've told Colonel Turner that I'm a poor soldier because I'm full of fear. He reassures me that he'd rather have a clear-headed officer who knows when to be afraid than a fool who always feels brave.

Beloved, take good care of yourself, and cherish our child for me. Kiss Matt for me, and reassure Minnie as best you can. The regiment leaves for Richmond in a few days. As soon as I have an address to send a letter to I'll write to you.

I miss you more than I can say. You are always in my thoughts and in my dreams. The moment that this war is over I will be home to be in your arms again.

Your Henry

Adelaide thought, If I'd learned of the baby this way, I don't know what I would have done. Her anger flared, like a headache, and when it subsided she felt sick and saddened.

Charlie dreaded the prospect of visiting Marse Mannheim to report on the crop and the place. The last time he visited Marse Mannheim was to beg him to sell Charlie and Rachel together. Since then, Charlie had never been in the Mannheim house.

Charlie didn't bother to put on his Sunday best. He washed his face and wiped off his boots, knowing how Ezra felt about keeping the carpets free of dirt. He presented himself at the back door, and told Ezra that Marse Mannheim was expecting him.

Ezra said, "I heard you the overseer on Marse Henry's place now."

"While Marse Henry's away." Charlie took off his hat. "I'm here to tell Marse Mannheim how we doing."

Ezra led him to the study. "Come on in, Charlie," Marse Mannheim said, in his loud voice, without inviting Charlie to sit.

Charlie stared at his boots—he could see how muddy they still were, despite his efforts to clean them—and the words that came so easily with Marse Henry, or with Rachel, died in his throat.

Marse Mannheim asked, "How is the crop coming along, Charlie?"

"Good, Marse Mannheim."

"Finished planting?"

"Yes, Marse Mannheim."

"Chopping now?"

"Yes, Marse Mannheim."

"Corn all right?"

"Yassuh."

"You fixed all right for supplies?"

"Yassuh."

"I heard you brought one of your mules over. Threw a shoe."

"Yassuh." Charlie thought, What kind of a report is this? How can he know what's happening, and how we're doing, if all I can say is "Yassuh"?

"Charlie, you never liked me, and you still don't." Was he joking? Through his sweat of fear and a fug of failure, it was hard to tell. "Nosuh," he said.

Marse Mannheim said, "You need anything, you tell me."

Sweating, miserable, Charlie retraced his steps to the back door, where Ezra waited for him. He said, "Go to the kitchen and Aunt Susy will give you something." As though he were a little boy who needed a piece of pone. He wanted a cup of water, but he said, "No thanks, Ezra, I'm all right."

It was no better the next week. He was as frightened, and as servile, as he had been as a boy. He walked back to the Kaltenbach place with an acute sense of failing Marse Henry. On the way back, he met Rachel, who took one look at his stricken face and asked, "Are you feeling all right?"

"Just came from Marse Mannheim. Acted the fool."

"You always did, with him. Never wanted him to know how smart you really are."

"One thing to do it on purpose. Another thing to be stricken stupid when you don't want it. How can he know how we do when I can't say a word to him? How can we make sure he does right by us?"

She shook her head. She knew, better than Charlie did, that they had no reason to trust Marse Mannheim.

He asked, "I promised Marse Henry I'd do this, but it won't help him if I can't say a thing to Marse Mannheim. Hate to ask, but would you come along with me to give that report? Give me courage?"

To help Charlie, she'd tamp down her fear and swallow her pride. "Promised Marse Henry we'd keep an eye on Marse Mannheim. Doesn't matter how we do it."

A week later, Charlie stopped for Rachel in the kitchen. She had put on a clean apron and a clean kerchief. It pleased him to recall how pretty she was. Carrying a baby gave her face an even prettier glow, even though she didn't show yet. He said, "Are you ready?"

She said, "Yes, I'm ready." No kitchen talk today.

As they walked through the woods, taking the shortcut to the Mannheim place, she said, "Are you worried about what you're going to say?"

"When I go into that house I can't say a thing. That's what worries me."

"You're still afraid of him."

"I was afraid every day on that place that he'd whup me or sell me. When I go back there I still feel it."

She thought, with considerable shame, of the way that Marse Mannheim had compelled Henry to join the Confederate Army. Charlie was right to feel his old fear. But she said, "Well, he can't. You belong to Marse Henry now, and he can't touch you unless Marse Henry says so. Which he won't."

Rachel, used to the ways of the big house, greeted Ezra at the back door as an equal. Used to the layout of the big house, she followed Ezra surely to Marse Mannheim's study. Used to the people of the big house, she raised her head to Marse Mannheim, and even though she didn't look him in the eye, she said, "Unless you plan on a short visit with us, you should ask us to sit."

Marse Mannheim looked surprised, but he roared with laughter and told Rachel she was still a forward gal. If he was still angry with her, he didn't show it. He asked them to sit.

Rachel's presence did Charlie no good. He sat tongue-tied, his eyes on the floor, while Rachel explained to Marse Mannheim how things were. The cotton crop looked good this year, all five hundred acres planted, the plants healthy. The corn was good too, all two hundred acres, and they should have a surplus again, which they could sell on the ear or make into whiskey. They were fine for provision. The smokehouse was full from last year, and there were enough shoats to get them through the coming year. The kitchen garden and the provision gardens were doing well. All they bought at Stockton's was flour and coffee. Mules and stock? All right. No visits to the blacksmith this week. Too many chickens to count, enough eggs for everyone to make pone with eggs in it.

Marse Mannheim asked after Matt. Marse Matt was fine, Rachel told him. Talking a little. Walking a little. Marse and Missus Mannheim should come to visit to see him.

And Adelaide?

Rachel would never be tongue-tied, but this question gave her pause. She answered carefully. Missus Adelaide was changeable, she said. Sometimes she had sick headaches and sometimes she was just fine.

Did Adelaide miss her husband?

Rachel answered the question sideways and then it was easy. She could put the proper feeling into it. "We all do, Marse Mannheim. We all do."

On the way back to the Kaltenbach place, Charlie said admiringly to Rachel, "He eat right out of your hand."

She had hidden her fear and he had acted as though he had never given her reason to be afraid. Suddenly weary, suddenly nauseated, she said, "I'm a Mannheim too. I know him better than anyone."

A week later, after they went to see Marse Mannheim—after she gave the report while Charlie looked at the floor, and occasionally nodded in agreement—Marse Mannheim sent him to wait in the kitchen while he talked to Rachel. He said, "Charlie's a good boy, but I can't get a thing out of him. Next time you come by yourself."

Now she had to appease Charlie. On the way back to the Kaltenbach place, she said, "Marse Mannheim asked me to give him the report next week. Just me. Would that bother you?"

Charlie said, "I promised Marse Henry. Feel like I'm not doing right by Marse Henry, letting you go by yourself."

She said, "You bring in the crop, like you're good at, and I'll go keep an eye on Marse Mannheim, like I'm good at." She reached for his hand, the old sisterly gesture of affection. He took it. He said, "I forgot how you could persuade me." He squeezed her hand. A slow smile crept over his face, the old brotherly look of affection. It was sweet to see it again. "All right. Now you got to report to me on what Marse Mannheim says to you."

Before Rachel left for her next visit to Marse Mannheim, she smoothed her skirt and tied her apron higher than usual. She wondered if Marse Mannheim knew that she was expecting, but even if he did she didn't want him staring at her and quizzing her. Marse Mannheim had been breeding slaves for thirty years. She was damned if she'd let him look at her the way he'd consider his prize mare.

Rachel had a few things to discuss with Marse Mannheim that Charlie hadn't been worrying about. She was certain that Mordecai hadn't sold the crop yet, and now that the Union navy was successfully blockading Charleston and Savannah, she couldn't see how the crop could get out to its buyers in the Northern cotton mills. The debt hung over her head as heavily as over Henry's. Everyone on the Kaltenbach place was in peril as long as Henry still owed Mordecai money. Charlie's promise to Henry was to bring in the crop. Hers was to settle the debt.

When she walked into Mordecai's study he gave her a long look, an up-and-down look, the appraising look of the seasoned slave dealer. Gruffly, he said, "You'd best sit down."

So he already knew. She wondered if he were thinking that she was worth more, now that she was carrying.

"Are you feeling all right?" he asked.

"I'm all right." But she began to feel hot, and cold, and queasy again, just as she had when the baby announced itself. He looked hard at her face and saw the ashen color that showed how puny she felt. He handed her the spittoon just in time.

When she was finished, he asked her again, "You're sure you're all right?"

Wouldn't want her to miscarry and lose Henry his property, she thought. She glared at him. "Yes."

He got up and poured water from a pitcher into one of the crystal glasses he kept for brandy. He said, "Rinse out your mouth and you'll feel better."

She took the glass, swished the water in her mouth, and spat it violently into the spittoon.

He said, "I never saw a woman so stricken by the carrying sickness as your mother. I don't think she kept her breakfast down until her fifth month. I saw her drink water to wash out her mouth and puke it right up again."

It unsettled her. He saw that too. She drank a sip of water, carefully, and felt him watching her. He said, "How are you feeling?"

"Better."

He waited until both of them were certain she wouldn't need the spittoon again. He asked, "How is the place? How is the crop?"

On the way back to the Kaltenbach place, she found a cool spot under a pine tree and sat heavily on the soft bed of pine needles. She sat for a long time, listening to the sharp cries of birds and the small sounds of the soft-footed creatures that ate pinecones and pine seeds. No longer queasy, she was uncomfortable in her mind. She wasn't sure she liked hearing about her mother from Marse Mannheim. Whether he'd loved her or not, he'd watched her mother carefully while she was carrying, just as he watched her now. She wished she could talk to someone who knew whether Marse Mannheim had taken her mother for his pleasure, or whether he had felt real affection for her. Was that why Henry had made him so angry? Did he see himself, and his biggest folly, reflected in Henry's love for her?

She missed Henry most at night, but at this moment, on a hot August afternoon, she missed him so sorely that she put her head down on her knees and sobbed with the pain of it. With each sob, she felt the weight of the baby in her womb. She felt an odd flutter in her belly. More than a flutter. The baby was moving. Startled out of weeping, she put her hand on her belly to feel it. She sat quietly, letting the baby do whatever it was going to do. It seemed to be rolling over, just like you'd roll over in your sleep. Was that the kick of a tiny heel? She laughed to think of the baby sticking her with its elbows and knees inside her womb. "You're a lively one," she said, taking pleasure in the movement under her hand.

After that, the baby moved all the time, and as much as it startled her, it pleased her, too. Minnie was elated. "It ain't just quick," she said. "It's sprightly!"

At five months along, she had started to show. When she came for her weekly visit, Marse Mannheim immediately told her to sit down. As soon as she sat, the baby began to move, and she put her hand protectively on her belly, still surprised at the sensation. Marse Mannheim gave her a glass of water to drink, and when she finished, he said, in a low voice unlike his usual loud tones, "When your mother was carrying she used to sit just like that. Cradling that child in her hands before it was ever born." That child, of course, being herself.

She blushed. Could he see that, too? For once, she couldn't meet his eyes for shame, instead of servility. He cleared his throat, as though he was afraid of the way his voice would come out, and he said, "Tell me about the place and the crop."

She didn't ask permission to raise her eyes to his. She did it, and she said, "I can tell you all about the crop, if you want, cotton and corn and stock and provision. Not much different from last week. But I want to talk about selling last year's crop and settling the debt."

"Cotton will go higher. I'm waiting to get a better price."

"How would you get it through the blockade?"

He was startled. "How would you know about the blockade?"

She didn't want to remind him that she read the *Savannah Republican* every week, with special interest in its commercial intelligence. "I've heard about it in town. Folks are talking. Worried and upset about it."

President Lincoln had ordered the blockade a week after the war broke out. Rachel had seen the cartoon in the *Savannah Republican* that portrayed the blockade as a great snake coiled around all of the ports of the South. Cotton couldn't get out, and nothing from the North was supposed to get in.

He said, "I'll sell when I'm ready. I ain't ready yet."

If he wanted to keep Henry, and everyone on Henry's place, in his grip, he couldn't have chosen a better way to do it. The baby rolled over and she put her hand over the bulge in her apron. "Can we sell? Or did we miss our chance?"

He was going to say something else, less blunt, more reassuring, but he knew he shouldn't bother. "Missed our chance to get it out the usual way through Savannah or Charleston. There are other ways."

"How?"

"Take it to Nassau first. Then get it to London."

"Get it through the blockade."

Again, he didn't mince words. "Yes."

Rachel savored Henry's letters, even though the ripped envelopes and unfolded pages reminded her that Adelaide had read them first. She never told him that Adelaide read them. She wanted his words and his feelings freely expressed. If it tormented Adelaide to read those words, so much the better.

She slipped away to their hiding place to read his letters. She read the words, and let his voice shape them in her ear. He had written since the day he left, and he always closed by telling her how badly he missed her, and she let herself miss him just as keenly, a pain she felt in her muscles and her bones. When she finished reading she kissed the pages, and wept over them, too.

August 7, 1861

> *Dearest Rachel,*
> *We left Camp McDonald with the kind of display that thrilled the hearts of the young volunteers—a grand display on the parade ground before the eyes of our senior officers, a sham battle, and a crowd to cheer us as we left.*

The men are full of excitement and think that it will be a quick business to beat the Yankees.

I've had enough time to think a lot about being in battle. I now understand what Colonel Turner said to me about hotheads who want glory. Most of the younger men are eager to prove themselves. Cat, who should know better, shares their romantic notion of glory and valor. I don't say this to my men, but I feel a cold dread at the thought of trying to kill people I would otherwise agree with, and to risk being shot to death by them in return.

We're now in Richmond, where we've been assigned to Camp Winder, which has become a hospital. We're guarding Union prisoners of war. They've all been wounded, and are recovering, and I can't imagine where the Confederate Army thinks they're going. They're very like my own men—very young and far from home for the first time. Some of our men work themselves into a frenzy, trying to think of them as the enemy. I look at them and feel sad, terribly sad, at being their adversary on the battlefield.

Cat, always the gentleman, has a busy life in Richmond society. He has friends and relations in Richmond, and they invite him to endless dinners and balls. He drags me along—I politely eat oysters and ham at these dinners, and dance a little with the young ladies who want to meet an officer—and I watch him tease and flirt. Like the young ladies, he's in love with the idea of being an officer. His first act, after unpacking his trunk, was to find a tailor to make him a dress uniform. He drinks more than he should, and games, too, habits that neither Marcus nor I approve of.

There's a photographer in the camp who takes pictures. I've had pictures taken and I'm having cartes de visite made. I'll send some to Adelaide, and some to you. I'm not as elegant as Cat, but I did put on my new uniform, a gray tunic with brass buttons, and before I marched off to the photographer, Marcus assured me that I looked all right.

Matt's progress delights me—that he walks by himself, and can say "mama," "daddy," "Ben," and "kitty." Kiss him for me, and read Minnie any part of this letter you see fit. I miss all of you more than I can say, and you most of all.

Your Henry

When the cartes de visite arrived, Adelaide had one framed and put it on her bedside table. Most wives kept a photograph of an absent husband, but this was a different kind of reminder. She kept it there to reproach her. In her spite, in her anger, she had never realized that he might die and never return. It still hurt that he loved Rachel and said so, in every letter. As her anger at Rachel began to diminish, her remorse for her conduct toward Henry grew and grew. It began to distress her to think that he would go into battle, to fight a war he hated, and he might never return. And that her words and deeds had sent him there.

Adelaide hadn't kept Yom Kippur for years—she still couldn't bear the thought of facing the Israelites of Savannah at Mickve Israel—but this year, she took the carte de visite and went into Henry's study. She sat before the unlit fire and listened to the hands as they sang their holler for picking cotton. She looked at the picture of her husband, the unwilling soldier in his Confederate tunic, and thought of everything that God would ask her to account for.

She looked at the carte de visite again, at the familiar face with the liquid eyes and expressive mouth. What did the Yom Kippur service say? That repentance and charity could balance the books against evil and for good? She was so heavily in God's debt that she didn't know if she could ever make it right.

She was sitting, not moving, not reading, when Rachel came into the room. "Did you know that today is the Day of Atonement?"

"Thought you had to go to synagogue in Savannah for that, ma'am."

"I reckon you can reflect on your sins, and let them trouble you, just about anywhere. This place is as good as any. Don't need a synagogue for that."

Rachel saw the photograph that sat on the little table at her elbow. "I believe you're right about that, ma'am."

Adelaide's eyes also rested on the photograph. "I hope that Henry will be safe," she said.

"So do I, ma'am. I hope and pray so."

"If he doesn't, I don't know how I'll ever forgive myself."

Rachel said, "Day of Atonement ain't over yet," and she left Adelaide alone before the unlit fire.

Charlie was pleased to tell Rachel that they would have six hundred bales again, maybe even a little more. Marse Mannheim received the news from Rachel impassively. He asked, "When is your young'un due?"

"Minnie says just after Christmas."

"Do you want me to send over Aunt Susy?"

"Minnie birthed Marse Matt. I trust she'll do all right for this one, too."

"How do you feel?"

"Fine. Baby's lively. Never seems to sleep when I try to."

He looked so wistful that she felt embarrassed for him. She said, "Do you think we'll sell the crop yet this year?"

Pulled back, he said, "I'm still pondering it."

As the crop came in, as Marse Mannheim watched the blockade tighten, as she waited for the baby to come due, Henry waited for his regiment's war to start.

Camp Fisher, Dumfries, Virginia
December 10, 1861

> *Dearest Rachel,*
>
> *We've had three false alarms—calls to battle that haven't come off. A few weeks ago, a battle was canceled, like a picnic, because of the weather. We're back in camp. We sit and wait while the war goes on elsewhere. The waiting seems harder than fighting would be. I'm at the point where I'm ready to fight—not eager, as the boys are. But ready.*
>
> *Camp life is very dull. We drill a little, but mostly we try to keep warm. It's bitterly cold here, and snows here as I haven't seen since I left Dresden. The men miss home and look forward to Christmas. Could you and Minnie send a package? I'm afraid that latkes wouldn't travel well, but all of us would welcome cake. Perhaps you could sneak in a honey cake? I miss all of you and hope that Saint Nicholas can manage to stop at our place again this year. If I could find an orange here I would send it to you.*
>
> *Take good care. I know the baby will come soon and it troubles my soul that I won't be there to greet our child and kiss your cheek. Have you thought of a name yet? Write to me to tell me. It will warm me better than whiskey.*
>
> *Your Henry*

Adelaide put down the letter, too sobered to weep. He was ready to fight. He could be in battle. If she became a widow—Out of jealousy! Out of spite!—it would be her own fault.

A few days before Christmas, as Rachel and Minnie sat at the kitchen table, slicing apples for Christmas pies, she asked Minnie, "What's it like to bear a baby?" The air was chilly, and there had been frost on the cotton plants, now stripped bare. Putting sugar and cinnamon on the apples, she said, "You don't have to sweeten it, like you did for Adelaide. I want to know."

Minnie measured out a few drops of cider vinegar to keep the apples from browning. She said, "Depends on how you take pain."

Rachel said, "I don't enjoy it. But I can stand it."

Many a night, Minnie had woken to hear Rachel weeping into her pillow, curled into a ball against the pain of Henry's leaving. And Minnie had crawled into Rachel's bed to hold her close, and to stroke her hair, on the nights that her bad dreams roiled through her and tore up her sleep.

Minnie sprinkled flour over the apple slices. "It can hurt a little or it can hurt enough to make you want to die."

"Anything to help?"

"Breathe deep. Breathe in deep, and breathe out deep."

"If that don't help?"

"Holler and moan."

Rachel laughed. "Did that to get the baby in. Guess I can do it to get the baby out!"

When Adelaide realized that Rachel was carrying Henry's child, her hurt and anger flared all over again. Rachel's pregnancy was a daily reminder of the way that her sister and her husband had betrayed her. But as Rachel came closer to her time, she felt concern. She knew what it felt like to be nauseated all the time, and to be so heavy on your feet that walking up the stairs was difficult. Was Rachel afraid—of the pain, and the possibility that the baby would die, or that she would die in bearing it? Her mother died in childbed. Did she think of that?

One morning, when she found Rachel in the kitchen, she asked her.

Rachel, heavy, weary, exasperated, said, "No, ma'am. I'm not worried. Minnie will help me and I'll be all right."

A few days after the first of the year, Rachel began to feel the twinges that signaled the beginning of labor. She said to Minnie, "Cramping started."

"You all right?"

Rachel gasped—more in surprise than in pain—and Minnie said, "You go on upstairs. I'll get Becky and Jenny and I'll be along shortly."

By the time Minnie came upstairs, her water had broken. Minnie felt her belly. "You doing fine," she said. "You feel all right?"

Surprised by another cramp, Rachel put her hand on her belly and said, "Should I lie down?"

"Not if you feel all right sitting up. You can walk if you want. Sometimes that helps."

It hurt, but it was tolerable. She said to Minnie, "Will it hurt worse than this?"

"Might. It's different for everyone. You remember about breathing deep?"

Rachel nodded. A pain gripped her and she breathed deep so she wouldn't cry out.

There was a knock on the door. Adelaide stood shyly on the threshold. In a low voice she asked, "How is she?"

Minnie said impatiently. "Laboring. All right."

"May I sit with her?"

"If she allow it."

Rachel's voice, hoarser than usual, came from the bed. "I'll allow it."

Adelaide sat by Rachel's bedside, in the little chair that had once been in her nursery. She asked, "How are you feeling?"

Rachel was suddenly racked by a pain, worse than before, but she clenched her teeth against it and said, "Tolerable."

Adelaide extended her hand to her sister, who looked at it with suspicion. Adelaide said, "Rachel. Let me help you."

Another pain, and a gasp along with it. "I'm all right."

Minnie said, "Don't pester her. You set there quiet, and if she wants to take your hand, she will."

Rachel, who had watched Adelaide sink into a haze of laboring pain, had promised herself that the same thing would not happen to her. She could bear pain. She would press her lips shut against it. But as her labor progressed, the pain overtook her, hot and searing. To her shame, she cried out, and could not help herself.

Since she first knew she was carrying, she had never let herself think about her mother. Now Eliza was close by, the pretty smiling woman who had known songs from Africa, and who would have borne Marse Mannheim a son, if she hadn't died in childbed. Had she labored like this? Who had sat with her, and bathed her forehead, and held her hand, as she slipped away?

Someone held a cup of water to her lips. How long had she been laboring? Between the fear and the pain it was hard to tell the passage of time. "Rachel." It was Adelaide's voice. Adelaide's hand that held the cup. "Drink a little water." Her hand was steady, but her voice shook.

Rachel raised her head to drink. When she lay back she reached for Adelaide's hand. At the next pain she clenched it tight.

Minnie said, "Ma'am, that baby's coming. You need to go so we can help it."

Rachel heard Adelaide say, "She stayed with me. I want to stay with her."

Minnie said, "It up to her."

Rachel clutched Adelaide's hand as though she were drowning. She said, "Don't go."

"I won't," Adelaide said, she never let go of Rachel's hand, even though Rachel squeezed it with all her strength, throughout the long haze of laboring pain.

She heard Minnie say, "Don't you cry, Missus Adelaide. She all right. Doing fine. Baby come soon." And finally, Minnie's voice, pleased and excited, a command for her. "That baby just about to come! You push!"

As the baby's head began to emerge, Rachel gasped with the effort. She pushed, and Minnie put out her hands to catch the child. She lay back against the pillow and asked, "Girl or boy?"

"Girl."

"Let me hold her."

"Clean her up first." As Rachel and Adelaide watched, Minnie gently toweled the baby and wrapped her in a clean cloth. Rachel propped herself up to take the child in her arms. A little dented from the effort of getting born, still a little slimy from the womb, she was a lovely shade of brown, a bit lighter than Rachel herself, with a round face and a dimple in each cheek. "She favor you," Minnie said.

Rachel felt a fierce love for her new daughter. She felt it deep in her womb, the spot that Henry had touched when she and Henry made this child.

Adelaide, whose eyes were wet, said, "What are you going to call her?"

Rachel said, "Call her after my mother. Eliza."

Camp Fisher, Dumfries, Virginia
January 12, 1862

Dearest Rachel,

I'm overjoyed to hear of the baby's birth, and relieved that you and the baby are well. I would trust Minnie to deliver a regiment of babies. Of course you know about naming a baby as to remember someone who's gone. We usually think of it for boys but I don't see why a girl can't be a memorial too. I can't think of a better name for our child than your mother's name, Eliza.

My heart is so full that it's hard to write. Kiss Eliza and Matt for me. Take care and rest, as Minnie tells you, and write again as soon as you can.
Your Henry

Adelaide put the letter down. Abashed, she thought, These letters are not mine to read.

After Eliza was born, everyone on the place made a fuss over both mother and baby. Minnie insisted that Rachel stay in bed, which lasted two days, until Rachel got so bored that she declared she felt rested enough to get up. She winced when she walked—she felt as though getting Eliza into the world had rearranged every bone in her lower body—but she told Minnie that she couldn't see lying in bed when she wasn't sick.

Everyone—all of the hands, even Davey and Harriet, who barely knew her, and Micah and Lydia, who didn't care about her or the baby—came by to congratulate her and to look at the new arrival. Everyone said the same thing: "She pretty." And then, immediately afterward: "She favor you." The words were a collective sigh of relief. Everyone on the place knew there was endless trouble when Marse's baby looked too much like Marse.

Matt was fascinated by the baby. Minnie brought him upstairs to the attic room, where Ben's old cradle now stood next to Rachel's bed. It was mid-morning, and Rachel still couldn't get used to sitting idle while the rest of the plantation worked.

Matt was tall enough to lean on the side of the cradle. At two, he was talking, and he made perfect sense, if you were used to his way of talking. "Baby!" he said happily, smiling. It broke Rachel's heart every time Matt smiled. He had the same bright smile as his father.

Minnie said, "That's your Aunt Rachel's new baby."

Matt called all of the black women who took care of him and doted on him "Aunt." There was Aunt Minnie, Aunt Becky, Aunt Jenny, and Aunt Rachel. It gave Rachel a twinge to hear the real relationship hidden inside the offhand endearment.

"Baby name?"

Rachel said, "The baby's name is Eliza."

"Liza," Matt said. "Touch baby?"

"Be gentle."

"Like the kitty?"

Rachel had taught Matt how to stroke the cat without startling or hurting her. She had never seen a child with such a gentle touch for an animal. "Even more careful."

Matt laid his hand on the baby's cheek. She opened her eyes and moved her head, not sure that she liked it. "Touch her hand, Matt," Rachel said. Matt touched his finger to Eliza's palm. The little fingers curled tightly around the slightly bigger hand. Matt laughed.

Watching them, Rachel thought, I wish I could tell him that she's his cousin and his sister. His blood kin. I do wish.

Adelaide came up the back stairs to the attic, where Rachel and the new baby rested. She had not been here since the baby was born. Despite the two big windows on either side of the room, it was not very light, and in January, it was cold here. She hoped that the baby had a warm coverlet.

Rachel sat propped up in her bed, the bundled baby resting on her breast. Her hair was loose and she wore her sleeping clothes, her chemise and petticoat. The arms wrapped around the baby were bare and goosefleshed in the winter chill. Adelaide had never realized that Rachel lacked a nightdress and a dressing gown.

Adelaide stood at the side of the bed and said carefully, "How are you feeling?"

Rachel looked up in surprise. She said, "All right."

"You ain't tired?"

Rachel smiled a little. "Weary. And sore. But all right."

"May I sit?"

Rachel nodded.

"How is the baby?"

"Just fine." She kissed the soft little head.

"May I see her?"

Rachel took this to mean "look at" and not "touch." She turned the drowsing child so that Adelaide could get a good look at the little brown face.

Adelaide said, "She's the spit of you."

Rachel said, "I reckon we'll be keeping her. Since she looks like me."

Adelaide turned her head away. If she felt repentant, she didn't say so. Instead she asked, "Would you let me hold her?"

Rachel tightened her arms around the baby. She took a long time to reply. Finally she sat up. "You be careful with her."

Adelaide held out her arms. "Of course I will." She took the wriggling, cooing bundle from Rachel and cradled her niece against her chest.

Adelaide found herself looking into the still-unfocused dark eyes and crooning, "Who's this pretty little baby? Who's this pretty little gal?"

Rachel watched. Adelaide could feel the unease that radiated from Rachel like heat. Reluctantly, she handed the baby back to her sister. Rachel took possession of her child and kissed her forehead.

Adelaide asked softly, "May I come back? To see both of you?"

Rachel laid back on her pillow, the baby in her arms. She looked tired and ashy. "Won't say no if you do."

Adelaide felt abashed, remembering her months of bed rest and the broths and custards that had come to her on a tray. She said softly, "Don't get up too soon. Minnie and I will manage without you. You take care of that pretty little baby."

Rachel was out of bed within a few days, and she brought Eliza and her cradle into the kitchen, to watch over the baby while she worked, and to nurse and hold her when she wasn't. As Rachel rocked the cradle, Adelaide walked into the kitchen, dirt from the Cassville road still on her boots. She drew something from her pocket. "These are for you," she said, handing Rachel a packet of letters.

Rachel looked up from the baby. "You ain't read them yet."

Adelaide looked away in shame. She said, "That was mean of me."

The closest she could come to sorry. Rachel held the letters in her hand. She said nothing.

"What are you thinking?" Adelaide asked.

Rachel looked up. "Just might accept your apology," she said, and she put her letters in her own pocket.

Chapter **16**

Through the Blockade

When Aggie Payne came to take tea on a warm afternoon in April, she noticed that Minnie brought the tray. "Where's Rachel?" Aggie asked.

Adelaide said, "She's over at the Mannheim place." She set down her cup. She was bothered enough to confess this to Aggie. "She goes there once a week."

"Why would she?"

Ashamed, Adelaide said, "She talks to my papa about our business."

"Why? Couldn't you? Or find an overseer to do it for you?"

"She says that she's the only one on the place who can figure well enough to do it."

Aggie set down her teacup, as though she would be too upset to hold onto it after she spoke. "Now that your husband is away, your nigger maid is running your place?"

Eliza had caused a big fuss at the Mannheim place, starting with Ezra, whose sternness evaporated at the sight of her. Rachel had never thought that Ezra might be a doting father, or uncle, or grandfather. But he evidently was, knowing to make faces at the baby and to croon to her, "Who's my little sugar bun?"

When Rachel walked into Mordecai's study, he rose, as he never had for her alone, and walked around the big desk so he, too, could get a good look at the baby. He bent down to give her a long, appraising stare. Rachel was suddenly furious. How dare you! she thought. Consider my baby like you plan to sell her! He straightened up and said, "Thank God. She looks just like you."

Rachel said, "So people say."

"I hear you named her Eliza." A wistful look passed over his big, red, coarse-featured face.

For the first time since she had come to report to him, he gestured to the two chairs that faced the fireplace. As in Henry's study, these chairs were for people who wanted to sit, and look at each other, and talk as equals. "Sit down," he said gruffly, seating himself. She sat opposite him, pleased and uneasy at once, looking at the baby because it unsettled her to look at him.

He said, "Have you watched cotton prices on the London market?"

"Last I looked, over a dollar a pound."

Because cotton was trapped on every place in Georgia—every place in the South—that grew cotton, the price had fallen and fallen in Savannah and Charleston and Natchez and New Orleans. It was at five or six cents a pound now. Because it was scarce in Lancaster and London, the price in England had risen to a level that made seasoned cotton planters dizzy and reckless. If you could get your cotton out to sell to a London broker, you could realize five hundred dollars a bale, paid in pounds, backed by silver.

He said, "It might go higher. But it's time to sell."

Rachel said, "How do you find someone to do it?"

"I've written to Jacob Pereira, of Pereira Brothers in London. They have shipping interests. They know."

"Is Marse William Pereira still with them?"

He raised his voice. "How do you know about that? God forbid you wrote to him, or anyone in that family."

"Of course not," she said. "I read the notice in the *Savannah Republican*." Eliza made a sniffling noise, and Rachel rocked her to soothe her. She said to Mordecai, "What did you hear from Pereira Brothers?"

"There's a great deal of money to be made, if a man is enterprising enough to take the risk. They know of a man who's willing to make the trip between Savannah and Nassau. He's a British naval officer who just left the service and has an eye for an opportunity."

"Can we trust him?"

He knew better than to say, Don't you trust me? "He stays in Savannah. I could invite him here to find out."

She cradled the baby and looked at Mordecai fiercely over the baby's head. "I want to meet him," she said. "I want to understand exactly what he's going to do, and how much it's going to cost, and how we're going to pay him." She thought, You could bamboozle Marse Henry, but you can't bamboozle me. I won't stand for it.

Every day, Rachel went into the study to sit at Henry's desk with the ledger and the account book open before her. Adelaide found her there, pen in hand, frowning. Without looking up, Rachel dipped the pen into the inkwell. Her middle finger was deeply stained with ink, as Adelaide's had always been.

"Rachel, what are you writing in there?"

"About the place. The hands, the stock, the crop. What we earn, if we earn something, and what we spend."

"Can I see?"

"Ain't much to see. Figures, mostly. Thought that figures made your head ache."

Adelaide said pleasantly, "I don't care much for figures, but shouldn't I know about the business of the place?"

"Thought you didn't care for business, either." Rachel's tone was sharp. She was unsettled and upset, and it was more than anything that she put in the ledger.

"Ain't it mine to care about, too?"

Rachel shook her head. "You wouldn't understand it."

"How hard can it be? Two columns of figures, debit and credit?"

Rachel set the pen in the stand and closed the ledger, keeping its mysteries for herself. Since she had begun to talk business with Mordecai, she had been closemouthed about what she said to him, and what he said to her. Yesterday, she had come back from the Mannheim place even more tight-lipped than usual, reporting that Mordecai thought Eliza was a pretty baby and that they would make six hundred bales this year, if the weather held. What you'd tell a child, if she asked.

Adelaide said, "What did you talk about with my father yesterday?"

Rachel had a secret, and she wouldn't give it up. Adelaide said, "Did he say anything about the blockade?"

Rachel looked sharply at her sister. "How would you know about the blockade?"

"Rachel, I ain't a ninny. I know perfectly well. Can't get anything in, not marmalade, nor toothpowder, nor laudanum, nor coffee, and can't get anything out. Especially cotton. Everyone knows that." She pressed her sister. "Is he thinking about running cotton through the blockade?"

"Why would you ask a thing like that?"

"Ain't every planter?"

Rachel closed the ledger and the account book. She put them into the desk drawer. If Henry had left her a key, Adelaide thought, she'd lock that drawer and take the key along with her. The better to keep the mysteries of the accounts for herself.

A week later, as Rachel settled herself in Mordecai's study, the stranger said, "I like to deal with Israelites. They're like Scotsmen. We both know the value of a penny." Captain Andrew Finlay McNeill spoke with a burr that was familiar to anyone who had lived with a Scots-Irish overseer on a Georgia plantation. He had a commander's forceful voice and a seaman's keen eyesight, which he turned on Rachel as he asked Mordecai, "Who's the lass?"

Mordecai answered for her. "She keeps house for my son-in-law, and she keeps his accounts, too."

"A slave?"

To her astonishment, Mordecai said, "She grew up on my place, and she has as hard a head for business as any Israelite. Or any Scotswoman."

Captain McNeill said, "Can she speak for herself?"

Rachel said quietly, using her best diction, "Of course I can, sir. But as a servant, I wait to be spoken to."

Captain McNeill looked from Mordecai to Rachel and back to Mordecai. He said, "Your domestic arrangements are your own affair. All I care about is that you can pay me."

"We can pay you," Mordecai said. "You can be sure of that."

Rachel wondered how.

"Where is your cotton?" McNeill asked.

Mordecai said, "In a warehouse on the Savannah docks."

"We'd best hurry. The Union Army is closing in on Savannah."

Aside from the risk, the transport itself was not complicated. The cotton would be loaded in Savannah. The *Phoebe* was a medium-sized ship, built to be swift, of four hundred tons. "Sir, how many bales of cotton is that?" Rachel asked.

"Four to a ton," McNeill said.

The biggest trouble was getting out of Savannah harbor. "We go on a moonless night," McNeill said. "We extinguish our lights. We blow our steam into the water, so we can't be seen."

More and more worried, Rachel asked, "What if a Union blockader sees you? What then?"

Captain McNeill's eyes gleamed. "Run like hell!" he said, laughing.

Once out of the harbor, once past the Union ships that ringed the entrance to Savannah by sea, the journey was short and likely to be uneventful. Within two days, at the very most, a ship could be in Nassau, five hundred and sixty miles from Savannah. Once it arrived, Captain McNeill would unload the cargo and it would await the next steamer bound for Liverpool, a merchant ship that could go undisturbed to England.

Rachel listened to Captain McNeill talk with growing alarm. Finally she asked the question that worried her most. "Sir, what will it cost us to get our cotton to Nassau?"

"Five hundred dollars a ton in gold. Half before I leave, the rest after I get to Nassau."

Henry's twelve hundred and thirty bales of cotton were three hundred and seven tons. She put her hand to her mouth in shock. A hundred and fifty-three thousand dollars to run the cotton from Savannah to Nassau! She could not imagine such a sum.

Mordecai asked her, "If cotton is selling for a dollar-fifty a pound, how much we will get for a bale?"

"Seven hundred and fifty dollars," she said slowly.

"How much will we realize for twelve hundred and thirty bales?"

When she figured it, and realized how much it was, she could scarcely get the words out. "Nine hundred twenty-two thousand and five hundred dollars."

If the ship was captured, or sunk, and the cargo was lost, Henry would be so deep in debt to Mordecai that he would never be free of it. If the cotton got through to be sold on the London Exchange, the return would be a staggering sum, even after everyone who was owed was paid.

Rachel asked Captain McNeill, "Have you ever lost a cargo? Or a ship?"

"Never." At her worried look, he said, "Is there anything you'd like? Anything you've missed? I'll bring it back for you."

"You ain't doing this for our pleasure!"

He smiled. "It would be a pleasure to oblige you," he said.

His attention and his boasting needled her. She asked for something small and homely that no one could mistake for a token. "Marmalade," she said.

As often as Adelaide had come into the study, she had never sat at Henry's desk to read the ledger. Rachel's smugness had stung her so badly that she opened the leather-bound book to see what was inside. The first pages were in her husband's handwriting, small and neat in the German style. Oh, pshaw, she thought. There's no mystery here. Instead of columns of figures, there were entries, just like the entries in her own diary, if she happened to write about mules and horseshoes and bushels of corn instead of what happened to her, and how she felt about it. She riffled through the pages to find the latest entries. She recognized that hand, too. It was the script she had taught her sister to write when they were girls, keeping a secret from her mother.

She read: *Tuesday, April 8, 1862. Met with Mr. Mordecai Mannheim. Captain McNeill, of the* Phoebe, *was there. Discussed selling the cotton. He can take it to Nassau and from there to England. It will cost us $500 a ton, which is $153,000 for 1,230 bales. Cotton is selling for $1.50 a pound in Liverpool.*

Adelaide closed the book, her cheeks flushed, her heart pounding. She had never thought about the sale of cotton, just as she had never thought about the sale of slaves. But she could understand perfectly well what was written in the ledger, even if she was a lady and supposed to be a ninny about money. Her father and her sister had decided a matter that could put Henry so deep in debt that he would be ruined, and no one thought to mention it to her, no more than they would have mentioned it to the kitchen cat.

She shut the book and put it away in the drawer, and went to find her sister, who was in the kitchen, mixing a batch of pone. It was warm for April, and the fire in the stove made the kitchen hotter still. Rachel's face was beaded with sweat.

Adelaide said, "When are you going to see my father?"

"Go every Tuesday afternoon."

"The next time you go, let me go with you."

Rachel said, "Don't think your daddy will allow it."

Adelaide thought, He'd let me sit in the corner and overhear, because he don't think I can understand. It's Rachel who won't allow it. Rachel, who had never had anything to herself, now had the business of the place as her own, and with it, Mordecai's full attention. She was loath to give it up. No matter how much she tried to hide it, her expression said, I'm capable, and you ain't.

Adelaide said fiercely, "I don't care if he allows it or not. I want to be there."

Rachel wiped her forehead with the sleeve of her dress. "All right, ma'am."

"Don't ma'am me. Don't mock me. And don't pretend you forgot, either."

On Tuesday, when Rachel left to see Mordecai, Adelaide went with her. Adelaide walked up the front stairs, as though she were making a call with her servant in tow. Ezra greeted them with a puzzled look on his face. "Miss Adelaide, didn't expect you. Are you here to see your mama?"

Adelaide said, "Rachel and I are going to talk business with my papa first." Ezra was too good a servant to question anything a master or mistress asked of him, or even to let a surprised look creep onto his face. He showed them both into the study.

Mordecai sat at his desk. When he saw Adelaide, he said, "Missy, why are you here?"

"Why is everyone so surprised? I want to know what you and Rachel talk about."

Mordecai said, "We talk business. It ain't for you to know. Why don't you go take tea with your ma?"

"It's my place, and I should know about its business."

"Business ain't a fit subject for a lady. Go on."

Adelaide rose, giving her father and her sister the same wounded look. "So a lady ain't fit to do business," she said. "But a slave is."

She sat in the parlor with her mother, who was also surprised to see her. She drank an impatient cup of tea, fuming that her father had cast her out of the study, where he and Rachel disposed of the mysteries that Rachel guarded so carefully in the ledger.

Even an angry woman remained a lady. She would save her temper for later.

When Rachel was finished, there were more pleasantries with her mother and with Ezra, but she and Rachel were finally on their way home, walking through the pine woods that separated her father's place from her husband's. It was a hot spring day and her dress stuck to her skin, where her corset didn't dig into it. She took Rachel by the arm, as though she were going to say something affectionate, and said, "You knew he wouldn't allow it. To let me talk business with him."

Rachel tried very hard not to grin. "I told you. Told you! Insisted on making a disappointment for yourself."

At Rachel's smug look, Adelaide said, "I looked in the ledger. I read what you wrote about going through the blockade. And believe me, I understood it just fine."

"You spied on it?"

"Oh, hush. Why is it I can only find out anything about the place by sneaking and creeping about? Why don't you trust me to tell me? If the Union Navy sinks that ship with Henry's cotton on it, we go so deep into debt that we'll never see the end of it. Shouldn't I know?"

"Ain't your worry. Or your trouble. Or your burden."

"God in heaven!" Rachel winced, and Adelaide recalled that Henry, who rarely swore, used *Gott im Himmel* as an oath. "If he's ruined because he can't repay my father, won't that be my burden?" She glared at her sister. "Won't it be yours?"

Rachel glared back at her. "Sell me!" she said. "Wouldn't that give you joy, to sell me to settle a debt!"

Adelaide lost her temper. "Sell you!" she said, with contempt. "I could sell all of you, and the house and the land, and everything on the place, and it wouldn't make a dent in a debt of over a hundred and fifty thousand dollars. I might as well drown myself, if the Union Navy is nimbler than the man who runs that ship through the blockade."

Rachel lost her temper, too. "How do you think we settle the debt, then? Hope and pray the war ends and the blockade lifts? When do that happen? Next year in Jerusalem!"

"This ain't a matter of business! This is folly! This is madness!"

"It's still business, selling cotton through the blockade, and if you decide to do it, you don't cry and carry on. You put that cotton on a ship. Even if it make you sick at your stomach. Even if it give you nightmares that it might sink. You hope and pray it get to Nassau. Because if it don't, some of us ain't lucky enough to think about how sweet it would be to drown. We get shackled up and we go to Mississippi. If there's still a Mississippi to go to after this war is over."

Angry, envious, ashamed, Adelaide said, "Don't talk to me like that. You ain't the mistress of this place."

Rachel gave her the dark, deep gaze that was more insolent than words. She didn't wait for Adelaide's reply. She shook herself free of Adelaide's grip on her arm and walked away, turning her back on her mistress and sister.

Adelaide stood unmoving, rage and common sense churning together in her constricted chest. It wasn't the insolence that bothered her. Neither of them, not the mistress nor the slave, ran the place. Mordecai ran the place. Rachel was right, and Adelaide hated that her slave and sister was right.

Henrico County, Virginia
May 29, 1862

Dearest Rachel,

I write to you not knowing if I will be alive by tomorrow night. What seems like a long time ago, Minnie once asked me if Jews believe in heaven and hell. I told her that we don't, which worried her. She wondered how I could live without the comfort of knowing that I would see those I loved after I died. I've never had that comfort. I've always believed that I'll live on in the memories of everyone who loves me. In that, I hope I'll have a heritage, in my family in Germany and in everyone who has come to care about me in my new home, so far from the home of my youth.

I know that I'll live in on my children, both of them, Matt and Eliza. You tell me that Matt has my looks and that you see my temper in his gentleness with his baby sister. My mother and father called me their Kaddish, after the prayer that a son says to remember them after they die. Matt is my Kaddish. And there is Eliza, who is living proof of the bond between us. If I'm gone, our love will live on in your memory and in Eliza. Does that offer comfort? I hope so.

Beloved, as I write, as I contemplate the chance that I might die tomorrow, I think of our love and all the joy it has brought me. I remember our vows to each other, that neither death nor distance would part us. I hope that whatever tomorrow brings—whether a reprieve to fight another battle, or death—that I will always be with you and that you will always remember me. If I die, that is the best memorial I can think of.

I won't tell you, don't be afraid. I know how afraid I am. I've told Colonel Turner again and again that I'm not much of a soldier, since I know so well how to feel fear. He tells me that a man who feels brave on the eve of battle isn't the hero. A man who can feel fear, and fight despite it, and take care of those he commands despite it, is the hero. So I will ask you to do the same for me—despite the fear, to face the hardships, and to carry the burdens, and to go on living.

Beloved, if I am still of this earth tomorrow, I will write to you at the first moment that I can. Whatever happens, I will love you forever.

Your loving Henry

Rachel put down the letter. It was the loveliest time of the year in northern

Georgia, the earliest summer, when the air was so sweet with magnolia that it seeped into the nose and lingered there, whether a person breathed it in or not. The wild birds nested, and brooded, and called to each other to protect their children. The cotton grew with such vigor that only the constant chop of the hoe kept it in straight, even rows, and everything in the kitchen garden burst forth to flower and bud and fruit.

In Virginia, the growing things would be trampled underfoot and the small wild creatures would flee at the smell of smoke and the sound of gunfire. Men would die tomorrow. She thought of the awful vision of fire and blood and death she had tried to conjure up when she read about John Brown's battle at Harpers' Ferry. Whatever would happen tomorrow in Henrico County would be worse, much worse, and Henry would be in the thick of it.

Even though Adelaide rambled over the Kaltenbach place, she never came past the old house. It reminded her of the betrayal, and she skirted it whenever she rambled. Today she changed her mind. She would walk up the stairs, and go inside, and see it for what it now was, tumbledown and abandoned.

She walked up the untended driveway, overgrown with weeds. She hesitated on the stairs, and chided herself for foolishness. She pushed open the door.

Inside was a bookcase, filled with letters bound with red ribbon. She felt a spark of anger. Even though it was left over from trimming a bonnet—from before the war, when there were bonnets to trim—it wasn't Rachel's to take.

And a book. Bound in Moroccan leather, with gilt lettering on the spine. *The Plays of Shakespeare*. Did Rachel take it back, or did Henry?

Holding it, she recalled all of the pain of the betrayal. She thought of the stricken look on Rachel's face when she first took the book away.

She held the book firmly in her hands, as though were a chicken squirming to get away from its fate as dinner. Slowly, she walked back to the main house, up the stairs, and into the study, where Rachel sat at Henry's desk with the ledger open before her.

She asked, "What are you writing in there?" as though Rachel were doing something to accuse her for.

Rachel looked up. "Mule threw a shoe and we owe your daddy's blacksmith for a new one. Is that all right?" Her tone was acerbic.

Adelaide held out the book so Rachel could see it. "Now I know where it went," she said.

Rachel rose. "Why do you have that?" she asked in alarm.

"Why shouldn't I?"

"Because it's mine."

Hers. Like the ledgers. Like the letters. Like her father's regard. Adelaide walked to the fireplace and plucked a match from the safe on the wall. She held the match in one hand and the book in the other.

"You wouldn't dare," Rachel said.

Adelaide struck the match on the safe and it fizzed and burst into flame. As Rachel watched, she brought the match closer to the book. "Wouldn't I?"

Rachel said nothing. Adelaide brought the match still closer. Rachel said, "You crazy."

Adelaide had never felt more clear-headed. She brought the match still closer, and she said, "Tell my father I need to know the business of the place."

"Do you?"

"Yes," Adelaide said. She brought the match close enough to lick at the binding, and Rachel flew at her, grabbing for the book, trying to wrest it from her hand. As they struggled together, they forgot the match. The smell of burning cloth startled them both, and at the sight of Rachel's burning sleeve Adelaide threw her sister to the floor and cried out, "Roll on the rug to put it out!"

Rachel stood up. She stared at the burnt cloth, so close to her skin, and said, "Did you intend to murder me?"

Adelaide was horrified, but her tone was sharp with anger. "Of course not! Just to persuade you."

Without a hint of servility—as though she'd been quarreling with Adelaide as a sister all her life—Rachel said, "Give me the book."

"Promise me first." Not a mistress' command. A sister's grievance.

"What will you do if I say no?"

"Keep it."

"Burn it?"

Adelaide turned away. She was in the wrong and she knew it.

Rachel said, "All right. Next time I go to see your daddy, we go together."

"You'll tell him? That I need to know the business of the place?"

Rachel let her voice show her own grievance. She said sulkily, "I tell him."

Fair Oaks Station, Henrico County, Virginia
June 2, 1862

> *Dearest Rachel,*
>
> *I'm alive and I'm whole, by God's grace or luck I don't know, and I don't care. Cat is all right, too. You can see how my hand shakes as I write. I have been in hell. I have been in battle.*
>
> *We advanced through a rain of bullets, a deadly rain, since the minie balls do so much damage wherever they hit. Infantrymen are wild shots; if the sharpshooters were in front, I would not be here to write to you.*
>
> *One of the worst things about a battlefield is the scream of wounded horses. Men choose to go into battle but the horses do not. The sight of the horses, fatally wounded, lying on the ground to die, affected me as much as the sight of the wounded men.*
>
> *As we advanced, more and more men fell. The ground grew slippery with blood, and the air was thick with the smoke from rifles and from the bigger guns father away. In brightest daylight, the air was gray with smoke. Men who were fighting were yelling, hoping to frighten the other side, and the men who had been wounded were on the ground, some moaning in pain and some screaming in agony. I saw men shot in the chest and shot in the gut die on the battlefield. Those shot in the arm or the leg were borne away to suffer worse in the surgeon's tent. Afterwards, I saw a great heap of amputated limbs, men's arms and legs piled up with no more regard than offal in a butcher shop.*
>
> *There was no thought of the cause for which we fought, or for the Confederacy. My only thought was to stay alive and to keep my comrades and men alive. We shot our rifles because someone was shooting at us. Every man we hit gave us a greater chance to live until the end of the day.*
>
> *When dusk fell, everything quieted. Armies settle and go to sleep at night. We found a spot to sit, and rest, and eat a little, and if we could, sleep a little. We could see the Federal soldiers do the same, huddle together to catch a few hours of uneasy rest before the sun rose and the battle started again. Seeing them, so much like us, I was struck by the folly of this war. I have no quarrel with these men from Vermont, or Indiana, or Wisconsin. For a moment I saw them as fellows, not as an enemy, and the thought of shooting at them again in the morning rent my heart.*
>
> *I feel half-crazed and I must sound that way, as well. I have been baptized by fire, a Jew turned into a soldier, and as little as I like the transformation, it will serve me well. We will fight again, and again, and again.*
>
> *Beloved, I write like this to you, of the worst and bitterest things I have*

seen, because I know you can bear it. In the thick of battle I thought of you, and my fondest hope was to live through it to be able to come home to you. I long for your embrace.

Don't read Minnie a word of this letter—tell her only that I was in battle, and I am all right. Kiss the children for me. I love you with all my heart.

Your Henry

The little boy from the Mannheim place had been told to give the note to Rachel, but he knocked on the front door instead and handed it to missus. Adelaide sent him to the kitchen and stood in the middle of the parlor, the note in her hands. Oh, pshaw, she thought. It's the business of the place. She tore open the envelope, ignoring the sound of hurried footsteps in the breezeway, and before she could read it, Rachel flew into the room and snatched the letter from her hands.

Rachel pulled the note from the envelope with shaking hands and scanned it. She sank onto the settee, her whole body sagging with relief.

"What is it?" Adelaide asked.

Rachel murmured, "Ship is safe in Nassau."

"Thought you'd be happy to know that." She sounded peevish, even to herself.

"Too worried to be happy." She shook her head. "Don't you worry?"

Of course she did. Henry wrote to her, too. But she said spitefully, "Why should I? You worry enough for both of us."

At six months, Eliza had started to look a bit like Henry. There was a hint of her father in her eyes, which were wide and liquid, and in her frame, which would be slenderer than her mother's. She had some of her father's disposition. She was a smiling, cheerful baby. She pleased everyone who looked at her.

Adelaide asked, "You're going to bring her with you?"

Rachel swathed her in a cotton blanket and said, "Why not? Your daddy like her, too. She soften him."

When they walked into Mordecai's study, Mordecai said to Rachel, "Bringing your baby along to do business. Trying to get the better of me." But there was a smile on his big red face. He turned to Adelaide. "Go along," he said.

Rachel stood before Mordecai, her baby in her arms, and she said,

"Missus Adelaide should know the business of the place. She need to hear what you have to say. She want to stay. I ask you, Marse."

Mordecai's eyes traveled from one daughter to the other. Gruffly, he said to Adelaide, "You can stay, as long as you set quiet and don't make a fuss."

Adelaide said, "I ain't a baby, Papa. I'm a grown woman, and I can understand business just fine." She sat in the nearest chair, her spine straight, and prepared to be attentive.

Rachel settled herself and Eliza. Mordecai said, "I have the contract that Pereira sent me."

At the name "Pereira," Adelaide sat upright with a start, as though she'd been jabbed by a pin. Rachel felt her skin prickle, but she ignored Adelaide's feelings and her own. She patted Eliza on the back. "Show me the contracts," she said. She pushed away the memory of the last time she read a factorage contract.

Adelaide rose to stand next to Rachel. "Let me see it," she said impatiently, holding out her hand.

Rachel raised her eyes to Mordecai's. "Marse?" she asked.

"Give it to her.

Adelaide grabbed the paper so roughly that she wrinkled it. Both Mordecai and Rachel watched as her eyes traveled to the bottom of the page. She asked her father, "Do I see right? That our factor in London is Mr. William Pereira?"

"Yes," Mordecai said, in a low voice like a growl.

She looked at her father. "Don't it bother you to do business with him?"

Mordecai said, "I ain't planning to marry him."

Adelaide stared at her father. She was so pale that Rachel thought she might faint. She crumpled the contract in her hand and flung it to the floor. "Weren't it bad enough to ruin our lives once?" Before either of them could reply, she walked swiftly from the room.

Rachel shook her head, trying to clear it of the memories of Savannah. Mordecai bent to the floor and retrieved the ball of paper. He smoothed it out. Kneeling, he handed it to Rachel. Their hands touched. "You read it," he said, his tone considerably gentler than before.

She balanced Eliza on her lap as she read it, relieved to turn her attention to business. Pereira Brothers, members of the London Exchange, agreed to broker the sale of the cotton. They would take ten percent in commission for their trouble. Rachel looked up. "They won't guarantee the price per pound?"

"Why should they? It floats, just like it does here."

"When will they sell?"

"I've told them to wait for the best possible price."

Eliza began to whimper. Rachel rubbed her back, trying to soothe her. "Better than what?"

"Don't you want to sell high?"

"I ain't greedy. I just want to sell."

Eliza's voice rose higher. Mordecai said sharply, "It's been as high as a dollar and sixty-three cents a pound. The difference between a price of dollar fifty and a dollar sixty-three is more than seventy thousand dollars. Worth being greedy for, by my reckoning."

Eliza began to wail in earnest. Mordecai looked at the baby and said to Rachel, "Can't you quiet that child?"

Rachel glared at Mordecai as Eliza howled. "All right. The best possible price."

After a year of drilling and waiting, Henry's regiment was now in the thick of the fighting. Rachel was afraid for Henry all the time, so afraid that it cramped her gut and gave her the flux, as though she were eating spoiled meat and weevily hardtack in the field. The pain she felt when he left seemed like a trifle compared to this new agony. Nothing reassured her. The newspaper reports were a week old by the time she read them. They only served to feed her apprehension, since the reporters and the illustrators showed her things that Henry hadn't mentioned and that terrified her afresh. None of his letters reassured her, either. By the time she received a letter the news was days old. Where was he now, as she read the reassuring letter? Was he fighting? Was he wounded? Was he dying? Was he dead?

Malvern Hill, Virginia
July 3, 1862

Dearest Rachel,

I'm alive and I'm whole. The fighting is over, for the moment. We are still in Henrico County, not far from Malvern Hill, where I've just seen the bloodiest and worst battle of the war so far. We marched through mud for days, massing for battle, fighting along the way, and by the time we arrived we were already battle-weary. Malvern Hill is really a hill. The Union men had gotten there first, cleared it of all timber, and from a fine vantage point, assembled to wait for us.

We charged up the hill, trying to overwhelm the Union men at the top. They put their sharpshooters in front, the men with the newest and best rifles

and with the deadliest aim. I saw waves of our men charge into what was a
firing squad. Our regiment was far in the rear, waiting for our turn to face
the sharpshooters. God smiled on us, and we were never called. In that
bloodbath, we suffered no losses.

I know that you wait and wait to hear that the cotton has reached
Liverpool. Write to me as soon as you have word.

I miss you more than I can say. I long to be home again.
Your Henry

Adelaide opened the door to a stranger, who looked at her with puzzled
eyes. He introduced himself as Captain McNeill, and asked her, "Where is
your servant Rachel?" Adelaide settled him in the parlor, and the mistress
went to fetch the slave.

When Rachel came into the parlor, Captain McNeill rose, and his hawk's
face burst into a smile. He said, "I told you I'd never lost a ship or a cargo!"

Rachel's face lit up. "We're grateful to you, Captain McNeill."

Captain McNeill said, "Write to me next year when you're ready to sell."

She said, "I hope with all my heart that the war is over and you're out of
business, Captain McNeill."

Without bothering to look at Adelaide, he said to Rachel, "I have a gift
for you." He handed it to her.

"Marmalade!" she cried out.

"None of your English guff. It's Dundee marmalade, the finest there is."

Adelaide said icily, "We'll put it to good use, Captain McNeill."

When he left, she glared at Rachel, who was still cradling the jar. "So
that's what you get for profiteering," she said.

Rachel said, "There's fresh pone in the kitchen."

Adelaide said, "That's mean of you." But she was wavering. Rachel
knew how much she had missed marmalade.

Rachel grinned. "Should we open that jar, or do you want give a speech
to it?"

As the cotton harvest began, Rachel grew increasingly impatient with
the lack of news from the Pereira Brothers in London. She knew why they
were waiting to sell, but she was weary, to the marrow of her bones, with
waiting to know what the crop would bring. In London they heard, every day

and every hour, how the price of a pound of cotton moved up and down. She read about it every week on the *Republican's* commercial intelligence page. Like all the news she received these days, it was old news when she got it, and none of it reassured her.

The cotton harvest dragged on, and the news of the battlefront in the *Savannah Republican* was worse than ever. Henry wrote nearly every day, telling her that they were on the move, that they skirmished with the Federals, that they suffered no losses, but they were massing for battle at Sharpsburg. He didn't try to reassure her, or to cheer himself. He sounded matter-of-fact and ready for battle. She was relieved that he didn't write another letter telling her that he feared he wouldn't be alive tomorrow. He was a seasoned soldier now. If he thought so, if he felt so, he didn't say so.

She was so much on edge that there were days when she wished she were at the front, rifle in her hands, waiting to shoot somebody. She was afraid all the time, but there was nothing she could do but wait. The silence from Pereira Brothers was as bad as the uncertainty about Henry.

September 18, 1862
Antietam, Martinsburg, Virginia

> *Dearest Rachel,*
>
> *Over the past three days we fought the worst battle I've seen—the bloodiest, and the hardest fought, even worse than Malvern Hill. We drove McClellan's men back, slaughtering them as we went. Thousands of our men were killed and wounded, men of the 18th among them. We fought from before sunrise to after sunset.*
>
> *After three days of fighting, both sides were too exhausted to fight any more. The Federals wanted to collect their dead, and we prevented them. Cat said it showed our advantage, but I think it was meanness. We Israelites are adamant about burial the day after death. It's wrong to let men fallen in battle lie on the battlefield. They should be laid to rest.*
>
> *We retreated under cover of fog back into Virginia, skirmishing with the Federals as we went. Our side called the battle a draw, but I suspect that the Union wants to call it a victory.*
>
> *I'm unhurt—I told you I'd live to settle the debt. Cat was grazed by a bullet, which made him feel like a hero. Marcus drenched it in brandy and bound it up with a kerchief, that's how trivial it was.*
>
> *I'm still wrought up, as if I'm in battle—can you tell? If we camp, and*

stop, and rest, I'll sleep like the dead, if I have to sleep on bare ground. I would give anything to sleep in your arms, pillowed on your breast.

Kiss the children for me—

Your Henry

A few weeks later, Mordecai sent for her. It's about the crop, she thought, full of anticipation and dread. Marse Pereira sold the crop.

Adelaide went with her, and they both walked quickly into the study, where Mordecai sat in his big chair and gestured to them to sit down. He said, "I heard from Pereira. They did the best they could."

Adelaide was silent. In a tone a slave should never use towards a master, Rachel said fiercely, "How much?"

He looked her in the eye and he started to grin. He said, "A dollar sixty-three. How much is that a bale, Rachel?"

"Eight hundred and fifteen dollars a bale." She began to shake.

Then he began to laugh. A real laugh. "How much did we clear?"

Shaking worse than ever, she figured. "One million, two thousand, four hundred and fifty dollars." She had never felt the weight of a silver dollar in her hand. She could not imagine a million dollars in silver. Astonished, she said, "Over a million dollars!"

He said, "That's what you get for selling at the top of the market."

Adelaide spoke. "That's what you get for doing business with Mr. William Pereira," she said bitterly, and she left the room.

Rachel struggled to find her voice. "Where is the money?"

"It's in the Bank of London. Henry can get it in gold, if he wants to, but I wouldn't put it in any Confederate bank. Confederate banks can't back it in gold. Confederate money is worthless paper."

"How do we pay you?"

"If Henry tells them to write a draft to me against it, I can get my money. I have an account with the Bank of London, too."

She said, "Explain to me what I should tell him, and I'll write to him so we can pay you."

"I'll write you an invoice for everything—the commission, Captain McNeill's fee, and the outstanding debt. And I'll write a letter for him about the draft for the bank."

"I want to read it before you mail it."

"Of course you do. As you should." He said, "I never saw a woman with a head for business like yours. And a spine for business like yours. I wouldn't trust Adelaide to settle her own account at Stockton's. I'd trust you to make a million dollars for me."

A million dollars. It hit her again like a summer downpour. She shook her head with the enormity of it.

Without waiting for Adelaide, Rachel left the Mannheim place on rubbery legs. She had to sit down more than once on her way home. A million dollars, she thought, and she shook again so badly she couldn't stand upright.

Sitting on the ground, pine needles sticking through her skirt and petticoat, she thought, Even after everything's paid off, there's more than half a million dollars left. Free of debt, she thought, weak with wonderment again. Free for good.

She was weary of Adelaide's bitterness and shame. She felt she would never be free of that.

She wanted to tell someone who would rejoice with her.

She got up, dusting off her skirt, and quickened her pace. When she saw the pine trees that grew at the edge of the cotton fields she hurried, and as soon as she crossed into the field, she saw Charlie, standing next to the cotton wagon. She broke into a run and began to whoop with joy. "Charlie!" she yelled. "Charlie! They sold the crop! You'll never believe what it cleared!" She sang it out, her battle cry of freedom. "A million dollars, Charlie! A million dollars!"

Chapter 17

Forever Free

S potsylvania County, Virginia
January 6, 1863

> *Dearest Rachel,*
>
> *Have you heard? That President Lincoln has declared that all of the slaves in the areas of rebellion, like seceded Georgia, are free? I've obtained a copy of the proclamation—it isn't easy to find, especially in an area in rebellion, like Virginia—and I've copied it out for you.*
>
> *Beloved, you're a free woman. I am bound to you forever, but in love. Now it's for you to choose, if you wish, to be bound the same way to me.*
>
> *Forever free! This year in Jerusalem!*
>
> *Kiss the children for me.*
>
> *Your Henry*

Rachel sat on the floor of their old hiding place, not feeling the chill of a gray January day. She let the letter fall.

To be able to say, along with the Israelites who had always owned her, We were slaves in the land of Egypt. President Lincoln's proclamation fulfilled the words of the Seder that had fortified her all her life: Next year we will be in Jerusalem. Next year we will be free.

Free. Free to read and to write. Free to come and go. Free to choose her path in life. Forever free.

She was too elated to weep. She rose, put the letter in her pocket, and ran back to the main house to find Adelaide.

Adelaide sat in the parlor, where the fire was never lit this early in the day. She stared into the hearth and shivered.

Rachel asked, "Do you want me to lay a fire?"

Adelaide shook her head. She picked up the letter and said, "It is the most terrible news."

Rachel said, "He wrote to me, too. About the Proclamation."

"It's happened, as we always feared. The North has taken our slaves away from us."

Rachel knelt and put her hand on Adelaide's arm. "We have to tell the people here that they're free."

"No!" Adelaide said, her voice sharp with fear.

"They deserve to know."

Adelaide raised her head. She looked pale and stricken, as though she'd received a widow's letter instead of Abraham Lincoln's words. "They'll rise up and take their revenge. They'll murder all of us, their former masters and mistresses, in their beds."

As Mordecai Mannheim, haunted by San Domingo, had feared all his life. Adelaide stared at Rachel as though she'd never seen her before. "What about you?"

It was too hard to set aside a lifetime of servility. Rachel said quietly, "I don't know, ma'am."

Adelaide's cheeks flushed red with anger. She tossed the letter on the floor. Rachel retrieved it and held it out to her former mistress. "Ma'am, you have to tell the people here that they're free."

Adelaide shook her head. Still trying to soothe, still trying to persuade, Rachel said, "You don't want them to hear about it in the street in Cassville. Or next Sunday at meeting. Do it proper. Tell them that they're free."

Adelaide raised her voice. "I can't! I won't!"

Rachel stood up. Holding the letter tightly in her hand, she said, "Then I will."

Adelaide stood up and came close. "You wouldn't dare."

For the first time in her life, Rachel spoke without intending to coax or beguile. She spoke freely. "I could. And I just might."

Adelaide stared at Rachel as though she were a stranger. "Get away from me," she said, turning away.

~~~~~)

Rachel walked into the breezeway and leaned against the wall, breathing hard. She felt as though she were drunk. She staggered a little as she walked toward the kitchen, and had to steady herself as she grasped the knob of the kitchen door. She stood there, shaking in the cold winter air, until she was calm enough to try to fool Minnie's observant eye.

Minnie said, "Missus didn't sit down to breakfast this morning. Is she all right?"

Sharply, Rachel said, "As far as I know."

"There's fresh pone. Maybe she want some. Take it upstairs for her."

Rachel went to the cupboard and yanked open the door. She took out the silver tray and set it down so hard on the counter that it rattled, and she pulled out the marmalade jar and banged it onto the tray. Minnie said, "Something bothering you?"

"Can't say." Except that we're all free, and I can't tell you.

Minnie grinned. "Is that why Missus ain't all right? You two fussing?"

Rachel leaned against the counter, weary with anger. "Don't pester me. Cut me some pone and put it on a plate."

"Don't bust the china. Can't get any more through the blockade."

Rachel breathed deeply and forced herself to handle the plate, the butter dish, and the jam pot more carefully. She picked up the tray and took the back stairs, letting her feet come down heavily on the treads.

She rapped on Adelaide's door and said, "I brought you some breakfast."

Adelaide sat at her dressing table, staring at her reflection as though her own reflection startled her. She picked up her hairbrush and watched suspiciously as Rachel set down the tray. Adelaide's stare bothered Rachel. Made her prickle. She let herself feel it.

Rachel picked up the hairbrush, as she always did, to arrange Adelaide's hair, and Adelaide shied away at her touch. "Put that down," Adelaide said, her voice shaky, as though she wasn't sure that Rachel would obey her.

Holding the hairbrush, Rachel thought, She's afraid of me. Afraid of what I might do. The joy in it burned out like a match. Known me all her life, known we were sisters since we were girls, and all she sees is a black skin. She put the hairbrush down.

Adelaide said, "What will you do, now that you're free? Take your revenge? Run away?"

The anger rose up in her, a crackling fire. Rachel controlled herself. She said, "Wouldn't be running away. Would be going away."

Adelaide twisted around to look at her sister. "Go! Where would you go?"

As though she'd been planning it for weeks, she said, "Atlanta. Take Eliza with me and go to Atlanta."

"What would you do? How would you live?"

Needled, Rachel said, "I can sew, I can cook, and I can do the wash, although I don't care to. Now that I'm free, someone in Atlanta can pay me to do it." She liked the sound of it. "Or go find the Union Army and join the contrabands." Contrabands were slaves who had freed themselves by running to the Union lines before the Proclamation. "I can read and write and figure and keep accounts, too. Maybe the Union Army would pay me to do that."

"Are you crazy? Pay you? Who would—"

"Pay a nigger gal who used to be a slave?" Rachel asked, her tone mocking. "I'm only half a nigger. The rest is Mannheim, and I have the Mannheim head for business. Good hard head. Put it to good use in Atlanta."

"You'll be begging on the street. You'll starve to death."

Rachel laughed, not at all pleasantly. "Look at you. If you went away, could you make a living? Scribbling in them notebooks? I think I know who'd starve to death, trying to get by. If I left you couldn't button your dress or cook a meal."

Adelaide felt furious, because Rachel was right. "That's why you ain't going anywhere. Because I need you here."

"If I left, you could get another nigger gal to take care of you. Someone who doesn't know that she's free. You don't need me for that."

"No, Adelaide said, tears of rage in her eyes. "I don't need an impudent gal who thinks she can say whatever comes into her head because she's free!"

Rachel walked to the door and paused, her hand on the doorknob. "You need a slave. And I ain't a slave, and won't be, not ever again." When she left she slammed the door.

Rachel had left the tray on the table by the bed, and at the sight of it, Adelaide stood up and swept it to the floor. The china shattered into slivers that glittered on the wooden planks, in the carpet, and on the bed. The butter and the marmalade smeared into a paste full of shards.

She couldn't call Rachel, who was no longer a slave, to clean it up for her. Adelaide stared at the wreckage she'd made and began to sob.

She couldn't leave it. She couldn't walk through the room or sit on the bed without causing herself harm. Still sobbing, she picked her way across the floor to the clothes press and rummaged for a clean cloth, forcing herself not to make it worse by flinging the clothes on the floor.

Cloth in hand, she stared at the litter. She bent to pick up the tray. It had dented when it hit the floor, and would never be right again. She sank to her knees and gathered the biggest piece of china. She cut her finger on a shard and the cloth went red with blood. She let it bleed, and the blood dripped onto the floor to add to the shards and the spoiled food. She sat in the midst of the mess, unable to call Rachel back to do her servant's duty, unable to clean up after herself. As blood dripped on her dress, she sobbed in anger and fear.

Later, when Rachel slipped into her hiding place, she opened the cupboard where she kept her most precious things, all of her letters from Henry, carefully bundled and tied with ribbon. They took up nearly a whole shelf in the cupboard. If she left, they would fill all of a satchel. She thought of carrying Eliza on her hip and the satchel in her hand, heavy with the letters, the burden of her relation with Henry.

She had never felt Henry for a burden before, but today anger welled up in her. She grabbed the nearest bundle of letters and threw it across the room. Then the next, and the next, until there was nothing left in the cupboard and the bundles of letters were strewn near the hearth.

She kept matches in the cupboard, to light a candle on the darkest days. She would put the letters in the fireplace to burn them.

She took out the box of matches, her hands shaking, and tried to strike a flame. Her hands shook so badly that she dropped the match before it caught. She tried again, without success. She tried once more, and the match caught, with the burst of flame and the smell of phosphorus. She ran to the hearth, ready to burn Henry's letters to a cinder.

Letters in one hand, match in the other, she stared at them both. Shocked, she dropped the match to the bricks of the hearth and ground it out with her foot.

She sat heavily on the floor next to the hearth and began to sob. She couldn't abandon the letters and she couldn't bear to look at them. She couldn't stay and she couldn't go.

Since she had found Rachel's hiding place, Adelaide often walked by it. Today, as she approached, she heard the sound of sobbing. She would not lurk outside to spy. She walked up the stairs, letting them sigh in warning, and pushed open the door.

She found Rachel sitting on the floor of the old house, the bundles of letters strewn about her, her face buried in her hands, sobbing. At the sound of footsteps Rachel lifted her tearstained face and said thickly, "You shouldn't be here."

It was like looking into the mirror. Behind the dark skin was a heart and mind just like her own. It was the most disquieting thing she had ever felt.

Adelaide said, "Rachel—"

Rachel said, "Leave me be."

Adelaide said helplessly, "Your letters—"

Rachel said bleakly, "Go on with you."

The mistress obeyed the slave.

Adelaide went back to her room, where she picked up the book of Shakespeare's plays, the book that had caused all the trouble between herself and Rachel. She thought of it as a book, not a love token, and she imagined Rachel reading it, taking pleasure in Shakespeare's words, delighting in the stories he told, just as she herself would.

Adelaide sat at her dressing table and looked into the mirror. She had never considered that a slave, even a slave bound to her by blood, would have the same thoughts and feelings as herself. She stared at her reflection, and instead of trying to see the echo of her own face in Rachel's, she looked for Rachel's face in her own. It was too disturbing a thought. She looked away from the mirror, queasy with the notion that a black slave and a white lady were sisters under the skin.

The next morning, after a sleepless night, Adelaide found Rachel in the parlor, dusting. Rachel looked up. Yesterday, she would have said, "What is it, ma'am?" but today, she said nothing. She waited.

Adelaide held out the book and said, "This is yours."

Silence. "If you go, you should take it with you."

Scornfully, Rachel said, "What am I going to do with it? Can't eat it and can't sell it."

Needled, Adelaide replied, "I can always rifle my jewelry box for you. Something silver or gold to sew into the hem of your dress."

"Don't want it and wouldn't take it."

"Suit yourself," Adelaide said, and laid the book on the parlor table.

Rachel went through the day in such a state of distraction that she dropped a bowl full of fresh-laid eggs and burned the dinner pone. Minnie shook her head, sure that she and Missus were fussing at one another again. Rachel sat at the kitchen table, a knife in one hand, an onion in the other. She wished she could tell Minnie about the book, but she didn't trust herself to keep the bigger secret. We're free, she thought. Free to go, free to do as we please, free to hate the masters and mistresses who owned us. Free to tell them how angry we are. Free to say so and not to care how they take it.

Free to feel the kinship that bound her to Adelaide, and to consider what it might be like to have a sister instead of a mistress.

Minnie said, "Give me that knife. You so bothered about something I don't trust you with it. Cut off your finger in that state you in."

Later that day, Adelaide found Rachel as she sat in the study. Her book lay in her lap, but she wasn't reading. She was staring at the cover, a look of distress on her face.

Adelaide said softly, "Are you still thinking about leaving?"

Rachel tightened her hold on the book, as though Adelaide might try to take it away again, and said sharply, "Haven't decided."

Adelaide sat in the chair opposite her sister, like two friends who wanted to talk intimately. She let her voice betray the heaviness in her heart. "Rachel. Please don't go."

Rachel was sharp. "Why not? You can find another nigger gal to lace your corset and do your hair and mend your dress. You don't need me."

"I don't need another servant. I need you."

"Whatever for?"

The Proclamation had set her free to say it. But she stammered as she spoke. "Because you're my sister."

Rachel said bitterly, "I'm your sister in the dressing room and the kitchen and the birthing room. Every place that's private and secret, I'm your sister." She drew a deep ragged breath. "But I'll ain't your sister at the Sabbath table, or in the parlor with the ladies of Cassville, or at the synagogue in Savannah, and I'll never be." She looked away, furious that Adelaide might see her eyes fill.

Adelaide saw it. She reached into her pocket and held out her handkerchief.

"I don't need it," Rachel said, but her eyes filled and she raised her arm to wipe them away.

Adelaide said, "I can't bear to see a free woman wipe her face with her sleeve."

Rachel stared at the scrap of lawn-trimmed lace, then at Adelaide. She took the handkerchief from Adelaide and used it to wipe her face.

Adelaide said raggedly, "I never let myself think it—I never let myself say it—"

Her eyes still wet, Rachel shook her head. "Ain't enough to feel it and to say it. Have to show it, too."

Adelaide said helplessly, "I don't know how."

Rachel drew a deep breath. She thought before she spoke. And then she spoke freely. "Tell the people on the place that they're free."

Adelaide was silent. Rachel insisted, "Read them the Proclamation. Let them hear it from you. That they're free."

Adelaide raised her eyes to Rachel's. She looked into the tear-stained face that echoed her own, in the shape of the eyes and the set of the jaw. With difficulty, she said, "All right."

Later that day, all of the people on the place assembled in the front yard, wrapped up against the chill. Charlie put his hands on Ben's shoulders, and Becky hugged Josey against the skirt of her dress. Minnie held Matt tightly by the hand. Adelaide and Rachel stood together on the front steps. Adelaide said, "There's important news. My husband wrote to me, and asked me to tell you."

Murmurs and worried looks. Rachel said impatiently, "Don't fret, any of you. Marse Henry is all right."

Adelaide pulled her shawl tightly around her. Her face very pale, she said, "Abraham Lincoln has freed the slaves."

She couldn't go on, because there was an outcry. Rachel put her fingers in her mouth and whistled as loud as a field hand. She called out, "Everyone hush! Marse Henry wrote us what President Lincoln said, and we want to read it to you." She looked at Adelaide. "Do you have Marse Henry's letter?"

Adelaide nodded. She drew a deep breath, and began to read. "That on the first day of January, in the year of our Lord one thousand eight hundred and sixty-three, all persons held as slaves within any State or designated part of a State, the people whereof shall then be in rebellion against the United States, shall be then, thenceforward, and forever free."

Her voice was pitched low, and it carried well, so that everyone, even those who were farthest away, could hear every word.

Even though Rachel had read these words to herself over and over, her eyes filled with tears again as she heard them, this time from Adelaide's lips: "Forever free."

All of them listened carefully, and when Adelaide finished reading, they were silent. Finally Minnie looked at Adelaide and said, "Begging your pardon, ma'am." She asked Rachel, "What does it mean, that we're free now?"

Adelaide said to Rachel, "It's yours to tell. You tell them."

Rachel let excitement creep into her voice as she spoke. "It means that we're free to come and go as we please. Free to live where we want to. Free to dress however we want, not like slaves. Free to work for ourselves and keep our money. Free to read, and to write, and to buy books. Free to get married. Free to fight so that everyone will be free."

Suddenly Charlie grabbed Becky and hugged her as hard as he could. Becky gasped. "Free!" he cried out. "We're free!" Micah and Davey began to whoop. "Day of jubilee!" Micah sang out. In the tumult, it was hard to hear Matt's little voice as he looked up at Minnie, still holding her hand, asking her, "Aunt Minnie, why are you crying?"

As the former slaves rejoiced, Adelaide watched and said in a low voice to Rachel, "There will be a world of trouble, now that they know."

They stood so close their shoulders touched. If Rachel would allow it, Adelaide could put her arm around her sister.

Rachel turned to look Adelaide in the eye. "We stand together for that, too."

Chapter 18

John Hardin's Band

On a pleasant Saturday in September, when the cicadas sang the buzzing song that foretold the end of summer, Rachel went into Cassville to retrieve Henry's letters from the post office and to stop in Stockton's. It was close enough to walk, but it gave Tom such pleasure to harness the horse and drive the little carriage that she never denied him. They went into Cassville together, and Tom waited outside Stockton's, fussing over the horse, while she went inside.

Stockton's was dark and musty-smelling. The barrel that once held flour and the jar that once held coffee were long empty. The bolts of cloth that still lay on the shelves were dusty, as were the nails and screws in their bins. The horehound candy on the counter had gone cloudy with age. Since the blockade, the price of life's necessaries had risen to dizzying heights. Rachel had heard that flour, when anyone could get it, was selling for two hundred dollars a barrel in Savannah. Even if there had been flour in Cassville, no one could have bought any. Everyone in Cass County was cash poor.

Marse Stockton said sadly, "Is there anything I can get for you, Rachel?"

Teasing a little, she said, "Do you have any coffee, Marse Stockton?"

"How many silver dollars have you got?"

She laughed. "I guess we'll have to go without this week."

She walked outside, where a group of men had gathered. She recognized John Hardin, who had little to occupy him since he'd come back from the war too badly wounded in his leg to stand behind a plow. A group of men stood in a rough circle with him. They were all pale, with lank, light hair and light blue eyes. Most of the hill country folk were kin; if they weren't Hardins, they were relations somehow. All of them carried rifles slung over their shoulders. A few of the men had old-fashioned muzzle loaders, and others—Confederate Army deserters—had left with their Enfield rifles. Hardin carried the long-barreled rifle that he could aim to shoot a squirrel through the eye at fifty feet. They were all flushed. Rachel saw the whisky jug making its rounds, from hand to hand and hand to mouth.

The hill country women had come with the men, a habit from before the war, when there had been things to buy at Stockton's, and money to pay for them. The women clustered together, their children around them, and they were oddly silent. Rachel saw John's wife Sarah, her dress patched and ragged, her shoes worn through, with her children. Johnny and Sally, their clothes worn, their feet bare, flanked her. Their younger brother Robbie clung to her skirt. She held the baby, little Mary, in her arms, wrapped in a quilt that was bright and pretty enough to catch the eye from across the street. The three older children, quiet and hollow-cheeked with hunger, watched their father. Their faces were shadowed with fear.

Rachel thought, I'd bet that man lays hands on all of them.

John Hardin took a swig of whiskey and passed the jug to the man on his right. Rachel recognized him as John's younger brother Jim, who had dodged the Confederate draft and now worked the farm as best he could. Hardin wiped his mouth with his sleeve and said to his friends and kin, loud enough for anyone on the street to hear, "Look at that nigger gal over there."

All of them looked at Rachel.

Hardin said, "Do she look hungry? Do she look ragged? Do she look like she and hers do without?"

The men were quiet, waiting to hear what Hardin had to say.

"Look at us. Look at our wives, and our little'uns. When was the last time your wife had a new dress? When your young'uns had shoes? When was the last time you felt a quarter in your hand, or earned a dollar selling your crop?"

"Too damn long!" said one of the hill country men.

He was preaching, Rachel thought. He was drunk—they all were—and he was firing them up.

"I was a fool and I went to war like they asked me. What did I get for it? Lame in the leg, too lame to plow or plant ever again." The whiskey jug came around again and he took another swig. When he handed it on he looked at

Rachel and addressed the next words to her. "What was I fighting for? A war for cotton, and for niggers to grow cotton. Anyone who has twenty niggers don't have to fight. Anyone who has two hundred dollars can buy a substitute to do his dying for him. A rich man's war, but a poor man's fight."

"Damn right!" shouted the man who had been too long without money in his palm.

Hardin said, "Now I watch my young'uns go hungry so rich planters can stay rich. So that their niggers can live better than I do." He looked hard at Rachel. He was drunk, as they all were, and he had a rifle on his shoulder, as they all did. She began to feel afraid.

He said, "I hate planters, and I hate their niggers, but I hate free niggers most of all. Look at her and hers. Niggers who feel free. Who have plenty in the henhouse and the smokehouse. Niggers above themselves. Thinking they're as good as us. Better than us."

He put his hand on the strap of his rifle, poised to shift it off his shoulder and into his hands. Rachel's heart beat fast in her chest. He wouldn't dare, she thought. Not here.

"John!" Sarah Hardin called out. Her high, clear tone carried in the pleasant September air. He turned to look at her, hand still on the rifle strap.

She started forward. Still looking at his wife, Hardin unslung the rifle and held it lightly in his hands. He didn't lift it to aim it. He didn't have to. He looked hard at Rachel, who thought, He won't shoot me today. But he'd like to try, someday.

Jim Hardin said, "Sarah, no." He touched his brother's shoulder. "John. Leave that nigger gal alone. She's minding her own business."

Still handling the rifle, John Hardin watched Rachel as she said to Tom, "Let's go." He watched as Tom slapped the reins on the horse's neck and drove the horse down the main street and back to the road to the Kaltenbach place.

Tom asked, "Miss Rachel? Are you all right? You look ashy."

Rachel shook her head.

The hill country men had always poached on plantation land. Mordecai Mannheim let John Hardin shoot squirrel and possum on the woods that were part of the Mannheim place. After that day in town, someone came onto the Mannheim place at night and stole vegetables from the garden, fruit from the trees, and ripe ears of corn from the stalk. Whoever was stealing got bolder. It was hard to know how many pigs they shot, but there was enough noise in the woods that the people on the place knew someone was trying. There was a night raid on the henhouse, which woke every chicken on the place. After that, Mordecai posted a guard on the grounds at night. Sam, who didn't want anyone breaking into the cow barn, and the carpenter Judah, who was a fine shot when he wasn't carpentering, stayed up nights to watch for trespassers.

On a night when the moon cast a sliver of light, when the two ex-slaves guarded the smokehouse, a band of hill country men came to the Mannheim place. They were on foot, but they were all armed with rifles, and they didn't care how much noise they made. When they saw Sam and Judah, they came running and yelling, "We're here to take what's ours!" They fired. None of the bullets were intended to hit or hurt, just to intimidate, but Sam and Judah, frightened and outnumbered, fired back. When it was over, one of the hill country men was shot in the shoulder, and Judah's arm was grazed by a bullet.

The news spread like wildfire from the Mannheim place to the Kaltenbach place. Minnie's eyes went wide with worry, and even calm Zeke and level Charlie were rattled. Adelaide was particularly upset. Rachel said, "The rest of you can fret, but I'm going to talk to Marse Mannheim to find out what happened."

Mordecai looked more distressed than she'd ever seen him. His face was gray. She had never seen a white person look ashy before. He said, "What brings you here today, Rachel?"

She settled herself in the chair. "Heard about that skirmish you had with the hill country men last week."

"Wasn't a skirmish. Just defending what's mine."

"You let them poach all these years."

"Taking a squirrel or a possum to feed your children, that's one thing. Stealing crops and livestock, that's different."

"How's Judah?"

"All right. Susy says he wasn't hurt much. He's shook up. Mad. He says they were seven men, and they were all shooting at him." Mordecai shook his head. "Hurting my niggers, that's even worse than stealing."

Her mouth went dry. "They wouldn't dare shoot at a slave. Now we're free, they feel different about it."

"Anyone who hurts my niggers will answer to me first. And to the law later." He looked at her, figuring something. "I'd be worried, if I were you."

"I am." She knew that the Kaltenbach place was next, a place where the only white people were a young woman and a little boy of three. A place where the gardens were full of greens, the trees were ripe with fruit, and the smokehouse was filled with meat. A place now run by black folks, whom John Hardin didn't mind shooting.

She took the familiar shortcut through the pine woods. So many people, slaves going back and forth, traversed this route that their feet had worn a path in the dirt. You could put down planks and make a road out of it. She often saw or heard someone on the path, so she wasn't alarmed when she heard the soft sound of feet on pine needles. "Who is it?" she called out.

She saw the glint of the rifle, aimed to shoot. They came out of the woods, all three of them, rifles in their hands. She recognized John Hardin and his brother Jim, and the angry man in town who wanted to feel money in his hands.

The angry man said, "Look what we found. A juicy nigger gal." He raised his rifle. "We could shoot her, right here." He looked at his companions. "Or have some fun with her." He laughed, a nasty sound. "Or have some fun and then shoot her."

John Hardin said curtly, "Will interfering with her feed your young'uns? Will shooting her? Put your gun down, man." Her relief was short-lived, because Hardin pressed his rifle to her side. He said, equally curt, "Don't you bolt. You're going with us to the Kaltenbach place."

They marched her there. As they neared the house, Hardin pressed the rifle into her side again. "Don't you call out to warn them."

With Rachel still in their midst, the three men strode into the yard and onto the piazza. They threw open the door into the house. The noise brought Adelaide into the hallway, but she was silenced when she saw the rifles. They walked deliberately through the rooms, looking around, their attitude half brigand and half interested visitor. In the dining room Hardin let Rachel go. He walked to the sideboard and picked up the candlesticks that stood there. They were the family Sabbath candlesticks, which had come with Rosa from Germany, and they were the only family heirloom that Adelaide cared about.

In a shaky voice, Rachel said, "You don't want those."

Startled, Hardin said, "Why not?"

"They ain't silver. They're pewter. Ain't worth anything like silver." Where had that lie come from?

Hardin hefted them. "They're heavy."

"Pewter's half lead. That's why they're heavy."

He put the candlesticks down and raised his rifle at her. "Find me some silver."

"Let me look in the sideboard." As she opened the doors and bent to look, she could feel the gun trained on her. She didn't think he'd shoot, not after what he said in the pine woods, but she didn't want to test him. She took out the Kiddush cup. "This is silver," she said, holding it out to Hardin. "Solid silver. You take that to sell, you'll get something for it. Feed those babies of yours."

He had to put down the rifle to take it. He hefted it. "If you're lying to me, you worthless nigger—"

"I ain't." She reckoned that they were even: he had saved her life, and she had saved him face.

He put it in his game bag. The angry man was still staring around the room. His eyes lit on the photograph of Henry in its bright ornate frame. "I'll take this," he said, and put it in his pocket.

Hardin said, "Let's go." He trained his rifle on Rachel again. "Don't you move, and don't you cry out."

They trooped out of the house, their boots leaving a trail of dirt on wood floor and Turkey carpet.

Rachel and Adelaide stood still as they heard an angry yell in the yard, Charlie's voice. "Damn you, you thieving trash!" And then they heard a shot, and a terrible scream.

They rushed out the door. The angry man was holding his rifle on Charlie, but the scream had come from a hapless pig that had wandered into the yard and hadn't run away quick enough. Jim Hardin grinned. "We'll have a barbecue today," he said, as he slung the carcass over his shoulder. Rachel and Adelaide sagged into the chairs on the piazza in their relief.

In a unsteady voice, Rachel said, "What do you think they'll do when they find out that picture frame is polished brass?"

Equally unsteady, Adelaide said, "Come back to shoot us, no doubt."

After Hardin and his men left, Charlie joined them on the piazza. They sat there together, angry and shaken. It was another lovely day, summer lingering into September, without the heat of high summer. The cicadas sang their odd buzzing song, overpowering the sleepy chirping of the crickets. The air smelled sweetly of ripe grass and clover, and this close to the fruit trees, there was a strong odor of ripe peaches.

Adelaide said to Charlie, "I thought they shot you."

Charlie said, "We need to defend ourselves, like they do on the Mannheim place. Zeke and I have rifles, and we're good shots." He would never be entirely easy with Adelaide, but he knew that she respected him, and now that he was free, he didn't mind speaking plainly in her presence if Rachel was there to bolster him.

Rachel said, "Charlie, we won't win a shooting war with these folks."

Charlie said grimly, "Shooting is all they understand."

He didn't know the half of it. She thought of John Hardin, rifle in his hands, but she also thought of Sarah Hardin in her ragged dress, and of her children, hollow-cheeked with hunger. Still trembling with the memory of Hardin's rifle poking her in the side, she thought of the words that began the Passover Seder. "Let all who are hungry come and eat." Jews, who remembered being slaves in Egypt, thought of those who were hungry and needy, too.

John Hardin, rifle in hand, had come to steal silver to feed his family. Even though he hadn't shot her, and had saved her honor, she had no love for him. But those hungry children of his haunted her.

Rachel said, "We aren't going to shoot anyone. I have another idea."

Both Adelaide and Charlie looked at her. Adelaide said, "What is it?"

"Br'er Rabbit," she said slowly.

Adelaide said, "With these ruffians? They would have killed us! Any of us!"

Rachel said, "If it don't work we can always try shooting. But I'd rather not."

On her next trip into Cassville, Rachel saw Sarah Hardin outside Stockton's, her youngest on her hip, the other three flanking her. Was she protecting them, or were they protecting her? Johnny, who was almost as tall as his slightly-built mother, moved protectively close as Rachel approached.

Politcly, giving all of them distance, as though they were rabbits about to bolt, she said, "How do, Miz Hardin."

Sarah said, "How do, Rachel."

"Miz Hardin, that's a pretty blanket you have wrapped around your baby."

"I made it for her."

"Missus Adelaide's little boy is the same age. Could you make a coverlet for him?"

She didn't hesitate. Didn't say, "My husband won't hold with it." She asked, "Do you have scraps?"

"Yes'm. Come by the Kaltenbach place, and we'll give you all the scraps and thread you need. We have needles, too." Needles and notions were a casualty of the blockade. These had been Captain McNeill's gift.

"I'll come as soon as I can."

Rachel realized how far Sarah would have to walk. "Should I send Tom to fetch you?"

Sarah shook her head. "I'll manage."

She managed to be there the next Tuesday. Tom, who knew her by sight, found her at the gate, hesitating. He brought her to the kitchen, telling her, "That's where you'll find Rachel. And Minnie."

Both women greeted her. She said weakly, "May I sit down?"

Rachel and Minnie looked at each other. Had she walked all the way from her place? Minnie said, "You set."

Rachel said, "Miz Hardin, Minnie just made a fresh batch of pone. We're going to have some, but there's more than we can eat. Would you like some?"

Sarah, pale and faint, said politely, "I wouldn't want to trouble you."

Minnie, understanding, said, "It's no trouble at all, Miz Hardin. It's just ready. Won't be any trouble to cut you a piece."

"If it isn't any trouble—"

"It ain't," Minnie said firmly. She brought the spider to the table, cut a generous piece of pone, and put it on a tin plate. "Rachel, do you want some buttermilk with yours?"

"I would. Miz Hardin, can we pour you some?"

Sarah swallowed hard. Before she could object, Minnie poured buttermilk from a pitcher into a tin cup. She said, "It won't keep on a warm day like today. You help us drink it up."

She took the cup. "Thank you," she said, her voice very soft. Minnie gave her the pone. "There's butter on the table. You help yourself."

Sarah broke off a small piece of the pone. Her hand trembled as she brought it to her mouth. She closed her eyes as she chewed, slowly, the way that ladies ate at picnics and dinners. She picked up the tin cup, and forced herself to take a genteel sip. Minnie and Rachel watched in surprise as she ate one small bite after another and took one small sip after another. When she was finished, she looked around the table for something. Minnie said, "What can I get you?"

"Do you have a napkin?"

Minnie handed her a clean dishtowel. "Excuse me," she said, carefully wiping her mouth. "A lady shouldn't eat so fast."

Rachel said tartly, "Most ladies don't come to the table as hungry as you."

A tiny smile played around the corners of her mouth. "Oh, la, my mother would turn over in her grave if I bolted my food."

Rachel and Minnie exchanged a look. Rachel said, "Whenever you feel ready, we can show you our scraps and thread."

Sarah's eyes flickered. "Could I have a bit more buttermilk?"

Minnie filled her tin cup. "We ain't ladies, either of us, and we don't mind how fast you eat. Or how much you eat. If you hungry, you eat. Won't bother us a bit."

Sarah smiled, a real smile this time. She picked up the tin cup and drained it, and she set it down with a sigh. After she wiped her mouth again—delicately—she said, "Oh, that was good."

Rachel fetched the basket that was full of scraps. Sarah's eyes lit up as she handled the cloth. "Such pretty calicoes," she said. "And fine white cotton. And silk! It's been a long time since I touched silk." She was pleased by the thread, and delighted to see the needles. She began to lay out pieces of cloth on the table. She measured them with the span of her hands, arranged them, looked at them, and arranged them again. "Broken dishes. If I cut it out today I can sew it at home and bring it with me the next time I come here. I won't bother you? Using your kitchen table?"

Minnie said, "I'm going into the dairy. You use that table all you want."

Rachel fetched a pair of scissors. Sarah began to cut out the pieces. She hummed softly as she worked. Rachel recognized the tune: it was the hymn that the freed slaves sang at meeting, "O Happy Day." Sarah's somber face cheered as the scraps turned into triangles, evenly cut, uniform as only a skilled needlewoman could make them. She laid them out again, to make sure she had cut enough for the pattern, and when she was sure, she smiled. "If you can give me some thread, and lend me needles, I can take this and go home."

Adelaide came into the kitchen, holding Matt by the hand. Rachel made the introductions. Sarah was too polite to say anything, but her face registered surprise that the mistress of the place would wear an old calico dress and a field hand's straw hat. Adelaide said, "You'll have to excuse me. I've been working in the garden." She looked affectionately at her son. "Matt helped. He dug up a potato for me."

Rachel said, "Miz Sarah is piecing together Marse Matt's coverlet."

Adelaide bent to look. "Oh, what a lovely pattern," she said. "Matt, do you want to see? No, don't touch, your hands are dirty." She lifted him so he could look. He said, "Pretty."

Rachel laughed. "He has his daddy's eye for dry goods," she said.

Adelaide laughed too. "He does."

Rachel said to Sarah, "We're going to get ourselves some dinner. Would you stay to share it with us?"

Minnie, who had come back into the kitchen, said, "Ham, and more pone, and a relish made of tomatoes. Can't make pie, not without flour, but we have peaches so ripe the juice runs down your hand when you bite into them."

Sarah struggled with herself. She tucked in her chin with the effort of trying to be ladylike enough to say no. Minnie saw it. "Do you know what would make my mama turn over in her grave?" She didn't wait for the answer. "Knowing that I wasn't getting enough to eat."

Matt and Eliza joined them at the table, eating and making a mess of their food. After dinner, Sarah put her hand on her stomach and sighed. "My mother's having a conniption, but Minnie's would be happy. I'm full."

Minnie said, "Miz Hardin, we have all this food left over. Can't keep a thing in this weather. Would you like to take some of it home?"

Sarah considered. Rachel said, "I reckon your children would enjoy it."

A look of pain passed over Sarah's face. "They would." She left with her basket laden with her cloth triangles and heavy with ham and pone and tomatoes and peaches.

When she returned a week later, she had dark smudges under her eyes. Had she stayed up late at night, straining her eyesight, to finish this quilt? The stitches were small and even, and the quilting was a lovely pattern against the colorful triangles. Adelaide smoothed it with her hand. "I never saw quilting so fine."

Sarah said, "I've been making quilts since I was a little girl."

Adelaide touched it and said, "It's beautiful."

"Thank you, ma'am," Sarah said shyly.

Adelaide looked up. She hadn't consulted Rachel, but she knew that Rachel would be pleased. She asked Sarah, "Would you make me a quilt?"

"I'd be glad to."

Rachel wondered how she had explained her effort to her husband. But Sarah was too genteel to say.

Rachel and Minnie went about their usual tasks and let Sarah look through the scraps, and lay them out on the table, and piece them together, and think of how they might become a quilt to please Adelaide. Engrossed in her task, she looked up in surprise when Minnie spoke to her. Smiling, Minnie said, "If you want me to feed you dinner you'll have to study them scraps somewhere else."

Sarah said, "I don't want to be in your way," and she gathered up her cloth. She rolled up her sleeves. "What can I do to help?"

Rachel and Minnie fed her a good dinner, and sent her home with the leftovers "for those children of yours." She said, "This one won't be as swift."

Rachel said, "Don't wait until you're done. Show us how you're coming along."

Sarah smiled. "I'll do that."

She came two weeks later, with the half-finished quilt rolled up in her basket. Rachel and Minnie admired it, and set the table for dinner. As she left, Rachel said, "When it's finished, bring your children along so we can meet them." Sarah laughed. "You mean feed them," she said. She looked at Minnie. "If it's no trouble."

Minnie said, "Feeding young'uns? Trouble? Makes my heart glad."

Sarah came back two weeks later, with all four children. The two eldest, pitifully thin, looked around the kitchen with wide eyes. They nodded when Sarah introduced them, but didn't speak. The baby buried her face in her mother's dress. The little boy, Robbie, looked up at his mother and said, "Do they have pone?"

Sarah said, "Robbie, where are your manners? Say how do first."

"How do," said Robbie. "Now is there pone?"

Minnie laughed. "We do have pone," she said. "Enough for all of you. Rachel, fetch Adelaide so she can see the quilt."

When Adelaide came into the kitchen, Sarah took the quilt from her basket and unfurled it on the kitchen table. It was a star pattern, made to accommodate the scraps. There was calico in it, and muslin, and watered silk, scraps from the Savannah dresses. The quilting was even more ornate than on the quilt Sarah had made for Matt.

Adelaide smoothed it with her hand. "It's lovely. It will cheer me every time I look at it. It's a rare gift," she said, meaning the coverlet as well as the needlework.

"Thank you, ma'am."

At the bottom of the basket was a glint of something metal, slightly tarnished. "I believe this belongs to you," Sarah said, picking up the silver cup her husband had taken. Her voice was courteous. She held the cup like someone used to handling silver.

Adelaide didn't speak, and Sarah went on, "It's one thing to shoot a possum on someone else's land. Or to pick up a windfall apple. It's another to steal silver." She handed it to Adelaide. "It isn't right for us to have it."

As Adelaide took it from her, she wondered who Sarah Hardin had been, before she was John Hardin's wife.

Minnie had gone to some trouble over midday supper. When Robbie saw the dishes come to the table, he cried out, "Mama! There's chicken! They're niggers and they have chicken for dinner!"

Sarah said, "Don't say 'nigger', Robbie. It's a mean word. Now you sit quietly at the table and wait until I say grace."

The older children, Johnny and Sally, were afraid to help themselves and afraid to eat. Their mother said quietly, "It's all right. There's plenty for all of us. You let Minnie serve you, and you eat as much as you want."

Their mother had taught them well, but they were too hungry for genteel manners, and they ate their chicken down to the bone, wiping up the juice with pieces of pone, and accepted a second helping. Robbie, too young to manage a fork, ate with his hands. Sally wiped her little brother's face and rolled her eyes. She unbent enough to talk. "They'll think you were brought up in the barn."

When everyone was replete—Johnny, leaning back in his chair, said happily, "I can't remember the last time I ate so much"—Sarah said, "Now all of you thank Minnie."

All of John Hardin's children raised their pale eyes to Minnie and thanked her.

After dinner, Sarah said, "I'm afraid there won't be leftovers, after the way my children ate their dinner."

Minnie said, "We have some bacon we can't keep."

Sarah put her hand to her eyes. "Oh, Minnie!"

Minnie put her hand on Sarah's shoulder. "It ain't charity," she said stubbornly. "You worked your fingers to the bone, making that beautiful quilt."

Let all who are hungry come and eat.

The kitchen was a comfortable place, but it was full of activity, and whenever anyone prepared a meal, it was full of grease and what Minnie called "mess." Sarah needed a better place to work. Adelaide said, "Would you like to come into the parlor to sew? It's quiet, and you won't be in Minnie's way."

Sarah came into the house. She wasn't overwhelmed, but she was wistful. She said, "If I had a room this lovely, I'd sit in here to sew every day."

Adelaide, who hadn't sat in this room for months, said, "I never was much for sewing, even before the war."

Sarah looked through the mending basket to see the work set before her. She shook out one of Matt's little shirts—he was hard on his clothes—and said, "When I was a girl, my mother and sisters would take turns reading while the rest of us sewed. It made the work go easier."

"Since I can't sew," Adelaide said, "I'd be glad to read to you. Let me fetch a book from the study."

When she returned, Sarah asked, "What is it?" sounding pleased that Adelaide would read to her.

"Thackeray. *Vanity Fair*."

"I read that, a long time ago."

Adelaide said, "Is there something else you would rather hear?"

Sarah said quietly, "When I can, I read the Bible, but I'll gladly listen to this."

Adelaide said, "Next time I'll bring the Bible for you."

Adelaide read, and Sarah sewed. When it was time for midday dinner, Adelaide closed the book and asked Sarah, "Did your husband miss the silver cup?"

"He thought his brother Jim took it." Sarah's pious face twitched into a smile. "I let him think so. They had quite a set-to."

"What do you tell him about the sewing? And the food you bring home?"

A real smile this time. "I tell him that Miz Kaltenbach needs some sewing done, and that she pays me in provision. He don't like it, not a bit, but he eats everything I bring home."

With each visit Adelaide wondered more about Sarah. After weeks of sewing, reading, and meals at the kitchen table, feeding Sarah and her children, it was surprisingly easy to ask.

Sarah looked up from her mending. "It isn't a happy story."

Adelaide looked at her with sympathy. "I've become used to sorrow. Tell me."

Sarah's father was a cotton planter who owned twenty slaves. When Sarah was a girl, her mother taught her how to embroider. Sarah still had the samplers she made, which showed off her ability to ply her needle. Her first, which she finished when she was seven, included the alphabet, her name, and two birds twined around the words of the 23rd Psalm. The other, which she made when she was ten, had a shepherd and a shepherdess in a landscape of mountains and trees, with pretty lambs at their feet.

Expected to marry a plantation fortune, Sarah began to sew her trousseau early. She sewed and embroidered handkerchiefs, pillowcases, tablecloths, and nightdresses. By the time she was sixteen, the cedar chest she would take to her new husband's house was full.

But when she turned eighteen, ready to court and marry, her father had two bad harvests back to back, went deep into debt, and had to sell his land

and his slaves. He became an overseer on an upcountry Georgia plantation, taking his humiliated family with him.

When her father died, the family was in desperate straits. Sarah married the first man who would have her. That was John Hardin, the oldest son of a hill country farmer, who had fifty acres in "hog and hominy." They were too poor to own slaves and too poor to grow cotton. He and his brother Jim were lucky to inherit the farm. The younger brothers scattered to scrounge a living however they could.

In twelve years of marriage, she had six children. One died at the age of three, and the other died in infancy. After that death, she turned to religion. Her faith was quiet, but she gave up many things she thought were too worldly—a love for finery, her book of Shakespeare's plays, and any show of temper.

Her skill with a needle came in handy. She sewed John's clothes and her own, and later made shirts and dresses for the children. The needle was constantly busy, mending and patching. The closest she came to embroidery was to take the scraps that couldn't be used any more, the bits and fragments past any other use, and to piece them together into quilts.

It was a hard life. John was a hard man. The war had made all of it harder.

Adelaide listened. She squeezed Sarah's hand. Sarah's face looked weary and calm, as it always did. Humbled, Adelaide thought, the trouble between Henry and me, as much as it troubles me, is so small next to hers. She said, "Let us help you."

Sarah smiled. "You help me more than you know. All of you."

A few weeks later, as Sarah sewed, Adelaide let the book fall into her lap—today it was her choice, *Vanity Fair*. She was still bothered by the story of Sarah's marriage. She asked Sarah, "May I ask you something private?"

Sarah, who felt easy enough to tease Adelaide a little, said, "Depends on how private."

"Do you love your husband?"

Sarah looked at the mending in her lap. "He's troubled in his heart and his soul. He needs my love more than someone who's sweet."

"Don't you ever feel angry?"

Sarah shook her head. "I ask God to help me love him. And to forgive him." She raised her soft blue eyes to Adelaide's. "I've met your husband. He seems like a kind man." She sounded wistful. "Was he not kind to you?"

Adelaide said, "He did his best." Tears rose to her eyes. "I wasn't kind to him."

Sarah waited to hear the rest.

"He has a loving heart, and I didn't love him. He fell in love with someone who did." Adelaide put her hand to her face. "I never have a handkerchief when I need one." She couldn't say who it was. Despite Sarah's sweetness, she was a planter's daughter, like herself, who knew that there was always a slave gal, somewhere. She said, "I hated her for it. I wronged her, too."

Sarah reached for Adelaide's hand. Her gaze did not waver. She said, "Whatever the wrong, don't you think that God would forgive you?"

"I'm a Jew, and I was raised a doubter. I'd hope so."

Sarah pressed Adelaide's hand with her own. "I dearly wish I had a handkerchief," she said.

John Hardin's band continued to harass the planters of Cass County. They shot pigs, raided henhouses, filched fruit, and helped themselves to corn. They continued to carry guns, and while there were no further skirmishes, they took potshots at planters and former slaves, who shot back in return. The Mannheim place, singled out as the biggest, richest, and stingiest in the county, was hit, over and over again. But they left the Kaltenbach place alone.

Their success in hindering John Hardin lulled them into a sense of safety. They slept at night without keeping watch, and went to and from town without fear. When Rachel and Adelaide heard footsteps in the pine woods as they walked home from Cassville, they weren't afraid.

Then they heard the cock of the rifle. Adelaide frowned. "They're still poaching," she said.

John Hardin stepped onto the road, rifle in his hands. He said, "I thought I'd find you here," he said, and he aimed his rifle at Rachel, as surely and easily as he'd aim at a squirrel in a tree.

Adelaide stepped in front of Rachel. She said, "You'll have to shoot me first."

Hardin hesitated. It was one thing to shoot a former slave. It was another to shoot a white woman, daughter of the richest man in the county. He lowered his rifle and said, "I ain't done with either of you yet." He turned and disappeared into the woods.

Adelaide began to shake. She turned to Rachel, whose face was gray. Adelaide put her arms around her sister. "I thought he would shoot you," she said, unable to control her voice. They clung together, trembling too much to move, until Rachel said, "We shouldn't linger. He might be lurking." Adelaide took Rachel's hand and they ran together, as swiftly as they could, back to the safety of the Kaltenbach place.

Chapter 19

The War Comes to Georgia

Since the beginning of the war, battle had been something far away, in Charleston, where the Union Navy blockaded the harbor, or in Virginia, where Henry was fighting. The conflict around Chattanooga, which had brought Henry's regiment to Chickamauga a few months before, hadn't been close enough to make the people on the Kaltenbach place feel as though Georgia was at war. Theirs had been a war of deprivation, because of the blockade, and of worry, because Henry was gone, and he was in danger.

In the spring of 1864 the war came to them in northern Georgia.

With the fighting so close, the human telegraph—the word that traveled from former slave to former slave, from former master to former master, from plantation to plantation—was swifter and more reliable than the newspaper. On a day early in May, Charlie came to sit with Adelaide and Rachel on the piazza at their accustomed time at noon. He sat heavily in his usual chair and told them, "I heard on the Mannheim place that there's fighting at Resaca."

Rachel felt a stab of fear. "Resaca's even closer to us than Chickamauga."

Charlie nodded. "They say the Union Army's following the railroad tracks."

Coming their direction. Adelaide said, "They'll be here. How soon?" It was as though they were talking about a bad storm, the kind that turned the sky green, then black, then opened a punishing deluge on the fields, and for good measure, sparked lightning that set any unsoaked boll to smolder.

"No one can say."

They sat together and took in the peaceful scene before them. The neat front yard, with the flower beds and lawn that Tom carefully tended. The kitchen garden, Minnie's pride, full of spring greens and new peas. The house, still gleaming white to deflect the summer sun. The new birds chirped and trilled and called at this time of year. The air smelled of the bright new shoots and the just-unfurled buds and the plants, all of them, bursting forth from the earth with the joy of warmth and water and sunshine.

Rachel thought of all the horrors that Henry had seen and had written to tell her in his effort to unload the burden of having been there, and having seen them. The earth churned to mud. The air full of smoke and fire. The horses, screaming as they fell. The men, crying out, wounded and dying. The ground running red with blood. Oh Lord, she thought. Not here.

Charlie said, "I heard the damnedest thing at the Mannheim place."

Startled, Rachel said, "What?"

"After the Union Army won the battle at Resaca, they tore up the railroad tracks. Why would they do that?"

Adelaide and Rachel looked at each other, equally perplexed. Adelaide said, "Can't imagine why."

The cotton crop was coming in lush and thick. Everyone chopped and chopped to thin the rows to let the remaining plants grow strong. Last year's crop was stored in the new cotton shed that had been built on the far reaches of the place, hidden near the pine woods at the edge of the property. Hardin's men hadn't tried to break into anyone's cotton sheds, but they'd set annoying fires in the cotton standing in the fields. Despite the success of Br'er Rabbit, neither Adelaide, nor Rachel, nor Charlie were taking any risks.

Last year's cotton crop sat ginned and baled in the shed. This year's crop grew lush and thick in the fields.

Spotsylvania County, Virginia
May 9, 1864

Dearest Rachel,

I've been wounded, but it's not serious, and I'm healing. The surgeon said that I was the luckiest man he'd seen that day. I was hit with grapeshot, not a minie ball, and it went into the meat of my thigh without hitting the bone. The leg looked a mess and hurt like hell after he cut out the grapeshot. I'll have a scar, and I may have a limp, but I won't lose the leg.

The battle was terrible, the worst I've ever seen. I'll write to you to tell you in a few days. I have to brace myself to recollect it.

My dear friend and fellow soldier Cat is dead. That is the least of the grief and the horror of the Battle of the Wilderness.

We hear that General Sherman's army moves through Georgia, hoping to take Atlanta. I am sick with fear, wondering if you are in harm's way. I hope with all my heart and soul that you are safe—write to me to let me know—

Beloved, how I long to embrace you—

Your Henry

Rachel laid the letter in her lap. Henry had been battle-hardened for a long time now. She had not read a letter from him so despairing since his earliest days on the battlefield. His leg had been little wounded. His mind and heart were the casualties of the Battle of the Wilderness. He was sick of war. He was wounded in his soul.

A few days later, Charlie came to find both her and Adelaide in the kitchen, with news too pressing to wait until midday dinner. His face was grim. He refused a piece of pone and a glass of buttermilk. He said, "They're fighting at Adairsville."

Rachel stared at him, catching his worry. "Too close."

"Battle's bad enough. I heard something worse."

What could possibly be worse?

He said, "When they ain't fighting each other, they don't hurt anyone in their way. Not people. But they're burning the crop."

Shocked into kitchen talk, she said, "They ain't."

"Burning it in the fields to a char, and whenever they can, busting open cotton sheds and burning what's baled and stored."

Nearly six hundred bales in the shed, and likely another six hundred in the field, with good weather and God's grace. She looked at Adelaide, who was as upset as Charlie. She said, "They can't burn the crop."

Charlie stared at her. His face was ashy. "How are you going to stop them? The Union Army? You going to Br'er Rabbit the Union Army?"

Thousands of blue-coated men, with artillery guns, and Springfield rifles, and torches in their hands to set fires. Worse than John Hardin's troublemaking men. Come to burn the crop to the ground.

How would they come? In a horde, whooping and shooting, killing livestock and setting fire? Or would they fight a battle here, turning their fields to mud, soaking their earth with the blood of horses and men, fouling their air with fire and smoke?

Rachel said slowly, "Don't know if it will do any good or not."

"What?"

"Remember that Union flag Marse Henry put up before he left? The one we stored away?"

"I do. You ain't thinking of putting it back up!"

Adelaide said, "At least it's something we can do."

Rachel had put the flag in Marse Henry's clothes press—it was a little wrinkled, but otherwise unharmed—and she asked Tom to help her hoist it up the flagpole. Tom pulled on the rope, and the flag rose, and unfurled, and fluttered defiantly in the spring breeze.

Tom said, "The Union Army's coming, ain't it."

Rachel said, "I believe so."

Tom looked frankly afraid. "Will we be all right?"

She put her arm around his shoulders—he was so tall now, she had to reach upward—and hugged him. "I pray to God that we will."

There was nothing more she could say. There was nothing more they could do. They would know soon enough.

Spotsylvania County, Virginia
May 12, 1864

Dearest Rachel,

I am able to sit up, after a fashion, and write, as long as I don't put too much pressure on the dressing, and the wound beneath it. The leg aches, but not badly enough for morphine, and if we had any, it would go to men in much worse pain than I am.

I've been in many battles, and I thought I was hardened to their horror. The Wilderness was the worst fight I've ever seen, and days after it's over, I still think of it, and see it in my mind's eye, and imagine that I smell it.

The Wilderness is a heavily forested spot, and unlike most of our battles, which we fought on open terrain, in the Wilderness we fought in a thicket. The trees were so thickly planted that horses couldn't pass through them. Any battle formation was immediately torn to shreds in those dense trees. The fighting was all at close range—by rifle, pistol, and worse, by knife.

The air was so dense with smoke from the guns that it was black, and nearly unbreathable. Minie balls and grapeshot flew through the air in a fatal hail. If you stood still, it was sure that something would hit you to wound you.

I lost track of my men, except for Cat, who was slightly behind me. We couldn't advance, in the press of men and the press of trees. We looked for a blue tunic, and we shot. I don't know how long we were there. It might have been minutes, or hours. I heard a cry behind me and turned to see Cat, bent over, holding his belly, blood running through his fingers. He'd been gut-shot.

Before he fell to the ground, in too much agony to stand, he looked at me in terror. We'd both seen enough gut wounds to know that they condemned a man to death. As well as we knew that it was a slow and agonizing death.

Then I was hit, in the right thigh, and I couldn't stand. I fell, too, and lay beside Cat. Now I was in an agony of my own, because I knew that a leg wound that shattered the bone meant the loss of the leg. Where I lay, I couldn't see how bad the wound was, and I couldn't rise to look, for fear of another wound, still worse than the one I already had. On the ground, I could see how many men had been hit and were stricken. Gut shot, chest shot, leg shot, and worst of all, head or face shot. All around me, men near death screamed in agony.

As I lay helpless on the ground, the smell of the place was the most vivid thing. It smelled of the coppery tang of fresh blood, and the sulfur reek of gunpowder, and the char of burned trees, and the decaying flesh of yesterday's dead. It was the smell of hell.

The crack of rifle fire contested with the groans and cries of the dying. My ears were keenest for Cat's voice. He was dying, he was dying in agony, and I could do nothing to help him.

From behind, I heard the crackle of fire—not gunfire, but the sound of trees on fire. Had the forest caught fire? None of us were able to move. Would we be suffocated and burned to death on the battlefield? I closed my eyes. I was sure that I would die, too.

I don't know how long I lay there. It was an eternity. Then oblivion overtook me—I didn't think I would wake from it—and the next thing I knew, I was awake, I was alive, and I was in pain in a cot in a field hospital far from the battlefield.

I raised my head and lifted the sheet to see that my right leg was swathed in a bandage, but it was still there. I never wept on the battlefield, but on that cot I sobbed with a hysteric's relief to know that I was alive and I was wounded, but whole.

Beloved, it's terrible to write to you like this, but it's too terrible to remember and not to tell. I hate to think that I'll remember it for the rest of my life. As much as I try to recall everything pleasant and fragrant—magnolia in full bloom, coffee brewing in the morning, Matt's brand new skin, your hair— the smell of the battle still haunts me.

I tell you of these horrors because I know how strong you are, and how brave you are. You are a soldier, too, one of the best I know, as well as being my friend and my beloved.

As Sherman's army comes closer I am as helpless to you as I was to Cat. I beg God to keep you, all of you, safe—
Your Henry

The Union Army was in Cassville, so close that they could hear the guns and smell the smoke. If you didn't know any better, you might think it was a summer storm, mistaking the artillery fire for the rumble of thunder and the burning cotton for the accidental strike of a flash of lightning. Everyone on the place knew that it was battle, and it was in Cassville, a place close enough to reach from their houses and fields on foot.

The battle went on all day, and the air smelled more powerfully of smoke and of burning cotton as the day wore on. It made everyone uneasy. The animals were uneasy too. The horse neighed and bucked in his stall, and the mules brayed in protest. The kitchen cat hated the sound and ran away to hide, in a place only a cat could find. The livestock, like the people on this place, were unschooled in the ways of war.

The guns stopped as dusk fell. Armies didn't fight at night, Rachel thought, remembering what Henry had written her. Tomorrow they would wake up and continue fighting. She slept badly, waking up to think about Henry in a field hospital in Virginia, and to worry about the coming day, when war would come to the Kaltenbach place.

The next day, Tom ran into the kitchen, where Adelaide was making a pone and Rachel and Minnie were shelling spring peas for midday dinner. All three women looked up. Tom's bright face was gray and grim.

He said, "They're here. The Union soldiers are here."

Part 4

Chapter 20

General Sherman's Men

Minnie brought both Union officers into the kitchen, where she bandaged Endicott's arm and put ham and peas and pone onto plates. "Nothing fancy," she said, "just what we eat every day."

Randolph said, "You don't know how good this is, after months of eating salted beef and weevily biscuits in the field." As Rachel and Adelaide watched, both men ate with appetite.

When they were finished, Endicott asked Adelaide, "May we look around the place?"

Adelaide said, "Charlie—" she corrected herself—"Mr. Mannheim can show you around and answer any question you put to him."

Rachel shot her a warning look. Except for the crop stored in the cotton shed, and the profit we made from running the crop through the blockade.

Randolph and Endicott, still wary after their skirmish that morning, took their rifles and their sidearms as they walked to Charlie's cabin. They had been on many plantations in Tennessee and Georgia, and everywhere they had gone, the houses were run down, the gardens were neglected, and the cotton fields were thick with weeds. Here, all of the cabins were recently whitewashed and well-tended, with carefully-swept steps and beds of flowers in front.

Charlie sat on the steps of his cabin with a little girl, who had the newspaper spread over her lap. He rose when he saw them approach. Endicott put out his hand. "Mr. Mannheim?"

"Always been called Charlie, and 'Mister Mannheim' sound odd to me," Charlie said. "Don't mean to be disrespectful, Captain Endicott, but I ain't used to it. Or to shaking hands, either."

Endicott bent down toward the little girl. "And who is this young scholar?"

Charlie beamed. "This my gal Josey. She read me the newspaper, until I learn how to read for myself. Show these men how good you read, sugar."

In a clear voice, without faltering, the little girl read her father the latest news of the war, about the battle at Resaca. Endicott smiled.

As they walked toward the fields, Randolph said to Charlie, "Your place looks prosperous and well-tended."

Charlie said, "Don't know about prosperous, because no one in this part of Georgia has any money for any purpose. But the place looks tended because we have people here who tend it. A lot of folks around here left after Emancipation. Half the people on the Mannheim place run off. But we stayed put."

Endicott asked, "Why? If you were free to go?"

Charlie said, "I show you."

As they walked past a field, they saw a man and a woman, each wielding a hoe, chopping the cotton plants. They worked so close together that if they raised their heads, they could smile at each other.

Charlie grinned and waved. "Davey, Harriet, if you can quit a moment, come talk to Captain Endicott and Lieutenant Randolph."

They came together, their heads up, smiling.

Charlie said, "These men are from the Union Army and they want to know how we work the place."

Randolph asked, "Who oversees you?"

Davey laughed. "No overseer. No driver. No gangs. Not anymore. Families work together. Husband and wife, like me and Harriet."

The woman smoothed her apron in a universal gesture: she was expecting. Her face glowed as she said, "After we got free we got married proper. Had the preacher and went to the county courthouse, too."

"Harriet, you feeling all right?" Charlie asked.

"Feeling fine."

Davey said, "Crop is fine, too. Wagered with Zeke that we'll outdo him." He laughed. "Aim to win it."

340

Charlie said good-naturedly, "Have to beat me, too. Harriet, you take care, you rest if you feeling weary."

With equal good nature, Harriet said, "Can't lose the habit of driving, can you, Charlie? I know when to rest. I'll be all right."

Davey and Harriet went back to their work, and Charlie said, "You see how we work, now that we're free. Let them drive themselves. Work their own plots, set their own pace."

Randolph asked, "Do the people here get paid?"

Charlie hesitated. "Decided to get paid like planters do, when the crop is sold. Keep an account of what everyone raise, how many bales. Can't get the money now, through that blockade, but when we can, everyone get their share."

Randolph said, "What did your people think about that?"

Charlie said, "Debated it mighty hard. Worried some folks. Can't predict what the crop will be. Could do well, could go bust. But that's part of being free. Like Rachel once said to me, we free to get rich or go broke."

Endicott said, "What kind of a crop did you have last year?"

Charlie hesitated again. He tried to speak lightly. "Not much. Couldn't sell it, and figured we'd need provision and fodder more than cotton. Had a fine corn crop, and plenty of cowpeas and taters and greens." He said, "Should do all right this year, if General Sherman don't stop by to burn it on the stalk."

They fell silent, and all of them heard the shot. Randolph and Endicott reached for their pistols and waited, listening for another shot. They all heard the sound of booted feet in the woods. "Confederates?" Endicott asked Randolph.

There was no further shot, and the sound of footsteps faded, as though the riflemen were running away. Randolph took out his pistol. "Let's go look."

In alarm, Charlie said, "Don't go after them."

Endicott asked, "Why not?"

"They ain't soldiers. They hill country men. Ruffians."

Endicott asked, "Bushwhackers?"

"Don't call them that. Nuisances. They don't like planters, or black folks, or the Confederate Army, or the Union Army."

His hand resting on his pistol, Endicott asked, "Do they bother you?"

Charlie said, "Haven't bothered the place. But they don't like Rachel. She helps out Miz Sarah Hardin, wife to the man who leads them. John Hardin ain't grateful. Hurts his pride."

Randolph asked, "What happened?"

"He tried to shoot at her. When she go into town, one of us goes with her, and we take a rifle."

That evening, when the two officers came downstairs for dinner, Endicott was obviously tired and even paler than before, wincing a little in pain as he sat down. But Randolph was alert and keen-eyed as ever, and as Rachel and Adelaide led both of them into the dining room, he looked around with interest. The table had been set with the damask cloth, the bone china dishes, and the just-polished silver. The candlesticks, which had not been lit for Friday Sabbath since the war began, were alight with the good beeswax candles from before the blockade.

Randolph said, "This room is beautiful. As it must have been before the war."

Adelaide wondered if it would be, next week. "Thank you."

Rachel said, "May I offer you some claret, Lieutenant Randolph? And you, Captain Endicott?"

Randolph's eyes were dark and very liquid in his ivory-skinned face as he accepted the glass from Rachel's hand. He tasted it and said, "It's good. Have some, Endicott."

Endicott asked, "Where did it come from?"

Adelaide laughed and said, "La, Captain Endicott, we ain't running it through the blockade. We've had it since before the war." She sipped from her glass. "Been keeping it for an occasion."

Adelaide filled their plates and Rachel refilled their glasses, and both men looked at the food with appreciation. Endicott bent his head and said softly, "Thank you, dear God, for your bounty." Tired as he was, he ate with appetite, and Randolph needed no encouragement.

As though she'd been entertaining Union officers all her life, Adelaide said politely, "Captain Endicott, where is your home?"

"Ohio. I grew up near a town called Elyria. Not far from Oberlin College."

Adelaide said, "I know of Oberlin College." At Endicott's surprise, she added, "I hoped to continue my education there, before the war."

Randolph looked at Endicott and grinned. "Oberlin College was a hotbed of Abolition before the war," he said. "As Endicott well knows."

Endicott said, "I was at Oberlin myself in 1861. We were all Abolitionists, at Oberlin, and we all hated slavery. So I rushed home to muster in." He realized who he was speaking to—yearning for Oberlin or not, she was still a Southern lady—and said, "I hope that doesn't bother you, ma'am."

Adelaide laughed and shared a complicit look with Rachel. Adelaide said, "Not a bit. Slavery's over now, for good or for ill."

With feeling, Endicott said, "I've seen ex-slaves turn into soldiers. They came to us as runaways, still slaves in their hearts and minds. Once they put on the Union uniform, they became free men. I hadn't realized I'd been fighting for that, but I've never been prouder than I was, seeing black men fight for the Union."

Rachel said, "One of our people left to join the Union Army. I hope they mustered him in."

"I'm sure they did, Miss Mannheim."

Adelaide asked them both, "Now that you've seen it, what did you think of our place?"

Endicott roused himself to a soldier's stance. "Ma'am, when we win this war, I hope to see more places like this in the South. Former slaves who work their own land. Former slaves who are paid for their labor. Former slaves who are learning to read and write. And a former slaveowner who has not obstructed their path to freedom."

Adelaide blushed. "Such praise," she said. "All we wanted was to keep the place going and to bring in the crop. We never intended anything more."

"Well, you have certainly achieved it."

"Can you speak to General Sherman, to tell him so?" she asked softly.

Randolph said sharply, "Captain Endicott, we can't promise such a thing, as you know."

Endicott looked more than weary. He looked haggard. He sighed. "That's true, Mrs. Kaltenbach. We can't promise such a thing."

Rachel asked, "Lieutenant Randolph, are you an Ohio man, like the captain?"

"No, I grew up in New York City. I never knew my father, but I heard he was a relation to the Randolphs of Virginia. My mother raised me."

Endicott said, "Lieutenant Randolph has had an adventurous life."

Randolph said, "I was a bootblack, and a cabin boy on a ship, and an apothecary, and a photographer. I lectured on Abolition before the war, in upstate New York, and I was a spirit medium for a while."

Rachel asked, "What does a spirit medium do?"

"We call to the spirits of the dead. Those who grieve are comforted to know that the dead remember them, and are happy in the world beyond."

"You called up ha'nts?" Rachel asked. "People wanted to see their ha'nts?"

Randolph's observant eyes gleamed in his swarthy face. "If we listen, those who are gone speak to us. They tell us their secrets."

Scouts were sent for secrets too, Rachel thought.

Randolph turned the conversation to polite praise of the buildings, the livestock, the fields, and the dinner, and neither Rachel nor Adelaide said anything more about the things that worried them the most—where the cotton was, and whether it would be spared.

When dessert was done, Endicott said to Adelaide, "Ma'am, you'll have to excuse me, but it's been a long and wearing day."

Adelaide said, "Of course, Captain Endicott. Will all of you excuse me, too? I should put the children to bed. Rachel, will you entertain Lieutenant Randolph?"

Randolph smiled at Rachel. "It would be my pleasure," he said.

Adelaide and Endicott left the dining room together. At the foot of the stairs, Endicott leaned against the banister and said, "Mrs. Kaltenbach, may I ask you a question—perhaps a bit ill-mannered?"

He was her guest, but he was also General Sherman's officer, here on the Army's grim business. "Captain Endicott, I'll answer any question you put to me."

He said, "I've been observing you and Miss Mannheim since I arrived, talking and laughing together, and I've never seen a former mistress and a former slave so familiar with each other."

Adelaide thought of all the half-truths she could tell him. She looked at her weary, wounded adversary, and in the words she had never spoken to a stranger, she told him the whole truth. "Of course we're familiar," she said. "We're family. We're sisters."

"I'll be damned," said Endicott.

Adelaide laughed. "It ain't as bad as that." She held out her hand. "Good night, Captain Endicott." She turned and ran lightly up the stairs, but he remained behind, lost in thought.

In the dining room, Lieutenant Randolph remained at the table with Rachel. She said, "I can offer you brandy."

"From before the war?"

She smiled and nodded. "Go into the study to have some."

His face was very dusky in the low light. He rose. "Look, Miss

Mannheim." He pointed to a little brown spider that sat at the edge of the table.

Rachel said in alarm, "Don't mess with it. It's a brown jumping spider, and it's poisonous. They like to nest in cloth. I should have thought to shake out the tablecloth."

"Watch." He held out his fingertip.

She said, "Don't! They bite! I've known men to die from a spider bite."

The spider crawled up his finger and came to rest in his palm. It sat there, quietly, without moving, like a pet. He watched it, and said, "They've never bothered me."

Rachel watched his face, shadowy in the candlelight, and thought of the African story she had heard as a girl from Aunt Susy. In Africa, Aunt Susy said, people believed in a spider god, who sat in the middle of his web, and watched and waited to play tricks on people.

The spider crawled down Randolph's finger and onto the table. "Don't startle it," he said. "Just let it go on its way." The spider made its way down the tablecloth and onto the floor.

Anansi, Aunt Susy called him. Spider and trickster.

They left the room to go into the study.

Even though she was in this room every day to write in the ledger, she had rarely come here at night since Henry left. The candles in this room were common tallow, but they'd do. She lit them. In the candlelight, the familiar room was full of shadows. She unearthed the brandy bottle from the sideboard and poured him some.

He tasted it and smiled. "From before the war." He set down the glass and said, "Mr. Mannheim told me that you're in danger."

"It's a danger for a former slave to be free," she said.

"From Mr. Hardin?"

"He's the one riled at me, and pointing a rifle. But he ain't the only difficulty."

"But you seem well accustomed to freedom."

The brandy sent its warmth through her, and added to the heat of her words. "All my life I yearned to be free. Dreamed about being free. Never knew how hard it would be, every day, to feel free and act free and have other folks treat me like I was free. You wouldn't know. You were born a free man."

Startled, Randolph said, "Why would you think otherwise?"

She leaned forward and let the brandy help her. "Your daddy was a Randolph, but I have a notion that it was a different matter with your mama."

He was quiet, looking down at the glass in his hands, then looking at her. He said, "My mother died before I was grown, but she was beautiful, and kind, and I miss her to this day. Her people were from France, and Ireland, and Madagascar."

"Where's Madagascar, Lieutenant Randolph?"

"It is off the coast of Africa, Miss Mannheim."

He had given her a secret. He would expect something in return. She nodded, wondering what he would ask of her.

He said, "You'd be a success as a spiritualist, Miss Mannheim."

"Calling up ha'nts?"

"Those of us who call the spirits can see the secret things, the occult things, the things that are hidden from view."

The spirits were a sham, just as they were when he called them up for the grieving mothers and widows. He was getting ready to ask her about the cotton, or about running the blockade, and even though she was tipsy, she would be ready for him. "Lieutenant Randolph, what do you think we're hiding from you?"

He looked at her with the limpid eyes that saw the hidden things. "If Mr. Kaltenbach hated slavery as much as everyone says, and loved the Union, why did he join the Confederate Army?"

The claret and the brandy she'd drunk deserted her, and she was suddenly clear-headed. Anansi thought he had caught her in his web and bound her there. But Br'er Rabbit knew just where the briar patch was, and how to get into it to escape and outwit Br'er Fox.

She would tell him. She said softly, "It's quite a tale, Lieutenant Randolph. How much time do you have?"

He put his ivory hand over her brown one. "As long as it takes you," he said, his voice equally soft.

In the middle of the night, the racket from the henhouse woke everyone on the place, so they were awake to hear the rifle shots. Rachel, Adelaide, and Minnie hastily dressed and ran outside, where they saw Randolph and Endicott, disheveled and a little flushed, with their rifles in their hands. Charlie, Zeke, and Davey had also roused themselves from bed, and Charlie and Zeke carried their hunting rifles.

In the cool night air, sound carried, and from the pines on the edge of the cotton fields, they all heard a snatch of drunken laughter and the words, "...we'll show them bluecoats... show them niggers..."

After breakfast the next morning, Randolph and Endicott slipped into the yard. Randolph said, "I want to patrol the place."

Rifles in their hands, they walked by the cotton fields, listening and looking into the woods, where Hardin's men had slipped away the night before.

Randolph said, "Did you hear that?"

Endicott nodded, and they both began to creep into the woods, after the sound of a man rustling through the trees.

"Damn, we've lost him," Randolph said. He and Endicott had pursued the sound into the thicket of pine that lay behind the fields on the Kaltenbach place. If it had been one of Hardin's men, he must have known a pathway through the trees, or else he had the power to disappear, because they could no longer see him.

This land was all scrub pine, the cotton planter's bane. Left untended, it grew wildly over open land, sending out deep roots and requiring the heaviest labor of man and mule to cut down the trees and drag out the stumps. If you weren't a farmer, it was pretty to look at, the slender trunks of the trees letting the light through, their canopies providing shade. A host of birds lived in these pines. Endicott heard a loud cry—chickadee-dee-dee!—and was startled to be reminded how tiny the bird was.

Through the thicket, they saw the building. It was low-slung, and although it was made of rough pine boards, it had been built and pitched to be weatherproof and watertight. It had a tin roof, which glittered in the morning sun, and no windows. Both men had the same thought and tried the door. It was padlocked.

His hand on the lock, Randolph said slowly, "Cotton shed. It's a cotton shed."

Endicott said, "So that's what they've been sitting on."

"Like a broody hen."

"Until yesterday they didn't give a fig about Hardin. He could burn and plunder the whole county for all they cared. As long as he left their shed alone."

Randolph said, "There must be hundreds of bales in there. Once the war is over, and the blockade is lifted, they have a fortune in cotton in that shed."

"That's what we're really here to find," Endicott said. "So we can burn it to the ground."

"Sherman's orders, sir."

"I know." Endicott looked beyond the shed, into the forest. Randolph knew him well enough to recognize the workings of Endicott's conscience.

"Sir?" he said.

Endicott said, "Think about this place. Peaceful, and prosperous, and run by ex-slaves who are paid for their labor. Isn't that what we're fighting for? To give these people the right to live as they please, and be rewarded for their efforts?"

"The owner's off fighting for the Confederacy."

Endicott said, "From what I understand, it was a matter of honor. Miss Rachel's honor, as you tell me."

Randolph laughed. "How are you inclined?" he asked, although he knew, from the set of Endicott's jaw, what he was likely to be thinking.

"We tell General Sherman to leave this place alone. If we have to go to him ourselves to deliver the message, we do it."

"Brewing a little sedition of your own, I see."

"No," Endicott said. "Just looking ahead. We'll need people like these— ex-slaves who want to build new lives, and ex-planters who are dedicated to the Union. After we leave, they'll be our allies here. After the war, they'll put this place back together."

The trees behind the sheds were full of birds, and their singing filled the air. Endicott, who was interested in birds, had made a study of them at Oberlin. The sweet songs were deceptive. Bird calls were about love and war.

"Will Sherman will say yes?"

"I'll do my damnedest to convince him. As far as I'm concerned, it's a matter of principle. If you'd rather do it for Miss Rachel's pretty face, that's up to you."

Smiling, Randolph said, "You have a low opinion of my character, Captain Endicott."

Endicott laughed. "Because I know it so well, Lieutenant Randolph."

"What do you make of it, sir? Former mistress and former slave, sisters?"

"I leave the ladies to you."

Rachel heard the pounding on the door, her heart pounding along with it. "Who is it?" she called out, terrified to open it.

The familiar soft voice was muffled by sobs. "Open the door! Hurry!"

Rachel flung open the door. Sarah's hair was tangled and her face was bruised and bloody. Rachel pulled her inside and shut the door. "What happened? Where are the children?"

Adelaide ran down the stairs. "Sarah!" she cried out. "What is it?"

Sarah's face was smeared with blood and tears. Between sobs, she said,

"It's John. He swears he'll come here to kill those Union men, and he'll kill you, too."

Adelaide said, "What in God's name did he do to you?"

"I've never seen him like that—so angry—so wild—"

Rachel said, "He'll kill you, too, if he finds you here."

Adelaide cried out, "Your children! Where are they?"

Sobbing, she said, "I left them with Jim's wife Janey."

"Will they be all right?"

Sarah buried her face in her hands and wept.

Rachel said, "Hurry! Take her upstairs. I'll find Captain Endicott."

Rachel ran down the front steps and toward the fields. She called out, "Captain Endicott! Lieutenant Randolph!" as she ran. She ran past the cotton fields, past the corn fields, toward the thicket of trees that hid the cotton shed. She called out again, "Captain Endicott! Lieutenant Randolph!"

She heard a rustling sound from the thicket and thought, What a fool I've been, making a ruckus so that Hardin's men could hide in those trees and hear me from miles away. She heard the sound of boots running on dirt, and thought, If it's Hardin I'm done for.

She saw the glint of metal. Were they armed? Then she saw the blue tunics and the familiar faces. Weak in the knees with relief, she said, "Hardin is coming here."

"Did you see them? Did you have word?" Endicott asked.

"Sarah Hardin is here. He told her he was coming to kill everyone on the place." She held herself rigid against the fear that coursed through her. "He beat her. He would have killed her, too."

As they ran back to the house, they heard the guttural yell, the sound of a troop ready to battle. They heard rifle shots. Randolph and Endicott let go Rachel's arms. Randolph shoved her away and shouted, "Run! Get inside!"

Hardin's men ran into the front yard, shooting and whooping. How could five men sound like a troop of hundreds? Were they drunk? The shots were wild. Rachel was afraid to move for fear she'd be shot by a stray bullet.

Randolph raised his pistol and aimed. He hit one of the men in the chest and the man fell, blood gushing from his wound, screaming in agony. Randolph aimed again, and the next shot ended it. Rachel recognized him. He was the man who'd wanted to outrage her.

The remaining men stared at their friend, whose chest gushed blood, even though he was dead. The blood soaked into the ground by the body.

Randolph said, "It wouldn't bother us to shoot all of you like that."

They lowered their rifles.

Hardin cried out, "You damned cowards! We ain't done here." He raised his rifle and ran toward Rachel. He grabbed her, holding her close to him and yelled, "Where is Sarah? I know she came here! Where are you hiding her?"

Rachel was too frightened to speak. This time he would shoot her.

He prodded her in the ribs with his rifle. "Tell me, you nigger bitch!"

Randolph raised his pistol, and Hardin said, "If you shoot at me I'll kill her."

The door flew open, and both Adelaide and Sarah stood in the doorway. Adelaide grabbed Sarah's hand, but Sarah shook her off. She ran down the steps, her voice an awful keening cry: "No, John!"

Still holding onto Rachel, Hardin pointed the gun toward his wife. "Damn you!" he said. "Damn all of you!"

Sarah stretched out her hands to her husband. Hardin, who needed both hands to aim his rifle, let Rachel go. Rachel backed away, a few steps, before her legs failed her and she had to sit heavily on the ground.

Randolph raised his pistol and took a sharpshooter's aim at Hardin. The first shot caught him in the chest, and he dropped the rifle and fell to his knees with the force of it. At the second shot, he slumped to the ground, dead at his wife's feet.

Sarah stood in silence, looking at her fallen husband. She knelt, and put her hand on his still-warm forehead, and closed his staring eyes. "God rest his soul," she said quietly.

Endicott and the men of the place turned their guns on the rest of the men. Endicott said roughly, "Hand over your rifles."

Jim Hardin stared at the men who encircled him. His face was white with shock. Endicott reached for Jim Hardin's rifle and Jim handed it to him, a dazed look on his face. The rest of the men handed over their rifles.

Rachel tried to stand, but her legs wouldn't obey her. Randolph came to her and asked gently, "How are you?" as he helped her up. Adelaide ran to her and embraced her. Rachel leaned against her sister, too shaken to weep. Adelaide stroked her hair with one hand and held her close with the other, her breath ragged with sobs.

When they broke apart, Randolph said to them both, "Go in the house and take some brandy." He gestured to Sarah. "And I don't care what she thinks about drinking. Make sure that she takes some, too."

Sarah looked at her brother-in-law Jim, who gave her a despairing look. "Take care of Janey," he said, as Endicott and Randolph led the captives away.

A few days later, an army of blue-coated men marched down the road that ran by the Kaltenbach place, and the former slaves stood at the end of the driveway to watch them. When the soldiers saw the Union flag flying, they waved and cheered. The next day, the people of the Kaltenbach place, safe and spared, listened to the guns booming fifteen miles away at the battlefield at Allatoona.

Chapter 21

Soldier's Heart

On a cloudless day in June, a few months after the war had ended, in the blessed lull between chopping and picking, a man came limping up the driveway. His uniform was in tatters, his beard was untrimmed, and his hair was long and tangled. From a distance, he looked no different from any of the returning Confederate soldiers they had seen in the past months. Most of them were hill country men, going home to the northernmost parts of Georgia or Tennessee. Rachel and Adelaide had given them a meal and let them unfurl their blankets on the ground. Most of them were so lousy that they weren't fit to be in the barn.

Rachel said to Minnie, "Another hungry soldier to feed." They sat on the piazza of the main house, resting after midday dinner. Charlie, who sat with them, said, "Can't deny them, but it's like locusts, one after another."

Then he got close enough, and she saw the breadth of the shoulder, despite how thin he was. The long thigh, even though he was limping so badly. She picked up her skirts and ran down the driveway, her heart pounding. He saw her and quickened his pace—he was too footsore and too hampered by his leg to run. "Henry!" she screamed. "Henry!"

Without caring who saw them, she flew into his arms and felt them tighten around her, the muscles ropy, the bones too close to the skin. She hugged him fiercely and felt how thin he was. "You're alive," she said, laughing and sobbing at the same time. "You're home."

"Beloved," he said. "Rachel, beloved."

Between words and sobs, they clung to each other and kissed, over and over.

When they broke apart, she said huskily, "Everyone will want to see you." She grasped his hand and pulled him after her, impatient to let everyone else know he was home.

He said, "I'm sorry, love. I've just walked all the way from Virginia and I'm too weary to hurry."

By the time he had limped his way to the piazza, everyone had gathered there. Minnie was the first to hug him. "I'm all over lice," he said ruefully, and she said, "I don't care," embracing him with all her strength and pressing her cheek to his. She stood back to look at him and said, "Marse Henry, fattening you up will be my life's work."

Rachel touched his long, tangled hair, so dirty with dust that it looked gray. He looked different bearded: older, thinner, more haggard. The whiskers had come in partly gray. He rubbed his face and said ruefully, "It was so hard to shave in the field that we all quit. After a few weeks we all looked like backwoodsmen."

"Let Minnie cut your hair."

"As long as she doesn't mind what's living in it."

Zeke hugged him too, and Charlie solemnly clasped his hand. "Good to see you home, Marse Henry."

"Charlie, the place looks beautiful. So many places in Georgia were burned to the ground. It does my heart good to come home to this."

Henry's eyes lit up at the children. He bent down to talk to the little boy. "You don't remember me," he said. "You were just a baby when I left."

Matt wrinkled his nose. He said, "You're right. I need a bath. We'll get acquainted after I get cleaned up."

He turned to the little brown-skinned girl. "And look at you! I never saw you at all!"

She looked straight at him, the dimpled face a miniature of her mother's. "My name is Eliza and I know my ABCs and my daddy ain't here because he's away in the war!"

Henry grinned. His eyes were wet. "Not anymore, he ain't."

He stood—his leg pained him, and everyone could see it—and said to Rachel, "I should see Adelaide. How is she?"

"She's visiting her daddy. She takes him a basket of food twice a week."

Henry said, "How bad off is he?"

"Like I wrote to you. Sherman's army busted up the place something terrible and they haven't had a crop since. Ezra's the only one left and he's too old to take care of anyone. They try to grow a kitchen garden but if Adelaide didn't go over there with provisions they'd starve to death."

Henry said, "I never thought Adelaide would take care of her father. Or that he would allow it."

Rachel said somberly, "The war changed all of us."

"I want to see the house." He hesitated at the base of the piazza stairs. "I need to go slow." She stopped. "Lean on me," she said. "I can't tote you, but I can help you." They made their way slowly up the stairs into the house and walked inside together.

He looked around with pleasure. "It's lovely. Untouched."

"Those two Union officers said it was the nicest house they'd seen in months of fighting. They ate at the table, and sat in the parlor, and slept upstairs. I hope you don't mind that I gave Lieutenant Randolph your room."

He laughed. "Beloved, I wouldn't mind if you gave General William Tecumseh Sherman my room, if it spared the house and the crop."

"Do you want to go upstairs?"

He gestured toward the lame leg. "I believe I need to sit down."

Rachel said, "You need a meal and a bath, more than anything. Lean on me and we'll get you into the kitchen."

In the kitchen, he sat gratefully at the familiar pine table. Minnie was already heating enough water to fill the porcelain tub in his room in the main house. He said, "Don't trouble yourself taking the water in the house."

Minnie said, "Where will you take your bath?"

"Can't walk much, and any stairs trouble me. Right here. Tin tub's fine."

"I thought you might like to be alone with Rachel."

"I would. Shut the kitchen door and tell everyone to leave us alone until I'm clean."

Minnie shook her head. Without asking, Rachel began to fill a plate. He said, "Whatever you have. I'm not the least bit particular. I haven't minded the kosher laws since the war started."

They gave him pone and peas with side meat, left over from midday dinner. He leaned over his plate, and like every famished person who had sat at this table in the past year, he wolfed the food. He sighed as he put down his fork. "No one had much to eat, from Virginia all the way home to Georgia. Everywhere I went, the crop was burned to the ground."

When the bathwater was hot, Minnie and Rachel filled the tub, and Minnie left them. Rachel helped him out of the clothes he wore. She said, "We'll burn those, if you don't mind."

"Please do."

She was horrified at how thin he was, and how bad his leg looked, red craters of scar on the skinny thigh. She helped him into the tub and bathed him as she'd bathe Matt. The hot water killed the lice on his body and in his hair and they floated to the top, sitting in the scum of the soap and the dirt. She washed his hair, relieved to see the brown color reappear as the dirt and dust came out. He closed his eyes as she ran the sponge, then the washcloth, over his weary, wounded body.

When he was clean, and wrapped in his dressing gown, she said, "Would you like me to shave you?"

"How steady are your hands?"

She held them out. They were wrinkled and soapy and they were shaking.

He grinned. "As much as I love you, I don't want to trust you with a straight razor," he said, and he shaved himself without a mirror, like a soldier in the field, by the feel of his face.

Clean and beardless, he began to look more like himself. Still too thin, and still too weary. But Henry again.

Rachel opened the door and Minnie came back in. She trimmed his hair, then she said, "Let me look at your leg." He arranged the dressing gown over his lap, for modesty, and let her touch the scars and feel for the muscle beneath the skin. "Looks worse than it is," she said. "You healed all right. Muscle's all knotted up."

Her touch roused him, much to his embarrassment. She saw it and laughed. "You save that for Miss Rachel." She tried to massage the muscle, but her hands were too small. "Rachel, get me that rolling pin."

He said, "You aren't going to hit me with it!"

"Goodness, no. Roll it to work out those knots in your leg." She worked the rolling pin, then took out the jar of salve with its familiar smell. Comfrey, for cuts and bruises, to treat the scars, and the blisters on his feet, for good measure.

Rachel brought him clothes from his press, and she was distressed to see how big his shirt and trousers were on him. He sighed to feel clean whole cloth against his skin. She handed him a pair of socks. He laughed. "Clean, whole socks," he said. "Worth fighting a war for." When he was properly dressed, he walked slowly to the piazza and sat there to rest.

He didn't recognize the tall, slender woman in the plain cotton dress and the plain bonnet until she put down her basket and came lightly up the stairs. He rose to greet her.

She was more wiry than she had been when he left, and a little tanned from the sun. She threw the bonnet back and the dark unruly hair was the same. She held out her arms and they embraced. Her arms were wiry and strong, like the rest of her. Like her former servants, she smelled of woodsmoke, harsh homemade soap, and herself, a sweet, musky odor. "Welcome home, Henry," she said, when they let each other go.

"You look well, Adelaide."

She laughed. "I look tired and weatherbeaten, like a woman who spends her days in the kitchen and the garden. You were right. A woman who runs a plantation needs to work as hard as anyone on it."

He said, "You've done well. The place looks beautiful."

Still holding his hands, she said, "It's so good to see you. When we didn't have word we feared the worst."

"I'm mighty weary, but I'm here."

She squeezed his hands and let them go. "You look done in. Don't stand on my account. Please, sit."

He sat, and she said, "Would you like a glass of whiskey? I'm sure Rachel would be glad to bring you one."

"If Minnie can spare her."

Adelaide grinned. "She can, if I get dinner. I'm a dab hand at peeling a potato now." He laughed. She said, "Don't get up. Take your ease, and we'll let you know when supper's ready."

Minnie wanted to serve in the dining room, but he was adamant. "I never enjoyed a meal I ate in that room. I want to eat in the kitchen with you." Minnie killed a chicken and cooked it in the most elegant way she knew, with tomatoes and shallots and a little claret to flavor it. "Poulet Marengo," she said, "almost like we had in the Butler house." There were new potatoes and new peas to accompany it, and Henry bent his head when he saw the food— not to say grace, but to weep at the sight of it.

"You" meant Minnie and Rachel, and Matt and Eliza, and Adelaide, and Sarah Hardin with her children, all of them together around the big pine table. Sarah Hardin would always be slight, but she had put on flesh, and there was color in her face. Her children, whom he remembered as frightened starvelings, were smiling and rosy. All of them were dressed in clothes that were worn, but they were clean and whole.

He said to her, "Rachel wrote to tell me about your husband. I'm sorry, Mrs. Hardin."

She said, "John was a troubled soul who brought pain to everyone around him. Now that he's gone I'm surrounded by friends, and I do God's work here."

"God's work?" Henry's Israelite skin prickled a little.

She lifted her soft blue eyes to his. "Isn't it God's work to teach children how to read and write?"

After dinner he got acquainted a little with Matt, who was shy around him, and Eliza, who was not. Adelaide kissed Matt goodnight. When he asked, "Kiss from Daddy?" she smiled and said, "He's right here. He'll kiss you himself."

Matt came shyly into his father's arms. Henry laid his cheek on his son's soft curly hair and kissed the top of his head. Eliza said, "Kiss from Daddy for me, too!" He pressed his face to her soft black hair, so like her mother's, and kissed her round little cheek.

Rachel said, smiling, "Just like you asked us, in your letters. Kiss from Daddy every night."

Sarah said, "Adelaide, would you like me to take Matt upstairs and get him settled?"

Adelaide said, "Please do. I'll be along soon to tuck him in." Sarah left with Matt and her own children in tow.

Henry asked, "Where does Eliza sleep?"

Rachel said, "She stays with me. In our house." Pleased, she explained, "We live in the old house. I want you to see it."

Adelaide said, "Henry, may I have a word with you outside?" He stood up slowly and followed her into the breezeway.

She stopped to face him. "I can see how much your leg troubles you."

It was good of her to say so. "It will, for a while." He met her eyes, which were sadder and older than they'd been before the war.

"We have a lot to talk about, you and I, but it can wait." She inclined her head toward the kitchen. "I know you have other business tonight."

"Adelaide, it ain't right."

He was surprised at the gratitude in her face. He said, "I'm bone weary. The only business I have tonight is to climb those stairs and sleep on a bed with a soft mattress." He took her hands. "We have a lot to untangle, all three of us, but it can hold until tomorrow."

She leaned forward and kissed him lightly on the lips. "Good night, Henry. Sleep well."

Adelaide walked upstairs to her room and sat at her old dressing table. She looked at her reflection, no longer seeing the face of the spoiled young wife she had been before the war. She had lost Henry a long time ago. But she hadn't been ready to feel so heartsore again. The old pain flickered at her temples.

She sat before the mirror, and thought of all the things that caused her regret. She tried to think of the things that gave her joy, these days. Tonight, the scale was too heavy with regret to balance. She bent her head and wept.

When Henry woke the next morning he didn't know where he was. He felt an unaccustomed comfort. He was in a soft bed, with a pillow. His leg didn't ache. He was hungry, but reasonably so. He must have been deeply asleep, because he hadn't heard the door open when someone left him a jug of hot water to shave with. He got up, marveling, to use it. It was still a luxury to feel shaved and dressed.

There were eggs for breakfast, and just-baked pone with fresh butter, and tea that Minnie made from peppermint leaves. No marmalade. Minnie said, "We had marmalade, but we finished it." Rachel said, "When we have money again I'm going someplace where they have coffee and I'm buying a heap of it."

Adelaide asked, "What are you going to do today, Henry?"

"Look around a little."

After breakfast he went to see Charlie. "Marse Henry, you shouldn't be walking, with that leg."

"Wish you wouldn't call me 'Marse'. I can walk as long as I go slow and I rest."

"What should we call you?"

"Not Massa, not ever again, and I can't stand the sound of 'Captain Kaltenbach'. Reminds me of the war. Wish you would call me by my name. Henry."

Charlie shook his head. "Can't see it."

He said ruefully, "Marse Henry will do, for now."

They wandered the place together. Charlie explained about the plots each family worked, and the wager, and Henry admired the rows of cotton, the stands of corn, and the provision gardens. He praised the flowers that grew so prettily outside each cabin. He was tired, and Charlie insisted that they sit on his steps for a rest. "Everyone looks houseproud, Charlie."

"We all are. Wanted to build better houses but we didn't have the cash for lumber. When I do, I'm going to ask Zeke to build me a proper house. Becky wants glass windows."

"Charlie, have you thought about what you're going to do, now that the war's over?"

Charlie said, "It ain't the time to settle it yet, but I have some thoughts about what I'd like to do, now that the war's over and you're home again."

"Tell me."

Charlie looked over the fields, the look of a man surveying his place. "I'd like to buy some land for a place of my own. Hoped you'd be willing to sell me a parcel."

Henry said, "I'd be glad to."

"Have to get my money from selling the crop first."

"Depends on how much I ask for it."

"How much would that be, Marse Henry?"

"A dollar," he said.

Charlie said, "Dollar an acre?"

"No," Henry said. "A dollar for the whole thing. Land, stock, equipment, seed. One dollar."

Upset, Charlie said, "That just ain't right. Ain't fair. Not to either of us."

"Charlie, I owe you more than I can ever repay. You brought in the crop that made all of us rich. You saved the place when the Union Army came through. It would be the least I could do for you."

"I won't take it as a gift. I'm free, and a free man pays what something is worth. I don't mind sitting down to talk to you to decide what it's worth. But I'll pay for it, and I want a contract to sign my name to, and a deed that says it's mine, and a note that tells you I'll repay you as soon as I get paid my money. Gratitude, that's a matter of conscience. But I want to do this right by all the laws of the state of Georgia."

"Will you let me forgive the interest on the note?"

"Is that customary?"

"When men who are friends, and who trust each other's word, lend money, it's customary."

"All right. I'll allow that."

Henry held out his hand. A handshake wouldn't seal a contract, but he wanted to show Charlie the courtesy. To his surprise, Charlie shook his hand. "I thank you, Marse Henry."

"Someday I will get you to stop calling me 'Marse.' It's my pleasure, Mr. Mannheim."

They walked slowly back to the main house. Charlie asked, "Did Missus Adelaide tell you about the school she and Miz Hardin keep?"

"Yes, she did."

"Right now they make do outdoors, but when we get lumber we're going to build a schoolhouse along with houses for us. Glass windows there, too."

"How many children do they teach?"

"We got a dozen now. Not just ours. Come from miles around to get schooled here. From the old Payne place, and Turner place, and from Cassville, too."

Henry said to Charlie, "Did you know that Rachel was Adelaide's first pupil? When they were little girls together."

Charlie said, "She a fine teacher. All the children learn to read and write and figure. She teach grown folks, too. Not just us, but anyone who wants to learn."

It was an act of bravery, even defiance, to educate freed slaves. He had seen the schools for freed slaves in Virginia, and met the Yankee women who ran them. They were as brave as soldiers, and in as much danger. He was proud of Adelaide's effort, and proud of her courage.

After midday dinner, Adelaide asked him if they could talk in private. She said, "I know you don't care to be in the house, but I thought we might sit in your study."

Surrounded by his beloved books. He could tolerate that. They walked into the study, which was tended and tidied, like everything else on the place. Adelaide said, "Rachel sits here to write in the ledger."

Henry smiled to think of Rachel sitting at his desk. "She does better than I did."

They sat in the wing chairs, Henry in his accustomed spot, Adelaide in the chair that Rachel had once claimed as hers. There were no hoopskirts any more—they were a luxury that had disappeared during the war, along with chocolate, or coffee, or flour—and Adelaide, in her narrow dress, took up a modest space in the big chair.

Alone, with serious business to discuss, they were more uncomfortable than they had been since he returned.

He said, "You're shaking."

"None of this is easy."

"Is it harder than four years of war?" He meant to tease, but the mention of "war" cast a shadow in the room.

She said, "I've had four years of war to repent of hating you so much I wished you dead."

"You weren't the only one. The whole Union Army felt that way about me."

"The Union Army was never married to you. I haven't been to a synagogue, I haven't gone to the Yom Kippur service, but I can't tell you how much I regret what I did."

He said quietly, "There was more than enough wrong to go around."

"Some people fall in love after they're married, and some learn how to rub along," Adelaide said, thinking of Aggie and Cat. "We didn't. We were never suited to be husband and wife."

He said, "I was always sorry for that."

"I once told Sarah that you have a loving heart. You always wanted a wife who would love you. I couldn't. Rachel could."

"Is it still a betrayal?" Henry asked softly.

"It will always hurt." She sighed. "But the war's over. Rachel and I have made our peace."

He reached for her hands and held them as they both listened to the sharp song of the crickets that came through the open window. The war was over, and peace, however troubled, was greatly preferable.

She asked, "What are you thinking you'll do, now that the war's over?"

"When I came home I came through Atlanta. Sherman burned it to the ground and it was coming back. Building up. Bustling. Busy. I liked to see it. Not like Savannah. I think Savannah's done for. Busted up for good."

"What would you do in Atlanta?"

"I wrote to Joe Meyer, and he wrote back. He's thinking of leaving Savannah and settling in Atlanta. Asked me if I'd consider going into business with him."

"Dry goods?"

He said, "I don't think I want to see another bale of cotton, as long as I live. But I think I could stand to see a length of cloth, and sell it."

Adelaide laughed. "Now that would suit you. Would Rachel go with you?"

"If she wanted to."

She got her pondering look. "There's no shame in a husband and wife living apart, if they're cordial about it. If you stayed in Atlanta to run your business and I stayed here, to look after the place, no one would think twice about it."

He said, "And in the old days, no one would think twice if a man brought his servant to town to live in his house. If Rachel comes with me, I mean to honor her more than that."

"It won't be easy for you." Was it that simple to say, I know how much you love her, and I won't stand between you? There was relief in it, along with the regret.

He said, "If you stay, to run the place and the school, it won't be easy for you either."

"I know. We've already had trouble. There are people who think that freedmen should stay as ignorant as slaves." She tucked in her chin in defiance. "I learned how kill a chicken with a hatchet and butcher a hog. I reckon I can learn how to shoot a rifle if I need to."

He laughed. "Look at you. How fierce you've become."

She said, "Didn't intend to. Didn't expect to fight a war at home, to end slavery. We all struggled, after Emancipation. I had to fight to be free of being Missus. Wish they'd stop calling me that."

He reached for her hand and laced his fingers through hers. "We ain't well suited to be husband and wife," he said, "but we may be very well suited to be friends."

She nodded. "Won't happen overnight. But I hope so."

That evening, after the supper dishes had been put away, and everyone had retired to the main house, Henry said to Rachel, "I want to lie in your arms tonight."

Rachel said, "Did you speak to Adelaide?"

He told her about the truce that he and Adelaide had reached.

"I know."

Surprised, he put down the dish he was drying and said, "Do you."

"Adelaide and I had our war," she said. "We made our truce a long time ago." She said, "Last year, at Yom Kippur, she told me she'd wronged me, and asked me if I could forgive her. I told her that she needed to ask God for that. Wasn't up to me."

Henry said quietly, "If you've wronged God—breaking the laws of Moses—you ask God for forgiveness. If you've wronged someone in particular, you ask them directly."

"That's what she said. Humbled herself before me to ask me to set it straight."

"What did you say to her?"

"Told her I'd never be easy in my mind or my heart about the wrong I did to her." She put her hand to her eyes. "But we're sisters. Sisters love each other and hate each other. Doesn't matter. Together, never to be divided."

He sighed and cradled her face between his hands. "Peace won't be a habit, not for a while." He kissed her, very gently, as he had the first time.

When he let her go, she said, "Come with me."

They walked through the pine woods. Early in the evening, the day birds were still making soft sounds, and the crickets had begun their song. The night sounds would come later, when the sun set. He knew where they were going: to the old house, their old hiding place.

Whitewashed, the yard planted with flowers, the stairs and piazza neatly swept, it looked better than he had ever seen it.

"I live here now," she said, and she waited as he made slow progress up the few front stairs.

Inside, the main room had also been whitewashed, and the windows were brightly clean. There was a rag rug on the living room floor, and a pine table and chairs before the fireplace. There was a kettle and a spider at the hearth, and a set of tin plates and cups on the table.

The biggest bedroom, where had they always lain on the floor, had a bed in it, with a cornhusk mattress and pillow. "Zeke made it for me. I told him it had to be big enough for two. He asked me if I was getting married." She laughed, and he delighted in the sound.

"That's a pretty quilt."

"Sarah made it for me."

The next biggest bedroom, where Zeke and his boys used to sleep, had a little bed with another pretty coverlet, and a little rocking chair. "That's Eliza's," she said. "When she isn't staying with her Aunt Minnie."

The smallest room had another rocking chair, with Rachel's mending basket next to it, filled with clothes to mend. There was a little table, with a candlestick on it, and an inkwell and a pen, and a pine bookcase with three shelves. Her book of Shakespeare sat there, and Dickens, and Sir Walter Scott, and a Bible. One of the shelves was filled with packets of letters, bound up with red ribbon. "Every letter you ever wrote to me," she said softly.

"This is your home," he said.

"Our home," she said, taking his hand, leading him to the bedroom and closing the door.

They sat on the bed and embraced, a little awkwardly, because it had been so long. He cradled her face in his hands and gently kissed her lips. "I've longed for this," he said softly. "Beloved, I have missed you so."

She began to sob, softly at first, then so hard she couldn't stop. He folded her close to his chest and stroked her hair. "What is it, love?" he asked tenderly.

Still sobbing, she said, "I was afraid all the time you were gone. I was afraid every day that you would die. When I didn't hear from you I was terrified, and when I did I was still terrified, because the letter was a week old when I got it. I didn't cry, not when you left, not when you were wounded, not when we didn't hear for months when you were a Union prisoner. Now that it's over, it isn't all right. I've let myself cry and I can't stop."

He knew what she meant. "When we were fighting, we couldn't let ourselves feel afraid. When it was over, there were men who cried their eyes out, or puked their guts out, or got blind drunk. But not until it was over. We called it 'soldier's heart.'"

She wiped her eyes. Still sobbing, she said, "This isn't the way I wanted to welcome you."

"You just laid down the burden of four years of fighting. You had a hard and lonely war, my love, and you just realized that it's over." He kissed her cheek, then the corner of her mouth, then her lips, until her tears stopped.

Later, they lay together, skin to skin, and even though he had yearned for her for months, he couldn't rouse to love her. She stroked his too-thin face. She said, "You're bone weary, and starved, and the war isn't over for you just because you cut the lice out of your hair and burned that uniform. Rest with me, and don't give it another thought."

The nightmare woke them both. Sobbing and shaking, he gradually realized where he was, as she held him and asked softly, "What were you dreaming?"

"Always the same dream. I dream that I'm back in the Wilderness."

"That terrible battle." She held him, gently caressed his face, murmured to him as she would comfort Eliza or Matt.

He said, "This wasn't the way I wanted to welcome you, either."

"Soldier's heart."

"It's over. I want to learn to live as though I know it."

She said, "Like you said, won't happen overnight."

He moved his leg and winced. She said, "Just like that leg. Give it time, give it care, and it will ease, and trouble you less and less. Once we have the habit of peace again."

"I hope so."

She held him close, to tightly that he could feel her heart beating against his chest. "I know so."

The next morning he opened his eyes to see Rachel, her hair unpinned and full around her head, wearing her petticoat and nothing else, washing herself with cold water from a tin pitcher. He stretched and sat up. "Good morning, love," he said.

She turned and smiled, at ease in her bare skin. "I look a sight with my hair loose."

"You look a lovely sight, all over."

"How do you feel?"

"Like I'd died and gone to heaven." He sat up and threw off the covers. She looked at his naked body, at his roused manly part, and laughed. "I can't linger. Will that keep?"

He said ruefully, "That will keep."

She came to embrace him. "I don't want to hurry, for our first time in a long time. I want to take it sweet and slow."

He kissed her. "Later."

That night, as everyone went to bed, Rachel took him by the hand and they walked together, unashamed at who saw them, to her house in the piney woods.

They sat on the bed together, in the room lit by moonlight, suddenly ill at ease, suddenly hesitant. She said, "I don't know where to start."

He said, "Would you unpin your hair?"

She smiled. She pulled out the pins and shook her hair loose. She said, "Did it keep?"

He knew what she meant. "Not from this morning." He smiled a little and said, "Perhaps we could read a contract to get us both roused."

She remembered, and she laughed. "Why? Have you got one handy?" At that they both laughed, all the way from the bottom of the gut. Afterwards it was easy between them. To kiss, sweet and slow. To unbutton. To touch. He ran his hand over her body and said, "You've lost flesh, my love. Was there enough to eat here? You didn't fib to me?"

"We always had plenty. But when I was worried it was hard to eat, and I was worried all the time."

She ran her hands over his chest, wincing at how thin he was. She wondered if he were still ticklish. He was. When he stopped laughing, he said, "What about you? Are you still ticklish?" His hand slipped from her belly to the hair on her mound of Venus.

She opened her legs for him and laughed. "We'll find out."

After he tickled her into a spasm, he moved to lay atop her. He winced. She asked, "Does your leg trouble you?"

"I'll be all right." He eased inside her, and she watched his face for signs of pain. But he sighed with pleasure. She wrapped her hands around his back, and as he went deeper inside her, wrapped her legs around his hips. They found their old rhythm, his pleasure heightening hers, until she spasmed and moaned with the bliss of it, and he spent in her, with a cry of joy.

He lingered until he faded inside her. "I'd stay there forever, if I could."

"You're always welcome back," she said, smiling. "You know that."

She lay with her cheek on his chest, and he pressed his face to her hair. He said, "I never want to be parted from you again."

She said, "I want us to be together forever."

"Husband and wife." He kissed her hair. "However we can manage it."

She kissed his mouth and laughed softly. "Managing it, that will be the thing!"

In July, a week before they planned to have their summer barbecue, a man walked up the driveway to the house. Rachel was in the side garden with Minnie, weeding the vegetable patch. Their visitor was tall and broad and muscular and ivory of skin. She straightened up. "Minnie, I think we'll need to set an extra plate for dinner."

Minnie put her hand on her back and straightened too. She shaded her eyes and said, "That's Lieutenant Randolph, and he's toting a mighty big box." Teasing, she said, "So you did write to him."

Rachel laughed. "I did. Told him he was welcome to visit, whether he took our portraits or not. But he brought his photographic equipment."

A photograph was an occasion, like going to Sunday meeting, and everyone retired to put on their best clothes for their portraits. Randolph, teasing, asked Henry if he wanted to be photographed in his Confederate uniform. Henry said, "What was left of it I burned after I got home. I never want to put on Confederate gray again."

Adelaide took Rachel upstairs to get ready for Lieutenant Randolph's camera. Joe Meyer had sent lengths from Atlanta and Sarah had sewed them into pretty new dresses, a blue sprigged muslin for Adelaide and a red and yellow plaid calico for Rachel. As she had done so many times, Rachel laced Adelaide into her corset.

Adelaide had a surprise for Rachel. She took Rachel's dress from the clothes press, and with it, a corset. Adelaide said, "You'll need this, with your new dress."

Rachel laughed. "I reckon I will."

Rachel's hands went to the fasteners in front, but Adelaide said, "You stand still and let me do that." Adelaide pulled on the laces in back, guessing at how tight they needed to be. "Are you all right?" she asked Rachel.

Rachel gasped, "Didn't know that being free meant being bound so tight into this thing!"

"That's too tight," Adelaide said, and she loosened the laces.

Adelaide buttoned her own dress, refusing Rachel's help, and she asked,

"Do you need me to button you?" Rachel said no. Each woman smoothed her own skirt. Even without hoops, skirts were voluminous again.

Rachel said, "Now you sit and let me fix your hair."

"Don't need to."

"Won't take but a moment." As she had done since they were girls together, she quickly combed, smoothed and pinned Adelaide's unruly dark curls. When she was done, Adelaide said, "Now I'll do yours."

Rachel said, "You don't need to wait on me."

"Just helping you, like sisters do for one another."

Rachel sat very still as Adelaide took off the kerchief and unpinned Rachel's hair. She held her breath as Adelaide carefully ran the comb through the long wiry strands, deftly twisted them into a knot, and pinned it at the nape of Rachel's neck. Rachel blinked back tears at the gentleness of her sister's touch.

Adelaide bent to kiss the top of Rachel's head. "You look pretty," she said, putting her arms around Rachel's neck.

Rachel struggled to keep the tears out of her voice. "Set next to me so we can both see if we're fine enough for a portrait."

Adelaide pulled over another chair so they could sit side by side before the dressing table mirror. They looked into the mirror, assuring themselves that they were ready to be photographed, and they both saw the reflected resemblance. The shape of the eyes. The curve of the lips. The set of the head on the neck.

"We should ask Mr. Randolph to take a photograph of the two of us," Adelaide said, reaching for her sister's hand. "Just like this."

Rachel turned to smile at her sister. "Yes," she said. "Just like this."

Historical Note

My earliest readers were surprised that Jews, with their long history of persecution in Europe, suffered so little from anti-Semitism in the South, and with their long memory of enslavement in Egypt, became slaveowners with so little difficulty.

The South's first Jews were assimilated Sephardim from London who did not seem like strangers to other newcomers from the British Isles. The German Jews who followed in the 19th century, European in manner and dress, were quick to learn the language, take on American customs, and intermarry with non-Jews. The few Jews in rural areas were highly adaptable. In the 1850s, a Jewish peddler in Alabama stopped with a farm family to share their dinner, which was the usual Southern meal of hog and hominy. As the farm wife watched her guest eat, she said, "I thought that Moses ordered the Jews not to eat hog meat." The peddler said, "Ma'am, if Moses had travelled through Perry County, Alabama, he never would have issued such an order."

Jews welcomed the freedoms they found in America: to make a living, own property, vote, and worship. They called the South their "Jerusalem" and felt very much at home there. They took on Southern mores. In a society that was divided between white and not, where the despised and oppressed "other" was enslaved and black, Jews were glad to take on the privileges of being white. They became slaveowners.

By 1860, about a quarter of the Jews in South Carolina and Georgia owned slaves. Most of Georgia's Jews were city dwellers, clustered into Savannah, working in mercantile pursuits, some profitable and some humble. Their slaves were primarily house servants. Only if their businesses were large enough did they put their slaves to work in the shop.

Jewish planters were a rarity in Georgia. Raphael J. Moses, who rose to fame during the Civil War as chief supply officer for Confederate General Longstreet, owned a plantation called Esquinale near Columbus and who had 47 slaves on the eve of the Civil War, was an exception. More typical of rural Jews was the real Mr. Levy of Cass County, who ran a general store in Cassville and who owned two slaves in 1860, a woman of 38 and a girl of 11.

Jews treated their slaves as other Southerners did. As masters and mistresses, their behavior ran the full gamut from cruelty to kindness. Some Jews sold their slaves for insolence or beat them; others educated them. A Jewish slave dealer was a rarity, but most Jewish slaveowners, like their non-Jewish counterparts, bought and sold slaves as they would livestock, selling them to fulfill a need for labor, raise money, or settle an estate.

However Southern Jews felt about slavery in private, they did not become Abolitionists. There were no Jews like the Grimke sisters, planter's daughters who renounced their upbringing to go North and join the antislavery cause. The only Jew to speak against slavery before the Civil War in the South was a rabbi from Germany, David Einhorn, a radical among Reform Jews, whose views got him run out of Baltimore in 1861.

Southern Jews, slaveowners and not, had interracial descendants. The best-documented example was in the Cardozo family. Isaac Cardozo, from a Sephardic family in Charleston, had a lifelong association with Lydia Weston, a free woman of color. They had six children together, and two of their sons—Francis Cardozo and Thomas Cardozo—rose to prominence as politicians during Reconstruction.

Most of the connections were more shadowy. Until 1830, when it became difficult to manumit a slave, there were Jewish masters who freed slaves in their wills. In a will that named a sole woman and her children, who received money and property as well as their freedom, it is safe to speculate—but not to assume—that the woman was a concubine or a companion or both, and that the children were his.

For the most part, any white Southerner's black children were a shameful secret that families keep to this day. We can hope that post-racialism may wash away the shame and let descendants tell the secret.

Two books are good departures for the topic of Jewish life in the South. For an overview from the 18th century through the mid-20th, see Marcie Ferris and Mark I. Greenberg, eds., *Jewish Roots in Southern Soil* (Brandeis, 2006). For a focus on the Civil War, see Jonathan D. Sarna and Adam Mendelsohn, eds., *Jews in the Civil War: a Reader* (NYU Press, 2011).

There are two well-known diaries by Jewish women kept during the

Civil War: one, by teenaged Clara Solomon in New Orleans and the other by Eleanor Cohen in Charleston. See Clara Solomon and Elliot Ashkenazi, Elliot (ed.), *The Civil War Diary of Clara Solomon: Growing Up in New Orleans, 1861-1862* (LSU Press, 1995), and Jacob Rader Marcus, "Eleanor H. Cohen, Champion of the Lost Cause, 1865-1866," in Marcus, ed., *The American Jewish Woman: A Documentary History* (Ktav Publishing, 1981).

On the black branch of the Cardozo family, see Euline W. Brock, "Thomas W. Cardozo: Fallible Black Reconstruction Leader," *The Journal of Southern History*, Vol. 47, No. 2 (May, 1981), pp. 183-206, for a negative view; and Joe M. Richardson, "Francis L. Cardozo: Black Educator during Reconstruction," *The Journal of Negro Education*, Vol. 48, No. 1 (Winter, 1979), pp. 73-83, for a laudatory one.